Praise for Erin Nicholas's
Just For Fun

"I'm wondering when Erin Nicholas sat down to write *Just For* Fun if she said to herself, 'I'm going to write the best damn book of my career.' I'm not saying her other books aren't good, because they are and I've enjoyed every one but this book is over the top, stay up until 3 a.m., cherry on the top of a pecan caramel fudge sundae good! With this book, Erin Nicholas firmly establishes herself as one of the most exciting writers to watch."
~ *Guilty Pleasures Book Reviews*

"*Just For Fun* was beyond my wildest imagination fantastic. From the detailed back story of Dooley's and Morgan's life to the ever present steamy, sexual chemistry between them as well, I felt that *Just For Fun* was probably the absolute best book out of the series."
~ *Sizzling Hot Book Reviews*

Look for these titles by
Erin Nicholas

Just For Fun

Erin Nicholas

Samhain Publishing, Ltd.
11821 Mason Montgomery Road, 4B
Cincinnati, OH 45249
www.samhainpublishing.com

Just For Fun
Copyright © 2013 by Erin Nicholas
Print ISBN: 978-1-61921-241-1
Digital ISBN: 978-1-61921-175-9

Editing by Lindsey Faber
Cover by Angela Waters

First Samhain Publishing, Ltd. electronic publication: July 2012
First Samhain Publishing, Ltd. print publication: June 2013

Dedication

To Nick, Nikoel and Derek—thanks for making every single day the best time I've ever had. And thanks for putting up with everything writing these books entails. It is fun, honest...in spite of the swearing you hear and the wine bottles and chocolate wrappers that pile up.

Chapter One

The sexy redhead who'd just stepped into the bar had been wearing far fewer clothes the last time he'd seen her.

But there was no doubt that she was the woman responsible for the hottest night of his life. Dooley Miller turned back to the bar and picked up his beer.

Well, shit.

This couldn't be good.

"Hi, I'm looking for Douglas Miller. Do you know him?"

Just as he would have expected, his friends and co-workers parted like the Red Sea. It wasn't that Dooley didn't ever have women looking for him or wanting to find him. But he'd never had a woman who carried herself with such smooth confidence and obvious sophistication looking for him. None of the guys in the bar had, for that matter.

She was in a whole different league.

He dated nice women, beautiful women, sexy women.

This woman was all of that times about ten thousand. Even the nice part. Though he doubted he was going to be seeing any of that in the near future.

He took a final fortifying swig, sighed and swiveled on his stool. He'd known, from minute one with her, that she wasn't actually a stripper.

"Hi, Sugar."

"You're already calling her *Sugar*?" Mac, one of his best friends, asked.

Calling a woman Sugar did imply a relationship, after all.

Though having hot sex in public and spending an hour in jail together probably didn't constitute a relationship.

"Sugar's her name."

"Actually it's not. It's Morgan." She put her hand on one hip and regarded him with a mixture of amusement and irritation. An interesting combination to pull off.

Morgan. Something about knowing her real first name made him take a deep breath. "Sugar fits." He took a drink of his beer as he watched her.

God he could still remember the taste of her skin against his tongue. And the way she moved. And the way she sounded.

All very, very sweet.

"I'm not sure that's a compliment, considering you don't know me."

"I know some stuff."

Her cheeks got pink and her eyes narrowed. "I suppose you're going to try to convince me you played baseball for the Arkansas Travelers."

He grinned. He'd known there was no way she'd recognize the name of his father's favorite minor league baseball player, but he'd been sure she'd known it wasn't *his* name.

"You Googled me?"

"I Googled, curious about the name you gave me. It didn't sound totally made up."

They'd agreed to use fake names. He'd pulled his out of his head right away. When she'd paused, probably trying to think creatively through all the Kahlua, he'd suggested Sugar. He'd also mentioned it sounded like a stripper name. She'd grinned and said, "Perfect."

Even thirty minutes into knowing her, he'd been aware that the woman was far too high class to have ever set foot in a strip club.

"So how'd you find me?"

"You told me you were the CEO of St. Anthony's Medical Center."

"Did I?" Crap, that had been dumb.

"Lucky for me the actual CEO's assistant immediately knew who I was talking about when I described you."

"You went to his office?"

"He wants to talk to you on Monday."

Dooley lifted his beer. He was sure he did.

"So—" she slid up onto the stool next to him, "—remember when you told me if I ever needed anything all I had to do was ask?"

He looked over at her, truly taking in the details now. She was wearing a pantsuit. A nice one that even showed a little cleavage, but a pantsuit nonetheless.

He preferred the cherry-red dress she'd worn to the fundraiser. The tight cherry-red dress that left her shoulders bare and clung to her curves.

That really didn't sound like him. "I said that?"

"No, but it's what you *should have* said." She scowled at him. "Especially after you got me arrested and left me in jail while you paid your bail and walked out."

Dooley didn't have to look at his friends to know their expressions ranged from shocked to downright entertained.

In fact, he stoically avoided looking at them. "You had to pay bail?"

She frowned harder. "Fine, they finally let me out without bail. You still left me there."

He'd paid her bail. That's why they hadn't asked her for it. But he didn't want her to know it.

The whole night with this woman had been out of control from the beginning, and getting arrested had been the sobering moment when he realized he was headed for nothing but trouble with her. He'd been in a cell before. Having a mark on his record didn't bother him. But it bothered him that he'd let things get so out of control it had affected someone else. Usually the other people with him in the cell were there because they deserved it.

In the jail cell it had become impossible to ignore that this woman was the complete opposite of the sexy-girl-just-looking-for-a-good-time she'd portrayed. He didn't get involved with classy women. They naturally needed things he couldn't give. Like money, for example.

That wasn't his type. He wasn't interested. It had been time to go.

Now she was here, had found him, in his regular hang-out. And the scene was all unfolding in front of an audience of his friends. Awesome.

"I need your help. And you owe me."

"You need *my* help?" He faced her fully for the first time. He'd been avoiding it because he knew the moment he looked into her eyes, he'd feel like he'd been punched in the stomach.

He was right.

She was stunning. Her auburn hair fell to her mid-back when it was down. She had a killer body with generous breasts and curvy hips, enough for a man to have something to hold onto. But her legs were long and toned and her butt was tight.

She should have been a stripper. It wasn't fair to humankind to not share every glorious inch.

She had a redhead's pale, creamy skin, but there hadn't been a freckle in sight. At least as far as he could tell. The lighting in the elevator had been good, but he hadn't gotten her completely undressed. Just enough.

Her startlingly bright green eyes could have easily been mistaken for contact lenses, but they were real. They'd looked at him as if he could give her the world. Which had been exactly what he'd wanted her to think that first night. It was supposed to have been their last night as well.

She wasn't looking at him like she thought he was a big shot hero right now.

He was dressed, as usual, in a pair of blue jeans and a T-shirt. His tennis shoes had seen better days, which made them his favorite shoes. They'd just come off a twelve-hour shift and he had some stubble going and knew his eyes were bloodshot from the lack of sleep he'd had last night.

He looked nothing like the man she'd met five weeks ago.

He did look great in a tux.

"Believe me, I'm not thrilled about it either," she said, referring to needing his help. "But, as unbelievable as this may sound, I need your sophistication and—" she looked him up and down in obvious doubt, "—charm."

There was a moment of shocked silence and Dooley braced

himself.

Then his friends let loose with three equally delighted and loud whoops of laughter.

Sophistication and charm were not adjectives most people would assign him.

But Sugar—well, she'd seen his best side for sure. The side he'd almost forgotten he had.

Dammit, it had been fun.

Suddenly Kevin Campbell, another of his friends, bumped into her. Sam and Mac had shoved him forward.

"Sorry," he mumbled, with the goofy grin that always had girls making goo-goo eyes at him.

"This is the best we can offer in the sophistication and charm department," Mac said, slapping Kevin on the shoulder. "There are no promises here either, but he goes to church and eats with utensils."

Dooley rolled his eyes. He deserved all of this. Had any of his friends been on the receiving end of the gorgeous redhead's attention he would have been doing the same exact thing.

He had to get her out of here.

But before he could tell her that, she turned and looked Kevin up and down. "The next time I need to pray or have dinner I'll keep him in mind. What I need right now, though, I need from him." She pointed at Dooley.

Mac, Sam and Kevin raised their eyebrows in unison.

"You sure?" Sam asked.

"Oh, yeah." She said it in a husky, seductive voice that had Dooley's blood pumping harder.

There were only three things she knew he was good at: dressing up, playing Blackjack and giving her orgasms.

"I think we should talk by ourselves," Dooley said, setting down his still half-full beer and sliding off his stool.

"Oh, no, no. We'll be quiet," Kevin said.

"Yeah, wouldn't want to miss any details about your class and charm," Sam added. Clearly the idea of Dooley having class and charm was intriguing. And hard to believe.

Well, screw them.

See? Totally charming.

He grinned in spite of himself. There was no reason for Sam or Mac to think he had class or charm. He never needed either with them around. Kevin knew him better. In fact, Kevin had been at the same fundraiser and had seen Dooley in his tux. He'd been properly surprised and amused by it, but he now knew Dooley could pull it off.

He hadn't, however, seen him with *her*.

"Okay, come here." He took a hold of her arm just above the elbow.

Touching her, even through the sleeve of her jacket, affected him. He felt his gut clench. Cripes. This was ridiculous. He had had sex with Lori, the lab tech he'd dated three or four times, just a couple of days ago. Or maybe it had been a week. Or two. Still, it wasn't like he was hard up.

But that was the biggest danger of this woman—she'd made him *want* in a way he'd never experienced. In an out-of-control, shake-up-his-world way that had, frankly, scared the shit out of him.

"What are you talking about?" he asked as he steered her around the end of the bar into a corner that had one important characteristic—it was far from his friends.

"I need your help. And you owe me," she repeated.

"You mentioned that."

She turned and faced him. "Do you deny it?"

Fuck. He couldn't. She'd participated in the getting arrested for public indecency, but he'd been the one to leave her in jail. It had only been half an hour, but he'd felt bad about it for weeks.

Also unusual for him.

So many things had been unusual about the night with Sugar that he'd wanted nothing more to do with her.

He was afraid that was no longer an option.

Looking at her now he was filled with a stupid, likely self-destructive, combination of lust, happiness and curiosity. She was here to find him. She needed him, wanted him for something. He liked that.

Definitely stupid.

He sighed. "I need a few more details before I agree to help out."

"Even considering you left me? In *jail*?"

Okay, she was clearly pissed.

"Thirty minutes. You were there for an hour and a half total. Relax."

"Relax?" she repeated. "You realize it shows up on background checks, right?"

"Maybe you shouldn't be involved in things where they need to do background checks on you," he suggested.

She narrowed her eyes. "It's still there. I still know it and it bugs me."

"Having my hand up your skirt didn't bug you."

Her eyes widened and she pressed her lips together. Then nodded. "You're right. That didn't bug me at all."

He appreciated—and was turned on by—her honesty. "It's a consequence. A risk you take to have what you want." He didn't have to drop his voice to a husky lower tone.

She stared up at him, her lips parting. Then she nodded. "You know what? I'd do it again."

"You would?"

"Definitely. Even knowing I'd end up in jail, I'd do it all again."

Heat swirled in his gut and he pulled her closer. "What do you need my help with?" Maybe she was here for a booty call of sorts. Maybe she'd missed him. Maybe she'd been thinking of him like had her. 'Cause he'd go for it. Without question. Right here and now.

"I need you to go to Chicago with me for three days."

O-kay. "Chicago?"

She sighed. "It's a work thing I have to be at, but I want you to come along. We're staying at a five star hotel, room service, massages...and I'm done by five every day, so then we'll spend the evening together."

"You want me to come to a work thing with you for three days in Chicago."

"Right."

"We barely know each other."

"All I need to know is you dress well, you can schmooze with the best of them and the sex is out of this world."

He grinned at that. "There will be sex in Chicago?"

She took a step back, looked him up and down and sighed. "Considering I'm in the middle of a bar and I'm annoyed with you and I still want to rip your clothes off...yeah, I'd say there will be sex in Chicago."

"When do we leave?" was what he would have expected to say in a situation like this. Not that he'd ever been in a situation like *this*, but if he would have imagined a situation like this that was what he would have said. Definitely.

Problem was, this wasn't his imagination.

He wanted to have sex with her. It was like her body had been made specifically for his.

He'd found her g-spot without effort, the simple smell of her hair made him hard and they both liked it upfront, honest, hot and fun.

But he didn't know her. Or her him.

What kind of woman asked a guy she barely knew to go to Chicago with her for three days to stay in the same hotel? Work or not, this was weird.

"While I share your appreciation of our sexual chemistry, there has to be a better reason for me to go along. We could have sex right here in Omaha and save some money."

"I have to go for work."

"I'll be here when you get back."

"I need you there."

Ah. Now they were getting somewhere.

"Why me? There's got to be a line of guys wanting to spend a weekend in a hotel with you."

She narrowed her eyes. "Does it matter? If you think I'm such a catch, why not just be grateful I asked you?"

Why indeed. Because he was pretty sure he knew why she'd picked him and that meant they needed to get some things out in the open right up front.

He signaled to Melissa, the waitress tonight. She headed straight for him. Clearly his little conference with Morgan had caught everyone's attention. Partly because Morgan stood out starkly in here and partly because she was with *him*.

"Hey, Dooley."

"Hey, Mel, I need another beer and a Kahlua and cream. A double."

Mel moved off and he focused on Morgan—who was staring at him. "You ordered me a Kahlua?"

"Yeah."

"Why?"

"It makes you talk."

Her mouth dropped open. "How do you know that?"

"I spent three hours with you at the fundraiser before the unfortunate incident with security," he reminded her. "Not only were you drinking it that night, but you told me it makes you talk. Right after confessing that you love men with blue eyes and lots of money, which meant, since I had both, I could talk you into doing anything with me."

Her cheeks got bright red almost instantaneously. "I said that?"

"Twice." He grinned at her appalled expression. He'd bought her two more Kahlua and creams after that.

"What else did I say?"

He shook his head. "Nope. I can see where it might be an advantage to surprise you with the things I know about you." She'd been flirtatious from the moment he joined her at the Blackjack table, but she'd become even chattier as the night progressed and the Kahlua flowed. It wasn't just the quantity of what she'd told him—there had been some true quality too.

Mel delivered their drinks and he watched as Morgan stared at her glass as if trying to make a difficult decision. But she did finally take a drink. Followed by sliding her eyes shut and sighing.

He chuckled and her eyes flew open.

"Okay, spill. Why do you want *me* to go to Chicago with you when I'm a virtual stranger?"

She licked her lips and he knew it wasn't going to take much for her to talk him into this.

"We had a fun, hot, crazy night. No strings attached. No future plans," she said.

He nodded his agreement.

"I need that while I'm in Chicago."

"Fun, hot, crazy and no strings attached," he repeated.

"Right."

"Sounds great." It sounded perfect. "But," he went on "there's something you should know."

"If you tell me you have an STD I'm going to scream. Just so you know."

He grinned. "Thanks for the warning. But no. It's worse."

Her eyes widened. "Worse than an STD?"

"Potentially."

"If you tell me you're married, *you're* going to be screaming."

His grin grew. He remembered this from the night of the fundraiser too. She'd been funny and he'd enjoyed the time they'd teased and talked *almost* as much as the time they'd spent moaning and panting. "I'm not married."

"Good. Then what?"

"I don't have any money."

She blinked at him. Then looked down at his tennis shoes, at his T-shirt and then around the bar. "You know, that's not as much of a shock as you might think."

He chuckled even though she'd basically disparaged his favorite outfit and hang out in one sentence. "You told me you like men with money."

"I do." Then she sighed. "But all you have to do is smile and I want to take my clothes off, which is more important here."

"This is sounding better all the time."

She sucked in a quick breath as he leaned in. "I don't think I can call you Dooley in bed. Is that what most women call you?"

"That or 'oh, God'. I answer to both."

She smiled and shook her head. "Dooley sounds like a frat boy name. Or a dog's name. I'll have to call you Doug."

He shook his head. Dooley *was* a frat boy name. "I'll be calling you Sugar for sure." Morgan sounded like a nice girl's name. You made love to a Morgan. But you could fuck a Sugar.

"You can call me whatever you want if you tell me you can *act* like you have money for three days like you did at the fundraiser."

"How do you act like you have money? 'Cause I'm not sure I can pull off acting like I'm better than everyone else."

She frowned at him. "Act...polished. Like you...know how to use utensils," she said, waving in the direction of his friends because of their earlier offer to send Kevin.

"I can probably pull that off," he said dryly. Hell, he'd spent twenty years of his life in polite society. He could remember how to pull out a lady's chair, not burp in public, tip the valets and make small talk.

"Good." She looked genuinely relieved.

"That's all you need? A date who won't embarrass you?" he asked. "Still seems you would have a lot of guys to pick from."

She stepped in closer and looked him directly in the eye. "I need a date who will be polite during the day and be downright indecent at night. Got it?"

Oh, he got it. He was undeniably the right man for this job.

She handed him a long, thick envelope. "Plane leaves Thursday at three."

"I still think there's more to this story," he said.

She shrugged. "Show up and I'll tell you everything."

Then she turned and sashayed her tight little butt right out of the bar.

Dooley considered going out the backdoor and avoiding his friends. But he'd have to show up for work again at some point. Besides, they all knew where he lived. And frankly, these guys were more than friends and co-workers. They were all a part of each other's lives to the point that avoiding them would be impossible and probably miserable anyway.

So he went back out front to the bar, braced for their questions and ribbing.

They didn't disappoint him.

They were now seated at a table in the center of the room. Ben Torres caught his eye first and waved him over. Ben was an ER physician at St. Anthony's, the hospital right across the street, where they all worked. As such, Ben was even keel, hard to rattle. He was also the newest addition to the group. But he fit right in.

"Damn, Dooley. You have way better taste in women than I've ever given you credit for."

Sure, if Morgan James—he'd learned her last name from the personal info in the envelope she'd given him, for a fricking background check of all things—was his typical type. But she wasn't. At all.

"God, I love redheads," Sam Bradford said.

"You love *all* women," Dooley muttered.

"Well, they all have something in common I really like," Sam said with a grin. "They're all *women.*" Sam hadn't discriminated when it came to women at all. His collection had been eclectic and extensive. But it was all past tense anyway. He was head over heels for his wife, Danika. Who happened to be a strawberry blonde. There were definite touches of red in her hair but nothing like the deep rich color of Morgan's.

Mac Gordon pushed a chair out with his foot. "Sit," he ordered.

Mac was the oldest of the group and functioned as an older brother. He and Ben were brothers-in-law, married to sisters Sara and Jessica, Sam's sisters. At one time, Mac had been the wildest of them all, so the sex-in-an-elevator-during-a-charity-fundraiser part of Dooley's story about Morgan wouldn't faze him. The leaving her in jail was going to ruffle all their feathers though.

Especially Kevin's. Kevin Campbell was the nicest of them all. By a long shot. He'd been an All-American defensive lineman for the University of Nebraska Huskers, he'd been a wild child in high school and he'd had his share of women warming his sheets until about eight years ago. But he was now a devout Christian who had sworn off fighting, gambling, sex and drinking. He'd tried to swear off profanity and impure thoughts too, but he was still working on those.

"You did actually get her arrested?" Kevin asked.

Dooley slumped into the chair across from the man who knew him better than the others. "Accidentally. Don't worry, I paid her bail."

Kevin shook his head. "Who paid your bail?"

"Jeni came down." Of his two younger sisters, Jeni was the one to call from jail at three a.m.

Actually, any of these guys would have been his first pick, but none of them would have let him leave a woman behind. Jeni hadn't asked. She was one of those people who loved him and just showed up. These guys loved him, showed up, then needed every detail of what had happened.

Jeni didn't want to know.

"The important part," Sam said, "is what did you get arrested for?"

"The important part," Ben disagreed, "is what does she want from you now?"

Dooley signaled for a beer and got comfortable. This might take a while.

Ten minutes later his friends were staring at him.

"So let me get this straight," Mac said, leaning in on his elbows. "You got her arrested for suspicion of solicitation, which didn't stick, and then for indecent exposure, which almost did. In fact, if Judge Rickman hadn't been such a good friend it might have been a different story. And she *still* wants you to go to Chicago with her to a work thing based on how you look in a tux and what you can do in bed?"

"Elevators anyway," Sam said.

Yeah, they'd never made it to a bed. Dooley took a long swig of beer and shrugged. "Guess so."

"You've known her for what? About an hour total?" Ben asked.

Four and a half. Not that it mattered. "I guess it doesn't take long for me to make a good impression," Dooley said.

The more they talked about it, the better he liked the whole thing. She'd remembered him. For over a month. She wanted him enough to track him down, even with a fake name.

Women like Morgan James didn't have to work for what they wanted very often. She was gorgeous, confident, and damned classy herself. That she'd tried to find him rocked.

He grinned and tipped onto the back legs of his chair.

"Then there are only two questions left," Mac said.

"I'm ready." He was feeling strangely full of himself.

"When's the plane leave?"

"Thursday afternoon."

"And are you Richard Gere or Julia Roberts?"

Dooley chuckled. "A *Pretty Woman* reference? Really?"

"Obviously he's Julia Roberts. She's the one paying for the hotel room, right?" Sam said.

"Definitely. Didn't she go with Richard Gere to some work-meeting-dinner-thing too?" Ben asked.

"Dooley's not gonna have a clue if they go to the opera," Mac said.

The legs of Dooley's chair *thunked* back to the floor. "We're not goin' to the opera."

"And Sugar will be the one lookin' hot in the slinky dress and bubble bath," Ben added.

"I'd get into a bubble bath with her," Sam said, "and Dooley will be the one with the colored and flavored condoms."

"I'm disturbed by how well you all know that movie," Dooley told them. "It doesn't matter which one I am, since I'm not going."

All four of the men who he considered his best friends in the world slowly set their glasses down and turned to face him.

"Why the hell not?" Sam was the first to demand. "That woman is way too good for you and she wants you anyway. Speaking as a man who is *with* a woman who's too good for him, grab this opportunity."

"Hear, hear," Ben raised his glass in salute of Sam's words.

"Amen, brother," Mac added, clinking his beer bottle against Ben and Sam's.

"While you are all completely right about being with women who are too good for you," Dooley said, "I can't just leave for three days out of the blue."

"We'll get the new kid, Conner what's-his-name, to fill in," Mac said. "No problem. The kid's dying to hang out and learn all we know."

Sam grinned. "I don't know. I think he's still scared of you," he told Mac.

"He should be scared of me," Mac retorted. "He was hitting on my wife."

Mac's wife, Sara, was Sam's little sister and quite a bit younger than all of them, especially Mac. They all felt like older brothers to her. Well, except Mac, of course. The way he'd growled at and threatened Conner left no question how Mac felt about the other man whispering in Sara's ear.

"You think he'll come work with you?" Sam wanted to know.

"If he's interested in being the best damned paramedic he can be, or in landing a woman like Sara, he should be hanging on my every word," Mac said.

They all laughed, but Dooley caught Kevin's eye. His buddy was the only one who knew there was more standing in the way of the trip than just work.

"Can't do it guys," Dooley said, feeling disappointed himself. "Not this time."

"Oh, so you'll just wait for the next random knock-out redhead to come along and ask you to go on an all-expenses-paid trip to have sex with her for three days," Sam said. "Sure. Probably sometime next month, right?"

He agreed it sounded idiotic but, as close as they were, the guys didn't know that beneath his laid-back, irreverent attitude, he had stress. A lot of it. He didn't like letting people get too close to that, so he put on the front of just not wanting any serious relationships. But the truth was, sometimes he felt held back from having everything he really wanted.

The guys knew that for the past eleven years, ever since his stroke, his dad had been living with him. They knew Doug helped his dad with the major things like finances and helping manage his healthcare, but they didn't realize the day-to-day details that kept Dooley tied down.

Doug Senior didn't need constant care, but he had trouble transferring safely in and out of chairs and bed because of the paralysis on his right side. Things like cooking and bathing were hard for him on his own too. Three days was just too long for him to be alone.

Dooley's sisters helped as they could, but they were both married with kids and worked. The stroke had happened while they were both in college and he'd taken over caring for their dad so they could both finish their degrees.

They'd fallen in love and he'd pushed them to live their lives, get married, have kids and everything. They and their husbands took turns helping out when Dooley couldn't be there, but part of the reason his shift as a paramedic was perfect was he worked twelve-hour shifts overnight. Dooley helped his dad get ready for bed before he left for work, then his sisters and their husbands came over later and hung out and eventually got Senior into bed. Then he slept all night while Dooley worked. It was during the day that he needed the help with moving around, eating and exercising.

"You can go," Kevin said, catching his eye again. "Conner can cover at work and everything else is a piece of cake."

Dooley frowned at him. Kevin helped him out when his sisters couldn't and he enjoyed hanging out with Dooley's dad. Senior's personality had also changed with the stroke and he was far more mellow now than he ever had been before. Being dependent on others for basic activities of daily life had a way of humbling a man.

"It's not important," Dooley insisted.

"You don't know unless you go," Kevin insisted right back. He pulled his phone from his pocket and slid the keyboard out. "In fact..." He typed something in quickly.

Dooley knew who he'd texted.

"Yep, everything's fine," Kevin said a moment later. He looked up. "Everyone thinks you should go."

His dad was surprisingly good at texting with just his left hand. The stroke had affected his right side and he had a hard time talking, but he understood everything and could communicate by writing, typing and texting.

The brain was an amazing thing.

"What are you doing?" Sam asked, watching Kevin and Dooley.

"Making sure Dooley doesn't have any reason not to get on that plane," Kevin said with a shrug. He pocketed his phone and took a drink of his soda.

"So you're going?" Sam asked.

Dooley sighed. His dad felt guilty and was constantly pushing him to go out more, meet more people, women in particular, and get serious with one. He hated that Dooley had put his life on hold for him.

But there wasn't any way around it. He would not put his father in a nursing home. He was perfectly capable of taking care of him and they got along great. His dad was cool. It was more like having a friend as a roommate than living with his dad.

It was just a lot to ask a woman to take on. Any woman who wanted to be with Dooley long term would be with his dad long term too. They came as a set. It wasn't even the same as hooking up with someone who already had a kid. Kids grew up, became less dependent, moved out eventually. That wasn't going to happen with his dad. He'd been young to have a stroke at age fifty-one and he was in great health in spite of the stroke. He was going to be around for a long time and Dooley was thankful for that.

He didn't have a wife and kids, but he wasn't lonely. He had a full, rewarding life, lots of friends, a great family with adorable nieces, and a job he loved.

He wasn't complaining.

"He's going," Kevin said firmly. "If I have to physically put him on the plane myself."

Kevin agreed with his dad that Dooley needed more in his life.

Kevin could physically put him on the plane too. He was an ex-football player—and a damned good one—who was in a lot better shape than Dooley had ever been. Plus he was determined. For Dooley's own good.

He looked at his friend, who raised a single eyebrow, as if daring him to say no.

He was being forced to go on vacation with a gorgeous woman he'd been thinking about for four weeks. He wasn't going to argue too hard.

"I guess I'm going."

If he remembered correctly, Julia Roberts had had a really good time in that movie.

Morgan dialed her sister's number as she drove away from the bar...and Doug Miller.

God, she'd just invited a guy wearing a T-shirt that read *Santa's jolly because he knows where all the bad girls live* to Chicago for the biggest professional meeting of her life.

Maybe not the best decision she'd ever made.

But dammit, she knew what he could do to a tux and it was too late for Plan B. Even if she had a Plan B.

In spite of the T-shirt, the beer mug and the obvious familiarity he had with the run-down bar and its patrons, she did hope he showed at the airport.

She was certainly still attracted to him. It seemed their chemistry didn't care if he was wearing Armani or denim. Out of the tux and away from the casino night fundraiser for the hospital's cancer wing, he'd looked like he'd be more at home on a California beach with a surf board in hand, but she'd still wanted to kiss him the moment she saw him.

He stood at just about six feet and had a slim, muscular-but-lanky build. His hair was a sandy blond that seemed perpetually wind ruffled and she had yet to see him clean-shaven. Instead he had that popular scruffy look going. His eyes were a deep blue and he carried himself with a lazy ease. He didn't walk, he sauntered. He didn't smile, his mouth slowly stretched into a grin. He seemed to think just a second longer than everyone else before replying to something someone said. He exuded laid back.

Which was a draw she couldn't deny. Most of the men in her world were determined, driven, goal-oriented, focused.

Doug Miller seemed to be a take-it-as-it-comes kind of guy.

She liked that.

"I found him," she said when her sister finally answered her phone.

"You're kidding," Maddie said. "How?"

"It wasn't hard." Morgan rolled her eyes. "He gave me the name of the hospital where he worked. Just not *his* real name."

"I can't believe you think this is a good idea," Maddie said. "So what if the background check turns out great? You're still taking a virtual stranger to Chicago with you."

"Well, I didn't tell him this but when I went to the CEO's office at the hospital I didn't just get the guy's real name. I got a character reference. He's a goof-off but he's a good guy. He's a paramedic. Been at the hospital for years with the same crew. They're the top crew in the city. They've done some amazing things. I mean you've got to know he's a good guy if he uses the CEO's name to get a girl into bed and the CEO is only mildly irritated by it."

Maddie sighed. "Okay, what's the plan?"

"He's supposed to meet me at the airport on Thursday."

"He didn't think it was strange at all?"

"It doesn't matter if he thinks it's strange. As long as he shows up and plays the part."

"You'll have to tell me all about it. Provided he doesn't rob you or murder you, of course," Maddie mumbled.

Morgan laughed. "I'll talk to you later."

She disconnected and took a deep breath. It might be stupid—okay, it was a little stupid—but she wasn't worried about being robbed or murdered. She was concerned about having the willpower to ever get out of bed once she had him in a hotel suite but other than that she was only taking him along to impress Jonathan Britton.

She frowned as she turned her car in the direction of her townhouse. Jonathan Britton. She'd worked for Britton Hotels for almost three years now but she'd never met the man himself until two weeks ago.

Her degree and background in hotel and restaurant management had gotten her the job with Britton's largest hotel in the Midwest—the Britton Towers in downtown Omaha, Nebraska—just as the glamorous structure had taken over a full square city block three years before. Under her management, the hotel had become *the* place to stay in the city for businessmen, politicians and celebrities alike. For one, she worked hand in hand with a city intent on bringing bigger and better entertainment and business to the area. The Omaha Britton Towers was the place to put anyone who needed to be pampered, catered to and buttered up. She was one of the Mayor's favorite people.

Yep, that summarized her whole job—making people happy so they'd say yes to things—and she was good at it.

She'd easily made the short list of potential managers of the new resort Britton was building in California. It was supposed to be the biggest and best yet. Which was saying something. Jonathan Britton had more money and took bigger risks than anyone in the business. It was why he had the absolute best resorts in the world and why he'd had some of the biggest flops.

Two weeks ago Jonathan had shown up in the lobby of her hotel and personally invited her to submit an idea for the grand west coast resort. They hadn't started building yet and he was looking for something different. He'd invited ten of his best managers to submit proposals.

Now it was down to two of them.

Her and Todd Becker.

Morgan pulled into her garage and stopped the car, lost in thought.

She hadn't seen Todd in a few months now. He managed the Minneapolis Britton Tower and they'd first met at a Britton management training. It was a three-day training requiring a two-night stay in Chicago—Britton's base of operations. She'd spent those two nights in Todd's bed having the best sex of her life.

The best sex of her life until she'd met Doug Miller.

Which was bizarre.

She let herself into her townhouse, locking the door and toeing off her shoes at the same time. Her heels landed near the coat tree and she tossed her purse and keys onto the small table near the door.

Then she padded barefoot to the kitchen. She needed tea. Or something.

"Tell me again why you have to take *this* guy?"

Morgan sighed as her sister let herself in through the patio's sliding glass door.

There were advantages to living in the townhouse next to her only sibling. And some disadvantages.

She would have told her younger sister to get out...but she did want to talk about it. "Okay, give me five minutes." She headed for her bedroom. This conversation called for cut off sweatpants and a T-shirt with no bra instead of a four-hundred-dollar suit and heels.

When she made it back to the kitchen, Maddie handed her a glass filled with Kahlua and cream.

Ah, yes, the magic elixir.

Maddie wasn't, unfortunately, the first to discover Kahlua had a way of making Morgan talk.

Still she took a drink. She loved it. Heaven surely served Kahlua and cream.

They took seats on opposite ends of Morgan's oversized couch and settled into the soft cushions.

"Now tell me why you need this guy to go along," Maddie ordered. "Why can't you take Landon? He'd go. Or Nate. He'd get a huge kick out of this."

"I don't want to sleep with Landon or Nate," Morgan said of

two of her sister's boyfriend's best friends.

"It's *required* that you bring someone you want to sleep with?" Maddie asked. "No way."

"No. But I have to *be with* someone I want to sleep with. Who I *will* sleep with."

Maddie didn't know this whole story. No one did. Until now there had been no reason to tell even the woman she told everything.

"This is a resort management job, right?" Maddie asked. "Or am I missing something?"

"It's not the job that's the direct problem. Todd's going to be there."

"Todd?" Maddie frowned. "Isn't he the guy from Minneapolis you hit it off with?"

"Right." But there had always been something she hadn't quite trusted. Or been comfortable with. Or something.

"So?"

"Okay, but you have to listen to the *whole* story before you tell me I'm crazy."

Maddie took a swig of her drink then drew a cross over her heart. "Promise."

"No laughing. Or eye rolling."

"Um...I'll try."

Morgan drank once more then set her glass on the coffee table and tucked her feet up underneath her. "Here goes. I've never been swept off my feet, ever. But he did it. In one night. He was charming, polished, classy, and amazing in bed."

She left out the part about not being completely comfortable with him because she couldn't explain it to herself. He did all the right things. He was the type of guy she wanted. He was driven, had goals, wore a tie to work every day. It sounded like a dumb qualification, but that was the guy she wanted. White collar. Steady, stable, financially secure.

"Sounds fantastic," Maddie said. "Not seeing a problem at all."

"I know. It wasn't a problem. At all. At first. I mean I've *never* had orgasms like I did with Todd. Plus, he had the whole romantic thing down. He could give seminars. There were roses and chocolate-covered strawberries, bubble baths and long, slow lovemaking."

Maddie sighed happily. "No. Problem. At. All."

Morgan grinned at her sister. "We parted on excellent terms and kept in touch via e-mail and occasional phone calls. Then the next corporate meeting six months later was a repeat of the first. Romance, dancing, expensive dinners and incredible lovemaking." She paused. "Then six months later the same."

"Still no problem."

"Well..." She took a deep breath. "I thought it was all great. I was excited to think there might even be a future."

"And he'll be in Chicago?" Maddie clarified. "What am I missing?"

"Todd has...a...power over me," Morgan said reluctantly. "I don't understand it."

"A power? How? Because he's a great lover?"

"Yes," she admitted. "But it's more like he'll...use it, I guess."

"Use it?"

"I don't know how it happened. I don't know if it's because he found this spot on my neck or just the right dirty words or just the right mixture of Kahlua and cream. Or worse, it might just be him. Something about him. But all he has to do is touch me and I'll go along with anything."

Maddie didn't laugh. Thank God. In fact, she set her glass down and leaned forward on the cushion. "Like he's hypnotized you or is doing something with your mind or something? Do you think he *drugs* you?" she demanded.

Morgan shook her head. "It's nothing ominous. I'm not scared of him."

"You obviously feel like it's a bad thing though."

"I do because..." This was the part she didn't want to admit. It made her sound weak. "I learned that in the aftermath of an amazing orgasm I have no inhibitions." She said anything that was on her mind, answered any question and told every secret. It was worse than her reaction to Kahlua. "Todd figured it out too."

Orgasms made her spill her guts.

"How?" Maddie asked quietly. "How did he figure it out?"

Morgan shrugged. "We'd start talking about work or projects and I start telling him about something I was going to be doing or trying at the hotel."

"Then what?"

"Then in the next corporate newsletter or announcements I'd find out he did the same thing and it was wildly successful and he was getting all kinds of kudos. In fact, the last time he did something he ended up getting a *bonus*."

Maddie frowned. "Why didn't you just make sure they knew about the idea from you first?"

"It took me awhile to realize he was blatantly getting information from me. I thought maybe he didn't *mean to* or something. That I just spilled things and he picked up on them. But the last time we were together we were lying in bed and he started asking me direct questions about my plans for the Christmas season. Suddenly it hit me." She covered her face with her hands. "I'm so dumb."

Maddie patted her knee. "Not dumb."

"Naïve, trusting."

"Maybe a little."

"*Easy*," Morgan moaned. "I barely know him but when we're dancing or he's talking in that sexy, husky voice on the phone, or when he's..." She stopped and cleared her throat.

"And now he's competing for the same resort job?"

"Right. He'll be in Chicago. I know what he's thinking."

"Of course he's thinking that." Maddie sat back against the arm of the couch. "This technique's been working great. Why *wouldn't* he be thinking that?"

"I don't trust myself. I swear if he kisses me I'll be mush."

"Morgan Rene James, you've got to pull yourself together. Tell yourself you can handle this. Now that you're on to him it won't happen, right?"

Morgan was already shaking her head by the time Maddie finished her sentence. "I can't risk it. This will be the first time

I've tried to resist and I can't take the chance it won't work and he'll walk off with this job."

"You're a strong, independent, intelligent woman," Maddie insisted. "Plus you should be *pissed* at him for this."

"I am." But she was feeling more mortified than anything. Here she'd been feeling like she was being romanced by Prince Charming while he was just using her to get her ideas. And it wasn't like he'd been having a bad time doing it. She wasn't the only one who'd left their weekends fully sexually satisfied. He'd ended up getting laid and promoted thanks to her.

She was mad. But she was obviously weak too. As soon as she'd figured out what he was doing she'd stopped returning his calls and e-mails, but she knew it would be harder to resist him in person.

She needed her defenses firmly in place.

"Then how does this new guy figure in?"

Morgan's body seemed to sit up and pay attention the moment Doug's image appeared in her mind.

"I met him at the fundraiser last month."

"Okay."

"We had sex in the elevator."

Maddie stared at her. "You're turning into a slut."

Morgan nodded. "I know. It's out of control. I totally intended to avoid him, never see him again. I mean we both gave fake names. It was a one-night stand that didn't even last all night. It was silly and hot and fun and stupid and never to be repeated."

Especially after the hour in the jail cell she was *not* going to mention.

"But?"

She breathed deep, feeling her blood heat thinking of that night. "He's the only guy who's had even more of an effect on me than Todd."

"Wow, no kidding?"

"Todd can touch me and I'm ready to go up to the room, but I've never been tempted to just hike up my skirt against the nearest wall. Todd uses flowers and lots of foreplay and romance. Doug just..." She licked her lips. "It's going to sound crazy but we looked at each other across the casino and I wanted him."

Maddie's eyebrows shot up. "Damn, you're so lucky. I want that."

Morgan grinned. "Anyway, if I take Doug to Chicago I won't have to worry about Todd. I'll want to be with Doug so I can get work done and not worry about being with Todd and spilling everything."

Maddie opened her mouth to respond. Then shut it. Then said, "I can't argue with that. It kind of, strangely, makes sense."

And it kind of strangely did.

Strangely being the key word.

Chapter Two

Dooley took a moment to appreciate the view when he first stepped into the airport ticketing area. There were, of course, dozens of people milling about but his eyes went immediately to the built redhead standing off to the side of the main doors, checking her watch.

Morgan was dressed down, he supposed. She wore jeans, anyway. But the silky green shirt and black jacket paired with the black heels made her look stylish...and hot.

He took a deep breath. He was on vacation. For the first time in years. With the sexiest woman he'd ever met.

He was going to make the most of this.

He strode toward her, coming up on her side opposite of where she was looking.

"Sorry I'm late," he said, just before he sank his fingers into the glorious ginger hair at the base of her skull, tipped her head and kissed her.

She wasn't surprised for more than three seconds. She dropped her purse, took the front of his T-shirt in both hands, rose on tiptoe and kissed him back.

It felt like he'd been waiting his entire life to kiss her, and he took advantage. He sucked gently on her bottom lip, and when she opened up with a moan, he stroked his tongue in deep, drinking of her, drowning in her.

When they finally pulled apart they were breathing hard. She stared up at him, seeming dazed.

"Responding like that is going to make you think it's okay to be late," she said as she let go of him, straightened her jacket and licked her lips.

"Couldn't help myself," he said, pulling the strap of his duffle bag higher on his shoulder.

She looked up at him. "Really?"

He grinned. Like men didn't want to kiss her all the time. "Really."

"Just keep it up," she said, retrieving her purse and extending the handle on her rolling suitcase. "That's what I need you for."

"Kissing? *Not* going to be a problem."

She gave him a smile that made him want to start all over again. "Be crazy about me, unable to keep your hands to yourself and we'll be good."

He watched her first several steps away from him. "Easiest gig ever," he muttered, starting after her. They went past the ticket counters and he caught up with her at the escalators to the gates. "You already have the boarding passes and stuff?"

"Don't need boarding passes," she said over her shoulder. "We're taking a private jet."

That pulled his attention from checking out her butt in jeans. "You have a private jet?"

"No, but my boss does."

He could so get used to traveling by private jet and acting like he couldn't keep his hands off of her.

The moment they stepped off the escalator, he grabbed her hand, threading his fingers with hers. Three days. He had three days with this woman. He intended to touch her for most of those seventy-two hours.

She didn't pull away, but slanted him a look. "You're not afraid of flying are you?"

"Will you sit closer to me if I am?"

"I'll sit close to you no matter what."

"Then no, I'm not scared of flying."

She laughed softly and he found himself grinning.

As they stepped out onto the tarmac, Dooley got his first view of the private jet.

He approved.

It was small, but sleek. Painted silver, it had Britton in black lettering along the side.

Dooley stopped abruptly, pulling her up short with him. "Britton?" he asked. "Not Jonathan Britton?"

Morgan looked surprised. "Yes, Jonathan Britton. I manage one of his hotels and this trip is to discuss his plans for a new resort."

It was a fucking small world.

Dooley wasn't sure what his part in this weekend was *exactly*, but if it had to do with hotels and resorts, he'd fit right in.

Fifteen minutes later they were seated in the private jet. It could seat six passengers but they were the only ones on board other than the pilot and a flight attendant. Once they each had a drink—beer for him and white wine for her—the flight attendant discreetly disappeared, leaving them alone as the plane taxied and took off.

Dooley turned in his seat to look at her better. The seats were certainly wide enough to get comfortable in. "You said if I showed up you'd tell me why it had to be me going along."

She took a long drink of her wine, then nodded. "I did say that, didn't I?"

"It's not a long flight. You should probably fill me in on what's going on these three days. What you want me to do. What you're doing."

She finished off her wine, then turned to face him too. "You want the long story or the short?"

"You have an hour. Let's see how far you get."

He was even more intrigued than last night. He wasn't sure why. It was a combination of her insistence *he* be the one to accompany her on this trip, that the trip was into a world he knew well, and just her.

She was unlike the other women he dated. Which was mostly on purpose. He liked girls who enjoyed shooting pool and watching football and thought a movie and burger were just fine on a date. He dated a lot of nurses and therapists and x-ray or lab techs. They were generally sweet, caring professionals, who were smart and low maintenance. Anyone who dealt with broken bodies, a variety of patient backgrounds and blood and other bodily fluids on a daily basis tended to be practical and down to earth. He liked girls with short nails, tennis shoes and ponytails.

Many times it had been pointed out that if he fell for a nurse or therapist he wouldn't have to worry about them accepting his dad. He'd dated more than one woman who would have been at ease around his father and his needs. But that didn't make it fair. He didn't want to be a package deal. Relationships were hard enough.

It was great that Morgan was not a woman to take blood or urine in stride. Her high heels, French manicure and perfect hair would be a constant reminder that he couldn't think of this as anything more than a weekend fling.

"I've been working for Britton for almost three years," she was saying. "I've done a hell of a job with his hotel in Omaha. But I want something bigger and this is my chance."

He'd only been by the Britton Towers in downtown Omaha. He'd grown up in places like that and they had no draw for him.

"He's building a new resort and you're up for manager?"

"I'm one of two people he's considering. That's where you come in."

Dooley leaned his arm on the armrest between them. "I'm listening."

"The other candidate is Todd Becker. He's from Minneapolis and he's..." Her eyes dropped to his beer bottle. "My ex."

Her ex was up for the same job. Interesting.

"You want to make him jealous while you steal the job he wants? Seems cruel."

She smiled. "No, I just want to avoid any...complications."

"Complications like what?" Dooley pressed. It was exceedingly stupid but he was all about showing Todd that Morgan had moved on. And upgraded. Temporarily, of course, but if it kept her out of the other man's arms—or bed—Dooley was all for it.

"Like left over feelings," she said, again not meeting his eyes.

"Left over feelings on his part or yours?" He didn't like the idea she might still want this guy. Which didn't make any sense at all.

She lifted her shoulder. "Either."

He reached out and tipped her chin up. "Mostly yours?"

"I don't have *feelings* for him," she said. "I just...find it difficult to...resist him. Physically. Like when he kisses me. Or touches me. Or in bed—"

"I got it," Dooley broke in. "I understand. Don't need to hear any more."

Dammit. She was attracted to Todd.

"So I'm here to what?" he asked.

"Make me want to be with you instead."

Her eyes went to his lips and he felt electricity arc between them. "I'll do my best." His voice dropped to a husky rumble.

"That's the thing." She leaned closer and her voice was a little scratchy too. "You don't have to try very hard. You're the one who makes it so I can barely remember his name."

Best thing he'd ever heard.

Cupping the back of her head, Dooley leaned in and claimed her mouth again. The kiss was hot, but lips only. At first. Within a minute though, he was urging her up out of her seat with his hands on her upper arms, then turning her. But she climbed into his lap, straddled his thighs, all on her own.

He peeled her jacket off, their lips never separating, then slipped his hands up under the silky material of her blouse to the silky skin of her back. She arched into him, deepening the kiss, holding his head. As if he'd think about pulling away.

Slipping his hands to the front, he cupped her breasts. He remembered everything about sex with her, in spite of the fact they'd drank plenty while playing at the fake casino tables. He knew her nipples were one key to making her crazy.

His thumbs brushed over the stiff tips and, predictably, she moaned. She wiggled, pulling her shirt up and the cups of the lacy emerald bra down.

Then he had to look. He pulled back. She was exposed to him, breathing hard, her hair rumpled. She looked sexy and a little wild. He loved her creamy skin, her pale nipples, the way his big tanned hands looked holding her waist.

"God, Morgan."

"More," she whispered hoarsely.

He leaned in and took her right nipple in his mouth, licking, then sucking, pulling a long moan from her.

"I want to make you come," he said against her breast.

"You're about halfway there," she panted.

"I love that," he rasped. His hand went to the button on the front of her jeans just as the plane hit a pocket of turbulence, jarring them hard.

She let her head fall back, pushing her hair away from her face. "Dammit."

"Give me two minutes," he said.

She grinned. "It would only take you one. But this is not the place for it."

He looked around. "I disagree."

"We have three days in a penthouse suite at a five-star hotel. I promise you there will be lots of this."

He licked his lips and looked at her breasts again. "We're going straight to the hotel right?"

"Definitely." She pulled her bra up, her shirt down and pushed herself off of his lap. She let out a breath, staring at his mouth. *"Definitely."*

Morgan stared at the man in front of her. Her whole body tingled. Looking at his mouth she could still feel his lips pulling on her nipple.

She wanted more. Intensely. Like she'd never wanted anything ever.

It didn't seem to matter that he'd gotten her arrested and left her in a jail cell. It also didn't seem to bother her that he would clearly be more comfortable in a beanbag chair playing video games and eating Cheetos than in a tux at a dinner party with her boss.

She could not let him overwhelm her. He was here with her because she'd let another man overwhelm her. She couldn't let the same thing happen with Doug. He wouldn't steal her work ideas, but she could easily see him talking her into skinny-dipping in a private pool. Or participating in a wet T-shirt contest. Or wearing a skimpy cheerleader's outfit and getting dirty in the backseat of his car.

She shook her head. Anyway, there was an aura of naughty fun and its-only-bad-if-you-get-caught about him that she liked and was wary of at the same time.

This was a business trip and she'd brought him along for protection. She couldn't let *him* be the one who got her into trouble.

"This is just for fun," she told him firmly, tucking her hair behind her ear. "No matter how intense this feels, it's just a good time."

"Okay."

"I mean, we barely know each other."

"Agreed."

"I don't think we have much in common."

"We don't. I'm sure of it," he assured her.

That mattered. It did. There was no way this could go beyond this weekend. She didn't play video games or eat Cheetos. "Okay. So..." She took her seat. "Just for fun."

He cleared his throat. "Tell me more about this job and project," he said.

She looked at him, surprised, as she fastened her seat belt. "You want to hear about it?"

"I *want* to strip you down and make you scream."

She sucked in a quick breath as heat and craving filled her. "I don't know much about the project," she started conversationally.

Dooley grinned and seemed to relax in his seat.

She tried to as well. "We submitted basic ideas about a month ago and he chose Todd and me as the final two from those proposals. We were supposed to include a target demographic, amenities, décor, things like that."

41

"What's your idea?" he asked.

"Um, well, okay." She hadn't let anyone see her ideas besides her sister and she hadn't explained any of it out loud. This might be a good chance to practice before she saw Mr. Britton. "My idea is about truly customizing the experience for the guests. They will go online and fill out a questionnaire about what they like, what they don't. Then we'll use it to make their stay personal and comfortable."

He was listening, seemingly interested. Which surprised her. A little. But she was already beginning to think there was more to Doug Miller than his dirty tennis shoes and unruly hair.

But she didn't want there to be more to him. He was a weekend date, a fling. She needed to concentrate on the Cheetos thing.

"For instance," she went on. "If someone likes lemon cake and not chocolate, then lemon cake will be offered with their first meal. Their favorite scent will be infused in their room, their bedding will be their favorite color, their favorite flowers will be on the table when they first enter their condo, their favorite movies will be offered on pay per view."

He was staring at her.

She tucked her hair behind her ear. "What?"

"You're going to need a ton of staff. And inventory."

She stared back. He was right. But most people wouldn't think of that. Her sister had said *Damn, I want to go.*

"Yes," she said. "But it will be worth it."

"What if the husband likes blue and the wife likes purple?"

She smiled. "I'll find a comforter with both blue and purple in it."

"So you'll also need a full-time shopper. Or fifteen."

"Dream job for someone, don't you think?" She crossed her legs and sat back. Britton already liked the idea.

"Think of the food inventory if everyone wants something different all the time."

"Think of the guests who will sign up to stay."

Finally he gave her a slow grin. "I want red sheets, don't

care about the flowers, but I need beef jerky, Pringles and blue Gatorade. And I'd love for the whole place to smell like chocolate chip cookies."

She couldn't help but smile back even as she shook her head. "You want race cars or fire trucks on those red sheets?"

His eyes widened. "Race cars are an option?"

"A twelve-year-old boy would ask for the same things."

"Twelve-year-old boys know how to have fun."

"Is that why you've decided to just essentially be twelve years old forever?" He exuded that little-boy-in-a-man's-body vibe.

He leaned in. "Being twelve was awesome. The biggest thing I had to worry about was whether my allowance was going to cover the candy bars and video games I wanted to buy. I'd be twelve forever if I could. Except, of course, for the sex thing."

She tried not to let it show how her breath hitched. Lord, the man only had to say "sex" and she reacted. "Twelve-year-old boys like breasts too."

"Yeah, but they don't know what to do with them."

But he did.

The rest of the statement hung unspoken but obvious between them.

Trying to distract them both she said, "You're telling me this because you want a free night's stay for coming along and helping me?"

"Definitely not," he said, sitting back.

"No?" She totally intended to give him some free time at the resort. But he didn't have to know that.

"I want two weeks. And I think I'll change my favorite color to black and white stripes for week two."

"Two weeks?" she asked. "That seems like a lot."

"How about I promise I'll earn it?"

His voice didn't change, his expression didn't change, but that sounded decidedly sexy.

She finally nodded. "You'll have to."

He reached out and grabbed a magazine from the rack on

the wall. "I'm not worried."

Um, yeah, he had nothing to worry about if the elevator and airplane seat were anything to go by. It gave her hot flashes to think what the guy might do with an actual bed.

They'd have an actual bed in less than an hour.

She fanned herself and looked out the window. Neither helped.

He flipped through several pages of *Money* magazine.

"I don't normally have one-night stands," she heard herself say.

"I know." He didn't even look at her. He grabbed another magazine and flipped through a few pages of that one too.

"You do?" She thought about that. Had she seemed inexperienced? She didn't have one-night stands, but it certainly wasn't her first time with a penis. "How?"

"The same way I knew you weren't a stripper."

He exchanged the magazine for yet another.

"I never said I was a stripper."

"But you didn't correct me." He'd made some comment about how he was sorry he'd missed her show and she'd decided to go with it.

"But you knew I wasn't anyway?"

"Definitely." He sighed as he stuffed the magazine back into the rack with the others.

"How?" She turned in her seat. She couldn't pull off stripper?

He looked at her. "Why do you care?"

"Curiosity." Her body wasn't good enough to show off?

"Okay." He shifted closer. "You've absolutely got a body for it."

Well, that helped.

"But you don't have the same confidence," he went on.

She cocked an eyebrow. She was nothing if not confident.

"Strippers know what they've got and how to use it. They want people to look at them." He looked her over from head to toe, the ripples of awareness seemed to awaken every one of her skin cells. "You're sure of yourself but you don't need people to look at you or acknowledge it to know it."

That was...nice. And true. Which startled her. He knew things like that about her already? Again she was hit with the idea Doug wasn't what he seemed. Which wasn't good.

Apparently satisfied he'd answered her questions, he reached under his seat and pulled out his bag. From the front pocket he retrieved a book.

She couldn't help it—she reached over and tipped the book to see the cover.

The first thing she saw was the hot, half-naked man on the front. The second thing was the name of the author. "Doug?"

"Yeah?" He opened to a page about a third of the way through.

"That's a Lori Foster book."

"Right."

"Do you know it's a romance?"

"The other four I've read were, so I assumed it was."

She put her hand over the page in front of him forcing him to look at her. "You read romance?"

"Have *you* ever read a Lori Foster book?"

"Well...no."

"So you're not aware of the hot women and hot sex scenes? I mean, she uses the word clit. Why *wouldn't* I read it?"

If the word "sex" made it hard to breathe, the word "clit" from him made her very aware of that part of *her* body. "Oh?" she managed. "How did you know she uses that word before you read the first one?"

"Sara told me."

Morgan looked away from skimming the first paragraph on the page he was reading. She saw nipples and tongue. There was a woman he was talking about clits with? "Who's Sara?"

"Sam and Jessica's little sister—Mac's wife."

"Who are Sam and Jessica and Mac?"

"Some of my best friends in the world."

She watched his face. There was something... affectionate...

in his tone. She liked that. "So Sara's just a friend?"

He nodded. "Almost like a little sister."

"How, then, did the subject of clits come up?"

His expression turned serious—and hot. He leaned in close. "Say clits again."

She couldn't take a deep breath suddenly. "Clits."

He slowly nodded. "I like a woman who can say words like that without blinking or blushing."

"You do?" She liked turning him on. She leaned closer to him too. "I can say other words too. Nipple. Cock. Fuck."

It worked. His pupils dilated and his gaze dropped to her mouth. "Yeah, I remember you can say fuck."

Then she did blush. She remembered asking him to fuck her in the elevator.

Wow. She *never* did stuff like that. She'd been naïve and easy with Todd, but she'd been downright naughty and dirty with Doug.

She thought she might prefer naughty and dirty.

"Tell me why you and Sara talk like this with each other," she said.

He shook his head quickly. "No, we don't talk like that. God, Mac would kick my ass, for one thing. Nah, she just mentioned men might get some insight from reading sex scenes women write for other women to read. Romance is the most popular book genre. Somebody's doing something right."

Considering she'd seen two words and was a fan of Lori's already, she had to admit he might be on to something. "What else do you have in your bag?"

He laughed. "No more books." He looked at her, amused. "Here, borrow it." He handed her the book while he reached into his bag again.

She wasn't going to argue. While she was tempted to start reading right where he'd left off, she decided to start at the beginning. She flipped to the front, but couldn't help looking to see what he pulled out next.

"A comic book? Seriously?" Just when he'd seemed more like an adult.

He grinned. "*The Guild.*"

"*The Guild?* Not even Spider-Man or something?"

"Love Spider-Man."

"What's *The Guild?*"

He showed her the front of the comic book. "It's a web show. About online gamers."

"Ah." She opened the book. "I think it's safe to say I know a lot more about what's in this book."

"There will be a test later."

She glanced at him but he seemed already absorbed in *The Guild.* She tried to ignore him. The book made it a little easier. But it was his book. What else was in his bag? More surprises, she was sure.

A thought occurred to her. "Um, Doug?"

"Yeah?"

"Is that the only bag you brought?" The duffle fit comfortably under his seat.

"Yeah." He flipped a page.

"I assume there's not much call for tuxedos and suits as a paramedic." Which she hadn't thought of until now. She wondered if he owned a tie. Or a shirt with buttons.

"It's hard to get blood out of Armani," he said.

"So you didn't bring anything more than jeans and T-shirts?" She hadn't dated a guy who wore a T-shirt that said, *I don't get drunk, I get awesome* before.

"Nope. But I promise you I look just as good in a suit as I do a tux." He flipped another page.

She wasn't worried about *that.* In fact, she shouldn't worry about any of it. She just cared what he looked like *out* of his suit, tux, jeans, etc. It had occurred to her to take him to dinner with her, but then thought better of it. She didn't know him. He was able to flirt but she wasn't sure he could make polite conversation. Regaling Jonathan Britton with tales of the things he'd seen and done as a paramedic might not be appropriate.

She was impressed with the I-save-lives thing, she could admit. It was sexy, in fact. But Jonathan Britton might feel differently. Either way, it was safer to keep Doug in the hotel

47

room waiting for her. Which would make her stick to business only with Jonathan and Todd and would ensure the only orgasms she had were with a hot paramedic who barely knew what she did for a living.

"Besides," he said. "I'm Julia Roberts."

"You're..." She didn't know what to say to that. "Do you have medication for these delusions?"

He looked up and grinned. "You haven't read Lori Foster and you haven't seen *Pretty Woman?* What kind of American woman are you?"

She frowned. "Of course I've seen *Pretty Woman.*"

"Then you understand. I'm Julia Roberts and you're Richard Gere. If you want me to have special clothes, all I need is a credit card and for you to tell the bitchy saleswomen to be nice to me."

Morgan looked at his T-shirt and then his lips. The lips she *really* liked and needed this weekend. He was just a big kid. But he held the record for the hottest, fastest orgasm of her life.

She sighed and opened the book again. "I'd have to worry about you spilling blue Gatorade on the suits."

The Britton Hotel, the original, was in downtown Chicago. Jonathan Britton didn't just own it. He lived in it. His home took up the entire top floor of the hotel. The luxury suites were the floor just below.

The moment Dooley stepped into the lobby he was assaulted by memories.

His dad's hotels would have rivaled Britton's any day.

Douglas Miller, Dooley's dad, had inherited the hotels along with his partner, Phillip Wyatt. Their grandfathers had been best friends and had built their first hotel in Omaha. The hotels had been the Wyatt-Morris hotels—Wyatt from Phillip's family and Morris from Douglas's maternal grandfather. By the time Douglas and Phillip took over they had over sixty hotels across the United States, including one in Hawaii.

Dooley had enjoyed every minute of his childhood in posh

hotels with room service and valets and maids. Right alongside Phillip's kids. He'd seen the kitchens, the laundry rooms, the security offices and the storage closets. He'd hung out with the groundskeepers and the delivery guys and the bell hops. He knew the ins and outs of how a hotel ran day to day and he knew how the overall, big business side ran.

In fact, he knew more about that than he wanted to.

"Isn't this gorgeous?" Morgan whispered as bellmen materialized, took their bags and seemingly disappeared.

It was gorgeous. The hotel was incredible, in fact.

It was precisely the type of place he'd been avoiding for the past eleven years.

"Look at the chandelier," she breathed. "And the flower vases are Waterford crystal."

Yup, probably.

Of course, the plastic thirty-two-ounce cup he had from the Omaha Stormchasers game held flowers just as effectively. Not that he'd ever put flowers in it. It also held iced tea and soda effectively, which was a lot more useful in his opinion.

"All of the lobby furniture is custom made in London by—"

"I like couches you can put your feet up on," Dooley interrupted as he took her elbow and steered her toward the front desk.

The hotel was beautiful and if someone was impressed by glamour and expense, then this place would do it. Morgan clearly was. Which disappointed him. Which was stupid. Of course she would look at and admire the décor. She was the manager of the most high-class hotel in Omaha. She worked for Jonathan Britton, for God's sake. Obviously she liked fancy, expensive and extravagant.

He was so not the guy for her.

All the more reason to be sure this was temporary.

"Ms. James?" A young woman stepped from behind the check-in counter and met them halfway across the lobby.

"Yes."

"We've been anticipating your arrival. Welcome to the Britton Chicago." The woman's smile was wide and bright and it was clear she'd been assigned as Morgan's personal greeter. She handed Morgan a key card and a bouquet of flowers. "We're so happy to have you here."

Morgan smiled at the woman. "Thank you for the warm greeting."

Dooley had to admit he was impressed. Especially when the woman turned to him and handed him a sparkly gold gift bag. "Mr. Miller, welcome to the Britton Chicago. I'm Beth. Please let me know if there's anything you need during your stay."

"Thanks, Beth, I'll do that."

"I'll escort you to your room if you're ready. You'll be in the North Suite."

"Wonderful," Morgan said, but as she turned to follow Beth she stopped.

Dooley followed her gaze to where her attention had been snagged by a well-dressed couple surrounded by suitcases, engaged in a hushed conversation. They looked worried and confused.

"Beth, have those guests been helped?" Morgan asked.

Beth turned to look at the couple as well. She frowned. "I don't recognize them."

"Can you check with someone please? We can wait."

"Of course." Beth headed for the front desk and soon had another attendant with her. They stopped by the couple but it quickly became clear there was a communication issue. The couple spoke what sounded like French to him and obviously Beth and the young man with her didn't.

Morgan, on the other hand, didn't have any trouble understanding the travelers.

Dooley sighed as he watched and listened to her talking with the couple and translating for the Britton Hotel employees.

She spoke a second language. Fluently. Dammit.

He loved bilingual women.

He shifted the flowers she'd handed to him to his other arm and leaned back against the nearest forty-foot high colonnade.

Within minutes Morgan had ascertained that the couple had been dropped off at the wrong hotel by their cab driver.

"Greg, will you please get a guest services manager from the Fairmont on the phone? I'll arrange for one of the Britton's cars to take Mr. and Mrs. Benoit to their hotel but I want to be sure someone is waiting to greet them."

Greg moved off to make the call while Morgan excused herself to the Benoits for a moment.

"I'm sorry. I don't mean to ignore you."

"I'm good," he said, with a shrug and a smile. "I can speak English so I'm fine on my own."

"The Fairmont is only a few minutes away. This shouldn't take long."

"That's nice of you. Especially considering they aren't your guests. Why not just talk them into staying here?"

She grinned. "I thought about it," she admitted. "But no, they just need a translator. If we'd known they were coming here we would have had someone ready to greet them in French. I'm sure the Fairmont will do the same."

"I'm impressed." He was. She was gracious and kind and spoke two languages. As if her breasts weren't enough to keep him at her heels.

"I traveled around Europe in college," she said. "I remember the feeling of helplessness that comes when you can't communicate and how grateful you are when someone takes pity on you and helps out."

She'd traveled. Great. He loved to travel. He loved women who loved to travel.

Dammit.

"I'm heading to the North Suite? No room number?" he asked.

"Only four suites take up the entire twenty-seventh floor."

Ah. "Okay, then I'll take the elevator up and turn north."

She smiled and rose on tiptoe, planting a quick kiss on the corner of his mouth. "I'll be up as soon as I can."

"You want me to wait?"

"No. Go on up. I can send a masseuse up."

He grinned and leaned in close. "The only person I want touching me is you."

Her cheeks got a little pink at that.

"Hurry," he said. He started to lean back, then thought better of it. He put a hand on her low back and nudged her forward at the same time he met her lips with his.

He was tempted to back her up against the colonnade and make her forget the French couple, but he didn't even open his mouth. He pulled back after only a few seconds.

But he memorized the dazed look on her face. He'd never done that so easily to a woman before.

This had the makings of the best weekend. Ever.

"Ms. James?"

She turned slowly to face Greg and the Benoits. "Yes?" She cleared her throat. "Yes?"

Dooley was feeling darned good about himself at this point.

"The car's ready."

"Okay." She spun back to face Dooley. "I'll just..."

"Hurry," he inserted with a grin.

"Right."

He watched her escort the Benoits out the front door to the car.

Then he headed upstairs.

In the elevator he dug into the gift bag, expecting lotion or coupons. Instead he pulled out a package of beef jerky, a can of Pringles and a bottle of blue Gatorade.

Amazing. He was still shaking his head when he stepped off the elevator. Morgan had something with these little special touches after all. Beth, who had escorted him up, opened the door and crossed to the fridge where she withdrew a bottle of water and filled a glass with ice from the ice bucket.

"Thanks, Beth."

"My pleasure." She laid a business card next to his ice water. "Call me if you need anything during your stay. My hours are eight to eight. Nathan will be your evening attendant. You can reach him at the same number from eight p.m. to eight in the morning."

"Great. Will do. Thanks." He wondered if everyone got a personal attendant or just the guys who traveled with the rising

Britton stars.

As Beth let herself out, he surveyed the room. The suite was amazing. High ceilings, huge windows, plush everything. There was a large living room, a dining area with a table that could seat eight, and a kitchen area with a half stove, full fridge and marble countertops.

In the bedroom there was a king bed in the center of the room, a loveseat and chair with a coffee table near the window, a full armoire and a balcony with two patio chairs and a table.

There were two bathrooms. The smaller one was basic, but then there was the master bath. It was nearly as big as the bedroom. The whirlpool tub was bigger than the bed. One entire wall was made up of mirrors and there was an enormous glass shower stall.

He could happily stay here for a year or two. He didn't live the high life anymore and most of the time he was fine with that. He insisted on being fine with that—after all, what was the alternative? He had enough money, just not extra money. No one *needed* five-thousand-thread-count Egyptian cotton sheets.

But he sure as hell wasn't going to complain about sleeping on them for a night or two.

He knew money didn't buy happiness, but it sure made happiness look, feel, taste—and even smell—better.

Returning to the front room, he noticed their luggage had already been delivered. His duffle sat next to Morgan's suitcase inside the door. Her *gigantic,* expensive suitcase.

"I'm here," Morgan called from the front room.

Dooley propped his shoulder against the doorjamb of the bedroom. "I guess this place will do."

She grinned at him as she kicked off her shoes, removed her watch and earrings, and slipped off her jacket. "Nice, right?"

She fit right in here. Everything on her and around her was expensive.

He sighed. "Better than nice." Good thing this was temporary.

When she turned to him with a sexy little smile though he knew, short-term or not, he was going to enjoy this woman.

"Dinner's at seven," she said.

"It's three thirty now."

"That gives us three and a half hours," she said, unnecessarily.

"Yep." He moved toward her, stopping a few inches away.

She was breathing fast now, her eyes were wide and she was clenching her hands at her sides.

"How are we going to kill that much time?" he asked, his voice husky.

The little hitch in her breathing and the way she pressed her hand to her heart definitely turned him on.

He started to reach for her. But then something stopped him. She was breathing *too* fast. She looked...nervous.

"You okay?" he asked, dipping his knees so he could look into her eyes when she glanced away.

"Of course."

He took her hand, holding her wrist, her pulse beating under his first finger. It was beating hard. "Morgan, I—"

"God, I want you," she breathed out, looking up at him. "I do. I feel..." She pressed her free hand against her stomach. "I almost feel sick."

Both of his eyebrows went up. "Sick?"

"Not *sick*. I mean excited. Jumpy. Itchy all over. I never get like this. It's not like this is our first time. I mean, obviously we've been...intimate before this."

She was talking way too fast too. Adrenaline was clearly pumping hard and Dooley felt a smile kick up the corner of his mouth. He'd seen this reaction in women before. But never to him. Sam got this reaction all the time. Women practically fell in Sam's lap, even now that he was married. They stuttered around him, they blushed, they giggled too much and talked too fast.

And now Morgan was doing it. Because of *him*.

An amazing surge of power came with that.

No wonder Sam had been such a ladies' man. This was fun.

Dooley tugged gently on her wrist, bringing her closer.

"This is so silly. I mean I *want* this, Doug. I do. I meant it in the bar when I said I knew this trip would involve this. Hell, I brought you along because I want you so much. I remember seeing you at the fundraiser. The minute I looked at you I—"

He covered her mouth with his hand. "Easy, Sugar." He hadn't used the name since the bar, since learning her real name. But it had the desired effect of stopping her words and making her smile. "I know you want me." He did. He could read it all over her. He could *feel* it just looking at her. This wasn't nerves, this was excitement. Intense excitement. Too intense.

"Breathe," he told her, moving his hand from her mouth.

She did.

"I like NASCAR," he said, still holding her wrist.

She looked at him, clearly confused, but he needed her to slow down, to relax, to enjoy this.

"I mean I really like it. So one year my dad arranged for me to drive with one of the drivers in his car around the track. They do it all the time for fans, to give you a taste of what it's like." He rubbed his thumb back and forth over the pulse point on her wrist that was still beating too fast. But she was listening to him, staring into his eyes.

They were standing only centimeters apart and he wanted her to get used to that, to being close to him, and he wanted it to be easy. Yes, they'd already been together, but it had been intense too. It had been fast and spontaneous. She hadn't had time to think, hadn't had time to get nervous. Hell, they hadn't even taken their clothes off. Yes, their chemistry was surprisingly hot, but a woman like Morgan didn't just lose her mind every time she got stirred up. Now she'd had more time to think everything through. This time it was going to be slow and deliberate. This time he was serious about seeing and tasting everything.

He was overwhelming her, and as much as his ego enjoyed the knowledge, he didn't want her to freak out.

"I remember being so excited about the ride," he went on about his trip to Daytona International Speedway. "I was all riled up, ready to go, couldn't wait. The first trip around was awesome. I was sure it would only get better, so I thought I was ready for him to punch the accelerator. The adrenaline rush was intense." Her heart was still thumping against his finger. "You know what I did?"

She slowly shook her head.

"I closed my eyes. And missed the whole thing."

Dooley watched Morgan process what he'd said.

"You want me to calm down," she finally said.

"Yeah." He smiled. "I don't want you to miss anything."

She looked embarrassed and irritated at the same time. "I don't know what's going on, but I promise you I'm fine. Let's just...do this."

"This?"

"Sex. Let's have sex. Lots of it."

"Okay. Come here."

She did, her breathing increasing even with the few steps it took. He smiled and shook his head, then lifted a hand and pressed his first two fingers against the pulse point in her neck.

"Your heart is racing."

"I know," she put her hand over her heart. "This is crazy. I never react like this. I'm cool under pressure. I'm never like this with men. I just... There's something about you... I mean, I've never had sex in an elevator before either. Every time I get close to you I just—"

He put his hand over her mouth again, stopping the babbling. "I have an idea. We need to take the edge off," he said firmly before dropping his hand. "And I need to wear you down some. If you're this energetic in bed you might kill me."

Morgan put a hand against her forehead. What the hell was going on?

As she'd told Maddie, Doug had the strongest effect on her she'd ever felt...ever. She'd looked at him and wanted him. Looking at him now, she wanted him.

At the fundraiser it hadn't been a risk. She didn't know

him. They hadn't spent any real time talking, at least not about anything important. They'd flirted. They'd talked dirty. But they hadn't *talked* and they'd known there was no future. Now though, just standing in a bedroom with him she was chattering uncontrollably. She knew she sounded stupid, but she seemed to have no control over her mouth. Or her heart rate, breathing pattern or thoughts. She could only imagine what she might say if they were naked, or making love, or lying in each other's arms, the sheets tangled...

Morgan forced herself to breathe.

"Okay, what's your idea?" she asked.

"Take this," he said, handing her cell phone over, "and go in the bathroom."

"What?" She frowned looking from the phone to him.

"Do it. I'm going to be right here." He sat back on the bed and she noticed he had his phone in hand.

"Go," he told her with a sexy half grin.

Well, what the hell? The moment the bathroom door shut behind her, her phone rang.

"Hello?"

"Lock the door. Then take your clothes off."

"Doug, what are you doing?"

"Taking the edge off in a way you can just enjoy and not get so worked up over."

"You're staying in the bedroom while I'm in here? With the door locked?"

"Right."

She had to admit, her heart wasn't racing quite as fast. She turned the lock. "Now what?"

"Are you naked?"

Her heart thumped. "No."

"Get that way. Tell me what you're taking off as you do it."

Phone sex. That was his idea. She should just march back into the bedroom, strip her clothes off and climb up on the bed beside him.

But she'd never done this before and she was intrigued.

And turned on. Okay, this was...safer. No, that wasn't the right word. This was...less intense. She didn't feel overwhelmed, just excited.

"Okay, I'm putting you on speaker." She set her phone on the counter top, turned the volume up and then stripped her shirt off. "I'm taking my shirt off."

"Me too."

Her eyes flew to the phone. He was stripping too? Images popped up one right after the other. Doug sprawled on the bed without a shirt, his bare chest and stomach...

"Morgan, you there?"

She cleared her throat. "Um, yeah."

"You still have your bra on?"

"Yes."

"What's it look like?"

She looked at her image in the mirror. "You saw it on the plane," she reminded him.

"I was distracted. Tell me what it looks like."

"It's, um, dark green, like my shirt."

"Lace?"

"The edges of the cups are lace."

"Can you see your nipples through it?"

Said nipples stiffened at his words. "No, they don't show."

"But you can tell they're hard right?"

She nodded, then realized she'd have to answer. "Yes." She sounded as breathless as she felt.

"Take it off now."

She licked her lips and reached behind her, undoing the tiny hooks and tossing the bra to the side.

"You've got perfect breasts and nipples," Doug said, his voice gruff. "They taste as good as they look."

She wasn't sure what to say to that. But he didn't wait for an answer.

"Lick your fingers and then play with your nipples."

She put her first finger in her mouth and then swirled it around the tip of her right breast. Ripples of sensation coursed from the simple touch straight to her clit. She loved having her nipples played with and had stimulated herself this same way before, but having Doug talking her through it and knowing he was out there imagining it made it so much sweeter.

"Are you doing it?" he asked.

"Yes."

"Are you looking at yourself?"

She lifted both hands to her breasts and toyed with the nipples, rolling and plucking them, breathing harder as she did it. "Yes."

"I'm picturing you now," he said.

"What are you doing?" She pictured him as well. Was he naked?

"I'm lying on the bed."

"Do you have your jeans on?"

"Yes." He paused a moment. "Do you want me to take them off?"

"Yes," she said huskily. "I want to know you're naked right outside this door."

"Whatever you want."

He must have set the phone down right beside him on the bed because she could have sworn she heard the zipper on his jeans and then placed the sound of denim brushing over the silk comforter. A moment later he said, "Okay."

"You're completely naked?" she asked.

"Yeah. Now you."

She wanted to peek out the door so badly. Instead, she shimmied her jeans off and then slid her silk panties off, tossing them on top of her bra. "Okay," she said.

"Gorgeous, right?" he asked.

She smiled. "I'd rather see you."

"If you need a mental picture right now, I'm lying on my back, buck naked, stroking my cock and thinking of how your mouth would feel on me."

She swallowed hard. Holy cow. Vivid images and major heat assaulted her all at once. "I'm liking that picture."

"I'm picturing you too," he said. "Are you still trimmed like you were at the fundraiser?"

She shouldn't have to look to answer his question of course, but she still looked at herself in the mirror. She got regular bikini waxes and kept things nearly bare there. "Yes." She could hear his quick breath. "But you never saw that."

"I felt it, girl," he said, his voice rough. "I've been thinking about it ever since."

Surprise hit her. Had he not been with anyone else since then? It had been a month since that night, which had specifically been a one-night stand. "You have?"

"Oh, yeah. Will you touch yourself for me?"

Somebody was going to have to touch her. She was burning up. "Yes."

"Good, slide your hand down between your legs. Are you wet?"

"Very." She slid her finger over her clit and imagined it was Doug's hand.

"Spread your legs and then spread yourself open with one hand. Can you see your clit?"

She did what he said, her breathing coming fast and choppy. "Yes," she almost whispered.

"I remember how that felt too," he told her huskily. "Sweet and tight and very sensitive."

"Yes," she breathed, circling over it as he talked. His voice was almost as addictive as his touch. Almost.

"Now slide lower. Slip your fingers inside."

Her inner muscles clenched as she slid two fingers inside. She knew just the angle that worked best and she immediately felt ripples of pleasure.

"Stroke yourself for me. Go deep. Make yourself feel good."

"I'd rather have your fingers," she gasped.

"You can have whatever you want. As soon as you come."

His words and voice combined powerfully. She loved the explicitness, the intimacy of it.

"Are you as hot and tight and wet as I'm imagining?" he

asked.

"Yes. Are you still touching yourself too?"

He chuckled. "Definitely. But I'm trying to hold back until you come."

"Are you going to come?" she asked, moving her fingers back to her clit.

"Oh, yeah. But I want to know if you want me to picture coming in your mouth or on your breasts."

She sucked in a breath. No one had ever said that to her before. No one had ever *done* that to her before. If she had given a blow job, it was never to the point of orgasm, just part of the general foreplay. The idea of doing that to him was intoxicating. "I can't decide. Either. Both."

He chuckled again, but it sounded almost pained. "You're amazing."

"This was your idea."

"I'm amazing too." There was a moment of silence, then he said, "Tell me you're close, Morgan."

"I'm close," she said, wishing she had her vibrator with her. Of course it hadn't even occurred to her when packing for this trip knowing Doug would be there.

"Are you standing up?"

"Yes."

"Sit up on the counter. Spread your legs wide."

Um...wow. She did it though. He had yet to give her a *bad* suggestion. The cool marble of the counter top seemed to heighten the sensitivity of all her nerves and as her knees parted and her fingers circled, then stroked, then circled, then stroked she felt the orgasm building.

"I bet you look so hot," Doug muttered. "I'll bet the counter is just the right height for me to step between your legs and sink deep with one thrust."

That was all it took. She gasped as the orgasm rolled over her. "Oh, *yes*." She wanted him to know, she wanted him to hear it. She wanted him there with her.

"Fuck, Morgan," she heard and she pictured his big hand on his cock, stroking fast and then the orgasm erupting from him.

Several beats passed as she sat on the bathroom counter breathing hard. She heard nothing from the other end of the phone.

Finally she said, "You still there?"

"Just wondering if you'd come out here and let me lick you now."

She had to clear her throat again before answering. "Um, yeah, I think I would. If I get to lick you too."

He groaned and she grinned as she slid to the floor and started for the door. Then she paused. They'd just been very intimate. They'd already had sex once. But he hadn't seen her completely, totally naked. Apparently he'd *pictured* it, but he hadn't seen it. Could she just parade out there without a stitch on? She grabbed a towel and wrapped it around her quickly.

He, on the other hand, clearly had no such reservations. He was lying back on the bed, completely naked. Gloriously naked. Breathtakingly naked.

Her mouth went dry and she stopped in the doorway.

He grinned. "You can't possibly be as surprised as you look. Did you think I was sitting out here watching TV and faking all of that?"

"No. I just... Wow." He was bigger than she'd imagined. Which was ridiculous since she'd felt as much of him as he had of her. But seeing it was different.

He looked damned good on the bed. His chest was nearly smooth with only a light dusting of golden hair gracing his pecs. He was muscular and tight...and she wanted to touch every inch.

As she stayed frozen in the doorway, trying to decide what she wanted to do to him first, he pushed himself up off the bed and came toward her.

"You gotta quit lookin' at me like that, Sugar," he said gruffly, stopping in front of her.

"Like what?" Like she couldn't remember why she'd had a single concern about getting close to him, in every way.

"Like you just forgot what you had asked me." He gave her a cocky grin, then reached for her. He got a finger into the top of the towel and tugged it loose. As the towel hit the carpet...the phone started ringing.

Chapter Three

Morgan was here for work. This wasn't vacation, it wasn't a date. She was here working and he was her...distraction. He knew she had to answer it. Still, he could hope she was so caught up in the moment that she'd let the caller leave a message. She sighed. "I have to answer it."

"Fuck." Dooley sighed too. "I know."

She grabbed the phone on the bedside table and, distracted by the call, she seemed to forget she was naked. He sat back on the bed and watched her.

She was gorgeous. He didn't mind that she had her attention on other things at the moment. It was the perfect opportunity to study her. And make some lists.

Like the list of all the places her wanted to lick and suck—the outer curve of her left breast, the sweet spot just below her belly button and her right hip bone. For starters. Then the list of all the positions he wanted to try out before they went back to Omaha. Then the list of all the places in the suite he wanted to make her come.

He loved that it was so easy to get her riled up. Whether it was just how she was wired or it was something chemical between the two of them, he didn't care. He loved how easy it was to turn her on. He was more than willing to take as much time as necessary, but with the responses she was giving him, it looked like multiple orgasms were in her future.

She crossed the room to her purse, then bent to rummage for something inside her briefcase... and Dooley about swallowed his tongue. *That* was a nice view. He wanted to cross the room, grab her hips and sink deep. No foreplay, no build up, just hot and *now*.

But before he could even stand, she straightened, hung up

the phone and tossed the cordless receiver onto the couch. "I have to deal with a crisis," she said, coming toward him.

It took him a moment to realize she was talking to him. Saying she had to do something else. Especially when her attention focused on the erection that was slowly gaining rigidity.

Just having her look at him made him hard.

"What?" he asked.

"There's a problem in Omaha. I need to head downstairs to the offices where I can get my hands on some contract copies and then get on a conference call with my department heads. The good news is some of the people I need to talk to are headquartered here."

"When?"

"Right now." She looked disappointed too. Damn.

"How long will it take?"

She sighed and pushed her hair back from her forehead. "Probably an hour. I'm sorry."

"It's not your fault." He looked down at himself. "Well, it *is* your fault." He chuckled at her look of chagrin. "But this is a work trip for you."

"I'll be back as soon as I can and we can—"

"It's fine," he interrupted. Talking about what they could do or would do later wasn't going to help.

Her eyes dropped to his groin again. "I'm so sorry. I wanted to—"

"Stop. Talking." He shook his head and grabbed his pants, stepping into them even though zipping them up over his erection was going to be difficult. And potentially painful.

"But I just want you to know I planned on—"

"I know."

"I feel bad that I got you all—"

"Morgan?"

"Yeah?"

"If you don't stop talking you're going to be late for your phone call."

"No, I have some time."

"It's not enough."

"I just have to go downstairs and get—"

He moved in, pulled her up on her tiptoes and kissed her until she melted against him, running her hands up his back and into his hair.

When he pulled back he said, "*That* is going to take another twenty minutes before we even get to the other stuff. So we don't have enough time."

She pressed her lips together and let him set her back on her feet. "Okay."

"Go do your business. Then get your pretty butt back up here a.s.a.p."

"Okay."

He waited a moment and when she didn't move, he turned and nudged her toward the bathroom. "Get dressed."

"Right. Okay. Dressed."

As she covered up her gorgeous body with clothes once again, Dooley wondered what he'd do while she was gone. He was on vacation. This wasn't work for him. He could get a massage, watch TV, read.

Except those ideas all sucked. He wasn't much of a sitter. He liked action. He also wasn't much for being alone. He was used to having people around him all the time.

"I'll be back as soon as I can." The woman who emerged looked all business. Still gorgeous. But all about the work.

Still, the first thing Dooley thought when he saw her was how the last time she'd been in that bathroom she'd been having phone sex with him.

"Please make yourself at home. Whatever you need, just call Beth."

He pushed himself off the bed and padded over to her. "I don't think so."

"Please." She was digging in her briefcase. "If you want something special to eat or..." Her gaze finally met his and realization dawned. "Right. Anything except *that.* That you're saving for me."

"Damned right." He hauled her up and kissed her again, long and wet and hot. Satisfied to see her breathing hard when he let go, he grinned then turned her toward the suite door and patted her on the butt. "Hurry back."

"What are you going to do?" she asked, tripping toward the door.

"I'll find something to kill the time."

She looked a little worried when she glanced back. "Okay, but remember," she said as she opened the door, "this carpet is white. Be careful with the Gatorade."

The business took an hour and forty minutes to wrap up. Of course. Apparently the moment she'd stepped out of her hotel, the Mayor stepped in. He wanted to plan the stay for everyone involved in bringing Tim McGraw to Omaha. In eight months. It could have easily waited until Morgan's return, but her assistant manager had done a poor job of reassuring him and he'd demanded to have a conference call with her, the hotel and event staff.

A long, detailed conference call.

Which she usually appreciated.

But she didn't usually have Doug waiting up in her hotel suite.

"Ms. James?"

She had just pushed the elevator button when she heard her name. She turned to find a man in a dark suit approaching. "Yes?" She was on the second floor of the hotel where all the administrative offices were housed. They included offices for the department head of the Chicago hotel as well as several offices for others who worked for Britton Hotels nationwide and worldwide. She'd been given one of the three large conference rooms Jonathan Britton used to meet with his Board of Directors, department heads and managers from all over.

"I'm Tim Arnet. I'm the head of security here."

Morgan extended her hand to the man. "Nice to meet you."

"Ms. James, because you're a special guest here I wanted to

address this with you directly rather than involve my staff and your guests."

She frowned slightly. "My guests?" She hadn't misheard the plural on the word.

"Yes. We've had a noise complaint from the east suite on the twenty-seventh floor."

Her neighbors.

"A noise complaint?"

"Yes. The guest in the east suite is a...musician."

Mr. Arnet seemed hesitant to share the information and she guessed the musician was rather famous and the hotel had, of course, promised to keep his identity and location under wraps.

"His schedule includes sleeping during the afternoon prior to performing at night. Apparently the gathering in your suite is disturbing him," the man finished. "I was informed you were not in the suite and wanted to give you the chance to address the issue."

She felt her cheeks flush. She was the one who helped take care of these things when they occurred in her hotel. She had certainly never *caused* a noise complaint. Nor did she invite people to stay who might cause a disturbance of any kind.

What the hell was Doug doing?

"I'm sorry. I will take care of it immediately," she assured the security team leader. "Please apologize to our neighbor."

She was scowling as she got off the elevator on the twenty-seventh floor.

She was less than satisfied with how the phone call with the Mayor of Omaha had gone. She was also worried about her assistant manager handling things while she was gone and she now barely had enough time to get ready for dinner. She was meeting Jonathan and Todd and who-knew-who-else in the dining room at seven and she wanted to be early. Now not only had she left a hot naked man in her room, but that hot naked man was causing a commotion.

Hopefully he wasn't naked anymore at least.

There wasn't any blaring music as she walked toward her

suite and she hoped that whatever had been going on was over. But just as she fit her key card into the door she heard a loud shout of "Motherfucker!"

Morgan pushed the door to the suite open and stood staring.

There were men everywhere.

Well, that wasn't completely accurate, she supposed. They weren't *everywhere*. They were gathered in the living area in front of the big screen TV.

There were only six when she did a quick head count, but it looked like there had either been more of them earlier, or the six had been there for a while.

There was a huge sub sandwich on the dining table, half of it gone, lettuce and condiment packages spread all over. There were also open chip bags and beer and soda cans all over the countertops of the kitchenette. She walked over and picked up an empty wrapper. Red licorice.

Wow.

Teenage boys had taken over.

Teenage boys were only more dangerous than little boys because they had access to money. That they spent on things like junk food.

The man sitting on the arm of the chair nearest the door noticed her first. "Hey, Dooley, we got company."

Doug pivoted from his seat in the middle of the sofa. When he saw her his mouth spread into a huge grin and he handed his game controller to the guy sitting next to him.

"Hey, gorgeous," he greeted as he climbed over the back of the couch. "Solve all the world's problems?"

"Um, well, Omaha's anyway," she told him. "What's going on?"

He looked over his shoulder with a smile. "Mario Kart."

"The video game?"

"Yeah!" one of the men shouted at the TV. "Suck it!"

She took a deep breath. "Doug—"

"You know what Mario Kart is?" he asked.

"Of course." She didn't want him to get distracted. "You've

got to tell the guys to stop yelling. There are other people staying up here."

"Son of a bitch!" one of them yelled. "Cocksucker!"

"Guys, tone it down," Doug shouted with a grin. "There's a lady here."

There were some glances in her direction and mumbles of "sorry".

"It's not just about me..." She broke off, deciding she needed more explanation of the root of the problem. "Why are you playing Mario Kart? Why are there so many people here?"

How did he even know five other guys in Chicago?

"I called Beth and asked if there was any way I could get a video game. She came through. When the guys came up to bring it to me, I asked what they were doing. They were just getting off their shift and they grabbed some other guys too. We ordered some food and started playing. Then Charlie and Dave showed up from housekeeping to get the grape soda out of the carpet—"

"These guys *work* here?" she interrupted. And they'd spilled grape soda on the ecru carpet.

"Well, yeah." He shrugged. "I don't know anyone else in Chicago. Mario Kart's way more fun with other people."

"But they *work here.*" Crap, it was a good thing the security manager hadn't come up. These guys would have been in enough trouble being in here, even without contributing to a problem with another guest.

"They're off the clock. They're just having some fun. I asked them to hang out until you got here."

"Why?" She was quickly trying to figure what she would do if some of her employees were partying in a guest's suite. That would not be good. Way too much potential for problems.

"This is Tony, Stan, Roger, Charlie and Dave. Roger's worked here for twenty-five years. Stan's been here for sixteen."

"Hi, guys," Morgan said, giving them a smile. "Very impressive." She glanced at her watch. She needed to get ready for dinner and she wasn't going to do it with five strange men in her suite. She looked up at Doug and corrected herself—*six* strange men in her suite. How could she keep forgetting that she didn't really know him? She knew he wasn't going to kill her or steal from her, she knew he didn't have any contagious diseases and she knew he had good credit. Other than that it was all a crapshoot.

This dinner meeting was important and she didn't want to be distracted. Or late. This was the first time she'd be seeing Mr. Britton and, more importantly, Todd since...the last time. "Doug, I need to talk to you."

He frowned at her. "Don't you want to chat with the guys, ask them some questions about their experience?"

"Whoo-hoo!"

"Yeah, man!"

They were still shouting but it was quieter now. As the guys were clearly into the game, Morgan took the chance to drag Doug into the bedroom. "I need to get ready for dinner. You have to get rid of them."

"Fine." He didn't look pleased. "I'll see what they're doing tomorrow."

"Tomorrow?"

"You'll be working all day tomorrow. I can hang out with them."

"Don't they have to work?"

He frowned. "I'll find out. If they do, I'll make some new friends."

Why couldn't he just hang out in the room? Get a massage? Have an expensive room service lunch? "I didn't realize I needed to arrange a babysitting service to keep you entertained."

His frown deepened. "I'm just hanging out with some nice guys. I thought it would be good for you to have a chance to talk with some people who have worked for this company for a long time. They know some things and have some ideas that could help you out."

"So you want *me* to hang out with them too? Can we have pizza tomorrow? Or Chinese food?"

His frown eased and he leaned back. "Sure, whatever you

want."

But she could tell he knew she wasn't serious.

"Tell me what time you'll be back up here tomorrow and I'll get everything arranged," he said.

Her eyes widened. "No. You can't have them up here."

"Why not?" He crossed his arms.

"They *work* here," she said, exasperated. "They can't be up in the suites, eating with the guests."

"I invited them."

"Still, it could be construed as them taking things from a guest. Which is against our policies."

"You could learn a lot from them. They've worked here almost longer than you've been alive."

"Which is even worse. They should know better than to accept an invitation into a guest's room. If something would happen, the liability is a mess. If someone would..." She had to get dressed, focus on the dinner meeting, be ready with her A-game. "Doug, I can't do this right now. I won't write them up or say anything, but no more partying with the employees."

He stared at her for a moment, then said, "Shit. You're going to be that girl?"

"What girl?"

"The girl I want to fuck even though I don't like you. I hate that."

She stared at him and swallowed hard. Okay, well, she'd asked. "Does that happen a lot?"

"Hot girls are often bitches," he said with a nod.

She needed to get dressed, but she couldn't let this go. "But you want to fuck them anyway?"

He shrugged. "I'm not proud of it."

She crossed her arms, feeling *something* she didn't particularly like feeling. She should be insulted, and probably turned off by the whole thing. Instead she was afraid she felt a tad jealous. "Do you?"

"Do I what?"

"Fuck them even if you don't like them?"

⁹ He seemed to be thinking. "Maybe twice a year."

She huffed out a quick breath. "Well, if it's any consolation, I don't like you right now either."

"I suppose that should be a deterrent to wanting you but it's not. Not with you."

She didn't have time for this. She rubbed the middle of her forehead and said, "I do need to get dressed for dinner. Can you clear the place out? Please?"

He nodded. "We'll just move the game downstairs."

She started toward the bathroom, then turned back. "Downstairs?"

"There's an employee lounge. A nice one. Couches and a TV."

He'd been down in the employee lounge? She pressed her lips together and counted to three to focus, then said patiently, "Doug, you can't go play video games and eat potato chips in the hotel basement with the employees. You're a guest. You're *my* guest. I want you to take advantage of the hotel amenities, enjoy yourself, relax."

"I'll enjoy myself down there." He started for the living room.

"Doug," she said quickly.

He turned back.

"I need you here. In the room." It wasn't about him getting into trouble when she wasn't around to supervise. At least, not completely. She needed to be thinking about him in the room. Naked. Like she had been all day. She had been excited to get back to the room all afternoon.

"Why?"

"I need..." She trailed off and took a deep breath, trying to figure out how to word this without sounding completely pathetic. "I need a reason to come back to the room. I need a...temptation."

He just watched her for a minute. Then he came back across the carpet, stopping directly in front of her. "I don't want to be accused of not doing my job here." He took her face in his hands and brought her onto her tiptoes for a kiss.

His lips moving over hers shot heat straight through her and she immediately arched closer, her arms going around his neck so she could press her whole body against him. His hands went to her butt and lifted her up close. When he let her go she found herself wanting so much more.

"Something like that?" he asked.

She blinked. "Um, yeah. Something like that."

"Then I've definitely got this covered."

He absolutely did. She didn't just want to hurry back to the room—she didn't want to leave it in the first place.

Morgan was nervous about the dinner with her boss and her jerk-thief ex-boyfriend. But she was almost more nervous about leaving Doug in the suite by himself.

Which served her right.

Bringing a near-total stranger to town for an important business meeting might not have been her brightest move.

As she curled and tucked and sprayed her hair into place, she debated taking him to dinner with her. She realized she did know some things about Doug that made him a great choice for the trip in general. First and foremost, she didn't want to be with anyone else after dinner. That was huge. That was key. She also knew he could flirt with the best of them and talk a woman out of her panties in less than twenty minutes. Also important.

But she didn't know if he could talk politely—not to mention intelligently—to a man like Jonathan Britton. She had no idea if Doug knew any entertaining stories or only dirty jokes. Somehow she was sure he knew a few of those.

Her phone was lying next to the sink on the counter top where only a few hours ago he'd made her come without even touching her himself. Exchanging her curling iron for her phone, she typed in *Do you know any dirty jokes?* and sent it to his phone.

How are women and tornadoes the same? his reply read.

She smiled and typed, *How?*

They both make a lot of noise when they come and they take the house when they leave.

She giggled. She knew he'd have a dirty joke ready to go.

Resuming work on her hair, she thought about how she liked him anyway. She just couldn't take him to dinner. What if he drank too much? Belched? Dropped the F-bomb in the midst of polite conversation? It wasn't incredibly bright to bring him along without knowing those things for sure, but at least if he was in the room it wouldn't matter and she would have a reason to come directly back to the suite after dinner. Before any Kahlua was served. Before Todd could be charming.

With a deep breath and a final look in the mirror, she grabbed her phone, tucked her lipstick in her handbag and stepped out of the bathroom.

"Holy crap."

She couldn't help the smile at Doug's reaction. It wasn't the most eloquent compliment she'd ever been given but she could tell it was heartfelt. He had been lounging on the sofa, channel surfing, but when she appeared, he pushed himself off the cushions, looking stunned.

"What?" she asked.

He wasn't even dressed up. He was wearing a T-shirt and shorts. His jaw was scruffy, as usual, his hair looked like he'd just run his fingers through it, as usual, and he was barefoot.

But it didn't matter. She wouldn't be putting in any extra time downstairs.

For that alone, she was glad she'd brought him along.

"Nothing," he finally said.

"Why aren't you saying anything else?" Was he still mad at her from earlier? Maybe she'd been too bitchy. But how did he not understand the issue with having the guys in their room?

"I'm just standing here trying to figure out what the hell you're doing with me," he told her.

Oh. She liked that. "I'm using you for protection," she said honestly.

He came around the end of the sofa. "Protection from falling into bed with another guy, right?"

That was the bottom line, yes. But this felt like...something more. Which was not a good idea, she knew. She needed him for a couple of days for very superficial—and naughty—things. Period. He wasn't someone she intended to date. Definitely not. She needed to date men she *could,* at some point, take to dinner with her boss. Hell, she needed to date men she could leave alone in a hotel suite and not worry about noise complaints or spilled grape soda.

"Right. You're here to keep me from doing something stupid with Todd," she said resolutely. She was going to simply ignore the risk of doing something stupid with Doug.

Doug frowned and moved in closer. "Something stupid? Like sleeping with him." He touched her shoulder with an open palm and dragged his hand down her arm.

Oh, yeah. His hand needed to keep up with that—in lots of places.

"Like sleeping with him," she admitted.

"I'm sorry he sucks in bed," Doug said.

She grinned. "He doesn't suck in bed. That's part of the problem."

Doug scowled, running his hand up and down her arm again. "But he's married?"

"He's not married."

"He's a dumb ass?"

She raised an eyebrow. "No. He's intelligent. In fact, that's also part of the problem."

"So what's the deal? Did he dump you?" He shook his head in disgust. "What an idiot."

She appreciated his opinion. She didn't appreciate his assumption. "He didn't dump me. I broke it off. I haven't returned a phone call or e-mail for almost four months."

"Then what's the deal? He likes to wear women's shoes? He's a racist? He has no sense of humor?"

She sighed. "He's a good-looking, charming, smart guy who's amazing in bed." She lifted a shoulder. "He'll be putting the moves on me. So I need a very potent Todd-suppressant. That's you."

✸ Doug's frown grew darker. "So he'll be trying to get you into bed?"

She sighed. "It's possible, yes. He doesn't know why I stopped communicating with him." She studied the whiskers on Doug's chin instead of meeting his eyes.

"Are you going to tell him?" Doug asked.

"Maybe." But probably not. She still felt like an idiot for letting it happen in the first place. Confronting him about it would be admitting she'd been fooled.

He tipped her chin up. "You don't have to tell me. I'm here with you no matter what. I'm more than happy to be your Todd-suppressant for the weekend. *More* than happy to keep you out of another man's bed. But I think you should tell him what he did wrong."

She took a deep breath. "What if he apologizes? What if he makes me see his side? What if I'm tempted to forgive him?"

Something flickered in Doug's eyes. "I sure as hell don't want that to happen," he said. "Not if it increases the risk of him getting you naked. But—" he moved his hand from her face and tucked them in the pockets of his shorts, "—you deserve the chance to tell him off. It might help you get him out of your system. Especially if he's *not* apologetic. Then you won't need a suppressant. I'm a short-term fix, you know?"

She did know that. Even if she didn't like it.

"He'll be apologetic," she said. "He won't want me to be pissed, because he'll hope he can get even more ideas out of me."

"Ideas?"

"Ideas for the hotel. I haven't talked to him in four months because he stole my ideas." It would be helpful if Doug agreed with her, shared her outrage, even got her a little worked up against Todd before dinner. She needed as much armor against Todd's effect on her as she could get.

"Ideas for this meeting?" Doug asked.

"No, our hotels. He's the manager in Minneapolis. He took my ideas and implemented them in his hotel. Then took credit and got recognition from Mr. Britton and the company."

"He claimed they were his?" Doug asked.

"Yes." She hated thinking about how dumb she'd been to trust Todd when she'd barely known him. But great sex made her stupid. She was in a suite hundreds of miles from home for three days with a guy because he'd been good against an elevator wall. Just for instance.

"Why'd you tell him your plans?" Doug asked with a frown.

"Hey, I didn't know he'd *steal* them. It's not my fault. I just—" It was too much to hope that he'd let her sudden break off go without asking more.

"You just what?" he asked.

"Nothing." Which was, of course, the sure-fire answer to give if you wanted someone to keep pushing for information.

He tipped her chin up again before she realized she wasn't making eye contact.

"You just what, Morgan? It would help me help you if I knew all the details."

She wasn't so sure of that. It was possible he'd use the knowledge against her too. "I didn't mean to tell him anything. It's just... I get talkative after..."

Doug's eyebrows shot up and she caught the curve to the one corner of his mouth before he hid it. "You get talkative after..."

"A good orgasm."

She could tell he fought another smile.

"First, all orgasms are good. Second, I'm feeling hurt I haven't noticed this."

"Clearly elevators don't lend themselves well to cuddling and talking afterward," she said dryly.

"Phone sex doesn't count?"

It was crazy but her body heated with just that much of a reminder. "Guess if *I* technically do it, it doesn't count."

He leaned close. "I look forward to testing that theory later."

She licked her lips. "Anyway. I got too talkative and told him some things he took and used to get noticed by Mr. Britton. I'm thinking this meeting would be a time when he'd be sure to find out my secrets."

Doug lifted a hand and dragged the pad of his thumb over her bottom lip. "I wonder what secrets you'll tell me. 'Cause I don't want to hear about the hotel."

"What do you want to hear?" she asked, her lips tingling from his touch.

"Your dirtiest fantasies, how hard you like your nipples sucked, the time you French kissed your college roommate."

She managed to chuckle even as she had a hard time breathing deep. "Never kissed my college roommate. Sorry."

"You can't make up a story for a nice guy?" he asked.

She smiled up at him. "I'll see what I can do."

"Thanks." His hands settled on her hips and pulled her close. "I also want to hear what you say or sound like when you come when I'm inside you and you're not holding back because we're in an elevator. I want to hear your words of encouragement when I put my tongue between your legs and—"

❧ She slapped her hand over his mouth, feeling wobbly in the knees. "Stop. I have to go to dinner."

He wrapped his big fingers around her wrist, kissed the palm of her hand then pulled her hand from his mouth. "I could make you forget all about dinner."

"Sure, for a half hour or so," she said with a shaky laugh.

"You, Morgan James, have been with the wrong guys," he informed her. "Half hour my ass."

She drew in a deep breath. "I look forward to you proving that. *After* dinner."

He grinned. "Eat fast."

This was exactly what she needed. There would be no dessert tonight. At least not at the table.

She stepped through the door, but hesitated and turned back. "Hey, do me a favor."

"'Kay," he said easily.

"Text me something dirty in thirty minutes."

"Dirty, huh?"

"Like 'I want to—'"

"Yeah, I got this." He gave her a grin that made her toes

curl. "This isn't going to be a problem."

She was sure dirty texting was just one of his many talents. "I might not be able to reply, but I'll read them all."

"The only response I'll need is your panties getting wet."

She wasn't sure what to say to that. Except *already there.* So she said, "Okay. See you soon."

The elevator hadn't even arrived before the first text chimed on her phone.

I can't wait to bend you over this couch and slide into you from behind.

She took a deep breath.

Definitely no dessert. She wasn't sure she was going to make it past the salad at this rate.

The woman was driving him crazy. This should have been the easiest thing he'd ever done. Ever. She was gorgeous and he was here specifically to be in her bed. A bed that was an oversized king, happened to be in a five-star hotel suite and had fifteen-hundred-thread-count Egyptian cotton sheets on it.

Piece of cake. Best weekend ever.

So why did he feel like he should fake the flu and get the hell out of here?

For a moment there when she'd been ticked about the guys hanging in the suite he'd thought, *Great, this will make it easier not to like her.* Unfortunately, he'd seen the vulnerability there. This was a big work weekend for her. She wanted it to go well, with no problems. Okay, fine. Maybe having some of the employees partying in the suite and making too much noise could be a problem.

But still, he had been careful to keep reminding himself that no matter how hot she was, no matter how easily he'd been able to talk her into phone sex, no matter how tight her ass was or how great her breasts were, that was *all* this was.

He was her boy toy for the weekend. He was fine with that.

Then she had to go and tell him Todd was more of a threat than just an ex-boyfriend. She had feelings for the guy. She thought he was great in bed.

The feelings of jealousy and possessiveness were *not* welcome. At all.

This was just a three-day gig. A vacation. Period.

What did he care if she was hot for another guy? After Sunday it wasn't his problem.

Hell, it wasn't his *problem* now. He'd come along on the trip at her request because he owed her a favor and because fucking Morgan James in a Britton Hotel was not at all a hardship.

She could have feelings for whoever she wanted to have feelings for. It didn't change that *he* was the one here now, propping his feet on a coffee table that cost more than everything in his living room put together. *He* was still the one who was going to be making her scream his name later. Maybe on that very coffee table.

But after Sunday she was going to have to figure something else out.

Which sounded perfect. It also *sounded* good to tell himself he wouldn't care if Sunday night she was on Todd-what's-his-name's coffee table.

Then, just when he was comfortable with this weekend being his only responsibility to her, she had to go and tell him about how Todd had stolen her ideas and used them to get ahead.

The surge of protectiveness he'd felt then had almost knocked him over. He'd hidden it from her, he was sure. He was good at making things seem superficial. But it had been strong and sure. Todd-what's-his-ass had not just fucked her—which was bad enough—but he'd fucked her over.

It made Dooley want to break the other man's nose.

He wasn't generally the kind of guy to break anything on anyone else. He was too laid back for that. He *could* help break up fights if needed at work or at the bar, but Kevin usually stepped in first.

This was not only out of character for him, it was also damned uncomfortable. He had enough on his plate, had enough people to worry about, without adding a hot little

81

redhead.

He needed something to snap him out of this. His first instinct to never see her again after the fundraiser had been right on. Now he was getting sucked in to all kinds of weird stuff. The fighting and desire to protect her worried him less than the urges he was feeling to put on a suit and tie, drink expensive wine and have *crème brûlée* for dessert.

God, he loved *crème brûlée*.

It had to be the view from the penthouse windows. And the whirlpool tub in the gigantic bathroom he could happily spend several hours in. Not that he'd ever admit any of that to anyone. He didn't need Egyptian cotton. He didn't even know what made Egyptian cotton better than every other kind of cotton. At least as far as anyone knew.

Truth was, he liked this stuff. He'd eat dinner with five forks every night if he could.

It was like a fantasy that the reason behind it all was a curvy redhead who was hot for him.

He needed a dose of reality before he did something stupid. Like consider actually dating her.

"Kev, it's me," he said when his friend answered his cell phone.

"Hey. Your dad is fine. You're in Chicago in a hotel with a hot girl. You don't call home to check in."

He smiled. "I'm not calling about Dad." He'd texted his dad earlier, before the Mario Kart tournament. Besides, he knew Doug Senior was fine. Between his sisters and Kevin, he would have better food and get the remote more than he did with Dooley anyway. "But I am calling about the hot girl."

"Oh, boy. 'Kay, just a sec. We're over at Sam's. I'll put you on speaker," Kevin said.

"No, Kev, I don't want..."

"Hey, Julia!" he heard Mac call.

Great. They were *all* over at Sam's.

"Her name was Victoria in the movie," Sam said.

"Yeah, yeah," Mac grumbled. "Whatever."

"No, that's not right," Ben said. "It wasn't Victoria."

"It was a V," Sam said.

"But not Victoria," Ben insisted.

Dooley rolled his eyes.

"You should be here," Kevin said, turning his attention back to Dooley. "Sam's trying to surprise Danika with a new countertop in the bathroom. We're missing you right now."

Dooley chuckled. Sam was worthless with power tools and fix-it projects. Which generally wasn't a problem around the house since his wife could do anything like that herself. But yeah, surprising her would require assistance from his buddies. Dooley was the best but Mac and Kevin could help a lot.

"Hey, I called for advice," he cut in.

"Flavored body powder," Mac said immediately.

"What's that advice for?" Ben asked.

"Anything having to do with a hot girl," Mac told him.

Ben laughed and Sam said, "I'd vote for butter. It's easier to get and is just as much fun."

"Have you *tried* flavored body powder?" Mac asked him.

"Who do you think you're talking to here?" Sam demanded.

Dooley rubbed his forehead. He totally deserved this. He had been on the other end of the razzing when Ben, Sam and Mac had all fallen in love. It was fun. On that side.

"Maybe he needs actual relationship advice," Kevin said. "Not just sex advice."

"Dooley isn't a food-during-sex guy anyway," Ben decided. "I see him being more straight forward and conventional."

Dooley sat up with a frown. He wasn't opposed to food with sex. He didn't use it—sex was damned good all on its own—but he wouldn't say no to it either.

"Well, maybe he should," Mac said. "That's advice."

"He hasn't even told us what the problem is," Kevin pointed out.

"I stand by my statement that flavored body powder is the answer anyway," Mac said.

"Butter," Sam called. "Or peanut butter. And jelly."

"Who does your laundry?" Kevin asked, evidently finally

distracted by the conversation. "That's *got* to be a mess."

"You get a naked girl and a jar of strawberry jelly and tell me you're worried about laundry," Sam said.

Dooley leaned forward and rapped his phone on the coffee table. "Hello?" he said loudly. "Guy with a problem here."

"You mean a problem strawberry jelly can't solve?" Kevin asked sarcastically. "Imagine that."

For a moment Dooley pictured Morgan spread out on the bed, sticky sweet jelly spread all over her. Yeah, he didn't give a crap the duvet was white.

"Tell me I like her and feel like I want to see her again only because I like and want to see the fancy hotel suite and free minibar again."

"The minibar's *free*?" Sam asked.

"How big is the suite?" Mac asked.

Dooley rolled his eyes. "It's bigger than Kevin's apartment. It's a penthouse. Free everything. Whirlpool, massages. We got here in a private jet."

A low whistle of appreciation came from one of his friends.

"Sounds great," Kevin said. "Not sure I see a problem."

"I'm starting to feel like I like her. Like I'd be okay with doing this again." There, he'd admitted it.

"That's a bad thing?" Kevin asked.

Dooley scowled even though his best friend couldn't see it. Kevin knew what Dooley's world was like. He should get this even more than the others.

"Yes. I can't afford this chick," he finally said. Which was completely true. Emotionally and financially.

Morgan liked expensive things. She fit right in here. She was not a beer-and-pizza girl, a Sunday-football-tailgate girl, a demo-derby girl. In his life, there would always be guys gathered around the TV on the sofa and in her way.

It would never work.

"But you're *Julia*," Ben said. "*She's* Richard Gere. Maybe she doesn't need you to afford her."

"Yeah, man," Mac said. "She'll afford you."

It sounded good. It might be true. He could get used to that. But... "I want a couch I can put my feet on. I don't want to have to wear a tie to dinner. I want to have carpet I can spill things on."

"What are you, five?" Ben asked. "Grown-ups sometimes have to wear a tie and shouldn't be spilling things."

"Really?" Dooley said. "Then why did I have to rent a carpet steamer after the last time you all came over to watch a game?"

No one answered him.

"In relationships you compromise," Kevin finally said. "You might have to dress up sometimes, but then she'll dress down sometimes."

Dooley shook his head but even as he did he could imagine Morgan in a pair of sexy cut-off sweat pants and a T-shirt with no bra, curling her feet up under her on the couch next to him as they shared popcorn.

Dumb.

"I don't want a *relationship*," Dooley said to the one guy on the phone besides him who didn't have one. "Tell me how stupid it is to even think about that this fast."

Total silence met his comment. He sighed.

Every one of the guys on the other end had fallen hard and fast for a woman. Three of the four were now married to those women.

Which meant they were no good to him.

"All I can tell you," Sam finally said, "is get her straight to bed and then out the door. Don't talk to her. Don't get to know her. Don't have fun with her outside of those sheets. That's when you're going to be sunk."

There were murmurs of agreement from the other men.

"If you just want sex, keep it just sex," Mac added. "Stay busy otherwise. You're basically living together. That gets nice and comfortable real quick."

"Maybe you shouldn't do anything," Kevin interjected. "Maybe you should just come home if you're so sure you don't want to be with her." There was the good Christian boy they'd all come to know.

"I can't leave." In spite of his temptation to plead illness earlier. "For one, we came on a private jet so I don't have a return ticket." Of course he could *get* one. "Two, I can't leave her to deal with her ex. Can I?" The truth was, being told he had to stay because it was the right thing to do would feel a lot better than knowing he was staying because he was concerned...and jealous. And because he just *wanted* to.

"It's because you care," Sam said. "Man, you're already getting attached."

"I care about the Jacuzzi tub and the prime rib on the menu tonight and the fifteen-hundred-thread-count sheets," he insisted.

"How do you even know what a thread count is?" Mac asked in the background.

"Vivian!" Sam exclaimed. "Her name in *Pretty Woman* was Vivian."

Dooley rubbed his forehead again.

"If you think you only like her because of the fancy stuff she can buy," Ben said, "then you need to prove you're right."

Dooley straightened. Ben was easily the smartest one of the bunch.

"By doing the opposite of what Sam said," Ben told him.

"Hey," Sam protested.

Ben went on, "Spend time talking to her. Hang out with her. Do things you like to do. Other than sex," he said as the other guys started to make comments. "You'll quickly see it's about the *things* instead of *her*."

"That's not bad," Kevin said. "Maybe you need to get her out of the suite and away from the minibar and Jacuzzi. Take her out of the hotel, hang out and do something you normally do and see if you still like her or if she just looks good because she's on fifteen hundred thread count sheets."

He wasn't going to mention that he hadn't had her on the sheets yet.

Do something he would normally do. Not a bad idea. As much as he liked smoked salmon and sending his suits out to be tailored, his real world was more fish sticks and worn denim.

"Hey, what was Gere's character's name in *Pretty Woman?*" he asked.

"Zack," Ben said.

"No way, that was in *An Officer and a Gentleman,*" Sam said.

"How do you even know that?" Mac asked.

"Me?" Sam asked. "Torres was the one that threw it out first."

Dooley hung up on the argument, grinning in spite of himself. It would take them a few minutes to realize he was no longer on the phone. It would be faster to Google the answer anyway. Or not. It didn't matter. That movie wasn't going to apply much longer. It wasn't like Richard Gere gave up his millions to become a pimp and hang out with Julia and the other hookers. Julia—*Vivian*—was the one who changed her life to be with him.

Dooley wasn't changing anything.

Except his clothes.

Dammit.

He wasn't sure if he was more upset that he was still the woman—the *hooker*—in the scenario or that it appeared he knew the damned movie as well as his friends did. His whipped married friends who had an excuse.

As he was pulling his jeans on, Richard Gere's character's name came to him too.

Edward.

Dammit.

Chapter Four

Jonathan Britton was sixty-four years old and had been king of the Britton empire since his father had died forty years before. It had been a major corporation when he took it over, but he'd doubled its size and tripled its worth in his time, and he showed no signs of slowing down.

He was active, vibrant and looked ten years younger than he was. He had a son and two grandsons in line to take over, but it would be at least another ten years until he was ready to step down.

"Morgan." Jonathan greeted her enthusiastically with a kiss to each cheek.

"Mr. Britton." She took the seat he indicted beside him. "It's good to see you."

"I'm looking forward to this," he said. "But call me Jonathan."

She smiled, hoping her nerves didn't show and trying not to dwell on the fact that this man held her life—or her career, at least—in his hands. "All right, Jonathan."

She ordered a white wine from the waitress and she and Jonathan chatted about her trip to Chicago and the jet until their glasses were set down in front of them.

"How's the room?" Jonathan asked.

"Gorgeous, of course," Morgan said with a smile. "Very comfortable."

"You have the same beds in Omaha, yes?" he asked, sipping his scotch.

"Yes. But I've never spent the night in one," she reminded him.

"Oh, that won't do." He shook his head. "You should spend at least a week in the rooms. A few days in each type, from the traditional to the suites."

"Maybe I will." He had a point, she supposed. Looking at the rooms, knowing the hotel layout and décor as well as she knew her own house wasn't the same thing as spending the night in the rooms, experiencing the sounds, even the service.

"Please do. Then I want you to personally call me and tell me how it was."

Morgan smiled. "I will. As soon as possible."

"Good evening, all."

She pivoted in her chair at the sound of the new voice. Todd was here.

"Todd." Jonathan stood and took his hand.

"How are you, sir?"

"Fine, fine." Jonathan gestured to the chair next to Morgan.

"Morgan." Todd's voice was low when he greeted her.

She tipped her head up and smiled. *He stole your ideas. He's a scumbag.* Still, he was a good-looking scumbag. Not fair.

"Hi, Todd."

"You look wonderful."

She slid her hands over the lap of her dress. It was a long way from skimpy, but the spaghetti straps left her shoulders bare and as Todd looked at her she was aware the dress came to a V between her breasts, creating some cleavage.

She should have worn a pantsuit.

But then she recalled Doug's reaction to her in the room and she was glad she hadn't gone with pants. His "holy crap" was better than Todd's "you look wonderful". Todd would say that no matter what she wore. Hell, he'd say it to any woman he was meeting for dinner. It was the polite thing to say. It was expected.

On the other hand, Doug said what he really felt at the moment he really felt it without filter. She supposed the no-filter thing could go either way, but when he was impressed by how she looked, it was nice.

Sipping her wine, she listened to the few minutes of small talk between Todd and Jonathan, but after the waitress took their orders, Jonathan turned the conversation to business.

"Both proposals were interesting," Jonathan said. "But now I want more. Drill it down. Give me details. This resort has to be the best we've done to date. A tall order, as I'm sure you know." He swirled the ice in his empty glass. "I've taken pieces I like from the other proposals submitted so I may ask you to incorporate some of those as well. You were both chosen for a number of reasons, but I've learned over the years that rarely does one person have all the answers. There is room for both of you on this project. Others as well. I'll bring in whoever and whatever is needed." He set his glass down and made eye contact with each of them. "But I am looking for a leader."

Morgan felt her phone vibrate from where she'd inconspicuously tucked it between her leg and the chair. She wiped her mouth with the napkin and leaned back for the waitress to take her salad plate, sliding the phone free and glancing at the screen.

I can't wait to suck on your clit and listen to you beg me to take you.

She squeezed her knees together and slid the phone back under her leg. Wow.

"What do you think, Morgan?" Jonathan asked.

She thought she was going to start taking her clothes off in the elevator on her way up to the room so they wouldn't waste any time with things like undressing.

"I'm curious if you want the new plans to follow the current brand or if you are looking for something entirely new with the California resort?" she asked, sounding completely normal and professional even though she was a hot wet mess of tingling nerve endings.

"I'm open," Jonathan said. "If the brand is the way to go, show me. If we need to shake it up, show me. I want a place to wow guests. Whatever that looks like. I want you to show me what that looks like."

"Obviously what we showed you already caught your interest," Todd said.

"Yes. The plans you both turned in showed me you two understand the business and thinking outside the box better than any of our other managers."

"But you're not looking at our plans as *the* plans," Morgan deduced.

Jonathan nodded. "That's right. There may be elements in those plans we need or want to keep, but show me."

Morgan studied her boss. Todd drank.

Finally she leaned forward in her chair. "Jonathan, are you using this as a test or do you honestly need our help?"

Jonathan looked up. His smile was slow. "I need your help. I've been doing this a long time, but I don't travel with a fresh eye anymore. The Board is largely the same way. We travel as people who have been in the business a long time. I have ideas, but I can admit I might be wrong. I was pleased with your plans, but also pleased that you're among our youngest managers. You're relatively new to the business, to our hotels and to the overall luxury travel experience. That's what we need."

"How do you feel about brutal honesty?" Morgan asked.

Jonathan smiled. "I'm for it."

"Then this will be great."

They continued to talk, but in the end Jonathan wanted them to work up ideas to present tomorrow evening.

"I brought you to Chicago because we are headquartered here," he said. "All of my department heads and administration staff know you're both here and why. Anything you need to look at or try is available to you."

Her phone vibrated and she pulled it out greedily.

I want you to ride me so I can watch you work yourself to orgasm on my cock.

Morgan passed on dessert and prayed for a good opening for ending the meeting.

"Morgan, dance with me," Todd said, pushing back from the table and extending his hand.

She looked at him in surprise. Dance with him? She wanted to go upstairs. She *needed* to go upstairs.

Which meant Doug was doing his job.

Which also meant she could dance with Todd and not be

afraid of acting like an idiot. They had to talk at some point, had to have some closure. With Doug upstairs and his texts in her mind there wasn't a single worry that this would turn into anything more than a dance.

"Okay." She let him help her from her chair, keeping her phone in her hand. "Excuse us?" She asked Jonathan.

"Of course. I'm just considering the dessert menu." Jonathan waved them toward the dance floor. "Have fun."

Todd folded her in his arms the moment they stepped onto the dance floor. He smelled great and she felt herself lean into him.

"I've missed you," he said against her temple. "We haven't talked in so long."

His muscular thighs moved against hers and she remembered the physical attraction she'd felt the first time they'd met.

The attraction seemed cooler now.

She smiled up at him. "How have you been?"

"Great." His smile was wide and gorgeous. "Could have only been better if I'd been talking to you."

No time like the present to face this thing. She took a deep breath. "Todd, do you know why I quit answering your phone calls and e-mails?"

He pulled her closer, bending to put his mouth near her ear. "No, but I want to."

His hot breath on her neck should have made goose bumps erupt. But it didn't. Which meant her Todd-suppressant was working.

She pulled back. "No. It's because of the housing drive you did in Minneapolis."

He pulled back too, with a frown. "The housing drive?"

"Where you asked people to bring donations for the local housing charity? People brought in furniture and old appliances and dishes and things and then got a voucher for a free night's stay? Remember?"

He'd done it a month after she'd told him her plans to do it in Omaha.

"Of course I remember. It was your idea."

She stared at him. "I *know* it was my idea. You stole it. You got a huge write-up in the company newsletter for that!"

He nodded. "I did. It got us some great local coverage too."

She gritted her teeth. "I'm sure it did."

"Britton loved it."

"I know. I read his quote in the newsletter. The same one where you were named hotel of the quarter."

"What are you so upset about?"

She pushed him back. "It was *my* idea. You stole it."

"I used it," he acknowledged.

"And got all the credit."

He shrugged. "I was the one who did it. Why didn't you?"

She frowned. "You got to it first. It would have looked like I was taking *your* idea."

"So what?" he asked. "We're all a part of Britton Hotels. We're not competitors. We're in two different cities. In fact, I was thinking it was something all the hotels across the country should do as a community service. Housing is the perfect charity for us to get involved with."

"But I..." She trailed off, not sure what to say. He wasn't her competitor. At least, he hadn't been until this new resort job had come up. She could have still done the housing charity drive, she supposed. "You shouldn't have taken credit."

Todd pulled her closer again, smiling softly. "I took credit for *implementing* a fabulous program at my hotel. I never claimed it was my idea."

She frowned. According to the write-up in the newsletter, he'd done a great job with the implementation. Of course he deserved credit for *that*. But...

"You also didn't go out of your way to point out the idea wasn't yours."

"No one asked, Morgan. I wasn't trying to hurt you. I thought you'd be happy I used your idea. For my sake and for Britton. I thought you cared about me. And I was trying to make my hotel more successful which helps make Britton successful. Isn't that your goal too?"

Morgan felt her frown deepen. What a guy. Stealing from her and then telling her she should feel good about it. "Of course."

"Just like the new resort," Todd went on. "We should all want it to be the best, no matter what it takes. Even if it means no one gets all the glory, even if we have to do things that mostly go unnoticed. As long as the overall result is magnificent, we all benefit."

Uh, huh. That sounded great. The fake sincerity was impressive. She wasn't sure she would have recognized it a year ago. Which ticked her off. Almost as much as wondering if he'd always been a lying, stealing jerk and she just hadn't noticed, or if it was a new thing since he'd realized she was a threat to his professional ambitions.

"Sounds like you have a plan," she said, trying to look innocent and sweet when really she wanted to smack him.

"Definitely." He gave her what she would have considered a sexy smile a few months ago. "I have all kinds of plans." He pulled her closer. "For the resort too."

The sexiness in Todd's smile didn't quite reach his eyes. Morgan studied him. She wondered if it had always been that way. Was it possible she'd just missed it? She'd wanted to see it so had believed it was there? Or was she aware of it now because it was such a sharp contrast to how Doug looked at her?

In any case, it wasn't there with Todd. And, best of all, it didn't matter.

"And I suppose you think we should compare notes," she said. "After all, the overall success—no matter whose idea it is—should be the bottom line, right?"

He leaned in. "Your suite or mine?"

The song changed and her phone vibrated. She desperately wanted to look at it. Even though she didn't *need* to look at it.

Todd Becker was no longer a threat to her career or her heart.

"Todd, I think you should know—"

"Who's the guy with Jonathan?" Todd asked.

She twisted to glance over her shoulder. Then turned fully and stared.

"That's, um, Doug Miller." Who was dressed in jeans, tennis shoes, a button up shirt and a jacket.

Oh, God.

Dooley easily picked Jonathan Britton out in the restaurant. For one, what he'd paid for his suit would have covered Dooley's house and car payment for a month. For another, he was the only older, distinguished-looking man sitting alone at a table for four watching the dance floor where Morgan was dancing with a man Dooley assumed was Todd.

Jonathan looked like he approved of the couple.

That wasn't good.

If Dooley's job was to keep her away from Todd, it wouldn't help to have her boss pushing them together.

It looked like he was going to have to pull out his charm and sophistication for a few minutes. Darn it. He'd been hoping to keep it under wraps.

"Mr. Britton?" he asked, extending a scotch refill procured from the waitress on her way to the table. "I'm Douglas Miller. I'm a friend of Morgan's."

Britton glanced toward the dance floor then back to Dooley. "Nice to meet you, Douglas." He took his hand.

"Please, call me Doug," he said, taking the seat without a crumpled napkin or half full glass of water. "You're hotel is impressive, Mr. Britton." He leaned back and propped an ankle on his knee.

"Thank you, son." Jonathan settled back in his chair. "I appreciate the compliment."

"Doug. What are you doing here?"

He looked up to see Morgan next to the table, Todd just behind her. She was worried. He got that. She probably assumed he was going to invite Jonathan Britton to a Mario Kart tournament tomorrow.

"Everything else here has been so amazing during our stay,

I had to try the restaurant too," he said. He didn't try to emphasize *our stay* but he knew both of the other men had picked up on it.

Britton turned and signaled to the waitress, who seemed to have been waiting in the shadows specifically for him.

Dooley handed the waitress the nearly full Kahlua and cream from beside Morgan's plate—needed to get that out of here with Todd around—and placed an order for prime rib, as she seemed to realize he was staying and took her seat. Todd followed, looking a lot less happy about it.

"So what do you do, Doug?" Todd asked, crossing his leg as Doug had.

"I'm a paramedic in Omaha. All I do all day is save lives, Todd," he said, lifting the beer bottle the waitress had placed next to him.

"Sounds...interesting," Todd said.

"Interesting. Exciting. Rewarding. All of that," Doug agreed. Truth was, if it weren't for working with three of his best friends, he would have died of boredom a long time ago. Exciting calls weren't all that common. Which was a good thing, in some ways.

"How'd you get into that field?" Britton asked.

"I was in the National Guard and trained and worked as a medic. When I left the Guard I still wanted to do that type of work, but didn't want to go to med school." Nor would he have had the time or money after his dad's stroke, but he didn't regret his choices at all.

He glanced at Morgan. She was watching him with a strange combination of surprise and interest. What did she think? That he was a paramedic because he couldn't do anything else? He forced himself to take a long drink of beer and then a deep breath. He didn't care what she thought and if she was comparing him to Todd then...well, it was what it was. All she had to approve of regarding him was how many orgasms he could give her before Sunday when they got off the plane and went their separate ways.

"Thanks for serving," Britton said.

Dooley gave him a nod. It had been his pleasure and duty to serve as a Guard but the thanks was always appreciated.

They went on to talk about some of his training, then where he'd traveled. He supposed he was lucky Jonathan Britton, and even Todd Becker, was too polite to *not* make casual conversation with him as he ate his steak and salad and watched Morgan.

She did look gorgeous. He had no doubt she could get any human male to do anything she wanted.

Her dress was some black silky material that seemed to cling to her just enough to hint at all the glory underneath without giving anything away. The front showed very minor cleavage, but her perfect breasts were cupped in a way that conjured tantalizing images. The skirt fell to mid-thigh, again showing just enough leg—especially when she crossed her legs—to make a man imagine a whole lot more about the smooth expanse of thigh up higher.

Her hair was twisted up on her head in some elaborate style, but a few strands were escaping, tickling her neck and throat. Mostly, though, he noticed her eyes. They were green. He was surprised he knew that. He was too far away and the lighting too low for him to see them now, but he remembered. That was unusual for him. He wasn't much of a detail guy. All he knew was that he hadn't seen an inch of her he didn't want more of.

That was all he needed to know for a weekend fling.

By the time Dooley had finished his meal they were discussing their favorite spots in Europe. His more extensive world travels had happened as a kid with his dad versus with the military, but once you'd been to Spain and Italy you had favorite places no matter your age.

Morgan said little and Dooley tried to pull her into the conversation. "Have you ever been to Italy?"

She shook her head. "No. I spent a short time in France when I was in college."

"I'll have to find a reason to send you over, Morgan," Britton said. "Doug can show you the best places."

Dooley and Morgan exchanged a look at his assumption they would be traveling together in the future. The ruse was working. He hoped. He looked at Todd. Todd was watching Morgan with an expression of disappointment. The ruse was definitely working.

Good thing.

Dooley didn't like Todd. He didn't like that the guy had used Morgan. He wanted to punch Todd for that. He hated that Todd had been in her bed. He wanted to punch him for that too. But just as much, he didn't like Todd because he was the kind of guy Morgan should be with. Other than the asshole part, of course. The truth was, both men understood the lifestyle she wanted, but Todd could actually give it to her.

Dooley shook his head and tipped his beer bottle back one final time. Not his problem. After this weekend, Todd would have to figure out how to be with her or Morgan would have to figure out a way to be without Todd. He'd promised to keep her away from Todd for this weekend, and *only* this weekend, and that's what he was going to do.

"We should go," he said, placing his napkin on the table and pushing back. "Jonathan, it was a pleasure to meet you and thank you so much for dinner, the room, everything."

Britton got to his feet as Dooley stood and shook his hand. "I'm glad you're enjoying it. I hope you'll take advantage of more of the amenities while you're here. Morgan's going to be working hard for the next couple of days, so feel free to check things out."

"I'll do that. Wouldn't want to distract her. Too much." He gave the older man a wink and Britton chuckled.

Todd was frowning when Dooley stuck out his hand to him. "Nice to meet you, Todd."

"You, too." Though it was quite clear he didn't mean it.

"Ready?" Dooley said to Morgan coming around the table.

"Sure."

He took her hand, linking their fingers and they headed for the front of the restaurant, but before they were past the Maitre d', Todd stopped them. Or rather, stopped Morgan.

"Morgan, just a minute." He grabbed her arm, pulling her away from Dooley. "I'd like you to stay."

"She's busy," Dooley said tugging on her hand.

"Morgan and I go way back," Todd said. "I think she should decide who she wants to be with."

Dooley tugged her further back and stepped up to Todd. "I know I seem like a hell of a nice guy. But I'm not. Don't push me."

Todd blinked and pulled back but said, "All the more reason I shouldn't let her go with you."

She pressed close to Dooley and he easily read that body language.

He laughed and slid his hand to her low back. "Oh, I'm going to be nice to *her*," he told Todd. "So nice she won't even remember your name...or her own. Again."

He wasn't going to physically keep her away from Todd. He was going to let her make the ultimate decision, of course. But he was going to make sure Todd deserved it.

Todd looked at Morgan, frowned, took a deep breath through his nose, then looked at Dooley. "If you do anything to hurt her, you'll have to answer to me."

Right. Okay. "What if she hurts me?"

Todd looked at Morgan again. "I'll buy the champagne."

Ah. Very good then. "We'll see you later, Becker." Dooley steered Morgan out of the restaurant with a hand on her back. She could easily change her mind, and her direction. But she didn't.

And Todd didn't come after them.

Idiot.

He really didn't like that guy.

Morgan started to turn in the direction of the elevator but Dooley turned her toward the front doors of the hotel instead. His friends were some of the best guys he knew and they were married to some of the best women he knew. They had to be doing something right and it sounded like even Sam had learned something about women through it all.

He was taking their advice.

"Where are we—"

He stopped at the concierge stand and shrugged out of his jacket. "I need to cleanse my palate."

"What are you talking about?"

"I made nice, used my manners and silverware for an hour. I need to hang with some real people to get that out of my system." He handed his jacket to the guy at the stand. "Hey, Mike, would you hold this for me?"

"Sure thing, Dooley."

"That name," he heard Morgan mutter. "Where'd the jacket come from?" she asked.

He turned to her. "I sent it to the hotel from home so it wouldn't get wrinkled on the plane." He started unbuttoning his shirt. "You ready?"

Her eyes were on his fingers and the buttons that were coming undone. "I'm ready," she said.

Dooley grinned and shrugged out of his shirt, draping it around her shoulders. "Put your arms in."

"What are you doing?" she asked even as she put the shirt on.

It, of course, engulfed her. But it covered her breasts, hips and thighs nicely. "Covering you up."

"Why?"

"We need to dress down a bit for where we're going."

"But I thought we were going to go upstairs and..." She trailed off suggestively.

He grinned at her as he reached up and started taking the pins out of her hair. "I'm afraid if I have too much polite in my blood I might not be a lot of use to you."

Her hair began to tumble down, but she was watching his eyes. "Why is that?"

"'Cause there's nothing polite about the stuff I want to do to you."

Her hair fell past her shoulders and he pocketed the pins, then pulled his fingers through her hair.

"Well then," she said, her voice husky, "how can we be sure to get rid of *all* the polite?"

Morgan wasn't positive what "dressing down" meant but considering the T-shirt under Dooley's dress shirt said *24 hours in a day, 24 beers in a case... Coincidence?* she had an idea.

"Where are we going?" she asked as he reached up and unclasped her necklace.

The backs of his fingers brushed the skin over her collarbones and she felt the shiver of heat wash over her. Just from a touch. Potent stuff.

He unhooked her earrings too and handed all her jewelry to Mike. "Somewhere less glittery," he said. "Somewhere we can relax. Have fun. Eat."

"We just ate," she protested as he threaded his fingers with hers. She did want to go right upstairs, but there was something about him right now, something tempting, that made her willing to do whatever he wanted.

He'd walked into that dining room, in tennis shoes no less, full of confidence. He'd introduced himself to her boss, made conversation, said the right things. He hadn't acted cocky, but he hadn't been a kiss-up either. He'd seemed perfectly comfortable holding his own, even in jeans. He'd just been...natural. His natural friendliness mixed with confidence and truly interesting conversation was intriguing. And hot.

It didn't make complete sense to her but his easy-going, I'm-nice-to-waiters-and-CEOs-equally attitude was amazingly attractive. She was used to men trying to make an impression on her and on anyone else around. They dressed to impress, they spoke in a rehearsed way, they were concerned with how they looked, acted and sounded.

Doug didn't have any of that. In fact, he didn't seem concerned about much at all.

"Jonathan, Todd and I ate," Doug said, looking down at his palm. She saw pen markings on his hand and peered closer, realizing they were directions.

"But you barely touched your food," he said starting down the sidewalk with her in tow. "Do you forget to eat a lot?"

101

She looked up at him, surprised. "You noticed?"

He gave her a smile. "I noticed everything about you." He stopped and turned to face her, moving in close. "I noticed there's this one strand of hair curling around your ear no matter what you did to it." His fingers touched the piece of hair just behind her left ear. "I noticed you drank from your wine glass only once for every three times you picked it up. I noticed your eyes got wide and you sat forward in your chair when Jon and I were talking about me being in the Guard." He ran his hand down the side of her neck, his thumb skimming over her throat. "Does that turn you on?" he asked. "The idea of me out there saving lives, being a hero, getting dirty and sweaty?"

The pad of his thumb settled on the pulse point at the base of her throat and, as she swallowed, she was sure he could feel it pounding. She nodded. "Yes." Hell, it seemed everything about him turned her on. "I don't hang out with guys who do what you do."

"If it affects you like this, I'm glad," he murmured just before touching his lips to hers.

She arched close, wanting to deepen the kiss but he held her back, just tasting her with his lips. No tongue, no fully body contact, no wandering hands.

She was still a wobbly mess when he lifted his head.

"Let's go have some fun."

She thought *that* had been fun, but Doug started walking again, her hand in his.

"I thought you'd want to go right upstairs too," she said as they reached the end of the block and crossed the street.

"You're wound up, but for all the wrong reasons," he told her. "You're thinking about work and you're irritated about Todd or something he said, so we need to get your mind off of that and focused on you and me."

She tripped along beside him on her heels, amazed. How did he know she was irritated? How did he know she couldn't stop thinking about how she might have been wrong about Todd and that she was worried about trusting him again? And worried about not trusting him again.

"Eating is going to help?" she finally asked as they crossed another street.

"Not just eating," he said. "I need you to be a regular girl for awhile. I think *you* need to be a regular girl for awhile."

He stopped in front of a building with neon signs in the window and big heavy red double door. But it wasn't a bar.

"Bowling?" she asked looking up at the flashing yellow arrow that read *Bud's Bowl.*

He was grinning when she looked at him. "You ever been bowling?"

"Sure. At a birthday party in third grade."

"Well, *this* is regular. Let's go." He pulled the door open and nudged her inside.

It was a typical bowling alley. To her right was an arcade, to the left a snack bar. In front of the counter where they offered hot dogs, pizza, nachos and drinks was the counter where they rented shoes, and in front of that were the racks of balls of all sizes and colors.

"Why here?" she asked just as she heard, "Dooley! Over here, man!"

It was the guys from the hotel. Well, that answered that.

Dooley waved at them then turned to her. "You're gonna have to lose the heels."

To exchange them for red, white and blue bowling shoes.

"I'll just watch."

He looked at her for a few seconds. "We'll just hang out for awhile."

She glanced over at the other guys where they were high-fiving, calling out good-natured insults and laughing. She sighed. "Okay."

Before heading for the guys, Doug stopped at the snack bar and ordered a super nacho and two sodas. He took the tray to the tall round table just behind the Britton guys' lane and helped her up onto the high stool.

"You bowling, Dooley?" one of the guys called.

"Maybe next game."

He faced Morgan again and picked up a chip. Then he

103

stopped and stared at her.

She sat up quickly and wiped her mouth. "What?"

"Were you just singing?"

Oh. "Maybe."

"This is Lady Gaga."

"So?"

"You know all the words to 'Poker Face'?"

She frowned. "I've got a radio."

He chuckled. "I'm glad to hear it."

She picked a chip from the plate and licked the cheese from the edge, thinking about how it seemed Doug had some preconceived notions about her too. And how it shouldn't matter.

They weren't dating. They weren't going to date. She was working on getting a job that was going to take her to California. He had a life in Omaha. They barely knew one another. She didn't care what he thought of her.

Except she did.

She loved finding out more about him. She was fascinated he'd been in the Guard and wanted to know more about what it was like to be a paramedic. She wanted to know what his friends were like and what his girlfriends were like. Probably that last one more than she should.

She started to ask him but found him watching her. "What?"

"Um." His gaze dropped to her mouth. "I've never gotten hard while eating nachos before."

She looked at her chip, then back to him. Then she slowly licked at the cheese again. His quick intake of air made her smile. It was fun to affect him too. "This makes you hard?" she asked. She dipped a fingertip in the cheese on the plate and put it on her lower lip, then slowly licked it off. Then she picked up an olive and sucked it clean of cheese before pulling it into her mouth.

"You're killing me," he groaned.

"This was your idea," she reminded him. Not that she was complaining.

"Just eat, for God's sake," he said, pulling his eyes from her. "You're gonna need your strength."

Grinning, she crunched on the chip. Then she sipped soda for the first time in over a year. She closed her eyes and sighed. God, she loved sugar and fat.

"What are you doing now?" Doug almost sounded annoyed.

"Drinking non-diet soda."

"Do you have to make it pornographic?" He shifted on his seat.

She stared at him. "My drinking sounds pornographic?"

"You moaned," he said.

"I did?"

"Yes. And it makes me want to make you moan a lot more...and louder."

She smiled. "Feel free."

He shook his head and ate three chips at once. "We're relaxing."

She looked around the bowling alley. No one here was trying to impress anyone else. No one here cared that the paint on the walls clashed horribly with the flooring. They were still having fun even though there wasn't a thing on the menu that cost more than five dollars and there was a strange smell in the air.

She leaned an elbow on the table and asked. "So what's a regular girl?"

He grinned as if he'd been expecting the question and leaned back. "A girl like I regularly date."

Oh, she wanted to know about this. She wanted to know what girls attracted Doug Miller. Obviously he was physically attracted to her, but she wanted to know what he *liked*, what he looked for in women he spent time with, not just the ones he took to bed.

She tried to get more comfortable on her stool. It was completely silly that she didn't like thinking about him taking other women to bed. Of course he did. He certainly didn't act like a guy who was unfamiliar with the whole seduction and sex thing. He'd go right back to it after they got back to Omaha. It was completely stupid that that bugged her too.

She still couldn't stop herself from saying, "What kind of girl do you usually date?"

He lifted a shoulder. "A girl who has simple tastes, who just wants to have a good time. No bells and whistles."

"Bells and whistles?"

He tipped his head to one side. "You know what I mean. I don't usually wear jackets to dinner, and dinner usually has one course and includes French fries. I date women who spend like twenty bucks on earrings, buy their sheets at Target and who have better bowling averages than I do."

Ah. She understood. Too well. He was warning her off. The girls he usually dated were nearly opposite of Morgan.

"So you only hang out with regular girls?"

"No. I said I only *date* regular girls. I hang out with...well, yeah, mostly I hang out with regular girls too. Jessica and Danika are regular girls. But Sara's not. She's a princess. Though she tries. Since she's married Mac she's a little more regular. But she doesn't bowl worth a crap. Too worried about her nails."

Morgan huffed out a frustrated breath. He had a definite look of affection on his face when he talked about these women. She'd already heard about Sara. The one with the romance books with the word clit in them. Great.

"Wow, you have a whole harem of regular women," she said, tossing a jalapeño pepper off her chip.

"Oh, they're not mine. Not like that. They're friends. Married to my best friends. But they are the best women I know."

Oh, really? "What makes them the best?"

He seemed to think about that. "They're beautiful, sexy, funny, intelligent."

"They sound downright perfect," she said with a frown. It also sounded like Doug had a few crushes.

He chuckled. "Nah. Jessica's too bossy. She's a nurse, super practical, willing to get bloody and dirty if needed. But she likes to be in charge. She's more like an older sister."

"What about Sara?" He'd already said she was married but Doug clearly had a soft spot for her.

"Sara's like a little sister to all of us. Except Mac, obviously." He laughed. "She's a lot of work. But she has a heart of gold."

How wonderful. Morgan picked a chip loaded with cheese, beans and salsa and took a huge bite.

"Then there's Dani. She's probably the closest to my type."

Even better. Morgan took another chip. It was one thing to hear about what he liked in women. It was another to have specific examples. That he spent a lot of time with.

"She's not too girly, likes to fix things, is more comfortable in T-shirts and jeans than anything. She's low maintenance for sure."

Right. There was the hint again, which wasn't very damned subtle, that *she* was not any of those things.

"But you do the not-regular thing well," she said. "You were a natural tonight at dinner with Jonathan."

"I *can* do it," he agreed. "I just prefer not to. I like things simple. Real."

And her life, her world, wasn't real. At least not to him. He *could* fit into it, but he didn't want to. Got it.

"You date a lot?" she asked.

"Enough."

"Lots of regular girls in Omaha?"

The corner of his mouth curled. "Enough."

"How come you haven't married one of these real regular girls?" she asked, breaking a chip into little pieces.

His eyebrows shot up. "Marriage isn't in the plans. I date girls who know that, who feel the same way. I don't date anyone exclusively, or too many times, for that matter. Things get complicated if you get to know a girl too well and vice versa."

"But you do have sex with them?"

"Of course."

She rolled her eyes, irritated by the conversation. Which made no sense. "You just keep things at sex and a few laughs and that's it?"

"Right." He said it more emphatically than was needed.

Okay, already. She got it. Hell, it was what they were doing—casual, sex, fun, period. He didn't have to act like she was getting too close for comfort. This was more or less a business arrangement. Even *more* straightforward than the relationships he apparently had all the time.

"So," she said, selecting another chip. "You worried about some performance anxiety or something?"

He set his glass down hard. "What?"

"You need to dress me down and take me bowling before we go to bed because that's what you're used to? You can't perform under different circumstances?"

He narrowed his eyes. "You think I need to see you with your hair down and eating nachos before I can get it up?" He laughed. "Uh, no."

"Then what is this? This wanting me to be a regular girl?"

"Regular girls have more fun. They're not uptight. They don't have big business deals nagging at the back of their minds keeping them from focusing on me. They don't have fancy lingerie so they don't care if I rip it getting it off of them. They don't worry about what other people think so they don't hold back on orgasms the neighbors can hear."

She swallowed hard. Having Doug rip her panties off sounded damned appealing. Even if they were expensive. "Is this wisdom based on experience with regular girls or...not-regular ones?"

Morgan could admit business was never far from her mind. But she wasn't sure she held back on the orgasms exactly. It was more... Oh hell, she didn't know. Maybe she did hold back. She had orgasms but she didn't lose her mind.

"I've been with enough of both to have formed an educated opinion," he said.

Of course he had. Why did she keep bringing this subject up?

"Meaning you've pegged me as high maintenance and too much work?"

"Pretty much," he admitted. "Life's short. Best to spend it

doing things I love. I'm not going to wait an hour for a woman to fix her hair to go to the grocery store or paint her nails or try on a hundred dresses. The best look for any woman is a rumpled old T-shirt, no panties and her hair in a ponytail."

He was talking about all the reasons he didn't think he'd like being with her and yet she couldn't help her smile. "You've put some real thought into this."

He nodded and shoved a chip into his mouth.

"What are some of these things you love that you want to spend your time doing?"

⸰ They were wrong for each other and that was wonderful. This was a weekend thing and the more reasons they had to cheerfully part ways at the end of it, the better.

"Being with people I care about and who care about me. Working a job I love and I'm good at. Sports, camping, being my nieces' favorite uncle."

"You have nieces?" She wasn't sure why that surprised her.

"Yep, three of them. One of my sisters has two girls and the other has one."

"What makes you their favorite?"

He gave her a grin that made her stomach flip. "I like to play. I'll get on the floor, get loud and messy and silly with them."

She had no trouble believing that. But all at once his childish tendencies were a lot more attractive. Plus, she knew now that he could turn it off. At least for long enough to eat dinner with her boss. He was interesting. And very, very hot.

"I'll admit I'm a little concerned about the ripped lingerie," she said casually, sipping from her straw.

He blinked as they changed topics. "Oh?"

"These were expensive."

"You can buy more."

She smiled. No promises of being careful or gentlemanly. "I have another idea."

"I'm open to suggestions as long as they come off."

She glanced around. Everyone in Bud's Bowl was otherwise engaged. Most had their backs to them anyway as they concentrated on the alleys.

Through her dress she felt the strip of her panties where they crossed her hip. The dress's material was thin and she was able to roll the edges of her panties down by sliding her palms over her hips through the dress. She had to lift her butt off the seat of the stool and wiggle but she was able to work the tiny bikini panties to mid-thigh. Then she crossed one leg over the other, grabbed the edge of the panties and pulled them to her ankles where she kicked them free.

Then she handed them to Doug. "Now there's no worry about ripping anything when we get back to the room."

Doug stared at the silky scrap in his hand. "I can't believe you just did that."

"Maybe regular girls don't do stuff like that," she said with a lift of her shoulder. She picked up her soda again. They wouldn't work out long term, but she was going to show him other girls could be fun too.

"I have to say, I've never had a woman hand me her underwear in a bowling alley before," he admitted.

"Stick around. I might surprise you again." She slid off her stool and headed for the Britton guys. She just didn't want to talk to him any more right now. She wasn't his type. Fine. Outside of this weekend he wouldn't want to hang out with her. Fine. Jessica, Sara and Dani were his favorite women. Fine.

But they were stuck with each other for the next two days and she still needed him. Todd was here and it was messing with her mind. She wasn't attracted like she had been before, but there was still a little...something there. Or maybe it was just a good excuse to keep Doug close. Either way it just seemed safer to stick with Doug—while *not* talking about how not his type she was.

"Hi, guys, can I play?" she asked, kicking off her heels.

The men turned as one. "Um, sure," one of them said. He glanced over her shoulder at Doug. "You can take my turn."

"Dooley, you want my spot?" another asked.

"Yeah," he called.

She stubbornly didn't turn to see what he was doing.

Instead she concentrated on studying the current bowler. She vaguely remembered the bowling birthday party she'd been to when she was eight or so. That had been a long time ago. She'd seen people bowling in movies and on TV but had never considered whether she'd be able to do it herself.

"You're gonna need these." Doug handed her a pair of shoes and then set two balls up on the return. "Guys, I ordered some fresh nachos and some beer, so help yourselves," he told the two who were giving up their spots.

Morgan slipped the shoes on and stood. "Here goes."

Doug chuckled. "You've got to wait your turn."

"Oh." She plopped back down on the chair. "When do I go?"

"You're taking Charlie's spot," he said, pointing at the score screen over their heads. "He goes third." He finished tying his shoes and straightened. "But I'm taking Dave's spot, so I'm up next."

She watched him chat with the other guys, pick up his ball and study the pins.

"You've got to be better than Charlie."

Morgan turned to find another man take the seat next to her. She thought this was Roger. He leaned back and smiled, watching Doug knock over all but one of the pins.

"I don't know about that," she said.

"We've been bowling together for thirteen years and he hasn't gotten one lick better," Roger said.

Morgan smiled. "You've worked together at the Britton that whole time?"

"Yep. Met the first day and he fit right in."

"You've worked at the Britton a long time," she said, remembering what Doug had told her when he introduced the group in the suite. "That's impressive."

Roger lifted a shoulder. "If you treat people right, they stick around."

She glanced at Doug. Was that true in all things? If she treated Doug right, would he stick around even after Sunday?

Morgan straightened. Did she want him to stick around? She let the idea settle in her mind and realized that yeah, she wouldn't mind seeing more of him.

When the hell had that happened? When he was eating chips and subs in their room? When he was giving her an orgasm over the phone? When he showed up at dinner with her boss with jeans and tennis shoes on?

Still, it was there. That I'm-not-quite-ready-for-this-to-be-over feeling.

Okay, so she had to treat him right to get him to stick.

Something in her gut said it would take more than great sex.

"So Britton's treated you right?" she asked Roger.

He nodded. "Definitely."

"In what way?"

"Appreciation goes both ways," he said. "When my wife got sick and I needed time off, Britton gave me the time without question. Told me to take as long as I needed, that my job would still be there. Whenever I do something nice for the hotel, you know go above and beyond, they tell me good job and thank me."

She pondered that. It was great business practice and she liked to think she did those same things in her hotel. If employees were responsible for someone having a great stay or for having a guest return to their hotel, she rewarded them, and if a loyal employee needed something, she did what she could to help them out.

Again her eyes went to Doug. Appreciation, huh?

She watched Doug laugh at something one of the other men said. She felt the warmth in her stomach that was becoming familiar when he was around. He was so at ease around everyone. His laugh, that sincere I'm-enjoying-myself laugh, was the same laugh Jonathan had gotten from him at dinner as they talked about their European travels.

And it hit her—she liked Doug. She was inexplicably drawn to how he could be comfortable bowling with some regular guys and sitting at the table with a hotel mogul all in the same night.

Or maybe it wasn't so inexplicable.

He reminded her of her dad.

She couldn't believe she hadn't seen it before this.

Her dad was just like Doug. He liked everyone, took things in stride, was all about the fun and not taking anything too seriously. She loved him dearly. Even though he drove her bananas.

Corey James had gotten his high school sweetheart pregnant and had happily abandoned plans for college to play house. He'd gone to work for some local farmers who had taken good care of the young couple with the cute baby girl. While it lasted. Corey got easily bored and changed jobs every few years, trying his hand at everything from bartending to contracting until finally settling in, of all things, daycare. When her mom, Mindy, went to nursing school and worked odd hours at the hospital, Corey was a stay-at-home dad who took care of both Morgan and Maddie—who'd shown up just a year later—along with a few other kids in the neighborhood for some extra money.

Being only seventeen years older than his daughters, he'd been more like a big brother or buddy than a dad. They played, they made messes, they got silly.

Like Doug said he did with his nieces. Morgan felt a little flip in the vicinity of her heart. Dammit. Why would that be attractive to her? She was a business woman. She had plans. She couldn't remember the last time she'd sat on the floor for any reason.

Maybe that was the appeal right there.

She could be like her mom and then maybe she'd need someone like her dad.

It had been up to Mindy to provide the stability and the money. Not only did she work as a nurse but she sold Mary Kay on the side and dabbled in other part-time jobs, saving everything she could. They lived on a shoestring budget so Mindy could put every extra dime in the bank. Initially it was because she never knew when he'd get bored or frustrated and quit a job. He'd gone into business with his brother once and a friend another time. Both required a large investment they never came close to recouping. Even after he stayed home, he was spontaneous enough to go out and spend large amounts on things that were difficult to return.

He'd put an above-ground swimming pool in behind their house one weekend when Mindy was working a double shift. By the time she got home and saw the surprise, it had been secured and filled with water. Another time, he'd brought two dogs home and the girls were already attached by the time Mindy got home. Then there had been the car he'd bought from a guy in the parking lot at the golf course. He didn't know the guy and never saw him again. Of course, the car had been a lemon and cost a fortune in repairs.

So, Morgan had thought she wanted a stable guy who could make a good living and was careful with finances.

But watching Doug now, she couldn't help but think about how much fun her dad was, how much she loved him, and how important it was to laugh and have a good time too.

Plus, trusting Doug wasn't an issue. She didn't need to trust him. She didn't have to worry about his drive and goals conflicting with hers like Todd's seemed to. As for him bringing a pool home without asking, well, she just wouldn't give him a debit card.

She could easily be the Mindy in their situation. She made good money, had some fantastic investments and a healthy savings account. Plus her job had a lot of fantastic perks like private jets and fancy hotel suites.

Why couldn't she keep Doug around? She wouldn't be depending on him for financial security. Knowing that up front would make it all a lot easier than her mom had ever had it.

And it would be fun.

Even Mindy would admit, with a laugh and a shake of her head, that Corey James was the most fun she'd ever had.

Besides, Doug was the one who'd said they were playing *Pretty Woman*. She knew Richard Gere had wanted to keep seeing Julia Roberts after their week was over. She couldn't remember the details of how it had played out, but they'd ended up together. She was pretty sure.

As Doug turned his grin on her directly she couldn't help

but think this was the first time she'd had a conversation even remotely about the Britton Hotels without her thoughts being consumed by her work.

Doug did that to her. He made her care about something else.

That should probably concern her. She'd brought him on this trip to ensure that she could concentrate fully on her job and not get into trouble with Todd and she was possibly in more trouble with him.

But it could work.

"Thanks for the insight, Roger."

"No problem. If you have any other questions about the Britton or anything just let me know."

She grinned at him, feeling lighter now. "I will."

He chuckled and gave her a wink as she got to her feet.

"Your turn, Sugar," Doug said.

"How many turns do I need to take?" she asked, taking her ball from him, letting her hands slide over his.

"Four."

She stepped up to the line as she'd seen everyone else do, pulled her hand back, then stepped and rolled the ball as hard as she could.

It was the worst shot in the history of bowling. Still, all the guys behind her cheered and applauded as she turned away from her ball rolling...slowly...down the left gutter.

Doug was grinning at her when she came back to the ball return. "You even look good bowling badly."

"Thank you. I guess," she said. "So three more turns like that, huh?"

"I think all the guys would agree to let you have twice that many. Your dress pulls up real nice on the back of your thighs when you throw the ball."

She tugged the back of her dress down and smiled. "Oops." She leaned in. "There are lots of great things to do without panties on, but I'm not sure bowling is one of them."

Heat flared between them and she watched him swallow hard. "Good point." He took her ball back and turned toward the table where nachos and beer were being consumed at a startling rate. "Charlie! Dave! You're up again!"

He gave Roger her ball and took her hand.

"Everything okay?" Roger called.

"Great," she called back. "Completely great."

They didn't talk as they hurried down the sidewalks and across the streets on the way back to the Britton. As they passed the concierge stand Doug said, "Mike, send our stuff up later. Much later. Like tomorrow morning."

Mike gave him a salute. "You got it."

They didn't stop until they stepped into the elevator and the doors swished shut.

"Doug, I just want to say that I appreciate you com—"

Then his mouth was on hers and his big hand settled on her hip and started gathering the skirt of her dress up until his skin touched hers. He sighed, as if he'd been waiting to do that for days.

She gasped as he stroked up and down the outside of her bare thigh, then around to cup her butt, bringing her closer. He lifted her leg so her knee was at his hip and his other hand slid between them, his fingers running up the back of her other leg and then between her legs.

"You're so hot. So wet," he groaned as his finger slid partway into her.

"Yes," she gasped.

His tongue was as hot and insistent as his hand was as he stroked into her mouth and into her hot folds at the same time. She ground closer to his hand and he added a second finger, filling her, stretching her and making waves of lust wash over her.

She was gripping his shoulders, trying to get closer, practically trying to climb on top of him when the elevator dinged, signaling they'd arrived on their floor. Thank God only one of the other suites was being used and it was by the musician who was out at this time of night. Had he been getting on the elevator just then he would have gotten an eyeful.

"You have thirty seconds to get naked and spread out on

that bed," Doug growled.

He wasn't kidding. When she pulled back to look at him, he wore the most serious expression she had yet to see from him. His fingers slid from her body and she shuddered at the sense of hunger left behind.

"I *will* do you right here in the hallway," he said in a low voice. "But I was serious about wanting to suck on your clit until you beg me."

Her knees went weak and she could only nod.

"On the bed, Sugar. Naked and spread out. You have fifteen seconds."

Chapter Five

She wanted to ask *or what?* but her body was throbbing and she wanted him to make her beg as promised.

She shed her dress the moment the door opened and she was on the bed ten seconds later.

Doug came toward her, his eyes roaming over her greedily. "I didn't think it was possible to get even harder, but I just did."

Morgan smiled. It wasn't flowery and romantic but it was the gritty real stuff Doug made so damned sexy. There were no practiced words, nothing to infer—he just laid it all out there.

She leaned back onto her elbows and pulled one leg up, while the other dangled over the end of the bed. "I've never begged for anything."

He half growled, half groaned and tossed his shirt to the side, then unbuttoned and unzipped his pants. But that was as far as he went.

"Hey, I want—"

He dropped to his knees at the end of the bed and took her hips in his hands. "I know what you want," he told her, pulling her butt to the end of the bed, "and I'll give it all to you. Over and over again."

Then he leaned in so she had to spread her legs.

This was promising.

He just looked at her for a long time, completely brazen in his study. Finally, he looked up at her with a half grin. "This is for spilling grape soda on the carpet." He leaned in and licked.

She thought she was going to faint.

One touch, one lick, and she would have agreed to dye the entire suite purple.

Then he said, "This is for inviting the guys up here without asking you." He licked again, but this time added a little suck on her labia.

She threw her head back and concentrated on breathing.

"This is for the noise complaint." He sucked again, then slid his mouth up to her clit. And sucked harder.

"This is for showing up tonight at dinner with your boss, uninvited." He slid two fingers into her as he sucked her clit into his mouth, rolling his tongue around it.

She arched her hips closer, gripping the bedspread with both hands. "*Doug.*"

"And this is for all the stuff I'm probably going to do tomorrow to frustrate you."

He licked and sucked and pumped his fingers as Morgan struggled to get closer and wider and...*more*. Just more. That was all she could think.

Then finally, all she could do was say, "Please."

"Please what?" he asked against her.

"Please take me. Do me. Fuck me."

With a soft growl he lifted himself slightly, not letting his fingers leave her.

Without his mouth on her, she whimpered, "Please."

"Say it again. Beg me," he said, shifting between her thighs and rolling on a condom.

She wasn't sure when or how he'd gotten rid of his pants, but she really didn't care.

"Please, Doug. I need you. Please. *Please.*"

Then she felt him lift her butt and pull her forward and the next thing she knew he was sinking into her, his cock stretching her and filling her. That was what she needed, that depth and girth.

She squeezed around his length, her muscles already beginning to milk him.

"Damn, girl, you feel incredible," he panted. "It's like you're sucking it out of me."

She loved the crude talk, loved how he thrust into her, holding nothing back. She loved the sweat on his forehead as he pumped into her, loved how he gripped her hips, making sure she took every one of his thrusts, loved the heartfelt groans of pleasure.

She wanted to pull him completely inside her. As her muscles flexed around him she felt the beginning swirls of an orgasm and she reached for it, arching closer to him and tilting just right, so he rubbed over her clit as he pushed forward and pulled back. That was all it took and the sensations built faster and faster until she was crying out his name, tumbling over the edge.

He was right with her. His cock throbbed heavy and full inside of her and with the waves of muscle contractions from her he was thrusting hard and faster until he thrust deep and groaned as he came.

Afterward, she sank into the mattress, her body was so relaxed and full. She could barely turn her head as he slumped forward and rolled to the side, pulling out of her, but keeping his leg tangled with hers.

She reached out and ran her hand over his chest, sweaty from the exertion and rising and falling with the deep breaths he was pulling in. "By the way," she said playfully, and breathlessly. "You're forgiven for all those offenses."

He chuckled. "I thought maybe I would be."

"But," she said, rolling to her side to face him. "If you want to do anything else nice for me, just in case there's a future need for my forgiveness, I promise to remember it when the time comes."

He laughed, pulled her close, tucking her head under his chin. "Good idea. I can just about guarantee there'll be a need for that."

He wasn't a stupid guy. Doug knew as soon as Morgan snuggled against his side and breathed a huge contented sigh, as if she'd never been as happy or satisfied, that he had made a mistake.

He'd just made love to a woman he could fall for.

Dammit.

There shouldn't have been any true risk here. He liked the

fancy hotel, the high-end beer, the plush towels. But taking her bowling was supposed to show him it wasn't *her* he liked.

She was the opposite of everything he wanted. He'd made a point of letting her know that too, and she was a smart cookie. He knew she'd caught on to what he was doing at the bowling alley. He'd been purposely pointing out everything he generally looked for that she didn't have or want.

Still, he'd watched her eating nachos as readily as she'd eaten the wild mushroom risotto at dinner. Actually, *more* readily. She'd picked at her food at the hotel, but on the tall stool in the middle of Bud's Bowl she'd devoured chip after chip. She'd been chatting and laughing with Roger. She'd slipped her panties off and given them to him.

She was full of surprises.

He wanted to know what else she might do. Or say.

Damn, she'd actually said *fuck me.* Again. That was probably when he'd lost his heart.

It wasn't particularly sweet or romantic, not a story he'd tell the grandkids about the moment he'd first known she could be the one, but he hadn't been lying when he'd said he liked things real. He liked down to earth, straightforward, simple.

It didn't get much more straightforward than *fuck me.* Especially in that voice, with that look on her face, that said she hadn't really been aware of what she was saying. She'd been purely *feeling* at that moment. It was the most honest thing she'd ever said to him.

Ben's advice had been to get to know her so he would see she wasn't right for him. Sam had said not to spend time talking but to focus on the sex and the sex only. It appeared brainiac Ben Torres had lost this round to former-ladies'-man Sam Bradford.

Dooley would have to remember that.

Not that it helped him right now.

He stroked his hand over Morgan's hair. He loved the feel of it. It was silky and smooth and a fascinating color. He let the strands fall over his fingers and tried to remember ever being fascinated by a woman's hair before.

121

It probably cost a fortune to maintain. He'd been around Sara long enough to know the cost of hair products and services varied widely from cheap to outrageous.

"How much does your shampoo cost?" he asked.

Morgan gave him a drowsy, "Huh?"

"It feels and smells amazing. Does your shampoo cost a lot?"

She lifted her head and gave him a quizzical look. "Um, I don't know. It's about twenty dollars a bottle."

He knew it. He spent something like two forty-nine on his shampoo. His hair gel was more like ten bucks, but it lasted him for months.

She put her hand on his chest and propped her chin there to look at him. "Of course, I use a lot more than just shampoo."

She seemed to be watching him for a reaction, so he kept his expression neutral. "Girl hair seems to be quite a production."

"It can be."

"So, total, what are we talking? Fifty bucks?"

"Per month? Probably more. Especially if you include the trip to the salon and stuff."

He sighed. "Figured."

"Is that a problem for some reason? I suppose *regular* girls cut and color their own hair? Oh, that's right, you like ponytails."

She sounded annoyed and Dooley realized he had two options at that moment—let it go or talk about it.

Letting it go would lead to more sex.

Not a completely horrible option, for sure. Definitely what Sam would tell him to do.

Talking about it would lead to more proof they wouldn't last. Probably what Ben would tell him to do.

Ben's idea had sucked earlier.

Except taking Morgan to the bowling alley hadn't sucked at all. It had been fun and even sexy and had proven there was more to her than he'd assumed.

He rolled toward her, sifting her hair through his fingers again. He knew for a fact it was her true color and it smelled and felt great.

"I like ponytails," he agreed. "I like the natural look."

"Why?" she asked, seeming genuinely interested. "You find lipstick and nail polish and hair highlights a turn-off?"

He thought about that. Her lipstick had been kissed off a long time ago, which was damned sexy. Her hair was gorgeous messed up as it was from the pillow. But her nail polish was intact and it looked good as she gently raked her nails over his chest, causing a shiver of want.

"It's not the final product," he said. "It's the process. The expense. Why spend the time and money? I'd rather see you naked in a shower, everything washed off, than all made up in a fancy restaurant."

She smiled, curling her nails into his chest again lightly. "What do the other women you date look like when you go out?"

He thought about it. He'd most recently taken Lori out a couple of times. Definitely low maintenance. She was an ER nurse with Ben's wife, Jessica.

"Jeans, shirt, basic shoes, no heels."

"Ponytail?" she asked.

He couldn't remember. "Sure."

"How do you know these women?"

"They work at the hospital." Almost exclusively. It was about the only place he spent time besides home. Or the bar, which was generally full of people who worked at the hospital.

"They wear scrubs and stuff when you usually see them?" she asked. "When you flirt and ask them out, right?"

"Right. Work clothes."

"So, jeans are dressing up for them," she said with a triumphant tone. "They're still trying to look nice. They're still putting more time and effort into it."

He thought about that. Hmm. Maybe she had a point. "They know me. They know they don't have to impress me."

"Maybe it's not about you."

He lifted an eyebrow. "Oh?"

"Maybe it's about them. I like dressing up. I like doing different things with my hair and changing my look with different make-up and accessories. It's fun. It makes me feel more relaxed and confident in a dating situation, which is different than being confident in a work situation. I wear pantsuits at work. I have to take care of lots of different issues for a lot of different people every day. Those people need to see me as their boss, or as the hotel manager. So when I go out, I want to look different from that. I want to be able to be confident in being a woman and having fun."

She pushed herself up to sitting against the headboard, tucking the sheet under her arms.

"Maybe the women you date are the same," she went on. "They work in a hospital. Scrubs make sense for what they do. People see scrubs and lab coats and think health care and see those people as competent and there to help them. Plus, scrubs are comfortable and the nurses can dive into whatever they need to do without worrying about ruining silk or breaking a nail or turning their ankle in heels. But when they go out with you they want to relax and be able to have fun and dress up differently than they do for work. Jeans make sense because you're taking them places where silk and heels aren't practical anyway."

She was looking at him with an expression that seemed far too smug.

"You're assuming I take them places that don't have a dress code?" He did. Definitely.

She didn't even blink. "Yes."

"Why?"

"Because you don't have any money. As you were sure to inform me the very first night in the bar when I asked you to go on this trip."

He had. He'd wanted it right out in the open.

"You like men with money."

"It's not a mark against them," she said with a shrug. "That bugs you about me, doesn't it?"

"Why do you say that?"

"You asked about how much my shampoo cost. No one has ever asked me that before."

"I was curious."

"You wanted to see if maybe I was a regular girl under all of this?"

He shook his head and pushed himself up to sit next to her. "I was positive, even before I knew about your shampoo, you're not a regular girl."

"Is that good or bad?"

"You tell me. I hang out in places like Bud's Bowl a lot."

She turned to face him more fully. "I can buy my own shampoo, Doug. I don't need a guy to do that."

There was something between the lines there. He didn't like between the lines.

"So you're *not* looking for a guy with money?" he asked. Straightforward, just the way he liked it.

"I'm just saying I can afford to hang out wherever I want, dress however I want." She took a deep breath. "You not having a lot of money doesn't make you any less attractive to me."

This sounded like trouble.

"That doesn't mean you want to hang out where I hang out," he said, wondering why in the hell he'd brought her shampoo up in the first place. But he'd started this conversation. He'd been wondering about how important the finer things were to her. But why?

Fuck. Sam was right *again*. He had to stop talking to her.

"How about you hanging out where I hang out?" she asked, waving her arm to encompass the suite. "This isn't bad is it?"

"This is great," he admitted. "But it's not...me."

"It's me," she said. "Stick with me and I bet it will grow on you." She gave him a sweet, probably unintentionally sexy smile.

He had no doubt the extravagance would grow on him. As would she.

About that time something would happen and it would all go away.

Good things never lasted.

"The money thing is important to you, huh?" he asked. Money especially seemed to not last. Jobs changed, the economy changed, the stock market changed. Learning to live with less, even when there was extra, made a hell of a lot more sense than getting used to the best of everything and having to adjust when it went away.

He'd been there. He'd grown up with money. A lot of it. When it was gone he'd tried like hell for awhile to figure out how to get it back. But the never-ending battle gave him an ulcer and insomnia and nearly cost him some important relationships. Finally, he'd learned to just accept what he had and protect himself from having it all taken away from him again.

"The money thing?" she asked.

"Having money. Spending money. Where's that come from?" he asked. "Did you grow up with money? You're used to being surrounded by all this stuff? You went to private school in a limo and ate sushi for lunch?"

She laughed. "Hardly."

"Ah, so you like all this stuff because you *didn't* have money."

She lifted a shoulder. "I grew up in a family where it was paycheck to paycheck."

"That could happen again," he said. His eyes dropped to her mouth and he realized sitting here talking finances was stupid. She was naked under the sheet. And he had only a few more hours with her in this bed.

"Britton is a very stable company. As long as I keep doing well, I have the security of a well-paying job with lots of great perks," she said, her chin going up.

"Even the most stable company can get into trouble," he said. "Somebody could be stealing from their accounts right now. Somebody could be planning a lawsuit against them. Or a takeover. That can change everything. What if something happens to Jonathan? What if he has a heart attack and dies? You're his golden girl now, but the next guy could decide he likes the girl in the office who gives him blow jobs on his lunch hour and promote her instead."

He looked from her lips to her eyes and found her watching him with wide eyes lit with a combination of panic and incredulity.

"What the hell are you talking about?" she asked, frowning at him and pulling the sheet tighter across her breasts.

Well, he hadn't been lying to her. He could have been more sensitive in how he said it, but it was all true.

"I'm just saying when you're on top, successful, popular, there's more of a chance of something going wrong. People are going to be targeting you as the competition because you're getting the raises and promotions they want. People are, of course, targeting Britton because this is a huge company. Others in the business would like nothing better than to see you—and Britton—fail. That's a risk of being successful."

Her frown had deepened. "So I should just stay in Omaha at the hotel because it's safer?"

"In some ways."

"Trust me," she said. "Being safe and secure and stable are all my main objectives. Money provides those things."

"Money is the worst thing to depend on. Sometimes—"

"I know all about money and what it can and can't do," she interrupted. "I loved the fun, frivolous, extravagant things my dad was always spending money on. But I hated watching my mom get mad and worry and work her ass off to make up for it. So I decided a long time ago I was going to have fun too, but I was going to be damned sure I could afford it."

Her cheeks were flushed and she was gripping the sheet against her heart. Dooley was enthralled. Not that she was upset, but by her obvious passion for the subject.

"When I was fourteen my dad woke us up in the middle of the night and took us on a surprise trip to the mountains," she said. "It was awesome and spontaneous and fun. Then it came time for going back to school and we couldn't afford new clothes, so the first two months I had to wear worn out jeans and shirts we got as hand-me-downs from my snotty cousin, Kaylee. I hated the idea that we couldn't have fun *and* have the things we needed. Hated it. Hated watching Mom work an extra job. Hated seeing Dad's disappointment when a surprise or gift would make Mom cry because we'd be further in debt. I also hated the year Dad decided to finally listen to Mom and not do anything spontaneous and fun. That sucked."

Morgan was staring at her lap and Dooley had no idea what to say.

Dammit, it was sucking him in, but he couldn't help it—he liked talking to her, listening to her, learning more about her.

"So your dad's idea of fun was big, crazy stuff?" he asked.

She smiled. "He was always fun. But he liked to spoil us. He liked to make us smile and give us good memories and he tended to go overboard. It wasn't that he didn't understand money and debt and everything, but I think he just believed life's too short and you can't take it with you and he'd worry about it later. But Mom worried about it right then. The truth was, their financial situation simply did not support the lifestyle he wanted to have."

She sighed. "They're still in debt. He works, but changes jobs periodically. They have little savings, no retirement fund. Stuff like that. So, like I said, I was determined I was not going to be in that position myself. I intend to have fun, enjoy things, have nice stuff and I'm going to be sure I can afford it." She looked over at him. "Maybe that sounds superficial or stuck-up, but I also give money to my parents and to charity. I work hard. I paid my way through college. So I think it's okay to want and have nice things. That doesn't make me a bad person."

Dooley knew he was staring, but he couldn't look away from her. She had been gorgeous from minute one. Now she was beautiful, with that proud, determined look on her face, that confident, intelligent look in her eyes and the way she met his gaze directly, challenging him to judge her. She was a hard worker who loved her parents and gave money to charity.

He was a goner.

"I need to know something," he said.

She took a deep breath. "What?"

"Is the sex so amazing with you because this is the best

bed I've ever been on, or is it you? This is way beyond the elevator at the fundraiser."

She looked surprised for only a moment. Then she smiled. "I think I know how to find out."

"Yeah?"

"One of your texts mentioned bending me over the couch."

As every drop of blood re-routed to his cock, all Dooley could think was, *Yep, definitely a goner.*

The next morning Dooley woke before Morgan did.

Thank God.

If she so much as rolled over and smiled at him, he'd want to have her again.

He wanted to anyway, but he wasn't going to wake her up for it. Probably. Still, he had to leave the suite to be sure.

Damn, the woman was messing with him. This was supposed to be a fun weekend fling. It had certainly been fun. But it wasn't supposed to be anything more. He wasn't even supposed to like her, really. No, he wasn't supposed to know her well enough to like her or not.

But not only was he getting to know her, he was starting to like her and he wanted her even more now that he'd had her.

As he pulled on his swimming trunks he was careful not to look in the direction of the bed and was thankful for the weird sleep patterns that kept him from getting more than five hours of sleep no matter what time he hit the pillow. It was a hazard of the night shift and of living with someone who was dependent on him at all hours.

This morning he was particularly thankful for not sleeping long and deep. He needed to get some space from Morgan. This was hardly a relaxing, laid-back vacation weekend at this point.

In fact, he was damned revved up.

He grabbed clothes for after his swim, not willing to risk coming back to the suite for at least a couple of hours. Jonathan had said something last night about wanting them to work for the day and then meet with him at four. Surely she'd be waking soon and getting to work. Somewhere other than the suite.

If not, he was going to have to find something to do in the great city of Chicago. Knowing she was in the suite, with the bed, the couch and the Jacuzzi they'd made good use of last night, would make him nuts.

He swam, pushing through a half hour workout without rest. Then he sat on the side of the pool, catching his breath. His thoughts went immediately to the redhead who was somewhere on the premises. Which was enough to put him back in the water for another twenty minutes.

It was stupid stuff that consumed his mind too.

It wasn't the exquisite feel of sinking into her from behind as she gasped and asked for more. It wasn't the way she'd ridden him while he sat in the Jacuzzi, her breasts bouncing as she lifted herself up and down in the bubbling water. It wasn't the way her back fit against his front perfectly as they lay in bed together.

It was the way she laughed. It was the way she had trustingly left her hand in his as he'd pulled her out of the hotel and into the bowling alley. It was the way she pulled the left half of her bottom lip between her teeth while she listened to Jonathan talking about the business.

He wanted to know what she liked for breakfast, if she brushed her teeth first or last in her morning routine, how long doing her hair actually took.

Fuck.

Dooley headed for the restaurant. He was going to eat a big, slow, breakfast. He was going to order whatever would take the longest to prepare. He was going for a walk after breakfast too. He was also going to have the front desk call up to the suite to see if she was gone before he went back up there.

Not because he was afraid of tearing off her clothes and putting her right back on the bed but because he was afraid he was going to *talk* to her.

This was a damned mess.

He rounded the corner to the dining room and came to a

stop.

Of course. The restaurant offered a breakfast buffet.

There would be no stalling with the preparation anyway. He could still eat slowly.

He was loading his plate with hash browns when Jonathan Britton came up beside him. "Good morning."

Dooley gave him a smile. "Morning."

"Morgan isn't with you?" Jonathan asked, reaching for the bacon.

"Sleeping late," Dooley said simply.

"Then join me," Jonathan said, gesturing toward the table that already had a pitcher of orange juice and a coffee carafe on it.

"Are you sure?" Dooley asked. "I'd hate to intrude." He was wearing a T-shirt that said *I'm multi-talented: I can talk and piss you off at the same time*, along with another pair of jeans. Jonathan was in a suit and tie, though his jacket hung on the back of the chair at the table.

"Of course I'm sure. I often have business associates over for breakfast but nothing today. I'd appreciate the company."

Dooley followed the other man to the table and took the seat across from him. After they'd each filled their coffee cups and taken the first bite Dooley asked, "Do you want to talk business or sports?"

Jonathan sipped his coffee and studied him. Then said, "Business."

"Your business or mine?"

Jonathan set his cup down. "Will it seem egotistical if I say mine?"

Dooley smiled. "It would seem egotistical if you assumed I had nothing to say about yours."

Jonathan gave him a nod of acknowledgement. "You're a guest in my hotel. I would love to hear any thoughts you have."

"All right," Dooley began, liberally dousing his scrambled eggs with hot sauce. "I appreciate you wanting to hear from your guests. I think that's great. But there are some other people right here under your nose who could give you a lot of

131

insight."

Jonathan dabbed the corner of his mouth with his napkin. "I'm listening."

"Your employees," Dooley said. "Did you know Roger, the concierge, has worked for you for twenty-five years?"

"Yes." Jonathan buttered his toast. "I'm aware, and appreciative, of Roger's years of service."

"I think Roger might have a few ideas for you, sir. I'll bet he's overheard everything from the highest praise to the biggest complaints about your hotel. I'm sure he knows how to make your employees happy as well. Which is important because, as I'm sure you know, in a hotel, happy employees make happy guests."

Jonathan was chewing as he watched Dooley.

He wiped his mouth with his napkin and picked up his coffee cup. "I don't suppose you're related to the Douglas Miller who was a part of the Wyatt-Morris hotel chain for years?" Jonathan asked.

Dooley knew he should have expected this. Jonathan Britton had been in the business a long time and knew everyone. "Yes, as a matter of fact. Douglas Miller, Senior, is my father."

Jonathan nodded. "I thought so. Plus I did some checking on you."

Dooley smiled. "That doesn't surprise me."

"I didn't check on you because of the hotel," Jonathan said.

"Because of Morgan?"

"Yes."

"I appreciate that, sir," Dooley said honestly. Anyone who cared about Morgan was good in his book.

"So, you have some insight into my hotels?" Jonathan asked.

"Yes. For what it's worth."

Jonathan signaled for the waitress. "Amy, I'm going to need a notebook and a pen, please."

Morgan spent the day in the offices, pulling data, making graphs and spreadsheets and meeting with anyone who might have valuable input to her project. She was going full-speed ahead with her idea about customized guest experiences with everything from menus to the soap guests found in their bathrooms.

Furthermore, she planned to present her idea to Jonathan by preparing one of the hotel rooms according to *his* personal preferences to show him what it could be like.

That meant also meeting with his personal assistant and other staff who might know his favorite foods, colors and routines. It wasn't as easy as having someone fill out a pre-stay questionnaire, but she was pleased with how much the people around him knew about what he liked.

She had a lunch menu prepared with a corned beef sandwich and potato salad, the bed made up in a maroon and cream bedding, Frank Sinatra playing on the stereo and two tickets to one of his favorite places, the Chicago Planetarium, laid out on the coffee table.

The whole thing would have been a lot easier if she had been able to concentrate fully.

Instead her mind kept wandering to Doug.

She'd been disappointed to wake up alone. Disappointed and sore. But the soreness made her smile. As she rolled over and stretched, every moment of getting sore played back in her mind making her tingly and hot.

The night had been amazing. It had been as if he couldn't get enough of her. She'd loved every minute. He'd been hot and dirty and delicious. There had been no rose petals, no candlelight, no sweet words. Everything had been sexy and erotic. He'd told her, graphically, how she made him feel and what he wanted from her. He'd made her say bold things, loudly, and make sounds she'd never imagined.

It had made her feel powerful to affect him so strongly and weak with want at the same time.

Even now, after everything, her body heated and started humming just thinking about him.

It hadn't been all sex either. He'd played with her hair a lot. Even after the shampoo conversation, he'd seem enthralled by her hair. He'd listened to stories about her sister, asked what music she liked and discussed how brilliant Robert Downey Jr. was as Sherlock Holmes. He'd also told her about the youth center where he spent time as well as a lot about his friends and sisters.

All in all, he'd made himself nearly irresistible and her even more sure that she wanted to continue things after they got back to Omaha. Julia Roberts hadn't even had it as good as Doug would.

She'd decided to work through lunch so she could finish and get back to the room sooner, but she did take a break to eat and make a phone call.

While he'd been in the bathroom last night, she'd quickly scanned the contacts in his phone and found Kevin's number.

She knew his best friends were Kevin, Sam, Ben and Mac but it seemed he talked most about Kevin. She was sure any of his friends could answer her question though.

"I told you, if you're in a hotel room with a hot girl who wants you naked, you don't call home to check in."

Morgan grinned. "I'll keep that in mind the next time I'm with a hot girl."

There was a long pause on the other end of the phone.

"Your voice sounds funny, Dooley," Kevin finally said.

She laughed. "Kevin, this is Morgan."

"I was afraid you were going to say that."

"You saw the strange phone number and assumed it was Doug?"

"Yeah. Sorry."

"No harm done. I do want him naked and I appreciate the hot girl comment."

"For the record, a hot girl with a good sense of humor is even better."

"Better than a naked hot girl?" she teased.

"There's very little that's better than a naked hot girl," Kevin said. "Though naked *and* with a good sense of humor is the epitome."

"I thought you were the good Christian boy who knows how to use utensils."

"Ah, Dooley's been talking about us."

"Maybe I saw the cross necklace around your neck that first night in the bar."

"Nah, you only had eyes for Dooley. Which I liked about you, by the way."

And she liked Doug's best friend. "Then maybe you'd be willing to help me out."

"I'm not telling you any of the dirt I have on him. Don't want to scare you off."

"How about telling me the best date I could possibly take him on?"

That made Kevin pause again. "Isn't this whole trip the best date you could possibly take him on?"

She smiled. "This is a business trip and a favor he's doing for me. I want to take him out somewhere great besides all this. Somewhere he'd love."

"I don't know that he's feeling this is a favor. Heard the hotel was amazing, the food's incredible and, well, there's the naked hot girl thing, of course."

"I know but... It's just..." She sighed. "I just want to do something *more*. What I can buy him or where can I take him that will be special?"

Kevin was quiet again for a moment. Then he said, "Okay, if you want something great, one of the things Dooley loves most is baseball. He hasn't been to a major league game since college. The Cubs are in town right now. You could take him to a game."

That was perfect. "Thank you, Kevin. Exactly what I wanted. I owe you a kiss."

He chuckled. "I'm writing that I.O.U. down right now."

As soon as they disconnected, Morgan headed for the administrative assistant, Nancy. "Nancy, any chance I can get a couple of tickets for the Cubs game tonight?"

Nancy nodded. "Sure. You want to sit in the box?"

"The box?"

"Mr. Britton has box seats to the Cubs."

"Are box seats nice?" Morgan asked.

Nancy laughed. "They're enclosed, air conditioned, you'll have your own waiter. Yes, they're nice. I think you'd have the box all to yourselves, too. Nobody's in town to see Mr. Britton since you and Mr. Becker are here."

"Even better. Who should I talk to about it?" Morgan asked.

"I'll call and let them know you'll be using it tonight. Do you want me to arrange a car for you too?"

"Thanks, Nancy." Morgan couldn't wait for the day to be over. She was taking Doug out and tonight his typical dress code would be perfect.

Box seats. A waiter. A limo. This didn't feel like baseball.

Baseball was the cheap seats, hot dogs and being surrounded by other fans.

But as Morgan sat down next to him, the air filling with the spicy scent he would forever associate with her, he didn't mind as much. She'd dressed down for him—denim shorts and a Cubs T-shirt with white tennis shoes and a white visor on her head. The shoes and hat were so white, in fact, he knew they were brand new.

And her hair was in a ponytail.

He wanted to do her right there in the fancy upholstered seats overlooking Wrigley Field.

"You're a Cubs fan?" he asked, shifting in his chair to rearrange his fly. Even with the ponytail and tennis shoes she didn't look like a regular girl. For one thing, she was acting like a little kid at her first circus. She was holding popcorn, her eyes were on everything and she was grinning widely, sitting on the edge of her seat.

"No. Why?"

"You have a T-shirt." Of course, it looked to be a size too small. The soft cotton hugged her breasts, her jeans hugged her ass and with her hair pulled back he could see that sweet spot just behind her ear where he could lick and get the best moans.

"Oh, Nancy sent someone out to buy this stuff for me today. I wanted the whole thing to be perfect." She turned to him. "You like this?"

She'd been so excited to give him the tickets he'd found himself grinning before she'd even told him the whole plan. Now, with those big eyes and the tennis shoes she was wearing, he knew she'd be crushed if he didn't think this was perfect.

"I love this. How'd you know?"

"Kevin told me you like baseball and the team was in town."

Dooley froze with his cup halfway to his mouth. "Kevin?"

"I called him today to get ideas for a good date destination."

He lowered his glass. "You called Kevin? To ask him where to take me on a date?"

"Yes. I wanted to do something nice for you and figured he'd be the best one to help me."

It would have been better if she'd asked it of a friend of his who could keep his mouth shut about it to the other guys.

Of course, he didn't have a friend like that.

They would all find Morgan calling one of his friends for information about him very interesting. He knew because he would have found it interesting if it had happened to one of the others.

"Did you tell him about the box seats?" The Julia Roberts jokes would never end.

She frowned. "No, why?"

"That's good. That's really good."

"Why don't you want them to know about the box seats?"

"They'll give me a hard time." He leaned back and stretched his arm along the back of her seat, fingering the end of her ponytail. He did love her hair.

"Why would they give you a hard time? It's a baseball game."

He chuckled. "I'm the last guy they know who would be watching a baseball game from a box seat. They're going to wonder what I've done to deserve this." He leaned in and kissed the back of her neck.

He'd never made out during a sporting event. There were two main reasons for that. One, sporting events were meant to be watched. Two, if he was with a woman at a sporting event she would be the type to feel the same way. But suddenly the idea didn't sound so bad.

But Morgan moved away from his mouth. "Will you tell them?"

"Tell them what?" He traced his finger along the back of the neck of the T-shirt. He couldn't seem to keep his hands off of her.

"What you've done to deserve this?"

No.

That was when it hit him. He was in way too deep.

No, he wasn't going to tell them about sex with Morgan. And they were going to know exactly what that meant.

"Well, I'm not sure which thing was the final deciding vote," he tried to joke.

She turned to face him. "I think it would surprise you."

"So there *is* something." That was bad too. He didn't want this date to be about rewarding him or paying him back for something. He wanted it to be...just because. Because she wanted to make him happy, wanted to spend time together outside the hotel, away from the business that brought her to Chicago.

She gave him a little smile. "No. There's not. I brought you to the game tonight because I wanted to do something nice for you. Because I like you."

God. He hadn't thought it was possible to want her more.

He tried to laugh. "I'm not sure they'll believe that."

Morgan just looked at him for a few seconds. Then she put her hand against his cheek, leaned in and kissed him. When she pulled back, he sighed.

"I don't care what they believe," she said. "As long as you believe it."

"This whole damned trip with you has been hard to believe."

She gave him a big smile. "Then I guess I'll have to try

harder to convince you." She turned and leaned back in her seat and up against him.

He kept his arm around her, content to sit and watch a baseball game he couldn't afford with a woman he couldn't afford in a box seat he couldn't afford drinking beer he couldn't afford.

Because she liked him.

Who cared what those jokers back in Omaha thought? He was going to let himself believe it. Because he liked her too.

Morgan liked baseball. It was America's game. There was no blood, for the most part. It was civilized, for the most part. There was no hand-to-hand combat and no body-to-body contact, for the most part. And of course, the baseball pants looked good.

But nine innings seemed a bit much.

Especially when the guy next to her wouldn't stop touching her.

She felt like she had that first day in the hotel when just being in the room with him made her heart pound and her body need to move and her thoughts and words come too fast. But now she had the memory of the loving from the night before to add to her reactions.

Every time he shifted in his seat, she thought about his hips thrusting. When he moved his hand from her shoulder to the back of her neck, she thought about his fingers thrusting. As he lifted his glass to his mouth to drink she thought about his tongue thrusting.

She crossed her legs and squeezed. She shifted. She tried to get into the game.

Nothing worked. She was reacting, head to toe, to being near him. Her clothes felt restrictive and she felt the wanting building and she wondered if she could just straddle him on the chair right here and now.

The night at the fundraiser she'd made the first move too.

It was official—she was the sex-crazed one.

She felt his hand lift from her neck to the back of her ponytail, then his fingers fasten around the ponytail holder and pull. Her hair fell to her shoulders and just as she was going to ask him what he was doing, she felt his hand cup her skull, massage her scalp for a moment, then pull away, her hair sliding between his fingers. Then he did it again.

It felt relaxing and stimulating at the same time.

He had a strange fascination with her hair, and her hair products, but she loved how he played with it, rubbing it between his fingers, twirling it, studying it.

It felt very intimate.

Maybe he had a thing for all women's hair, but she somehow doubted it. He seemed more the type to barely notice something like someone's hair.

"Just so you know," he said conversationally, still playing with her hair and watching the game. "This game was a nice idea and I do believe you like me."

"Good." That made her happy. She did like him. More than she should.

"I like you too," he said. "So when I get you back to the hotel and go down on my knees in front of you, I hope you'll spread your legs and make all those delicious sounds you make for me. Nice and loud."

She opened her mouth, but didn't know what to say to that. Besides *of course* or *how about now?*

"And when I make you come, I want you to know it's just because I like you. Just because I want to. Not because I'm keeping you away from another guy, or because you got me these tickets, or because you brought me to Chicago."

His eyes were still on the game, his fingers were still in her hair, they could have been talking about the error the third baseman made.

She, on the other hand, couldn't get a deep breath in.

"I, um... I'll be right back." She lurched out of her seat and headed for the hallway that ran behind the boxes.

She didn't turn to see his reaction to her sudden exit and she moved fast enough that he didn't say anything before the door shut behind her, cutting them off from one another.

Morgan slumped against the wall and put her hand to her head.

He was too much.

She'd never been with a guy who just told her what he was thinking like that. All the time. No matter what.

She had to figure out how to handle him or he was going to reduce her to a quivering pile of Jello and then their weekend would be over and it would all be a blur. Then, if he said no to her proposal to see each other again, she'd be out of luck. She had to pull herself together or she wouldn't get to half the stuff she wanted to do with and to him, and she wouldn't remember the details of what they *did* do.

"Maddie, it's me," she said, as soon as her sister answered. "How do regular girls have sex?"

There was no answer, or sound, from Maddie's end of the phone for several long seconds. Then she said, "What the hell are you talking about?"

Morgan sighed. Maddie was the only person she could say this to. Well, besides Doug, which was weird. "You were way more sexually active than I was in high school and college. And now," Morgan said.

"Hey."

"I need to know what you do... How you do it... With what."

"Morgan, have you been drinking?" Maddie demanded. "This is bizarre. Or is this a dare?"

"No. I need your help." Morgan rubbed her forehead again. "I think I've been dating and having sex with too many men who have money," she said.

"You've dated and had sex with like three guys in the past three years."

"Four," Morgan said.

"Okay, four. Anyway, who cares if they had or have money? It's not like rich guys have sex differently, Morg."

"How do you know? You've never been with a guy who has money."

Maddie paused. Then said, "Yeah, good point. *Do* they have

sex differently?" she asked. "They're not hiring someone else to do it for them like they do the garden, right?" She laughed.

Morgan rolled her eyes. "I don't remember how *regular* guys have sex. Even in college I was drawn to the guys whose *families* had money."

"That makes you sound shallow and gold-digging," Maddie told her.

"I know."

It did and it wasn't something she was proud of. It was more like an accidental truth. It wasn't like she'd been sleeping with guys to get their money or because of their money. Those were just the men she found attractive. She liked how they dressed, how they handled themselves. There was a confidence that went with money. Not that they couldn't be real pricks. Many of them had been, which had led to their eventual break ups.

But she couldn't deny she liked being taken out to nice restaurants versus fast food joints, liked spending the weekend at a cabin on the lake or on ski vacations versus hanging in the dorms, liked being given earrings and necklaces with real gems for Christmas versus bubble bath and body spray.

She thunked her head against the wall behind her. God, she did sound shallow and gold-digging.

But she also remembered the Christmas her dad had bought her mom a real diamond necklace. Her mom had gotten tears in her eyes, and not the I'm-so-touched-I-love-it kind. Her tears were always more the oh-shit-how-are-we-going-to-pay-for-this kind. A month later Morgan could remember their fight in the kitchen and her mom threatening to leave if her dad didn't stop spending the way he did. Eventually they'd had to sell the car Morgan and Maddie shared and they started catching rides with friends.

Her mom had stayed. She truly loved him. He was a great guy. He just didn't have the means with which to treat her mom the way he wanted to.

Morgan liked guys who could treat her well and afford it. It wasn't about the jewelry. It really wasn't. She'd always seen the feelings, the desire to make her mom feel special, behind the spending.

That was what she wanted.

Without having to sell cars and wear hand-me-down clothes.

"That's why I have to tone it down some," Morgan said. "I want to show Doug I don't care if we're in a fancy hotel room with champagne and strawberries and sexy lingerie."

Again Maddie didn't reply right away. Then she said, "What is it about this guy?"

Morgan shook her head. "I don't know. It's so crazy. He keeps warning me about not being his type and about not having money and all of that. Instead of just accepting it, I want to find a way to show him it doesn't matter."

Maddie laughed softly. "Oh, boy."

Morgan frowned. "Oh, boy? What does that mean?"

"Nothing," Maddie said quickly. "But I'm all for helping you figure out how regular girls have sex. I assume by 'regular' you mean 'not rich'. Like me?"

Morgan almost said yes, knowing she wouldn't offend her sister, but she realized that wasn't at all what she meant. "No, it's not about money. Regular girls are...not uptight." She remembered Doug's comment about regular girls not holding back. "They like things down to earth and real." At least by Doug's definition. "How do I do that?"

Maddie laughed again. "For you, it will be a stretch," she agreed. "With your job you're paid to be uptight, to worry about if the flowers are arranged just right and if the windows are perfectly polished. In your job everything is about appearance and impressions. 'Regular' people don't worry about those things so much. We're not slobs, but not everything has to be a production."

Morgan breathed with relief. Yes. Maddie got it.

"You think I'm making a production out of this?"

Her sister snorted. "Yes."

"So how do I dial it back?"

"You said it yourself," Maddie told her. "You don't care if

you're in a fancy hotel or have champagne and strawberries. Seduce him. Wherever you are. However you can. Don't plan it. Don't think about it. Just do it."

"Wherever we are," Morgan muttered wondering if she had the guts to do it in the box seats at Wrigley Field with the big glass windows. That belonged to her boss.

"Oh, and Morg?"

"What?"

"I don't care how much money a guy has or doesn't have... You can never go wrong with a blowjob."

Chapter Six

By the time she returned to the box, the last batter was up.

"You get lost?" Doug asked as she slid into her seat beside him.

"My sister called. Sorry. Got distracted." A little lie. And a big one. She hadn't been distracted from him for a second. He was all she was focusing on, in fact.

"You ready to go?"

"Sure." She jumped up from her seat. "I'll call the car." They had to ride in an elevator from the sky box to the street, but they weren't alone. Which was probably good. Though throughout the conversation Doug had with the two other men about the game, she was imagining going down on her knees, unzipping his jeans, pulling his cock from his underwear and taking him in her mouth...

"Morgan?"

She shook herself. "Hmm?" She found herself needing to look up from the front of Doug's jeans to his face.

He looked pointedly over her shoulder.

She glanced behind her to find the door to the elevator open and the rest of the Cubs fans waiting for her to step out onto the sidewalk. She felt her cheeks flush as she hurried off and turned to the right to find where the car was going to meet them.

As she raised her arm to wave at their driver who was parked four cars down the curb, she felt Doug's hand settle on her low back. "You okay?" he asked in her ear.

"I'm completely fine." Wound up. Feeling crazy. Probably on the verge of doing something stupid. But fine.

"What were you thinking about on the elevator?" he asked, moving her hair to one side and kissing the back of her neck.

She swallowed as her eyes slid shut. "Giving you a blowjob."

She felt him jerk with surprise and opened her eyes. They weren't alone on the sidewalk anymore.

Carefully avoiding eye contact with anyone, she stepped off the curb as their car came to a stop in front of her. She didn't even look at the driver as he opened the door for her. But the moment the door slammed shut behind Doug she felt his arm snake around her waist and pull her up against him. She turned just in time for his lips to find hers.

The kiss was hungry and she wasted no time in climbing onto his lap. The partition was up between them and the driver and he already knew they were on their way back to the hotel so there was no reason to worry about it coming down.

Morgan slid her hands up under the front of his T-shirt, her own nipples tingling as her palms slid over his. He groaned into her mouth and his hands went to her hips, pulling her down as he pushed up. He was already hard and every detail of her recent daydream played back. But this time it could go further. All the way.

As for plans... Well, she didn't have one. She was no blowjob expert, but Maddie was probably right—not everything needed to be all planned out.

She wiggled in his grasp, trying to slide backward. His fingers curled into her hips tighter. "You're staying right there," he muttered. Then before she could promise he wouldn't mind, his hands pulled up the front of her shirt.

"I can't get enough of you," he said, reaching behind to unhook her bra. "It's like every time makes me want you more."

She loved that almost as much as the feel of his mouth on her nipple. He didn't work up to it, he didn't start gentle, he just sucked. Spears of heat shot through her and she cried out.

"Yes. More of that," he said, switching sides. "Louder."

"I can't be louder," she gasped. "We're not alone." She instantly regretted the words. That wasn't letting go. That wasn't less uptight.

Doug released her nipple and sat back, his hands up as if

he was surrendering. "You're right. Okay, we're on our way to the hotel. It's only a few more minutes."

But the heat in his eyes when he looked down at her made her look too. Her nipples were prominent and wet, the cups of her bra just barely out of the way. She looked...wanton.

She wanted more of that.

"Hearing you say blowjob made me crazy."

She wanted more of that too.

Over Doug's shoulder, out of the back window, she saw something interesting. Pulling her T-shirt down, she slid onto the seat and punched the button to lower the partition. "Jeff, I need a hot fudge sundae. Any chance of turning around?"

"Sure thing, Ms. James." Jeff immediately pulled into the turning lane.

"A hot fudge sundae?" Doug asked. "You're trying to prolong the trip back?"

"Yes." She laughed at the look on his face. "I haven't eaten a hot fudge sundae in at least five years."

"And right now, all of a sudden, you have to have one?"

"Yep. And I didn't plan it. I didn't think about it and weigh the pros and cons. I didn't think about how it doesn't fit into any diet plan or that I'm not even hungry. I just want one and I'm going to do it. That's a huge step for me."

The corner of his mouth curled up. "I'm all for self-growth."

"There's something else I haven't had in a long time that I want," she said.

"There're a few things I want too," he muttered.

"I think you'll approve of this." She moved to kneel in front of him on the floor of the car.

His eyebrows shot up again. "What are you doing?"

"Going for it. Without a plan or a pro and con list." She unsnapped his jeans and lowered the zipper.

He sucked in a quick breath. "I can't think of a single con."

She smiled up at him. He wasn't going to protest, or try to tell her to wait. He wanted this too. There was a definite thrill that went along with just doing something because it felt good. He lifted his hips as she tugged on either side, pulling the denim to mid-thigh. He was hard and hot and didn't make a single move to cover himself. In fact, in true fashion, he was the one to pull his underwear down.

She felt the car bump to a stop. The back windows were tinted. Very tinted. So she leaned forward and licked the head of his shaft.

His head went back and he arched toward her. "Damn, Morgan."

She heard the muted voices of Jeff talking to the person in the restaurant and she licked again, adding a suck at the top.

Doug's breathing was ragged and he was pressing his palms into the seat on either side of him. She took another lick, then lifted herself and pivoted in time to accept the ice cream sundae and block the view of Doug at the same time. "Thanks, Jeff."

"No problem, Ms. James." The partition went back up without further comment and the car moved forward.

Morgan turned back to Doug. She looked from him to the ice cream and back. "I just don't know where to start," she said.

"Morg—"

"Oh, I know," she interrupted with a sly smile. "I can have my cake and eat it too. So to speak."

She took the spoon from the dish and leaned toward Doug. Ice cream and hot fudge sauce trickled from the spoon to his shaft and his eyes slid shut. "Morgan," he groaned.

Oh, she liked this. Leaning in, she took a bite of ice cream, then took him in her mouth too. The combination of sweet and salty, smooth and hard, hot and cold was delicious and she swallowed the ice cream, sucking on him at the same time.

His hand tangled in her hair, but he let her lift her head. She put the dish on the floor, but dipped her finger in the sauce. Watching his face, she drew a line of fudge along the length of his erection, loving the way it affected his breathing. He seemed to be holding himself still, one hand pressing hard into the seat, his chest barely moving. She put her tongue to the sauce, dragging it up to the tip and then back down. She swirled her tongue around his balls, then up to the tip where she circled before sucking.

Finally she had to feel him completely. She wrapped her hand around his shaft, sliding it up and down as she let him slide into her mouth again. She felt his fingers tighten against her scalp and she increased her speed, loving the obvious reaction to her actions.

Apparently it didn't matter that she was no expert.

"Morgan. God, Sugar," he panted. "I want this. But I want you. I want to be inside you."

She wanted him to lose control. She wanted to push him over the edge. But she also ached for him, her body protesting not getting more of him than this. She lifted her head, also breathing hard. "Okay." But she couldn't take her hand off of him. She watched her hand move on him, stroking his full length.

"Morgan."

"I know. Just a minute." She moved up and down again, then squeezed gently.

"Morgan...things are about to get...interesting," he said.

She grinned. "Think you can make it inside?" The hotel was coming up on their right.

"I'll find a way," he said through gritted teeth.

She still hadn't moved her hand. "I love doing this to you."

"I promise you'll love the stuff I'm going to do to you just as much."

A shiver of desire went through her.

The car rolled to a stop and Doug struggled to make himself presentable. "Don't even think about leaving that ice cream out here," he said.

She snagged the bowl just before she slid across the seat. She was more than happy to pick up where they'd left off. As they emerged from the car, he put her directly in front of him as they walked into the hotel and through the lobby.

She giggled as they stepped onto the elevator. "Do you think that looked strange?"

"What you walking in front of me or me walking like someone just kicked me in the groin?"

He sounded irritated. She slid closer. "Does it feel that bad?"

"Trying to zip a zipper over one of the hardest erections I've ever had?" He asked with a frown. "Yeah."

She looked at him with surprise. "This is one of the hardest erections you've ever had?"

He groaned. "Even hearing you say erection makes it hurt."

"But it's one of the hardest?" she pressed. Did she have *that* much of an effect? Truly?

He took her hand and pressed it against his cock. "Absolutely. And though I'd dearly love to lick *you* until you're about to lose your mind, I'm not sure I can last that long."

She swallowed hard, letting her hand run up and down his fly. "No need to worry. I'm right there with you."

They stumbled to the suite and the moment the door swung shut, she pulled her T-shirt and bra off. She was aching everywhere. She wanted his hands, his mouth and yes, definitely, his cock.

She went back to her knees in front of him, unsnapping and unzipping him, but he quickly hauled her back to her feet. "I need you, Morgan. Every damned time I think we're going to take it slower. Every damned time I think I can't possibly get this crazy again. But it happens." He popped the button loose on the top of her shorts. "Every." The zipper came down. "Damned." He skimmed the shorts off of her hips along with her panties in one swoop. "Time."

She kicked the shorts and underwear free and stood in front of him naked.

"Yes," he said to no question in particular as he studied her.

He pushed his jeans and underwear to the floor as well, his erection straining toward her. He managed to get out of his shoes, jeans and underwear before he reached for her. His hands went to her breasts as hers went to his shoulders and he was kissing her.

She lost track of where they were as he possessed her mouth. Until her back came up against cool glass. Her palms pressed against the smooth surface and she recognized that she was against the sliding glass door leading to the balcony off the living room.

"Doug," she gasped as his mouth trailed down her neck to her collar bone.

"I have this overwhelming urge to be sure the world knows you're here with me like this," he said against her skin. He tugged on her nipple causing a heartfelt groan from her gut. "I think that's why the elevator happened. I want everyone to see how much you want me, what I can do to you."

She had never considered herself an exhibitionist before but a thrill danced through her. She knew it wasn't the thrill of getting caught or being watched. It was the possessiveness he was showing. Like he wanted to advertise she was his.

And she was afraid maybe she was becoming a little bit his, a little more every minute.

"I want to show off what I can do," he said, running his hand down her side. "I've never been like this before. But I want everyone to know you're with me. That I can make you scream. That I can give you absolute pleasure, can overwhelm you, can be all you want."

Before she could respond he spun her to face the glass. She braced her hands on the door. The darkness outside turned the glass into a mirror. She could see her reflection with Doug behind her, passion on both faces. Beyond that she could see the lights of the city. Other buildings were lit but none that had floors this high were close enough to see them. Still, it made heat swirl in her blood the way Doug seemed to want this, them, on display.

"I can be all you want, right, Morgan? I can make you hot, make you crazy," he breathed in her ear, one hand cupping her breast, the other sliding low, his fingers sliding into her.

"God, yes," she groaned.

Watching him do this to her in the reflection, seeing it as she was feeling it, was amazing. His big hands were everywhere, owning her, making her sure she'd never want another man to touch her like this.

"When I have you like this, is doesn't matter where I come from or what I have or don't have as long as I know how to give you something no one else can give you."

His words were muffled by his kisses and licks along her shoulder blade and middle of her back as his fingers stroked deep. But she heard them. She wondered if they were coherent or just mumblings in the heat of the moment.

Either way, she wanted him to know for certain that how she felt with him was like nothing else she'd ever experienced.

"If I could keep us out of jail, I'd take you down to the middle of this fancy-assed hotel's lobby and make you moan and beg and scream for everyone to see."

Lust shuddered through her. She would never want to do that, but somehow she understood the sentiment for what it was.

"Spread your legs," he murmured as he stroked over her clit.

She gasped and did as he asked, feeling him press close, his cock against her butt. "Don't make me beg," she practically begged.

She heard a soft chuckle. "You've got *me* at *your* mercy," he said.

His fingers slid free and she heard the sound of the condom package ripping, then his hands were back on her hips. "Push back, babe," he said.

She did and he slid deep.

They groaned together.

He tried to go slow. He really did. It would have been nice to make love to her, to take his time, to indulge and enjoy and draw it out.

But like he was wired for a quick detonation the moment he was fully inside her, he seemed to have no control. His body took over and he had to move, fast and hard and deep. Once she started gasping and moving against him he was done for.

He meant every word. Every damned, pathetic word he'd

said. He wanted the world to know that she chose him, let him be like this, do these things to and with her.

He couldn't explain it. Wasn't sure he even wanted to analyze it too much. He'd never felt this way about a woman. Sex was sex. Nice, fun, satisfying. But never so crazy. He wanted to possess her, drive her mad, make it so she'd never want anyone else and never...forget him.

As the realization hit him he surged forward, burying himself deep. Her muscles clenched around him, holding on, pulling everything out of him. It felt so much more than physical. It felt like she was demanding all he had on every level and, God help him, he wanted to give it to her.

The city lights shone outside of the window and he felt, again, that he was showing her, and what he could do to her, to the world. That made him thrust faster and when he focused on her reflection in the glass, the desire on her face, her gasps, the way she pushed back, arched and met his strokes, as if she couldn't get enough of him either, made all the heat, the lust, the emotions he was feeling coil tightly in his gut. He wouldn't last much longer.

"Morgan." He reached for her clit again, circling and pressing. "Come for me, Sugar."

"*Yes.*" She pressed closer to his fingers. "How do you know... How can you always..." She gasped. "Find...*that* spot."

He didn't know, or care. He just loved that he could. He thrust forward while rolling her clit and she came apart just moments before he did.

She leaned forward, resting her forehead on the glass, breathing hard. Dooley pulled away from her, running his hand down her back as he did.

He was totally addicted.

And totally screwed.

How was he supposed to never see her again? Never taste her? Never touch her?

Then she turned with a smile that made his whole body react with *again!*

"We didn't even use the ice cream."

He looked around and located the dish with the brown and white swirls of melted ice cream and fudge sauce in the bottom. Looking back at Morgan leaning unabashedly naked against the sliding glass door he knew they weren't going to get any sleep tonight.

"We haven't used the ice cream *yet*," he corrected, crossing to the dish.

She met him at the door to the bedroom.

Dipping his finger into the dish, he swirled the sweet liquid around her nipple. "I'll never look at another hot fudge sundae without thinking of you."

He hoped the same would be true for her.

Of course, she'd admitted in the car that the last time she'd had one was five years ago. So she'd think of him in five years. Maybe.

His gut clenched at the thought and that pissed him off.

He was worried about her not thinking of him when this was over? Why? Who cared? He might think of her but it wasn't like he was going to do anything about this hunger to be with her, see her, know how she was and what she was doing.

He needed to only remember three words. Just. For. Fun.

He lifted the dish and tipped it over her chest.

She gasped as the sticky stuff dribbled over her breasts and nipples. Wide-eyed she looked up at him, then her eyes narrowed and she took the dish from him. He thought she meant to set it to one side and he started to lean in to lick the ice cream from her skin, but instead she poured the rest of the concoction on her lower stomach.

Brown rivulets ran toward her mound and lower.

Then she stepped close, pressed her body to his and kissed him.

They were both covered in sticky sweetness, almost literally stuck together, as they made their way to the bedroom, Dooley walking backward until he felt the edge of the bed at the back of his legs.

He sat and she climbed up, still spreading the ice cream between them by moving and sliding her body against his.

Finally he clasped her hips, stalling her movements.

"I sincerely doubt you could taste any better, but I can't help but find out," he said laying back and bringing her hips up his torso until she had to move her knees over his shoulders.

He felt her body shudder as she moved so she straddled his face.

"Just a minute," she said hoarsely.

He watched her move her hand, circling the pads of her fingers through the ice cream smeared on her stomach, then sliding lower until she painted it over her clit. She gasped as she rubbed over the spot made even more sensitive by their love-making just minutes ago.

Dooley couldn't believe how much he wanted her again. Still. It seemed like it would never be enough.

Her finger dipped a little lower, then circled her clit again, right in front of his eyes. He grasped her wrist in his hand and brought her fingers to his mouth. His eyes on hers, he sucked each finger clean of ice cream and the sweet taste that was all her.

Then he lifted his head as he clasped her butt bringing her forward until he could taste the spot that would make her scream for him.

Her hips bucked as he licked and sucked, but he held her still, wanting to make her wild. Finally, her moans and begging trailed off to gasps as she came.

Before the quivers in her body had even quieted he flipped her to her back. "So much sweeter than hot fudge," he said. "See?" Then he kissed her deeply, making sure she could taste herself on his tongue.

He moved between her legs, once again overcome by the need to possess and claim. *Mine*, he thought as he barely remembered to don a condom before surging into her as hard and driven as if it had been months without sex rather than barely enough time to catch his breath.

The fact he'd given her three orgasms in less than an hour didn't escape him for a moment as she came around him only minutes later and his own orgasm roared through him.

They lay together, panting, sticky, spent—and one of them was afraid he was now mostly in love with the last woman he should be.

Being sore and sleep deprived didn't slow Morgan down in the morning. She was humming as she left Dooley sleeping in the suite and made her way to Jonathan's office for the final meeting before heading back to Omaha.

"Morgan."

She came up short when she realized Todd was right in front of her. She hadn't even noticed him. "Hi, Todd."

"I'm glad I caught you before we go in. I just wanted to tell you I think your ideas for California are great. Good job. You deserve the position."

She narrowed her eyes. "How do you know about my ideas for California?"

"Jonathan and I had dinner last night. You know, while you were at the ballgame with Doug."

"Right." She wasn't going to feel guilty about her time with Doug. Or panicked. There had been no dinner plans with Jonathan. If the two men had met spontaneously, there was nothing she could do about that. Then she thought about the rest of what Todd said. "I deserve the position?"

"I made sure to tell Jonathan I feel you have what it takes to run the resort."

"You did?" Did she believe him? Why would he have said that? Even if he meant it? It would mean *he* wouldn't get the position if Jonathan agreed.

"Of course. Like I made sure he knew I enjoy working with you and I think we have a real...chemistry. If he needs me to help out in California in any way, I'm happy to."

Ah-ha. Todd was showing Jonathan he wasn't threatened by her. That they were a good team. That he was gracious enough to build up a co-worker, even one competing for a position. That had to have gotten him some points. Dammit.

"I appreciate that, Todd. I'll be sure Jonathan knows I feel the same." She pulled the door to the office suite open with more force than was necessary. She could play the games too. If Jonathan wanted to hear how fantastic Todd was, she could be his biggest cheerleader. Even if it made her want to gag.

Two hours later, her head was spinning. Thoughts, ideas, and questions swirled.

The wrap-up meeting had turned into a brainstorming session. Jonathan had picked the pieces of each of their proposals he liked best and asked them to combine them. Right then and there.

Ideas had blossomed.

She couldn't believe it. It turned out she and Todd did have chemistry. One she noticed Jonathan watching with interest and pleasure. It just wasn't sexual chemistry anymore. In fact, she could honestly say she could now look at Todd without a single thought to their past relationship. The truth was, she and Todd worked well together. Every angle she suggested, he could build on. Every idea she tossed out, sparked ideas in him.

It had been an exhilarating experience.

But she wasn't stupid. At least not where Todd was concerned. Anymore. He wasn't just using her to get ahead—he *needed* her to get ahead.

"Morgan."

She stopped and turned. She'd been expecting him. "Todd."

"Great meeting." He was smiling widely as he caught up to her halfway across the lobby.

"Yep. Great meeting."

"I was hoping maybe I could buy you dinner and we could build on some of the ideas further. I think Jonathan would appreciate us developing some of them more. Together."

They had a lot of great starts, but they hadn't finalized anything. And it was clear Todd was worried. He could implement ideas. He could get people to show up. He could do the PR and make the plan seem like the best thing since someone had first added chocolate syrup to coffee. But he couldn't put it all together by himself.

"I don't think so, Todd."

He smile wavered, but he caught himself before his expression went into full frown-mode. "Okay, we can Skype. Or I could come to Omaha. When would you be free?"

"Never."

He frowned, but then quickly smoothed it out. "What's wrong? Let's talk about it."

He reached for her, but she dodged.

He still didn't frown but he definitely wasn't smiling. "Morgan, we're a team."

She sighed. She'd figured him out. It was a relief really. Yeah, he'd found her vulnerabilities and used them against her, but it was over now. She didn't even need Doug anymore.

Okay, that wasn't entirely true. She needed him. Just not to keep her away from Todd.

"I'm done, Todd."

"Done? With us? Look, Morgan, it's obvious you and Doug have something going on but I'm not giving up so easily. Let's spend some time—"

"Yes, with us. For sure."

"Because of Doug?"

She thought about that. Doug was a factor in a few things, but not this. Not really. Not anymore. "No," she finally answered. "Because of you. I'm done giving you ideas, Todd. I'm done helping you get ahead. I want this job too. You're going to have to get it on your own. Good luck."

He let his frown show this time. "Giving me ideas?"

"I figured it out. You're charming, you're smart, you're one of the best schmoozers I've ever met. You'll always have connections and you'll always look good making other people's ideas work. But you're going to have to find someone else to give you the ideas, since you clearly can't come up with anything on your own."

His frown deepened. "I can help you too, you know. I can make your ideas bigger and better. I can give glitz and glamour to what you come up with."

"I don't need your glitz and glamour, Todd."

"You sure about that? I can find someone else with good

ideas. Do you have someone to take your ideas and actually make them work?"

She frowned now. "*I* can make them work."

"Maybe. Maybe not. You have yet to implement any of the big stuff you've come up with."

She opened her mouth, then shut it again. Dammit. He was right. She had ideas, lots of them, but he was the one who had actually done something with them. Why was that?

The answer came almost immediately. She wasn't confident enough. She couldn't risk it not working out. She had ideas but Todd had showed her they were *good* ideas, ideas that worked. Security was a big deal for her, being sure of things before jumping in.

"That's going to change." She *sounded* confident anyway.

"If you say so."

"Goodbye, Todd."

He gave her a smirk and a wink. "You know where to find me when you realize you need me too."

She wasn't going to need him. That she knew for sure. But that was about the only thing she was sure of.

Todd turned and sauntered down the hall as she continued on to the elevators. She pressed the up button, lost in thought.

"Hey."

The deep voice and warm body behind her, made her turn with a smile. "Hey."

Doug looked great.

She sighed. Would he ever not look great to her?

His hair was familiarly rumpled, his eyes looked tired, and his shirt read *Cleverly disguised as an adult*, but his smile was sexy and warm.

"I already packed us up." He indicated their bags resting by the closest colonnade in the lobby. "You said you just needed to call the car and the pilot and we could leave right away, right?"

She'd mentioned that as they dried off from their shared shower last night. But she hadn't expected him to be so anxious to leave. Her heart twinged and she had to shake her head. Her business in Chicago was over. That's why they were here. Since the meeting was done, their reason for being here was done.

That shouldn't make her feel so miserable.

"How did you know I'd be done now?" she asked, trying to keep her disappointment from her face. One of the great things about a private company jet was that they didn't have a scheduled departure time. They could have made use of the suite a little longer.

"Oh, I've been hanging out down here for about an hour," he said, waving toward the valet stand. Roger and Stan were on duty.

She gave them a wave too.

"Okay, well, just let me call the car." She pulled her phone out, knowing it was childish to hit the numbers more slowly than she usually would have. This didn't have to mean things were over. The trip was over, but she could see him again. They were headed back to the same city. Where they both lived and worked.

At least for now.

That was the part that hung her up. A high-paying job with travel and great perks and benefits was what she'd always wanted. It wasn't shallow or materialistic. Her job meant security. It meant she didn't have to worry about having adequate health insurance, or a dependable car, or enough money in the bank to cover unexpected things like repairs to her house after a bad storm.

She'd lived through all of those things with her parents.

At age ten, Maddie had flipped over the handlebars on her bike and needed stitches. Morgan had heard her mom on the phone with the doctor's office afterward trying to set up a payment plan for the x-rays and other expenses. She'd seen her mom's tears.

Morgan had been fourteen when she and her dad were stranded on the highway in ninety-degree heat when their transmission gave up. They'd had only one car for almost a year after that and she remembered her mom's stress, and even embarrassment, when arranging rides with friends and co-workers.

She'd lain awake at night listening to her parents fight about how they were going to replace everything their home owner's insurance wouldn't cover when their basement flooded.

The job in California meant she never had to worry about how to take care of herself and she'd have enough to help her parents or Maddie if they ever needed anything.

She knew there was more to life than money. Her sister didn't make the kind of money Morgan did, and she was perfectly happy. Her father was the perfect example of not needing money to enjoy life.

And as long as Morgan had money she could sit back and let them enjoy things, knowing she could bail them out of anything that came up.

So did she want to pursue a relationship right now?

As she waited to be connected to the car service she watched Doug. He was conversing casually with the two guys from the cleaning crew who were polishing the front windows and he hurried forward to help two older women get through the revolving door as Roger and Stan loaded what appeared to be a dozen suitcases on a valet cart.

No, she didn't want to start a new relationship right now.

She wanted to keep having one with Doug.

Yes, it had been three days. Four if she counted the fundraiser. But she could not deny that this felt very relationship-like. It had been intended just for fun, just a fling, sex only, but it had turned into more. Surely he had to feel it too?

Still, she was sure flat-out asking him, or telling him her thoughts and feelings on the subject, would do nothing but send him running. This had been a weekend agreement, short-term, nothing serious just three days ago. She couldn't jump ahead here. He dated casually. That's all he wanted. So she'd keep this casual, simple, straight-forward. But fun and sexy too.

They got into the car only five minutes later and headed for the airport. It wasn't the same car, but she couldn't help but think about kneeling on the floor in front of him in the limo last night.

Strangely, it wasn't just about the physical, sexual thrill it gave her but the idea that she could make him feel that way. She loved that in that moment she was all he was thinking of, all he wanted or needed.

Which all sounded a lot like what he'd been saying when he had her up against the sliding glass door last night.

The desire to be the most important thing to him, to fulfill every one of his fantasies, had to be more than she was supposed to feel for a fling.

In fact, she'd thought she'd had a relationship with Todd and she'd never felt that way for him.

"How'd the meeting go?" Doug asked as they turned on to the street.

"Um, great." It had been. "Great. But the position is still up in the air. He said he would be talking more with both of us."

"That's a good thing," Doug said, taking her hand.

He did it so casually, she wondered if he realized he'd done it.

"It's good he's carefully considering everything. But I think in the end you have nothing to worry about."

She smiled, warmed by his loyalty. "Thanks. Based on what?"

"He's a down-to-earth guy. I don't think you truly get ahead in a service industry unless you're a people person...or you recognize you're not and you surround yourself with others who are. Todd might have good ideas but when it comes to making it happen, it's going to take someone like you."

He squeezed her hand and she again wondered if he was aware of it.

"I'm flattered," she said. "But how do you know this? About Jonathan or me?"

"I've seen it in you," he said with a grin. "You like people. When you're not worried about smudging the crystal and silver, you can be quite sweet and charming."

She smiled in spite of herself. He'd pegged her—at least about the worry over smudges. She hoped the sweet and charming was true too.

"Jonathan is the same. At breakfast he was talking to all the waitresses and even the bus boys. He impressed me."

Morgan sat up straighter. "At breakfast?"

"Yeah, the other morning... Geez, was it just yesterday?" he said with a little frown.

"You had breakfast with Jonathan yesterday?" she repeated.

"We both happened to be having breakfast at the same time in the same place and so we sat together," Doug said.

"Then what?"

"We drank orange juice."

"What did you talk about?" she insisted, squeezing his fingers. Oh, Lord, was this when he'd pulled out the raunchy jokes? Or had he divulged how he'd met Morgan? That *she* was the one to jump on him first?

"We talked about the hotel."

She stared at him for a few seconds. "The hotel?" she asked.

"All the hotels."

"What do you mean?"

"I just gave him my opinion on some things."

Oh...boy. "Like what, for instance."

He turned to face her more fully. "What are you afraid I told him?" he asked, a knowing look in his eyes.

"I, um, don't know," she hedged.

"Uh-huh. I told him what I told you. That he should be talking to his employees if he wants good ideas about how to improve things."

"What did he think?"

"He loved it." Doug leaned in closer. "I'm sure it would impress him if you incorporated that into some of your stuff for him."

She wasn't one to let a golden opportunity pass her by. She leaned in too. "We should spend some more time together so you can fill me in completely. You know, so I can impress him."

Doug jerked back as if she'd spit on him. "Um, oh, no. That's not necessary. I mean, I told you...just talk to the employees. Empower them to be part of it. That's all you have to do."

She watched him with surprise. And a little hurt. The idea of seeing her again was *that* bad?

She narrowed her eyes. "But I'd *like* to see you again."

"Maybe I'm only good in fancy hotels."

She could tell he was trying to make light but now he wasn't looking at her, holding her hand, or sitting comfortably, at least it seemed that way with all the shifting on the seat he was doing.

He had a point. The fundraiser had been at a fancy hotel too. One of her competitors, incidentally. But she knew it wasn't where they'd been that made her feel like...well, whatever she was feeling.

"That's not a problem," she said flippantly. "I happen to *have* a fancy hotel we can use whenever we want."

He gave her a weak smile. "Right. How could I forget?"

"Or we could test the theory and go to my apartment. Or yours."

"That would be a test all right," he muttered.

Morgan frowned. Well, that had certainly lacked the enthusiasm she'd been hoping for. In fact, it sounded decidedly *un*enthusiastic. She was offering more naked time. Doug really liked naked time with her.

She wasn't even asking him out. She wasn't planning on bringing an extra toothbrush to keep at his place. She wasn't asking him to meet her parents.

She just wanted more time with him. Even if the only talking they did was between the sheets.

If this was how he responded to that offer, she could only imagine how he'd react if she confessed her oh-crap-I-could-be-falling-for-you feelings.

Watching him stoically keep his eyes everywhere but on her, she thought about her offer. Maybe going to her apartment felt too real-life to him, too serious. Maybe the locations they'd been in were a part of why *he* was feeling whatever he was feeling. Or maybe he *thought* the fancy hotels were part of it, anyway.

She didn't love that idea. She wanted him to be crazy about *her*, like she was about him. But the hotel, the box seats, the private jet all certainly contributed to the sense that this was just a fantasy. And who wouldn't like that?

Fine.

She wanted more time with him, period. If the only way she could see him again was to keep the fantasy going, she could do that.

But before she could say anything more, they turned into the airport. Okay. They had another hour on the plane. Just the two of them. She was going to be the best Richard Gere ever.

She wanted to see him again.

Dammit.

Dooley got into his seat and pulled his book out immediately, hoping to curtail further conversation.

She wanted to see him again.

Why? That was stupid. He wasn't just complimenting her when he said he was sure Jonathan was going to eventually choose her for the California resort. She was obviously the better choice. Anything Todd had to contribute to the project could be done via conference call, frankly. The on-site person had to be Morgan.

He might just have to call Jonathan up and tell him so.

Which meant she was leaving. *Why* prolong this...thing they were doing? No matter how great it was, there was no future. He already knew all good things had to come to an end, and this end was already set up.

His dad had been—and still was—a vivid reminder that things like health, marriages, jobs, friendships, security and wealth could be snatched away from you without warning. Dooley preferred to stay on top of those things so he knew, and had some say in, how they were going to go.

He drank and ate too much junk food, but he also worked out, took vitamins and visited his doctor twice a year. He had been at the same job since his dad's stroke and he worked his ass off to be the best he could be at what he did. At the same time, he never felt totally settled. He knew things could change suddenly and so was exceedingly careful with his savings and investments. He also barely spent. He was a minimalist, always prepared for a time when he might not have any extra.

As for his relationships, well, he tried to keep them simple. He had surrounded himself with a small, tight group of friends he knew he could trust completely. With women it was even simpler. He kept it straightforward and superficial. It was easier than worrying about investing time, emotion and money and then having it end.

He did not want to get in any deeper with Morgan.

No, that wasn't entirely true. He *wanted* to—and he was more tempted with her than he had been with any other woman ever—but he *wouldn't*. As soon as Jonathan said go, she'd be gone to California.

Why then get all caught up in liking her and wanting her and making memories he'd miss when she was gone?

It was like getting used to eating lobster every night, knowing it wasn't going to last, but getting so used to it that the cravings nearly killed you after there was no more left.

Well, it was kind of like that.

Morgan turned in her seat. "I want to offer you a job."

He frowned. "I don't need a new job."

"It's very part-time and will mostly not conflict with your regular job. If, on occasion, it does, I'll make up any pay you're losing."

He really didn't want to know what she was talking about. He really didn't. It didn't matter. "What are you talking about?"

"Okay, just hear me out," she said quickly. "My life is crazy right now and it's going to get crazier as I work on this project. If I get chosen for California, I'm going to have a wild schedule. Besides my hours and travel, my focus has to be about work. I can't do a relationship right now."

She *didn't* want a relationship? Dooley felt tight in his chest and told himself it was relief.

"Still," Morgan continued, "I need someone to take to dinners and parties here in Omaha, as well as to go with me on any short trips to California. I need someone who can hold his own at a dinner with big shots, but I want it to also be someone I enjoy spending time with. It has to be someone who understands what my business entails, but who isn't competing with me."

Like Todd. Dooley was relieved to hear she wasn't interested in a relationship with Becker. Todd was more her type in many ways, but she was right not to completely trust the guy.

But she didn't want a relationship with *him*?

"I need someone who won't be upset if I have to work late instead of seeing him and who won't be hurt or jealous if I choose a dinner meeting with a business colleague over going somewhere with him." She took a deep breath and met his eyes directly. "I don't need a boyfriend. I need you."

His first reaction was *what the hell does that mean?* He and *boyfriend* were two different things?

Then he took a deep breath. He and *boyfriend* were definitely two different things. It was a good thing she realized it.

That he didn't want her to have anyone else as a boyfriend didn't matter at all.

Okay, so if she wasn't looking for a boyfriend but needed a date, he could agree he seemed like the perfect choice.

The only real problem was he knew every minute he spent with her was a chance for him to fall harder and deeper. A chance for The End to be all the more depressing.

"And how is this a job, exactly?" he asked, instead of saying *no fucking way* like he should have.

"I'll pay you to be at my beck and call for whatever I need, whenever I need it."

He just blinked at her. That was certainly...direct.

"Just like that? You snap your fingers and I show up?" He

didn't hate the idea as much as he would have expected.

"Right." She gave him a smile. "Of course, you'll have all expenses paid for everything, and a stipend."

A *what*? "A stipend?"

"Sure. It needs to be a win-win situation."

She was planning to not just pick up the tab but to *pay* him to date her?

His lack of response must have made her think she needed to go on. "Of course, I'll try to schedule trips around your days off. But there will be times when I need you to do something that conflicts with something else. It's only right I make it worth it to you to choose me."

As if there was anything he'd rather do than her.

"It's a business arrangement, Doug," she continued. "I need your time and talents, so I pay you for providing them. Just like I pay..." She trailed off, perhaps realizing her next choice of words wasn't the best.

"The delivery guy who brings you Chinese food?" Dooley supplied, trying to keep the bite out of his tone. He didn't think he succeeded. "Or the guy who changes the oil in your car. They do something for you and you give them money for it. It's easy enough to understand, Morgan."

"Not exactly like that," she said weakly.

But it was. She wasn't asking to see him again because she liked him or wanted him or was crazy about him. She was asking to see him again because she needed him. Not in the hot God-I-need-you-Doug-I-can't-live-without-you way but in a practical, business-like, not-completely-satisfying way.

"What about dating other women?" he asked, just to see her reaction. He couldn't imagine dating anyone else. Maybe ever. Which sucked.

"You want to date other women?" she asked.

"I'm just trying to understand the details of the arrangement," he said nonchalantly. "Can I date other women or am I all about you?"

She took a deep breath through her nose, then gave him a sweet smile. "You can date other women. As long as you're willing to cancel on them if I need you."

"I see," he said. There was a twinge of jealousy in her voice that made him feel a lot better.

"Do I get paid extra for the nights we have sex?" he asked.

She frowned at him. "I'd like to think it's a win-win without any money changing hands. Oh, and it's illegal to pay for sex."

In spite of himself, he grinned a little at her clear offense. And yeah, it had been an offensive question. But he was feeling offended by the whole damned thing for some reason.

In actuality, it was a perfect solution for her. They'd already traveled together and clearly got along just fine. He fit into her social and business situations well and they enjoyed each other's company. She didn't want to get involved in a relationship with anyone, but she would need the occasional date. It actually made sense for her to ask him to do this.

A practical business arrangement was a far cry from madly-in-love, so he should be happy too.

And there were the Egyptian cotton sheets to think about.

It wasn't like he'd be suffering.

"But we *are* going to have sex?" he asked, because he couldn't help himself.

Her eyes widened. "I certainly hope so."

He appreciated the way she'd phrased that. At least she liked him enough for that.

He frowned at that thought. He was worried about her liking him? She liked him just fine. Just enough. It didn't matter anyway. This wasn't about *liking* each other.

Apparently this was about doing *business* together.

"I don't think so. Thanks anyway," he said, pretending to focus back on his book.

"Thanks anyway?" she repeated, clearly with disbelief. "You're saying no?"

"Yeah, I am." He couldn't win here. Not seeing her again would suck, but seeing her as she was proposing might just suck more. They'd be playing at a relationship, and though he'd *never* admit it to *anyone*, he wasn't so sure his heart would be able to tell the difference.

"I *need* you," she said. "You're the only one. You can fit into my world, make sure I'm having fun, and hot sex, and not care if I can't make time to see you or call you every day. It's impressive."

He almost laughed. He'd been worried about how to let her down, how to explain he didn't want a relationship with her and now she was listing that fact as one of the reasons she wanted him around.

Awesome.

"I can fit into your world, Morgan. But I don't want to. I've been in this world. I know what it's all about and it's not what I want now."

It was all true. Sort of. It wasn't that he didn't like her world. He just knew it was more fantasy than reality. And reality always showed up eventually.

"Even for me?" she asked, her voice quieter now. "You *can* do it, but you *won't*? Even for me?"

"There are about a million men who can do what I can do and who will *want* to. Don't you think you should find one of them?"

Even as he said it, he gripped the book hard. The idea of her with another man, even if it was just at dinner, made him want to break something. Like some unknown, unsuspecting guy's nose.

Wasn't that just one more fantastic reason not to get further involved? Another man, probably more than one, could do things for Morgan he couldn't. He hated that. *Really* hated that, but it was the harsh truth. He wasn't the guy to live the lifestyle she wanted. He *could* golf and make small talk and use the right fork at dinner.

He just didn't want to.

Baseball, raunchy jokes and pizza were more his style now. He could maintain that style. He could relax in that style.

"Is it an ego thing?" she asked. "You have a problem with a woman being the one to pay for everything, buy you stuff, take you places?"

He looked at her with wide eyes. Then laughed. "Uh, no."

He didn't care who was paying for the dinner with too many forks. "In fact, I enjoy other people paying. Especially gorgeous women who only want sex in return."

"So you just don't want to do it," she finally said.

"Right." She needed to stop talking about it. Damn her for being so tempting.

He couldn't look at her. He concentrated, or pretended to, on his book. It was better this way. If she was a little hurt, maybe she'd stop talking. Maybe she'd even get up and move to another seat. Because every second he sat next to her, smelling her, wanting to touch her hair, wanting to make her laugh, was one second closer to never getting over her.

"Right," she finally said, pulling a magazine out from the seat pocket in front of her. "It was just for fun."

"Right."

But she didn't move seats and by the time they landed in Omaha, Dooley knew he'd never forget her smell, the six different shades of red and gold in her hair, or how much he wanted her.

He didn't want her.

The words kept nagging in her mind for the rest of the flight.

Well, he *wanted* her. Physically. Sexually. But he didn't want to spend time with her, travel with her, be with her. Not even for money.

It was her own damned fault. What had she been thinking? He had been essentially a stranger when she'd met him at the airport three days ago. In fact, even now, there were a million and a half things she didn't know about him. Important things.

But she did know *some* things about him. Important things.

He was a great guy. Someone she enjoyed immensely. Someone she genuinely liked.

Until he said no to her.

Morgan did not like the word no.

She was grateful they didn't have to claim bags. She was mad, and yelling at him right now was likely not the best approach to convincing him to take her up on her offer. She was trying to be low maintenance. What was less complicated than what she was suggesting? He'd get to go great places, have great sex and didn't have to do any of the normal relationship stuff.

Once outside the airport, they were headed in opposite directions to claim their cars. He was clearly feeling awkward.

She gave him a big smile. "Thanks so much for coming to Chicago, Doug."

"Um, yeah, you bet." He didn't quite make eye contact.

She handed him one of her business cards. "Call me anytime," she said, leaving it wide open for what that meant.

He took the card and slipped it into his front pocket. "Okay."

He wouldn't call. She could tell.

Fine. This still wasn't the last time they would talk. "See you," she said, meaning it.

"Goodbye, Morgan."

Oooh, goodbye was right up there with no on her list of least favorite words.

As she watched him cross the street toward the parking garage she realized she had a new motto: What Would Richard Gere Do?

Chapter Seven

It wasn't like the bastards he called friends would have left him alone regardless of how he acted upon his return from Chicago, but his refusal to talk about Morgan made it obvious this was more than a weekend fling. Which, of course, it was. Or had been anyway.

He'd considered making up some stories, just to shut them up, but when the time came, he just couldn't. He couldn't blow this off convincingly as a hot weekend and nothing more.

Fuck.

He was in trouble. And deserved every bit of it. If it had been any of the other guys—hell, when it *had* been the other guys—he had been merciless in talking and taunting.

When a guy fell in love, it was a big deal.

He should know.

"I like this girl," Sam announced as he came into the break room with a huge basket tied in a deep red bow. "'One dozen reasons you should say Yes'," he read from the card. "I don't even know the question and I want to say yes," Sam said.

Dooley groaned. Maybe the basket was for Mac.

But he knew it wasn't.

"You've said yes to too many women as it is," he said, dropping his feet from the coffee table to the floor and reluctantly getting up. "Thank God Danika came along."

He should have known Morgan wouldn't just let it go. In fact, he *had* known that.

"You're getting gift baskets from Morgan?" Mac asked, also coming to his feet. "Damn, boy, you must be even better than we thought."

Yeah, well, it wasn't about what he'd already done so much as it was about what she wanted him to do in the future. "Of course I'm that good," he muttered, taking the basket from Sam. In it were a dozen bottles of beer. He groaned.

"What?" Kevin asked.

"It's beer," Dooley said.

"It's *good* beer," Mac corrected.

"Oh, yeah, this is high-end stuff," Sam said, grabbing a bottle and holding it up.

"Dammit," Dooley added. She was trying to sweeten him up, show him the perks of being her *mistress*—for God's sake— were damned nice ones.

"Oh, yeah, what a bitch," Mac said, taking the beer and studying the label. "She obviously has no idea how to get to your heart."

She didn't need to try too hard. But Dooley kept the thought to himself.

"So what's the question you're going to say yes to?" Sam said, settling himself in the chair Dooley had vacated.

"None of your damned business. And I'm not saying yes."

"Why the hell not?" Sam asked.

"Did I mention it's none of your damned business?"

"You did. When did that ever stop us?"

Mac laughed. "At least tell us what it is." He put a hand on Dooley's shoulder. "If it's something you don't know how to do, we can help."

Dooley knew he should just let it go. The less he said, the less ammo they would have for giving him a hard time.

But they thought he needed help *sexually*? Wouldn't it be sweet to tell them that was definitely not the problem? That, in fact, sex was all she wanted? That she was even willing to pay?

Sure, she'd said the sex was on the side, not part of the job she was offering, but his pride wouldn't quite let him believe that. The sex was certainly part of why she liked him. Yes, he'd been charming with her boss and had given her a few good business ideas, but he'd also hosted a party in her suite and threatened to punch her co-worker.

As far as he could tell, the only good thing he'd *really* proven to her was that there wasn't a sexual position she didn't like. That was why she wanted to keep him around.

No, he could definitely not tell the guys that. He shouldn't tell them anything. They knew him very well and he was afraid it would be painfully obvious he'd gone and fallen for her when all she wanted was a piece of ass.

His friends would not miss the irony.

"Sure. Thanks. I'll keep that in mind."

"Seriously, man," Mac said. "There's no shame amongst friends. Some of the toys can seem intimidating at first, but once you know where to put everything, they can be fun."

Dooley stared at him. "You're honestly going to talk me through how to use sex toys with Morgan?" In spite of his annoyance, he felt a surge of heat thinking about it. They hadn't been there yet. Maybe seeing her one more time wasn't the worst idea in the world.

"That's what friends are for," Mac said with a nod. But his smile gave him away.

"You think she wants me to do something with her sexually that I don't want to do and she thinks the best way to convince me is to send me a basket of beer?"

"Well what else could it be?" Mac asked with a big grin.

Dooley leaned back against the counter and crossed his arms. "What the hell would I not know how to do or not *want* to do to the most beautiful, sexy, fun and sweet woman I've ever met?"

He knew immediately he'd screwed up. His friends' eyes got wide and their knowing grins followed.

"I think I'm good, thanks," Dooley said.

But of course they wouldn't drop it.

"She's fun and sweet, huh?" Mac asked.

"Which meant you *talked* to her, right?" Sam asked. "Told you not to do that."

"That's not really helpful right now," Dooley said.

"Because now you like her and you can't undo it." Sam nodded thoughtfully. "Been there, done that, man."

He sure had. Then he'd married the girl. The difference there had been that Danika had liked him back. Not that he thought Morgan didn't like him. She did. She'd even said so at the ball game.

But just when he thought he was going to have to talk her out of liking him too much, she went and asked him to basically be her boy toy. At least when Sam and Mac had fallen for their girls, the girls had wanted it too.

Fuck.

"It doesn't matter if I like her. That's not what this is about," Dooley said. "I'm saying no and that's all you need to know."

"I disagree," Mac said.

Of course he did. Nosy fuckers.

"Are you having trouble being creative?" Sam asked. "I can tell you some things to shake it up in the bedroom. I wasn't kidding about the strawberry jelly. Now, if romance is the problem, maybe Kevin can help you. Since romance is *all* he does with his ladies."

Kevin smiled and linked his fingers behind his head. "I haven't had a single complaint, boys."

"That's because you date virgins who don't know any better," Mac said.

"Hey, hey," Sam broke in. "As far as I'm concerned *your* wife was a virgin when you married her."

Mac chuckled. "Right. Of course." He winked at Dooley. "Still is."

Dooley couldn't help his smile.

"Maybe Dooley should talk to Ben. He's the one who can prescribe," Kevin said.

"Prescribe?" Dooley asked. "What's that mean?"

"You know, if you're having trouble keeping up with Morgan. They make pills for that."

"You're hilarious." He didn't believe his friends thought he was having trouble getting or keeping an erection around Morgan, but that was no joking matter. "I'm not talking to Ben." Dooley rubbed the spot between his eyes that was starting to pound. "I'm not talking about it period. Could have sworn I mentioned that."

"Come on, Dooley, what's she want you to say yes to?" Sam said. "Is it a threesome? 'Cause you should so do that."

"Maybe she's into leather and stuff," Mac said. "Don't be too quick to rule that out either, man."

"Is the threesome with another girl or another guy?" Sam asked.

"Leather's okay. But get specifics because there's a whole spectrum there," Mac added.

"With another girl, it's easier. You just do what feels good. With another guy, you want to lay down some ground rules," Sam said.

"And when it comes to being tied up and blindfolded and stuff, it's good to take turns," Mac told him.

That was it. "Maybe it doesn't have anything to do with sex," Dooley finally burst out. "Did that ever occur to you?"

It had occurred to *him*. Because it had everything to do with sex. Okay, she wanted him to go to dinner, maybe dance with her or something at a party, but mostly it was about sex.

Which should thrill him. But didn't. And that was a problem.

Sam, Mac and Kevin were all looking at him funny.

"That was fast," Sam said.

"Damn, sorry, man," Mac said.

Dooley frowned at them. "What?"

"She wants you to meet her parents or something?" Sam asked. "*Why* can't women just be happy with a sexual relationship for a while? If everyone's having fun, why does there always have to be more?"

Dooley took a deep breath. Indeed. A purely sexual relationship should be wonderful. Something most guys would give anything for. With a woman like Morgan, for sure.

"Or is it even worse?" Mac asked. He was looking at Dooley with worry.

If he looked as bad as he felt, they were right to be worried.

"She wants a key to your place?" Mac guessed. "Or to move in together?" His eyes widened in horror. "Is she crazy?"

"She hasn't said anything about tattoos has she?" Sam

asked, then shuddered.

They all knew the tattoo story—a girl named Debbie fell madly in love with Sam and tattooed *Sam's*—with the possessive s—over her heart. Then she'd gotten him drunk and into a parlor for a matching tattoo with her name. Mac and Dooley had showed up just before Sam signed the consent form.

The thing was, the idea of his name permanently inked on Morgan's skin sounded...well, not crazy.

He decided keeping his mouth shut at this point was his best defense.

"So she just wants more than you're willing to give right now," Sam said with a shrug. "It happens. You can't feel bad."

Dooley did appreciate his friends' support. Even if they didn't know what they were talking about.

"Man, it's been three days," Mac agreed. "What'd she think? You'd fall madly in love and spend the rest of your lives together?"

Right. That was crazy.

Like it was crazy that he didn't want the "perfect" situation she'd offered—sex, luxury and no commitment.

Like it was crazy that he wanted all or nothing from her.

"You'll have to be strong, my friend," Sam said. "It looks like she's willing to put some money and effort into winning you over."

"It's just beer," Dooley finally said.

"For now."

He glanced at Sam. "What do you mean?"

"I realize I don't know Morgan real well, but she impressed me as a woman who is used to getting her way," Sam said. "I don't think the basket of beer will be the last attempt."

"Crap." They were right. She was going to keep sending him stuff.

"I'm guessing it's all going to be nice too," Mac added. "Expensive, high-end stuff. Like the beer."

"Fuck," Dooley said. "That's low."

"Oh, yeah, poor you," Kevin said dryly. "A hot girl takes you away for the weekend and then is so enamored she sends you gifts? Wow. I feel so bad for you."

"I just..." Dooley thrust his hand through his hair. He didn't want to think about her all the time. He didn't want her buying him stuff. He didn't want to think about how she had paid attention and knew things he'd like.

"Well, when the hot girl's crazy, you don't want her sending you stuff, you know?" Sam said. "Sometime it might be boiled bunnies."

Dooley frowned at him. "She's not crazy."

"She's a snob though," Mac said. "Look at this beer."

He knew they were trying to be supportive but he couldn't let them say—or think—that. "She's not a snob," Dooley said. "She's..."

His friends grinned at him.

"Yeah?" Mac prompted.

Dooley sighed heavily and said the closest thing to a confession as he was going to get. "She's frickin' Richard Gere."

Fuck.

"I'll be outside." He needed some air. Or something.

"Okay, Julia," Mac called. "Don't scuff up your nail polish."

"It's Vivian," Sam reminded him.

"Whatever."

Not even a phone call.

She'd sent baskets of beer, beef jerky and Gatorade and then, thinking food wasn't doing it, she sent several Lori Foster books and finally baseball tickets. She'd included enough of everything for all of his friends too.

A few days later she'd sent a basket of panties and thongs, attempting to remind him of the night at the bowling alley.

She hadn't even gotten a phone call.

Dammit.

Morgan sat back on her couch and scowled at the phone. Now what? She was running out of ideas. She figured by now he would have called and they'd have plans to get together.

She'd presented a reasonable, mutually beneficial partnership suggestion. She hadn't been clingy, she hadn't pushed for more emotionally or even asked him to date her. She'd asked him to be her...well, employee.

She'd offered him a job.

A good job.

And now he was ignoring her.

Dammit.

Maybe that's how he ended things with other women, but she was not other women.

She dialed the number she somehow remembered from dialing it in Chicago.

"Hello?"

"Hi, Kevin. It's Morgan James."

"Morgan?" He didn't sound shocked to hear from her.

"I need Doug's home address," she said, getting right to the point.

"Sending something more personal than a basket of panties?" he teased.

This was Doug's best friend. He might tell Doug her plan but she needed his help and she had an idea he might be protective of Doug if she was vague or secretive. She needed to be honest with him and hope her sincerity won her a favor or two. "I'm sending myself this time," she said.

Kevin was quiet for a few seconds and she just waited.

"Tonight?" he asked.

"Yes."

"It's twenty-six forty-seven Hamilton Ave. Seven o'clock would be a good."

She nearly wilted with relief. "Thanks, Kevin, I owe you."

"Oh, let's just wait and see how things go before you get too grateful," he said.

Right. Okay then. No pep talks from Doug's BFF. "I'll be there at seven."

Doug's house was nice. It was a modest ranch in a nice, if slightly older, neighborhood. A big black Ford F-150 sat in the driveway, shining under the light over the detached garage.

After she parked at the curb across the street and got out of the car, she smoothed the front of her trench coat, making sure it was closed all the way to her knees. She swung her bag over her shoulder and then reached for the giant hot fudge sundae she'd picked up through the drive-through a few blocks away.

It took a few seconds for her to hear footsteps in the house after she rang the doorbell.

If it wasn't for the ice cream, her palms would be sweating.

The door swung open and Kevin stood grinning at her. "Hi, Morgan."

Okay. The naked-under-the-trench-coat idea seemed less brilliant now. "Hi."

"How are you?" he asked, pushing open the screen door and motioning her inside.

She quickly understood what was going on. She could see Doug, but not without his bodyguards. Good grief. What had he told them to make them so protective? She sighed and handed him the hot fudge sundae. "Wishing I'd brought tequila instead of ice cream."

Kevin laughed. "We're not *that* bad."

"Ah, there's a 'we'". Why did she feel she'd just showed up to an interrogation? "So, you're staying?" she asked.

"You better hope so. I'm making the enchiladas."

He turned and headed into the house. "Now that you're here we can start the game."

"The game?" She started after him.

"You play thirteen-point pitch?"

"Um, no."

"Give me an hour and you will. Want to take your coat off?"

She stopped in the doorway to the living room. It was...a house. A home. So typical, so classic, so like where she'd grown up she had trouble swallowing for a moment past the lump.

Everything was clean, but clearly old and well-used. The

furniture was mismatched and a little ragged around the edges, but the chairs looked perfect for curling up with a book, and the couch was the ideal spot for weekend napping.

For a moment she could picture everything from a Christmas tree in the corner to friends gathered around watching a game. On the massive flat screen TV.

A person's home truly showed what was important to them, she thought with a shake of her head. She was guessing there was an elaborate game system somewhere close by as well.

She followed Kevin into the next room, which turned out to be the kitchen.

It smelled good. The whole house smelled good. Like home cooking, laundry soap and...Doug. Good Lord. She knew his *smell?* But she did and this house embodied it. Which seemed rational, but her senses were so overwhelmed by the feeling of *him* that she felt a little fuzzy looking around.

A circular table with three chairs sat to her left and the appliances, cupboard and countertops were to her right. It was also quintessential. Canisters for flour, sugar and the like sat on the countertop next to the coffee pot which was next to the microwave. The fridge was covered with crayoned pictures and photos she assumed were of Doug's nieces. There was a stack of mail next to the base for a cordless phone and the little hooks on the wooden rack that read *Keys* held a huge assortment of, well, keys.

Obviously the enchiladas were already in the oven and there were bowls of chips and salsa on the countertop closest to the kitchen table. Dishes were sitting out on the counter but had not been put on the table yet and she had to resist the urge to set the table. That had always been her job growing up and again, the feeling of home hit her and she took a deep breath.

"Why don't you toss your coat over the couch?" Kevin suggested as he pulled a glass from one of the cupboards and plugged in the blender.

Her coat. Right. *That* would be more than awkward. "Um, no. I'm good."

He looked over at her. "You're going to keep your coat on?"

"Yes, definitely."

He turned to her, his eyes running over her, the coat, her bare legs below the hem of the coat, and back up to her face. A knowing smile pulled up the corner of his mouth. "He really is an idiot."

"Excuse me?" She felt itchy under the coat.

"He's got a girl who will show up on his doorstep naked under a trench coat but he's not even calling her? Total idiot."

She felt her cheeks heat. "I should have asked more questions about what tonight was about, I guess."

"Doug's bedroom is the third door on the left down the hall. Why don't you borrow something to put on?" Kevin said, turning back to the blender. But not before she saw the grin on his face.

She had no better ideas, so she headed down the hall.

Doug's bedroom hit her harder than the rest of the house the moment she stepped through the door. The first thing she noticed was the furniture was way too big for the space. The headboard on the king-sized bed took up one entire wall. There was barely space to walk between the end of the bed and the dresser, which stretched across most of the wall it sat against, and was covered with papers, receipts, books and magazines. The wall opposite her had a window with plain blue curtains covering it. The curtains matched the blue of the comforter that looked to have been just tugged quickly into place.

It was cramped and obviously the last place Doug spent time tidying or straightening up.

Which made her happy.

He clearly wasn't trying to impress or entertain women here.

She scrounged through the dresser drawers of underwear, socks and stack upon stack of T-shirts. The man had a real addiction.

Not wanting anything even remotely see-through, especially since she didn't have a bra, she finally settled on a black one that said, "Come to the Dark Side. We have cookies". The shirt fell to mid-thigh but she also slipped on some dark gray boxer shorts. In her purse she found the ponytail holder from the night at the baseball game and used it to gather the loose waist of the shorts and tie it so they wouldn't fall off as she walked. Lastly she pulled on some of his socks. She wasn't going to walk around in this get-up with high heels on.

It was far from a fashion statement and she felt ridiculous, but at least she was covered as she headed back for the kitchen.

Kevin took in her outfit but said nothing. He even successfully resisted the smile she was sure was threatening.

"We've got some time before dinner. Want something to drink?" he asked.

"Very much." He had no idea.

As he started the blender she thought about this whole thing. Why was Doug's friend making her dinner and playing host to her in Doug's house? When Doug wasn't even here. "Do you and Doug live together?"

Kevin laughed. "No. It feels like it sometimes. I'm over here a lot. But I have an apartment closer to the hospital."

"Oh." She looked around. "So Doug's not coming?"

"Good grief, no," Kevin said. "He'd kill me for inviting you over."

Well, that didn't sound so great. "So why did you?"

"I think there are some things you should know about him." Kevin handed her what looked suspiciously like a margarita. Which would make him one of her favorite guys at the moment.

"Things I should know that will make me like him less and not pursue anything beyond Chicago?" she asked, knowing that wasn't the case. "Because that's what he wants." She sipped the drink and found it was indeed a margarita. A very good margarita.

"I guess that's something I'd like to find out," Kevin said, taking a swig of the soda he'd opened for himself. "I'm curious how it makes you feel about him."

"But he won't be here?"

"No. He's over at Katherine's. She'll make him stay for

dinner anyway and I put a bug in her ear about coming up with something to keep him there longer."

"Katherine?" One of his sisters maybe? She hoped. Rather than an ex-girlfriend. Or a current girlfriend, for that matter.

Kevin was leaning against the counter, sipping his soda and watching her closely. "Katherine is one of the three older ladies we take care of."

Morgan leaned against the counter across from Kevin and took a big drink. "What do you mean older?"

Kevin grinned. "She's seventy-eight."

Okay. "What do you mean by take care of?"

"It started a few years ago. There were four gals who were good friends and played cards together once a week. We met Katherine when we picked her up in the rig one night and met her friends when they came to see her in the ER. Long story short, we decided they needed someone to look after them." Kevin smiled. "We all help all the gals out. Sometimes we'll all be together for dinner or something. But we each have one we're especially close to. Dooley is Katherine's favorite."

She could understand that, Morgan thought. He'd quickly become her favorite too. "What stuff do you help them with? Besides eating their meals?" She smiled. She could imagine the older ladies loving having these guys to feed and fuss over.

"Trust me, eating their meals is a pleasure," Kevin said with a chuckle. "We do repairs—change light bulbs or bigger things if needed, do the heavy lifting, or yard work, cleaning, things they can't or shouldn't be doing for themselves."

She sipped again. "This isn't helping me like him less."

Kevin nodded. "Good."

"But you said 'we' earlier. Are the other guys coming over too? Are you going to ask me my intentions with Doug or something?" she asked.

"Oh, I wouldn't subject you to everyone just yet," Kevin said, pushing away from the counter and setting his drink down. "It's just me and Senior tonight. But yeah, your intentions are of interest to me. To us."

"Senior?"

Someone cleared their throat and Morgan turned to find an older man, in a wheelchair, sitting in the archway into the kitchen from a room at the back of the house. Kevin crossed to him.

"Douglas Miller, Senior." Kevin smiled at her. "Dooley's dad. Senior, this is Morgan."

Morgan stared at the older man. He smiled at her, but didn't say a word.

Doug's *dad*? She was having dinner with Doug's dad? And best friend? Wow, this *was* an interrogation.

She could handle his full-of-it, rowdy bunch of friends wanting details about their weekend in the hotel. Parents were a whole other level.

"Mr. Miller, it's a pleasure," she said, also crossing to where he sat and extending her right hand.

Doug Senior put his left hand under his right forearm and lifted it. It was clear he couldn't move his right arm, hand or fingers, so Morgan took a hold of his limp hand and gave it a squeeze.

"Thanks for having me over for dinner," she said.

Still looking at her with a smile, Senior lifted his left hand and moved it over his face.

Kevin chuckled and nodded. "She is beautiful. That shouldn't surprise you."

Senior shook his head.

Kevin looked at Morgan. "He had a stroke about eleven years ago. He can't use his right arm and his right leg is...a challenge." He glanced at the older man. "Talking is tough too. He can say a few words. Like beer and no." He grinned at Senior.

"Pizza," Senior said, with some effort. Then gave her a smile.

Kevin laughed. "Right. The important words." He looked up at Morgan again. "But he understands everything and can make himself understood. We do some basic sign language but a lot of it is just hand gestures we've developed over time."

Wow. Okay. "You're here a lot then?"

"Senior lives with Dooley. But obviously he needs another pair of hands once in a while. Besides, Senior and I like the same TV shows. Dooley likes the History Channel and stuff."

Senior rolled his eyes and Morgan laughed.

"You have two daughters too, right? And some adorable granddaughters," Morgan said to Doug's dad.

He grinned widely with a nod.

"The girls help out and so do their husbands," Kevin offered. "But I'm more flexible. They've got the kids and activities and stuff. I'm single so I can come more easily and whenever. And I'm here to watch *Castle* no matter who else is here."

Senior gave Kevin a high-five and then Kevin gestured to the table. "Okay, we gotta get your first pitch lesson over before dinner's ready," he told Morgan. "Take a seat."

It occurred to her that she could leave. She could have left the moment she realized Doug wasn't going to be here. She could have left as soon as Kevin answered the door. Definitely before she changed into a T-shirt, boxers and socks.

But she didn't want to. She was curious.

Morgan surreptitiously watched Doug's dad maneuver his wheelchair with one hand and foot smoothly and easily around the table into the space where there was no chair. Kevin made no move to get things out of his way or to help so she didn't either. Obviously if the man had been living with the effects of the stroke for eleven years, he knew what he was doing by now.

So Doug's dad lived with him and Doug was more than just a roommate. He was a primary caregiver. Plus he took care of Katherine and the other ladies. He'd also told her about the Bradford Youth Center while they were in Chicago.

The man was...amazing.

Kevin set a bottle of beer down for Senior and refilled Morgan's glass from the blender while Senior dealt cards one-handed.

Kevin explained the general rules of bidding and taking tricks, while Senior jotted the point system down on a scrap of paper for Morgan to refer to as they played a couple of practice hands.

She'd caught on by the time the timer on the oven went off.

"So you have a big job opportunity coming up?" Kevin asked as he got up to get the food.

Morgan took her glass and the empty beer bottles to the sink. "I hope so. It's still in the air."

"Dooley said the trip to Chicago went well."

She shot a glance at Kevin but he was removing the casserole pan from the oven and didn't seem to be referring to anything other than business. "Yes. I was pleased with how everything went." She *was* referring to things other than business and she wondered if Kevin would pick it up.

The hot fudge sundae she'd brought with her was still on the counter and she felt warmer just looking at it. She was standing in the middle of the kitchen, getting ready for dinner, dressed in Doug's ridiculously too-big-for-her clothes with his best friend and dad, and yet her thoughts still went easily and immediately to her last night with Doug in Chicago.

She missed him.

In the middle of his house, wearing his clothes, hanging out with the most important people in his life, she *missed* him. More than his body, more than the orgasms, she missed him, wanted to see him, wanted to talk to him. Even if he didn't kiss her or touch her. Even if they didn't end up under the blue comforter together, she wanted to see him.

"Morgan?" Kevin asked, waving a hand in front of her face.

She shook herself and looked over at Doug's dad. He was watching her with a contemplative look. "Yes, fine." She could see Doug in his dad's eyes and chin and forehead. Doug Senior was a handsome man. More, he had a kindness in his eyes that drew her.

Kevin handed her a plate. Two chicken enchiladas and a lettuce salad. Her stomach rumbled and she felt like crying.

So stupid.

But it was there and not easily swallowed or blinked away.

She didn't know what it was. The food she would have never made for herself, the kitchen table that was worth thirty bucks at a garage sale, the way the T-shirt she wore felt and smelled, or that these men had asked her here to check her out because they loved Doug. Or that they were treating her like an honored guest without even really knowing her.

Whatever it was, she was blinking hard as she headed for the table with a plate for herself and for Senior.

"Doug," Senior said, as she set his plate down.

She looked at him, waiting for more. Senior rubbed his hand over his heart, then pointed at her.

Her heart thudded. "He likes me?"

Senior nodded. "A lot."

She smiled. "How do you know?"

"He..." Senior trailed off, then put his fingers to his lips and mimed locking his lips and throwing the key away.

"He's not talking, huh?" she asked. Did that mean something? Seemed to her that was a bad sign.

Senior shook his head. "Talks," he said. "A lot."

She glanced at Kevin. "Doug talks about the girls he dates a lot?"

Kevin put his plate down and sat. "He does." He shrugged at Senior. "He talks about what they do anyway."

"What they do?" Morgan took a bite of enchilada and thought she was going to pass out. It was delicious.

"What they do on their dates," Kevin said, taking a big bite.

Morgan coughed and stared at Senior. "He tells *you* about what they do?"

Senior winked. "Not that."

Kevin laughed and drank his soda. Then said, "He talks about where they go. Like if they go to a movie or shoot pool or whatever. But he won't tell us anything about you. I know you went to the game but only because you called me."

"He didn't tell you about bowling?"

"You went bowling?" Kevin looked over at Senior. "No kidding."

Morgan frowned. "Is that a bad thing?"

"No offense," Kevin said. "But you don't seem like the

bowling type."

"He said he wanted me to be a 'regular girl' that night. He'd come to dinner with my boss and then wanted to go bowling."

"Ah." Kevin nodded as if he'd just figured out something important. He chewed thoughtfully.

Morgan also ate, but watched the two men carefully.

"Are you a bowler?" Kevin finally asked.

"Not in the least."

"Did you have fun?"

She thought about it. "Definitely."

"Uh-huh." Kevin chewed another two bites.

Morgan drank another half glass of margarita.

"Were there other people or just the two of you?"

"Other people too. Some guys who work at the hotel," she said.

That also seemed to interest Kevin. "So he took the advice," he said to Senior. "And he's still tied up in knots over her."

Senior nodded, seeming pleased. "It's good."

Kevin nodded too. "It is good."

Morgan waited for them to fill her in. When they just kept eating she finally put her fork down. "*What* is good?"

Kevin smiled at her. "He thought maybe he just liked you because of the fancy hotel, good food, private plane and stuff. So Ben told him to take you out to do something more like he usually would with a girl. Then he would find out if it wouldn't work out."

Morgan wasn't sure she was particularly happy with Ben. "Oh?"

"But clearly that didn't make him like you any less at all."

"Clearly?" she asked looking from one man to the other.

Senior rubbed his hand over his heart again with a wink at her.

"He likes you, Morgan. It's obvious. So we wanted to meet you and see if you were worth it."

"Worth liking?" she asked, feeling a little offended.

"Worth pushing him toward."

She frowned. "What does that mean?"

"Senior wants him to see you again. Me and the guys agree. At least we think we do. He hasn't acted like this about a girl before. But we had to be sure you're worth it."

Morgan sat back and crossed her arms. "Well?"

"Definitely worth it," Kevin said.

"Definitely," Senior added.

"Really?" That made her feel better. "You'll help me get him to say yes?"

"Yes?" Kevin asked sitting up straighter. "Maybe. What's the question?"

"He didn't tell you about my offer?"

Kevin looked at Senior who shook his head.

She sighed. "I want to see him again too. But he didn't like my suggested...arrangement." Out loud this sounded bad. Especially in front of Doug's dad.

"What arrangement?"

"He makes himself available to me whenever I need him— parties, business dinners, work trips out of town. In exchange, I pay for everything and give him...extra."

Kevin stared at her. Senior stared at her. Then they looked at each other. Then they both burst out laughing.

She sat and watched them, waiting for it to pass.

Finally Kevin took a swig of cola and then asked, "You want him to be your mistress?"

"There might be another term for it," she said dryly. Though she certainly didn't know what it would be.

"But you don't want to move in or get matching tattoos or marry him, tie him down? You just want him to stay in fancy hotels and eat lobster and sit in box seats at baseball games?" Kevin said.

She shrugged. "Yes." The word *marry* made her mouth go dry. But she'd known Doug for only a few days. There was no way they could talk about something more serious. Plus she might be moving. Halfway across the country. For a job that would be very demanding with crazy hours. "Just for fun."

Senior touched Kevin's arm to get his attention. His eyes

were wide and he pointed toward the door leading to what Morgan assumed to be the garage.

"Okay. Here we go," Kevin said.

Morgan knew immediately what they were hearing. Someone had just pulled into the garage.

Even if she was fully dressed, which she obviously wasn't, she wouldn't have time to escape.

"He's not going to be happy with me," Kevin said. "But even if he yells, he only means half of it."

"I'm not worried," she told him. Doug might not like finding her here without warning, but he wouldn't be *angry*. Probably.

"It's just, he's been...edgy," Kevin warned.

"I got this," she said just as Doug came through the door.

His eyes landed on her instantly and he froze.

She felt like someone had hit her in the chest. He looked great. She wanted to throw herself into his arms, feel his scratchy jaw against her neck, feel his arms around her, hear his husky voice calling her Sugar.

"Hi," she said brightly, staying firmly in her chair instead.

Kevin took a deep breath. "Dooley, I—"

She kicked Kevin under the table, silencing him and earning her a scowl.

She pushed her chair back and stood. She wasn't dressed sexy, for sure. But maybe this outfit would make her seem more like a regular girl. "Surprise."

He took in every detail of her ensemble, but his expression stayed neutral. Then he took inventory of everything from the food they were eating to his father sitting across from her. "What the hell are you doing here?" Doug asked, tossing his keys on the counter.

"I need you for something." Showing him how much she needed him, and vice versa, had been her original intent tonight.

His eyes locked on hers and she saw the muscle in his jaw tighten and relax. "Is that right?"

"Kevin and your dad have been keeping me company while I waited."

"I thought I told you I wasn't interested in being your sex slave."

She straightened her spine. "Slaves don't get paid."

"I didn't agree to any terms that included gift baskets in exchange for sex."

"But you haven't returned anything," she pointed out. He was just surprised to see her. Probably less than pleased to find her entrenched in his life like this—his house, his clothes, his food—without invitation. But she wasn't going to let him get rid of her that easily.

"You should go, Morgan."

She wanted him. Not just *wanted*, but wanted. Standing here surrounded by all of this that made her miss him had been bad enough. Now seeing him, looking at him only a few feet away, she knew she wasn't leaving here without touching him.

"Geez, I'm not asking for a kidney. I want to invite you to a party," she said.

"So you're not here for a booty call?"

"I didn't say that." She turned toward the hallway to his room, pulling the T-shirt up as if she was getting ready to slip it off. It was just enough to display the boxer shorts.

"Kev?" she heard him say.

"Yeah?"

"Take Dad out for dessert."

Kevin's chair scraped back. "Be nice, Dooley."

She was just far enough down the hall to be out of sight but she heard Doug say, "No promises."

"She just wanted—"

"I know what she wants, Kev. Get lost."

She scooted into the bedroom and shut the door. It was less than three minutes before Doug came through the door.

"I can't believe you came here," he said, stripping his shirt off and tossing it toward the closet.

"I miss you," she said simply. "I wanted to see you."

The minute he'd come through the door and seen her in his house, in his *clothes*, with his dad, all he could think was *Yes!*

She was the least put together he'd ever seen her and he wanted her more than ever.

Had he known she was going to be there, his mind would have tried to reject the idea. He wanted to keep her away from this. He wanted her to stay the fun, hot piece of ass from Chicago who only wanted him for his body and charming business dinner conversation.

In his T-shirt, though, she became the woman he was very afraid he was falling in love with.

He had never missed someone like he'd missed her.

And now she was here. *Here.* In his house, in his *bedroom.* In his heart.

He couldn't believe it. If this was a drunken dream, he was going with it. If it wasn't...he was going with it anyway. He unzipped his jeans and pushed them down.

She wanted sex? She wanted to just have him show up and be up whenever she wanted and needed him? Fine. He was up.

Morgan was watching him undress, her breathing quickening. He could see her nipples hard under the cotton of his shirt.

"Come here, Morgan."

He slid his underwear off, tossing them into the pile by his closet.

She moved toward him immediately, her desire clear in her face. He wanted to go slow, but as usual his body was running far ahead of his brain.

He slid his hands under the bottom edge of the shirt she wore, then drew it up, his palms against the hot skin over her rib cage. She sucked in a quick breath as he skimmed over the outer curves of her breasts. "You're naked under all of this?"

"I showed up naked under a trench coat. Thought I should put something more on for dinner with your dad."

Naked under a trench coat on his doorstep.

He pulled the shirt off, watching her gorgeous hair settle back on her shoulders. Her breasts rose and fell with her breathing and her nipples beaded even further under his gaze. "How'd you get my address?"

"I'm very resourceful," she said.

That was good enough. He didn't know who'd given her the address but it didn't matter. It wasn't like it was a national secret. It would have been easy to find if she wanted it.

"You're not mad I'm here?" she asked as he slipped his thumbs into the waistband of the boxers. The hair tie holding them tight popped loose and he pushed them over her hips. They were baggy enough that they easily fell to the floor, leaving her completely naked.

"I am mad you're here. But if you're going to stalk me, at least I'm going to get laid."

Well, he *should* be mad. But if this was stalking, he was a huge fan.

Before she could respond, he cupped her breasts, brushing his thumbs over her nipples, causing her to gasp and lean into him. He loved watching her face as he affected her. He tugged on her right nipple and she moaned. He pinched it gently and she moaned louder. He bent and took it into his mouth, sucking hard and her hand tangled in his hair.

Turning slightly he nudged her and she went down onto the bed. An advantage of having a small bedroom was he was never far from the bed. He thought he should hate that she was here, seeing his modest home, his middle-class surroundings, his seen-better-days furniture. But with her naked on his bed and the raging erection he'd been walking around with nearly constantly because of the dreams of her that plagued him at night, he just couldn't work up enough ire to send her away.

"I want you," she said, sitting on the edge of the mattress.

He stepped close, his cock nearly bumping her chin. "I know." He cupped the back of her head and urged her forward.

She came readily, taking him into her mouth without hesitation.

The silky heat made blood surge through his cock, and it throbbed heavily. She ran her tongue up and down his length, sucking when she got to the top, then letting him slide all the way in, taking him deep.

He tipped his head back and concentrated on not moving. She couldn't take all of him and he couldn't thrust or she'd gag. He let her hair slip between his fingers over and over, and just absorbed the feel of her sucking and licking, almost greedily.

One hand cupped his balls, the other encircled his shaft at the base.

Dammit. This was all she wanted from him and he hated that, but he couldn't deny this was very, very good.

It was almost worth his pride. Almost worth the risk of wanting more and having her eventually leave. Almost worth upsetting his life. He deserved some fun, some travel, some time off.

Could he turn it all inside out for nothing more than the best sex of his life?

She sucked hard as her hand squeezed him and he thought, *Yes, I really think I could.*

He wanted to come in her mouth. Something primal in him wanted to just lose it like this. Her doing this to him. Her working him over, *her* pleasuring *him.*

But he couldn't in the end. He wanted inside her. He wanted her moaning and begging and arching into him, wanting more.

She made love to him like she gave head. Greedily. Like she couldn't get enough. He needed that.

Finally he pulled away from her mouth and just stared down at her, his hand still in her hair. "Ride me."

She nodded and moved over for him to join her on the bed. The moment he lay back, she climbed on. "Condom?"

"Bedside table."

She leaned to retrieve one and put it on as he linked his hands behind his head. He was going to make her work for this. She was going to do him. She'd shown up here, this was what she claimed to want, *all* she claimed to want. So she could have it.

And if she left a twenty on the bedside table, he'd fucking spend every last dime.

Screw it. He was weak. If this was how she wanted this to be, he didn't think he could keep saying no.

He could say no to the gifts. But he couldn't say no to her. Not when she came to his house, sat at his table as if she fully belonged and made his dad smile.

Eventually she would leave and he could have his balls back then.

Morgan took his erection and positioned it so she could take him in as she lowered herself over him.

He had to grip his fingers together as he slid into her. The tight heat sucked at him, the intensity growing as she took him deeper and deeper. Finally he was fully sheathed in her and she just sat for a moment, her eyes closed, her breathing shallow and quick.

"Morg…"

Then she started to move.

Dooley thought he was going to die.

His body *needed* her like it needed water. More than it needed water.

He wanted desperately to take over the rhythm, the depth of the thrusts. But part of him needed to watch and feel her do it.

She looked gorgeous. Her breasts bounced, her lower lip was pulled between her teeth, her hands were braced on his chest as she moved her hips up and down. Then she leaned back. She sat upright and her hands moved to her breasts. She closed her eyes and started playing with her nipples as her hips moved.

Dooley knew he was going to die.

But he'd have the biggest smile in Heaven.

Morgan started making those moaning sounds that indicated she was feeling the beginnings of an orgasm.

"Your clit," he rasped as he finally gave up. His hands came from behind his head to her hips and he thrust up hard. "Do it, Morgan."

Her eyes slid open and she looked like she was having a hard time focusing.

"Touch your clit, Morgan," he groaned.

Her eyes locked on his as she put her middle finger in her mouth, wetting it, then slid it into her folds, circling over her clit as he slammed his hips up into her.

In the midst of having her, of fucking her, he still *wanted* her more than he could remember wanting anything.

He felt her muscles begin to tighten around him, the waves small at first and building. Her breathing and gasps matched and he gripped her ass, moving her up and down, grinding against her, then lifting her again, before thrusting hard again and again.

Finally her muscles grabbed him and wouldn't let go and he felt the orgasm tighten in his balls and then erupt upward and into her.

"*Morgan*," was all he could say.

But it was all he needed to say.

Chapter Eight

Thirty minutes later he was still holding her. She'd slumped forward, resting her head on his chest. He was still inside her and her body fit against his perfectly. He wanted this to last. Forever.

If only there wasn't a real world. If only there weren't two different real worlds—hers and his.

In fact, part of his real world would likely be back soon. Dessert didn't take that long.

Yes, Morgan had come here tonight. Yes, she now knew some of what his real world looked like and she obviously hadn't run screaming from the house. And yes, she was comfortable right now and he knew she'd had a good time.

But his real world consisted of loading and unloading a wheelchair whenever they went anywhere, doing laundry and grocery shopping, balancing a checkbook that at times didn't allow many extras, and working a job that involved picking pieces of people off the pavement when they decided not to wear a seatbelt. Things like that. Not glamour, not luxury.

It wouldn't take more than one time for her to realize spending the night was about a lot more than sleeping and sex. If Senior needed the bathroom in the night, Dooley would have to take him. There would be no sleeping in or breakfast in bed. He was up, or just getting home, in time for his nieces to come over so his sister could get to work. He fed the girls and his dad, got the girls ready and on the school bus, then helped his dad shower and get dressed for the day. It was chaos, pure and simple. He loved it.

Being with him meant being with all of them too.

Morgan hadn't signed up for that.

Besides, if he was gone all the time, jetting to California

with Morgan, what would his dad and the girls do? Morgan hadn't promised any perks for them.

Worst of all, not only would he want her *in* his life, he'd want to be more than the guy on her arm at social functions and warming her bed in the hotel. He'd want it all.

And that wasn't what she was offering.

"Morgan. Sugar. Time to get up."

She squirmed against him, her breasts against his stomach. "Don't wanna get up," she mumbled.

He cupped her head, rubbing her hair. "Kevin's probably already eaten two pieces of pie for me. Not sure he's willing to go three."

"Okay." She slid to the side, then sat up next to him on the bed, moving her hair away from her face. "I guess I know the answer to the question of you coming to my house for the night."

"Things are...complicated," he said.

"I know." She nodded. "Why didn't you tell me about your dad and your situation?"

He raised an eyebrow. "Not a great first date conversation, you know?"

"I told you about my mom and dad."

She had and it had explained a lot. "I don't know," he finally answered. "I guess I'm used to keeping that separate from my..."

"Social life?" she supplied when he trailed off.

He gave her a half smile. "Yeah, my social life."

"I like Kevin and your dad," she said.

He was sure the feeling was more than mutual. Talk about complicated. "They're the best," he agreed. He wouldn't trade either one of them for anything. But he was sure in the next few days he was going to want to. If they liked Morgan and if she'd said anything to them about wanting to continue seeing him, they were never going to shut up about it. His dad could be very assertive—and annoying—even without the full power of speech.

"I get that they're your life. Girls are on the side, right? A necessary evil?"

That got a full smile. "Right."

He liked dating. He liked spending time with women. They smelled good, he never needed to make them breakfast, if they were in the shower together the soaping went both ways, and if he couldn't be there for them he just said sorry. He also enjoyed talking to people who didn't already know everything about him and who had some stories he'd never heard before.

But he'd never believed he would have someone permanently in his life.

He didn't consider his dad a burden. Or his sisters, his nieces, his friends or all the other people he'd collected over the years. He loved every one of them. And they didn't *just* need him. They made him laugh, they loved him, they listened to him, they cared about every detail of his life.

But—and until that moment he wasn't sure he'd ever completely realized it—he didn't combine his dating life with his home life for the simple reason that sometimes he needed a break and dating provided that.

"What about your mom?" she asked, running her hand up and down his arm.

He stared at her. No woman had ever asked about his mom. Or his dad. Or anything that personal. They didn't get that far. Now Morgan had played cards and eaten dinner with his dad. How would it feel to tell her everything?

He hadn't told anyone this story in a long time. He'd never told Sam, Ben or Mac. Kevin was the last one he'd opened up to and it had been years ago, after Kevin had forced him to tell. For the most part, all of this was a secret he kept from everyone. He didn't want to talk about it.

But he wanted to tell Morgan.

Fuck.

"Mom left Dad after the stroke. After he lost his company technically. His partner stole the business from under him while Dad was in the hospital recovering. His partner had been his best friend for years, so there were no provisions anywhere for what would happen if one of them couldn't do his job for an extended period of time, or permanently. The stroke was massive and the doctors didn't expect Dad to recover to the point of being able to make major decisions. So his partner convinced the Board Dad was incapacitated. Dad basically lost everything overnight. Mom couldn't handle it, so she left."

Morgan's hand had frozen on his shoulder. "Wow. Doug, I'm sorry."

"Yeah. It sucked." It had been eleven years and he only spoke to his mother when she called on his birthday and Christmas. His sisters stayed more in touch, with the girls and all, but Dooley had a hard time forgiving her selfishness.

He shifted uncomfortably on the bed. He didn't like talking about this and it certainly wasn't perfect post-coital conversation, but he still found himself saying, "I think it was a combination of things that made her leave. She wasn't really the nurturing type, so the idea of taking care of Dad freaked her out, I'm sure," he said. "But it was also..." He sighed. "We had money."

Morgan just raised an eyebrow.

He wet his lips. "Dad was worth millions—literally—at the time of his stroke. I grew up with the best of everything. Limos and tuxedos and Egyptian cotton sheets aren't exactly new to me."

Morgan's other eyebrow went up, but she said nothing.

"Losing his business and his wife all at once did a number on him." Dooley chuckled slightly at the understatement. "It was a major lifestyle adjustment for all of us. It took us some time to figure things out—like how to actually live on a budget and that instant gratification was no longer an option. But," he lifted a shoulder, "we made it. It works now. And Dad's doing well."

There were several seconds of silence and Dooley wondered what was going through Morgan's mind.

"That's what you meant when you said you've been in my world," she said. "On the plane when we were leaving Chicago."

Yeah, when he'd stupidly said—and tried to believe—that he didn't want any part of her world.

He nodded.

"And why you can talk business so confidently, and how you thought to send your suit jacket ahead in case you needed it, and why you weren't overly impressed with the Britton hotel."

He gave her a smile. "I was impressed with the hotel."

"Okay, you weren't...surprised. You took it all in stride."

Dooley ran his hand over her bare leg. "I've learned that no matter how much glitter you put on the surface, it's still just on the surface," he said.

"Which is why you were so insistent about making me believe things can go wrong, even with the most stable company."

He sighed. He knew he'd been overly serious and cynical during that conversation. He tried not to be. Things had worked out for him and his family. His dad was alive and healthy, his sisters were happy. They were richer now in so many ways than they had been before his father's stroke. "I've just learned that no matter how much you plan and work and even succeed, you never know for sure what's going to happen."

"Ain't that the truth."

At her soft statement, Dooley looked up at her. He was naked in bed with the sexiest woman he'd ever met and he was talking about the most frustrating and depressing time in his life. Something about the smile she gave him, or the look in her eyes, or something, made him feel like she really did get it. And that made him way happier than it should have.

"Though meeting you and your dad certainly hasn't convinced me that all of the unplanned things that happen are bad things." She smiled softly and brushed her hand over his head in the most affectionate gesture a woman had ever made toward him.

He had to swallow hard. "No. There are some very good unplanned things that have happened to me."

Like her. Most definitely her.

"But I understand," she said, moving to the side of the bed and reaching for the trench coat he'd noticed over the chair.

She shrugged into it. "You have a lot going on here."

"I do. I really, really do."

"I see why you said no to the idea of traveling with me." She slid her arms into the coat and tied the belt at her waist.

He opened his mouth to agree, then realized that wasn't why he'd said no. At least it wasn't the whole reason. It would take some juggling to make it happen, but it wasn't impossible. Instead, he'd said no because that was all she wanted.

He didn't want to travel with her because he didn't want to *just* travel with her.

Dammit.

"I'm glad you understand." She didn't need to understand it all. She just needed to leave it alone.

"I do." Morgan leaned over and kissed him. "But I still want to see you again. Will you please come to the party at the Britton on Friday? It's our three year anniversary celebration."

Of course, she needed a date.

She understood his life, she knew more about him than any woman ever had other than his sisters. And all she wanted was a date to a party.

She hadn't even argued about not spending the night.

She was probably even more certain that all she wanted was a date now that she knew more about his life.

Okay, she thought she knew what she wanted? She thought this was how it should be? Fine.

More annoyed and maybe even a little hurt, he tried to sound casual even as he said, "I'm going to need a suit for that for sure."

"Yes, it will be formal." She picked up her purse.

"I'm sure I don't have a suit nice enough." He put his hands behind his head and watched her.

She paused and looked at him. "Um, yes. A new suit is a great idea. Why don't you go to Henry's downtown? I'll take care of it."

She'd "take care of it"? She'd just call Henry up and say "whatever my guy wants"? As long as he was dressed appropriately and showed up, that's all she cared about?

"Great. I'll call Henry tomorrow."

"Great."

They just looked at each other for a moment. And he just couldn't help it. "What else?"

"What do you mean?"

"What else do I need to do besides look nice and show up?"

She wet her lips and for a moment he thought she was trying to stay calm. Then she gave him a smile that could have even been real. "Make small talk, drink champagne, tell me I look nice, don't get upset if I don't talk to you much because I'm schmoozing a bunch of other people and then make me come at least twice before you go home."

He took a deep breath. "Sounds like I'm the perfect guy for the job."

"That's why I asked you."

"It's important to make sure things are perfect. Isn't it?"

She took a deep breath and put a hand on her hip. "You know, Mr. Straightforward, it seems you'd like to say something to me."

"I told you on the plane I didn't want to do this."

She frowned at him. "Okay, what will it take?"

He frowned right back at her. "What do you mean?"

"What do you want in exchange for going with me?"

Everything.

That was the problem.

But what the hell? You missed one hundred percent of the shots you never took. "Come over here every day this week."

Her hand dropped from her hip and she stared at him. "What?"

"Come over here for dinner tomorrow night and watch TV with us until I need to go to work. Tuesday afternoon after school we'll go to Jeni's for Josie's birthday party. Then Wednesday—"

"Um, I don't think that's a good idea," she interrupted.

Was that right? Hanging out with him and his family, doing regular stuff, stuff that didn't include champagne and limos, wasn't a good idea?

"That's what I want."

"You want me to spend time with you and your friends and family?"

"Yes."

She just looked at him. Finally she asked, "Why?"

Why indeed? Why make it worse? Why ingrain her in their lives? Make them all miss her when she left?

Then he'd at least have company when he was miserable without her.

Maybe it would give her something more to miss as well.

"If you want me to fit into your life, make things easier on you, then I want the same."

"How does me being here make things easier on you?" She was studying his face carefully.

Because she fricking made him happy. In spite of him knowing it would be short-lived.

"There are dishes that need to be done, laundry that needs folding...all kinds of ways you can make my life easier."

She looked suspicious. "You're going to make me do dishes?"

He couldn't help it—the thought of Morgan in an apron, elbow deep in a sink full of dishes, made him smile. "Maybe."

"Fine," she said. "I'll come over tomorrow." She opened the door and pulled her purse strap up on her shoulder. "But the only way I'm touching your underwear is when I'm taking it off of you." Then she blew him a kiss and disappeared through his door.

Not falling in love with him was getting more and more difficult to pull off.

She was fully and completely addicted to him. Meeting his dad and seeing more of his life made her like him, and want him, even more. It also helped her understand why he'd said no to her proposition.

But the suit comment had hurt. If he would have just come to the party with her, as her date, it might have meant something, but he was doing it because she was paying.

Which should have been fine. That was what she'd said she would do. Besides, she hadn't been lying to him about this being a bad time for a relationship. She was working hard, hoping for a promotion that would take her almost two thousand miles away.

But it wasn't fine.

She was falling for him. Or had already fallen. She also loved his best friend and dad, and she wanted to meet the rest of the people important in his life. It was a bad idea. She knew that. The more she knew about him, the harder it would be to leave him when it was time. But there was a draw she couldn't resist. She wanted to meet these people, experience the people who knew him best, the ones who had his love and loyalty. Because one thing was clear about Doug—when he cared about people, he went all in.

It reminded her a lot of her dad.

A lot. "Hi, Dad." Morgan propped herself up on the couch as the phone in her parents' house only rang once.

"Hey, muffin!" He was always excited to hear from her and Maddie. He answered immediately when he saw their numbers. "What are you doing?"

"Checking in with my favorite guy."

"Honey, if I'm your favorite guy, you need to get out more."

She smiled. "I love you, you know that."

"Of course I do. But you need a favorite guy your age."

She sure did.

"What have you been up to?" she asked. One thing about her dad, he always made her feel like she was amazing.

"Working with Ted and Wes again."

That would make the third time. They usually managed to get along for about eight months at a time. Then someone would do something, they'd fight and her dad would quit.

"Great, how's it going?"

"Fine, fine."

Work just wasn't something her dad was particularly interested in.

"I'm taking your mom away for the weekend in a couple weeks."

On the other hand, fun and frivolity was something Corey James could have long and detailed conversations about.

"Where are you going?"

"Kansas City. We're going to stay in a great hotel, eat room service, shop. She'll love it."

She would *want* to love it, Morgan conceded. "Dad, you know I *work* in a great hotel right? I can get you a room any time."

"Oh, sure, honey, I know. But we want to get out of town."

"We have hotels in a lot of great cities, Dad."

He should know that. Maybe he kind of did. But Morgan knew the family dinners where they talked about her and Maddie's jobs were the ones Corey listened to with only half his attention.

"I can get you room service, tickets to shows, all kinds of stuff." She could send her parents to Chicago for the weekend for practically nothing.

Morgan thought about that. She'd always wanted a job where she could have stability but have the money and benefits to afford to have fun too. But she hadn't just gotten a job that paid well. She'd chosen a career in a field where luxury and fun were what she did every day, what she created for others and what she surrounded herself with. She made good money and was able to enjoy a lot of great things—hotel suites, fabulous food, private jets—all guilt free because it was work.

Wow. She'd just saved some big money on having a shrink show her that.

"Okay, well, I'll call you next time," Corey said.

Morgan figured the chances were about fifty-fifty he'd remember.

"Is Mom home?" she asked.

She needed her mom to tell her the job in California was the best thing to happen to her, that she'd be crazy to think about staying in Omaha, that the fun needed to come *after* the stability.

"Hang on. Love you, muffin."

"Love you too, Dad."

She did, but she needed to talk to the practical one.

"Hi, honey, how are you?" Mindy James asked a moment later.

"Good. Okay. I'm up for a promotion." With her mom, she could not only talk about it, but lead with it.

"Oh, Morgan, that's wonderful!" her mother gushed predictably. "Tell me about it."

"It would be for manager of a new resort in the San Francisco area," she said.

"California, wow. That's great. It includes a pay raise, I assume?"

Morgan frowned. It was great. It did include a pay raise. And her mom's enthusiasm about those things was what she'd thought she wanted.

"It does. But I don't have it yet."

"When will you know?"

"I'm not sure." She shook her head. "That's not why I'm calling," she said.

"Oh?"

Morgan knew her mom wanted to know more but her mom also respected that Morgan was busy. A workaholic who hadn't fallen far from the tree. So when Morgan tried to change the subject it was usually easy. "I need your recipe for tuna casserole."

There was a long pause on the other end of the phone. "Tuna casserole?"

"I haven't had it in years and I'm feeling...nostalgic." Ever since stepping through the door of Doug's house she'd been thinking more about home and family.

"It's easy." Mindy rattled off the few ingredients and the instructions while Morgan scribbled. "You're going to make tuna casserole?" she asked at the end.

Morgan smiled at her notes. "I think I am."

Erin Nicholas

Her mom probably wasn't going to be the only one who was surprised by that.

She'd had to buy a casserole pan and a sleeve to keep it warm as she drove to Doug's, but she proudly rang the doorbell with her very first homemade casserole in hand.

"Hi."

He looked great.

"Hi." She handed him the pan. "I brought dinner."

She brushed past him as he took the pan and stared at it.

"Where did you get this from?" he asked, shutting the door behind her.

"What? The pan? I had to go shopping," she confessed. "Williams Sonoma."

He chuckled. "Of course."

"What's that mean?"

"Ever heard of Walmart?" he asked, heading for the kitchen.

"Sure."

"Never mind." He set the casserole on the counter and lifted the lid. His eyes widened as the aroma hit him. "Tuna casserole?"

She grinned and nodded. "What do you think?"

He put the lid back down and came toward her, a strange look in his eyes. He looked...turned on. Which was, of course, ridiculous. Instinctively she backed up but she was stopped by the table.

"I think," he said crowding close, "that's the sexiest thing you could have done."

Okay, maybe that *was* desire she saw on his face. "Better than naked-under-a-trench-coat-on-your-porch?" she asked.

He cupped her face in his hands and said huskily, "Strangely enough, yes."

Then he kissed her. He kissed her until she was hot all the way to her toes and wanted to smear tuna casserole all over her

210

body so he'd start kissing other parts.

"Hi."

She tore her mouth from his as Doug Senior rolled into the kitchen. She pulled her eyes from Doug Junior, somehow, and turned to smile at his dad. "Hi."

The man had gone out for dessert last night so she and his son could have sex. It's not like him catching them kissing should embarrass her. But it did. "I brought dinner tonight," she said, waving toward the counter where the casserole sat.

"Yum." Senior gave her a thumbs up.

"Best I've ever had," Doug said near her ear.

He couldn't have been talking about the casserole, because he hadn't even tasted it yet.

Half an hour later, though, Morgan thought maybe she'd managed to make the best tuna casserole ever. The way the men ate it they were either starving to death or she was a tuna casserole genius.

Either way, it was fun watching them eat.

Doug had thrown a salad together and they had a package of Oreos in the cupboard for dessert. It was the best meal Morgan had eaten in a long time. The chef at the Britton Towers in Chicago would be appalled to hear it, she was sure, but putting Oreos on the menu might not be a horrible move.

When they moved to the living room to watch TV, Doug pulled her down on the couch next to him. She cuddled up immediately. Leaning against him, with his arm around her, his fingers toying with the ends of her hair felt so natural, like they'd done it a million times.

Doug Senior laughed at something on TV then and it hit her that she wanted to do it a million more times.

Morgan suddenly had to blink rapidly and knew she'd be unable to talk if they asked her a question. She was choked up over tuna casserole and evening TV. Bizarre.

The hour went quickly. They talked about nothing important and laughed easily. When the final commercial ended, Doug shifted.

"I need to get up," he said.

Disappointed, she glanced at the clock. "Time for work already?"

"No, I have some time. Need to get Dad ready for the night."

Senior was rolling down the hall, leaving them mostly alone. "Oh, so he just sleeps while you're gone?" That made sense, she supposed. "What if he needs help with something?"

"He's got his cell and can call me or my sisters. But everyone helps out. I work seven to seven, so leave around six thirty. Lisa and Kaitlyn, my sister and niece, come over around seven-thirty or eight and hang out and help him get to bed. Then Lance stops by around midnight when he's getting home. Everybody rallies."

"Who's Lance?"

"Lisa's hubby. He's a cop. His shift ends at midnight so he swings by here on his way home. Then Jeni goes into the hospital at seven so she and the girls come by around six and wake Dad up and the girls watch cartoons or play until I get home just after seven. I do breakfast, get everyone ready for the day and off to school and stuff."

"Wow, you have quite a system, don't you?" His hesitation to travel with her made more sense all the time. Not just because of his dad's needs but because of all the people affected. It was all balanced and it all worked. As long as everyone did their part.

"We do. It's a good thing." He leaned over and kissed her temple. "Stay? I'm gonna help Dad, but I'm not done with you yet."

She grinned. "Definitely." She wasn't even near done with him either. Nor did she think she would be any time soon.

Doug stretched to his feet and grinned. "Make yourself comfortable."

She watched him head down the hall and wondered if she'd ever met a guy like him before. She couldn't imagine any of the men she'd dated in the past few years taking care of their fathers, especially if their fathers were in wheelchairs and needed special care.

He couldn't just pick up and travel with her. That was

clear. Dammit.

She wanted that. Now that it couldn't happen she wanted it even more.

Morgan headed into the kitchen. She was restless. There had to be a way to do this. She could figure this out. Why couldn't she have Doug and her job?

Pouring dishwashing liquid into the sink she got the bubbles going and started scrubbing dishes.

So, she wanted it all. That was nothing new. She'd managed to have it all so far. She had stability and fun, security and extravagance. She would do anything to have Doug and her promotion.

She was drying the last plate when he came in.

"Glad you got those done. The laundry's in the laundry room already." Doug slid his arms around her, his hands flat on her stomach, rubbing in little hot circles. "The vacuum is in the hall closet." His lips met the side of her neck.

Heat shot through her instantly and she arched against his hands, resting her head back on his shoulder. "I told you about how I intended to touch your underwear."

He chuckled, the sound rumbling through her body too. "Wish I had time for that."

"Me too." For the first time, the need to connect with him wasn't out-of-control-heat-and-need.

She wanted to do something for him, the way he did for all the people in his life. Even her. He'd dropped all of this to come to Chicago. They'd been near strangers then, so it wasn't like he'd done it because he cared or was trying to take care of her, but still... Doug made other people's lives better. She wanted to make his better too. She was trying to figure out what all that meant. What did he need? What could she give him?

But sex wasn't a bad start. She knew it was great for him too. They could start there and something would come to her, she was sure.

His hands kept rubbing, the circles getting bigger. She reached a hand up to the back of his head which pulled her shirt up away from her waistband. His palm met bare skin and he groaned softly. Slipping his hand under her shirt, he stroked her stomach.

"Come to Jeni's house tomorrow with me?" he asked in her ear.

"Josie's birthday?" she asked.

"The big number five," he said.

He nipped at her neck causing shivers to dance down her spine. "I'd love to," she said breathlessly. "What time?"

"Four thirty all the kids show up and then dinner at five so I can get to work."

"The whole family, right?" Her heart tripped as she realized he was introducing her to his sisters and their husbands.

"Right. And about twenty five-year-olds. So bring your ear plugs and Ativan."

She laughed. "How about wine instead?"

"Wine might work," he agreed, pressing into her.

She felt his erection against her butt and pushed back, desire spreading through her. He could just take her pants down and take care of this right now. "Doug," she moaned.

"I know. I shouldn't have started this," he said gruffly. His hand slid higher to tease her nipple. "But I can't help it."

"When do you have to leave?" She could make do with ten minutes. She needed him.

"Two minutes ago," he said regretfully. He let his hand fall away and he stepped back, sucking in a deep breath. "Damn, you're addicting."

She turned with a smile. "I know the feeling."

"Now that you've cooked for me I'm not sure there's a cure."

He was watching her closely and Morgan wondered what he was looking for. A reaction, apparently. But was he trying to scare her? Or tempt her?

"Wait until you see how well I vacuum," she said. Also not sure if she was trying to scare or tempt him. She would love to help him out. If vacuuming and dishes and casseroles were what he needed, then she'd do it.

"Do *not* vacuum this house, Morgan," he said, stepping close.

"I don't mind," she said quickly. "I may have a cleaning lady now but housework isn't completely foreign to me."

Doug chuckled and shook his head. "I was protesting only because it's Molly's job and she'll be mad because then she won't get her allowance."

"Molly is another niece?" Morgan guessed.

He grinned. "Her job is to help clean Grandpa's house."

"How old is she?"

"Molly is going to be eight, Josie is five and Kaitlyn is seven. Molly and Josie are sisters. They're Jeni's girls. Kaitlyn is Lisa's. But they all act like sisters."

She sighed. She loved his family already.

"Okay, no vacuuming. Break my heart."

"But if you want to dust, knock yourself out. Molly's not so good at that."

She smiled. "Noted."

He just studied her for a heartbeat, then leaned in and kissed her. It was hot and sweet and she found herself almost whimpering when he pulled away. "Got to go."

"I know." There were people out there—his crew and potential patients—who needed him more than she did. In a way, at least.

Doug grabbed her bag and the clean casserole pan and escorted her to the door. She bent and kissed Senior's cheek as she passed. "See you soon."

He gave her a grin and thumbs up.

Her heart felt light as Doug opened her car door, kissed her again and then gently pushed her into the car.

"Tomorrow," he said.

"Tomorrow," she answered with a nod.

He was watching from the driveway as she drove off.

On her way home, she called her mom for her lasagna recipe.

Dooley knew glowering and grumbling was not appropriate

for a five-year-old's birthday party. But he was going to have to fake happy and excited.

Josie wouldn't care that Morgan couldn't be there. Josie had never met, or even heard of Morgan. But she'd care if her favorite uncle was being an ass.

Still, ever since Morgan's phone message informing him something had come up at work and she couldn't make it to the party, he'd been in a pissy mood.

Like it mattered.

It was Josie's birthday party. Two weeks ago, he'd intended to come alone. Josie would still be thrilled with the real china tea set he'd gotten her. There would still be cake. Why did it bother him that Morgan couldn't be here?

That was the million dollar question. The one that made his heart pound.

He wanted her here because he wanted her here. He wanted her in his life and little girl birthday parties were part of his life.

It was also bothering him because she was ditching the party for work.

Her work was important. He knew and understood it. And Josie wasn't *her* niece. But he'd thought she'd be here to see him too and clearly something at work was more important.

He sighed as he stalked up his sister's driveway. He shouldn't be so dramatic. It wasn't *his* birthday, she wasn't truly letting anyone down, the party could certainly go on without her. No big deal.

Shaking off the irritation, Dooley rounded the corner of Jeni's house to the backyard.

And froze.

There was a gigantic blow-up bouncy castle in the middle of his sister's yard.

"Uncle Doug!" Kaitlyn saw him first and came running with Josie and Molly right behind her.

He squatted and was tackled by three of his favorite females. He was laughing within seconds as he gathered them all up in his arms together. "I was told someone here was turning twenty-five today. Do you know who that might be?" he asked, finding ticklish ribs and planting a kiss on the closest cheek.

"Not twenty-five!" Josie said with a grin. "Just five!"

"Five what?" he asked. "Five toes?"

"No!"

"You don't have five toes?"

"Yes I do!" she said giggled. "But *I'm* five."

"You are? When did that happen?" he asked with mock surprise.

"Today! I'm five today!" She grabbed his cheeks in her hands. "You're silly!"

"*I'm* silly?" he asked, stretching to his full height. "I don't have a big old castle in my backyard."

Molly bobbed her head up and down. "It's *so* fun!"

"Thanks for sending it, Uncle Doug!" Josie said. She waved and turned to run back to the castle and her friends.

She thought *he'd* sent it? He looked at his oldest niece. "Where'd your mom get that thing, Molly?"

She shrugged. "Don't know." She ran off as well.

Kaitlyn grinned at him and then followed her cousin.

Dooley went in search of his sister. She was just emerging from the sliding glass door to the patio with a tray of cupcakes. "Hey!" she said with a big grin.

"Hey. I knew the theme was princesses but didn't know you'd get a castle," he said, plucking a cupcake from the top of the tray.

"Right." Jeni laughed. "But there's one here anyway. You know Molly and Kaitlyn will want one for their parties too now, right?"

He frowned. "I didn't send it, Jen."

"I didn't say you sent it," she told him as she set the tray on the table covered with a sparkly pink tablecloth, pink plates and napkins, pink plastic forks and spoons and a pink crown at each place setting. Even the lemonade was pink.

"Josie thanked me for it."

"I told her it was here *because* of you. Subtle difference."

He paused with the cupcake at his mouth. "Because of me?"

"I don't know a Morgan. Neither does Tim, Lisa or Lance."

Dooley lowered the cupcake. "Morgan?"

"That's what the note from the delivery guy says." Jeni pulled it from her pocket and handed it to him.

Morgan. With trepidation, he unfolded the paper.

Happy Birthday, Josie. Have a great time! Love, Morgan

He looked up to find Jeni watching him with a knowing smile. "Who's Morgan?" she asked.

"A girl." Who had him tied up in knots, slowly going crazy.

"A girl who knew about Josie's birthday?"

"So?"

"So you never get girls involved with family stuff."

She was absolutely right. "I was waiting for one who could afford to send a little girl she doesn't even know a bouncy castle."

Jeni raised an eyebrow. "I see. I hope you at least invited her for cake."

"I did. She had to work." Dammit. She was buying his family's affections instead of showing up in person.

"You invited her?"

"Yeah."

"To a five-year-old's birthday party?"

"Yeah."

Jeni said nothing for a few seconds, then she asked, "How long have you been in love with her?"

He thought about lying. For about three seconds. Instead he said, "About a week. Give or take."

Jeni gave him a huge smile. "That's what Dad said."

Dooley thought he was surprised for a moment. But no, he wasn't. "For a guy who can't talk well, he sure has a big mouth."

Jeni laughed. "It's the quiet ones you have to look out for."

Dooley knew his moments of peace were numbered—his

sister Lisa was around here somewhere—so he headed inside and pulled out his phone. He texted Morgan, *I want to see you tonight.*

He was going to explain to her that in his life *things* didn't take the place of *people.* She was going to have to *be* there, not just buy them things.

I should be done in an hour or so, was her reply.

His heart rate picked up. He'd just seen her last night, but he felt hungry for her. He wanted to see her face, hear her laugh. He had it bad.

Meet you at my place. He could talk Tim, Jeni's husband, into bringing his dad home later. He and Morgan needed to have a talk. Among other things.

Bring me some cake, she replied.

He grinned. He was going to have his cake...and eat it too.

"A bouncy castle?" he said as he opened the door for Morgan an hour and a half later.

"Did she like it?" she asked, her smile big.

"It's a bouncy castle. She's five. Of course she liked it."

"Oh, good. I wanted to be there."

She moved past him and he took a deep breath of her scent, growing hard immediately.

He grabbed her wrist and she turned to face him. "A bouncy castle?" he asked again.

"What?"

"What about a card? Maybe a balloon bouquet?"

"She's five," Morgan said with a smile. "A bouncy castle will always be better than balloons and cards."

He sighed. "That's not the point."

"Her liking it isn't the point?"

"No, of course her liking it is good."

"Right."

"But a bouncy castle is...too much."

Morgan tipped her head to the side. "In what way?"

"In every way," he said. "It overshadowed everything else. It was too expensive."

"Overshadowed what?"

Dooley thought about it. Actually, during the party his sister and her husband sat at the picnic table and chatted with him and Lisa and Lance and seemed very relaxed. More relaxed than he'd ever seen them at one of their kids' parties. Probably because all the kids were occupied in the fricking bouncy castle.

"It was too expensive," he repeated.

Finally she propped a hand on her hip and sighed. "Doug, I like to spend money on people. I have the money to do it. And it's not your business who I write checks to."

"But..." Okay, she might have a point. "You don't even know Josie."

"I don't need to know Josie. I know you. You love her." Morgan shrugged. "In my book that means she deserves a bouncy castle on her birthday."

Something about how matter of fact she was with that statement stopped Dooley's breath. Knowing him was enough for her to feel an allegiance to the people he cared about? Looking into her eyes he realized yeah, that made sense. Knowing her was enough for him to like anyone she cared about too.

Damn, this love stuff was strange.

"For what it's worth," Morgan added. "I would have sent the bouncy castle even if I could be there. That was my gift. Instead of a Barbie or an Easy Bake Oven, I gave her something that made her and her friends laugh and have fun and burn off some of the excess sugar they ingested. The kids and parents were both winners there." She put her hand against his cheek. "It wasn't a replacement for me showing up."

"Okay," he conceded. That all sounded good. "But If we're going to do this," he said, pulling her close. "Then we're going to really do this. I'm in your life, you're in mine. If I'm available when you need me, then you need to show up for me and my stuff too."

She put her lips against his jaw. "It might be easier if I just keep giving you gift baskets."

He could tell she was kidding, but he wanted to hear her say she'd be there. "Tell me you get this. This isn't a business arrangement. This is a relationship."

She pulled back and looked up at him. She didn't say anything at first but finally she nodded. "Okay. I'm in your life and you're in mine."

Something about hearing that from her, something about that reality setting in, turned him on faster than tuna casserole.

"The other reality of my life," he said as he started walking her backward down the hall, "is that we should try to spend all of our alone time naked because there won't be a lot of alone time."

Laughing, she started unbuttoning her blouse. "I'll keep that in mind."

They made good use of the forty-five minutes before Doug's dad and brother-in-law came back to the house. But Morgan stayed to watch TV again and then for bedtime.

Doug called in sick to work for the first time in over two years.

Not that anybody at work believed he was sick. She'd heard his responses and seen his eye rolls and grin while talking to Sam. But he still took the night off.

They made love that night again and then in the morning before she helped with breakfast for his dad and two of his nieces. While Doug helped his dad get dressed, she occupied the girls by French-braiding their hair. Apparently no one else ever had the time or the talent and she instantly had two new best friends. When she walked to the corner bus stop with a girl on each side, holding her hand, talking a mile a minute and making her promise she would do their hair again, she even promised to paint their nails.

She was a hero.

And she had a *relationship*.

Morgan had been rolling that around in her head all day. It still amazed her the guy she'd intentionally tried not to have a relationship with was the one she'd fallen for.

But it also made her smile. Big and stupid.

Like she was now.

She was standing on his porch with another casserole dish and grinning like an idiot.

"Lasagna," she said when Doug answered the door.

He held the screen door open for her. "Wow, I could get used to this."

So could she. It was a far cry from the hotels and restaurants she was used to but she could imagine doing this on a regular basis. Even better if she was making the lasagna in Dooley's kitchen instead of just bringing it over.

Which was a big jump forward.

She needed to try to resist those kinds of thoughts. For so many reasons. She'd known him for two weeks. His life was incredibly complicated. California was still on her horizon. And probably fifteen other things she couldn't come up with at the moment.

"Hey, Morgan."

Kevin came out of the recliner next to Doug Senior as she came into the room.

"Hey, Kevin. Is it *Castle* night?"

He grinned. "Nah, Senior needs some cash so he invited me over to play cards."

"You lose?"

"More often than seems possible without someone cheating," Kevin admitted, angling a glance at Senior.

The older man just smiled and shrugged.

Morgan laughed and followed Doug into the kitchen.

They managed to get the lasagna into the oven to heat and the dishes on the table, but every time they passed each other one of them had to touch. She was up against the fridge with Doug's hand over her breast when they heard the doorbell ring.

He paused, but he stayed pressed against her. "Who the hell is that?"

A minute later the noise level in the front of the house increased ten-fold.

"Fuck." Doug pushed himself back from her, his hand slipping from her shirt.

Before she could respond, the kitchen was filled with people. Three big guys led the way, each carrying plates and sacks. Three women followed, laughing and chatting. Everyone was talking at once and without direction from Doug they moved all the dishes they'd just set on the table and laid container after container of food out on every available surface. The toaster and coffee pot were shoved to the side as a crock pot was slid onto the counter, the aroma of garlic hit her from a basket of bread, a huge bowl of what appeared to be a Caesar salad was uncovered, and brownies and an apple crisp were set on top of the stove.

Morgan turned wide eyes to Doug. "What's going on?"

"Kevin made a couple of phone calls," he said, looking perturbed.

"Hi, Sugar, I'm Mac," the big man with the shaved head said, nudging her and Doug out of the way.

Doug scowled at him. "Hey, nobody calls her Sugar but me."

Mac laughed, clearly unconcerned as he stowed a pitcher of iced tea and a case of beer in the fridge.

Doug sighed. "I guess you get to meet my friends tonight."

"It's lasagna night," Mac said, as if that explained everything. "If the girl can make tuna casserole amazing, we had to see what her lasagna was like."

"Who told you about the tuna casserole?" Morgan asked, grinning. She'd been proud of that tuna. To know it had gotten rave reviews made her happy.

"Senior told Kevin who told us," Mac explained.

"Convenient how you all just happened to have things on hand that went with lasagna," Doug said, his hand still on Morgan's lower back.

He didn't seem surprised to see all of his friends. A little annoyed, yes, but resigned too.

"Now that's a funny story," Mac said, popping the top to one of the beers.

"I bet it's not," Doug said.

Mac grinned. "Maybe not *funny*, but clever."

"I bet it's not that either," Doug said. "What I think is Kevin told you I've been seeing Morgan for dinner every night and you nosy fuckers all got together and planned to have stuff ready tonight that would go with whatever we were having." He gestured to all the food. "Garlic bread, salad and brownies... All good with lots of main dishes."

Mac shook his head and looked smug. "Well, you'd be wrong," he said. "Kevin texted us all what you were having and we stopped at Giovanni's, bought everything, dumped it into our own bowls and showed up."

Morgan giggled as Doug scowled at him, crossed to the crock pot and lifted the lid. "More lasagna?"

"There's a lot of us," Mac said with a shrug.

A pretty, petite blonde with long spiral curls came up beside Mac and slid her arm around his waist. "You weren't supposed to tell him we've just been waiting to pounce."

"I don't think he's shocked," Mac said, putting his hand possessively on his wife's butt and pulling her up against him.

For just a moment, Morgan had to swallow hard past the lump that formed at their display of affection.

Doug sighed. "Morgan, this is Sara. Mac's wife."

Morgan extended her hand to the woman who'd convinced Doug to read romance novels because they had the word clit in them. Seeing her with her husband made Morgan feel a lot better about how much Doug cared about her. It was obvious Sara and Mac belonged together.

"Nice to meet you," she said as Sara took her hand.

"Oh, you too." Sara said it with enthusiasm. "You have no idea."

Morgan raised an eyebrow. "About what?"

"Dooley dating a woman who wears shoes like that?" Sara pointed to Morgan's feet. "It is truly a pleasure."

Morgan glanced at her shoes as Doug said, "Shut up,

Sara."

"I'm *complimenting* her," Sara told him. "I *love* those shoes. I *love* that you're dating someone who knows about shoes. I *love* that I have someone to go shopping with who might know as much as I do, if not more, about fashion."

"Sara," Doug said through gritted teeth. "Back off."

"Hey, I shop." Another blonde joined them.

Sara rolled her eyes. "I know."

The other woman laughed. "Geez, I see I'm about to get dumped."

"You always make us stop at Home Depot, for God's sake," Sara said. "Dani, I love you, but no woman should know that much about caulk."

A good-looking guy Morgan recognized from the bar the night she'd found Doug came up behind Dani and wrapped his arms around her. "She knows a lot about a lot of c words."

Morgan felt Doug cough slightly, then said, "Morgan, this is Danika and Sam Bradford."

"Hi." She wasn't sure if she should be grinning, considering how irritated Doug seemed, but she couldn't help it.

"Hi." Danika was smiling as she said, "So you're the one Sara's going to cheat on me with."

Morgan glanced at Sara who nodded eagerly. Morgan laughed. "Sorry."

Danika laughed. "Don't be. If I can avoid a shoe store or two I'll be forever in your debt."

"Why are you avoiding shoe stores?" A beautiful brunette and another good-looking guy joined them.

"I'm avoiding going to shoe stores *with Sara*," Danika clarified.

"Ah, how can I get in on that?" the other woman asked.

"Hey," Sara protested.

The brunette sighed. "Sara, the only place you spend more time is Bath & Body Works. I can hit six stores in the time it takes you to sample all the new scents."

"That's because you don't appreciate finding just the right scent for all occasions," Sara said.

"I think she smells great on every occasion."

Sara rolled her eyes. "Oh, Ben, you're biased. You even think she smells good with baby puke down the front of her."

He laughed. "Well, less so then."

The other woman elbowed him, but he kissed the top of her head and she smiled.

"This is Jessica and Ben Torres," Doug finally interrupted. "You've now met all of the people who meddle in my life."

Everyone laughed.

"You deserve all of this and more, man," Sam said, grabbing an olive out of the salad and tossing it into his mouth.

"Definitely," Mac agreed. "We've been keeping score, you know. Just waiting for this day."

"Dammit," Doug muttered.

"What day?" Morgan asked him under the noise of the continued conversation and joking.

"The day when they get to have input into a relationship of mine."

For some reason her heart tripped at that. "You've had other relationships, haven't you?" she asked, wondering why this seemed so significant.

Something flickered in his eyes as he seemed to be considering something. Then he turned, caging her in against the countertop, blocking her off from the roomful of people. "But I've never been in love before," he said for her ears only. "And they know that."

Morgan stared up at him. Everything seemed to spin for a moment, until she took a few deep breaths, and it all settled. On Doug. On the fact she felt *more* steady than she ever had before.

She cleared her throat. "You're in love with me?"

"Completely."

"I, um, wasn't expecting that."

He gave a low chuckle. "Me either."

That made her smile. "By the way, I'm in love with you too."

His smile was quick and bright. "That's the best thing I've

heard in a long time."

She became aware the kitchen was completely quiet. She peeked around Doug's shoulder. "Even if it means a lot of torture and teasing from your friends?"

His head dropped and he sighed. "Yeah. Even then."

Chapter Nine

It was worth putting up with Ben, Sam and Mac to have Jessica, Dani and Sara at dinner, Dooley decided. They managed to pull information from Morgan that Dooley hadn't even thought of.

They found out her birthday was May sixteenth, she hated blueberries and she had been to Tease.

"You've been to Tease?" Sam asked.

She nodded. "Sure."

"The sex shop? With the vibrators and lingerie and stuff?"

She nodded again. "Yes. Over on Fifth."

"On a dare? Or for a bachelorette party gift?" Mac asked.

Morgan shrugged. "No. For me. They have the best stuff in town. Everyone knows that."

"So," Sam said, sitting forward in his chair and leaning an elbow on the table, "you're telling us you've gone in there, by yourself, to buy stuff. Like you stop by the grocery store for milk."

"I don't go in there every week or anything," she said.

"You've been like once? Or twice?" Sam clarified.

Morgan swallowed her bite of lasagna, wiped her mouth and gave Sam a smile. "Let's put it this way, I have a VIP punch card. For every nine purchases, I get twenty dollars off."

The guys just stared at her.

Dooley barely resisted laughing. God he loved her. He had no doubt Morgan had been to Tease and bought herself some toys—which he fully intended to have her bring over next time— but he knew she was messing with Sam about the punch card.

It was fantastic. She'd pegged his friends within an hour of knowing them.

Dani laughed. "Close your mouth, Sam, you're drooling on the table."

"But she goes to Tease, to shop, for stuff..."

"I know." Dani patted his arm. "It's truly amazing a woman figured sex out without your help," she said dryly.

"I would have totally gone to Tease if I'd known about it," Sara said, finishing off her wine.

"Thank God you didn't know about it. And I mean that on behalf of all the men of Omaha and the surrounding area," Mac said, putting his arm over the back of her chair. "Once you figured that stuff out you were downright dangerous."

She leaned close. "You seem to handle me just fine."

"La, la, la," Sam said loudly, shoving his chair back and carrying his plate to the sink. "I'm not hearing this."

Sara rolled her eyes. "Morgan's right. They have great stuff. Their lingerie is gorgeous. Not like some of the cheap stuff you can find. You ever been in there, Jess?" she asked her sister.

Jessica had just taken a bite of garlic bread, and started coughing. Ben thumped her on the back as he grinned at Sara. "We have a VIP punch card too."

Dooley was grinning and shaking his head as he stood and started clearing dishes. He loved these idiots. A lot. And they didn't seem to faze Morgan, which was a huge mark in her favor. If she was going to be in his life, she would have to put up with this bunch.

As he loaded the dishwasher he thought about how he'd told her he loved her. He hadn't meant to say that at all, but certainly not the way he had. Still, the moment had seemed right. The gang had never before insisted on spending time with any of the women he dated. It was almost as if they sensed this was different.

It hit him then that if *they* knew it was different, it was official—he was past the point of no return.

"She's awesome."

Dooley looked up to find Kevin handing him plates.

"You have a bigger mouth than I ever realized," he said easily.

"They forced me," Kevin said. "They threatened to duct tape me to a chair and make me watch porn if I didn't tell them everything I knew."

A few years ago the porn would have hardly been a threat. Kevin was as red-blooded and male as any of them. But once he'd found God he'd tried to clean up his act. Not that he would have *hated* the forced porn-watching, but he would have felt guilty.

"So you caved." Not that Dooley minded. He liked that Morgan fit in with them and that they were accepting her. In fact, tonight made it all feel very real. And very good.

"Paybacks are a bitch, as they say," Kevin told him.

He was right. Dooley deserved all of this. In fact, it could have been worse.

"I think Ben, Sam and Mac are all enjoying that fact a lot right now," Kevin said.

Dooley glanced over at the table. The guys had Morgan laughing and blushing about something. But he wasn't too worried. For one thing, Morgan James could more than handle herself. For another, the girls would intervene if the guys got too out of hand. Probably.

"She took her underwear off in the bowling alley?" Mac called over to Dooley. "Why is this the first I'm hearing of this?"

Dooley looked at Morgan, who seemed to be proud to have told them yet something else that amazed them.

"For the same reason we never did get the story about the pink fur wedge that showed up on your kitchen table once Sara moved in," Dooley said.

"Careful with the Sara info," Sam warned.

But the guys all nodded their understanding. It was because you didn't talk that way about the woman you loved.

Damn if it didn't feel good to admit he was in love with Morgan.

"Dooley?" Jessica called. "Could you bring Dani a beer? She hasn't had anything to drink yet."

"I'm good," Danika said quickly. "I'm ready for dessert. Beer doesn't go well with brownies."

Jessica pinned her with a direct stare. "You've only been drinking water."

"So?" Dani shifted on her seat.

"For days," Jessica added. "What gives?"

The whole room was quiet. Dani looked at Sam who, even if his life depended on it, couldn't keep a secret.

"She's pregnant," he announced with a flourish.

"I knew it," Jessica said triumphant, coming out of her chair to hug her sister-in-law.

Sara bounced up as well, throwing her arms around her brother. "Yay!"

Congratulations continued and Dooley caught Morgan's eye over Ben's head.

It almost knocked him on his ass.

He wanted that. With her.

"Damn," he breathed as the strength of the emotions hit him.

"Yeah."

Kevin's tone drew Dooley's attention. He was smiling for their friends, but he looked a little sad. "What's up?"

"I want that."

Dooley looked back at Sam. His friend was beaming. The notorious playboy looked ecstatic about being a soon-to-be dad. "I want that too."

"Morgan's the one?" Kevin asked.

"I think so." No, he *knew* so.

"Then you have to go for it."

Dooley looked up at him again. "You'll have it too someday."

Kevin sighed and leaned back against the sink. "I don't know. I think I had it and it got away."

Dooley turned to look at him squarely. "Seriously?"

"Yeah."

"The girl in high school? You think she was your only chance?"

Kevin shrugged. "I have watched all of my best friends fall

in love. I see them with their wives, now I see you with Morgan..." He sighed again. "I can't imagine feeling that way about anybody else."

Dooley didn't know what to say. All he knew about this woman from Kevin's past was it had been a long time ago and his pre-Christian lifestyle had been a part of the problem. He also suspected the girl had something to do with Kevin's reformation, but Kevin didn't talk about her much. Dooley didn't even know her name.

"You ever think of finding her?" he asked.

But just as Kevin opened his mouth to reply, Sara shrieked, "*Really?*"

Dooley turned.

Morgan was nodding. "Of course. I'd love to have you all. It will be a great party. I'll put you all on the list."

Sara grabbed her sister's hand. "We have to go shopping!"

Dani groaned. "We do?"

"We can't show up at the Britton in jeans and tennis shoes," Sara admonished.

The Britton party? Dooley stared at Morgan. She'd invited them all to her anniversary bash?

She was a brave woman.

And if he wasn't careful, he'd end up proposing to her before he'd known her for a whole month.

Finally, it was time for the guys to get started for work. The kitchen was cleaned up in record time and leftovers packed up.

"Oh, hey, I brought this for you," Mac said, handing what looked like a magazine to Morgan.

She looked at the front. "*Cosmo?*"

"I marked the article for you," Mac said.

She opened to where the sticky note stuck out. "Top Ten Best Sex Positions," she read out loud.

"Dooley likes number four."

"The Couch Canoodle?" she asked.

"Okay, time to go." Dooley clapped his hands together. "It's been great. Don't let the door hit you in the ass on the way out."

Laughing Mac started for the door.

"But hey, we haven't gone over the anti-ogling rules," Sam protested as Dooley tried to herd them toward the exit.

"Ogle her all you want," Dooley told him. "As long as you're on your way *out* as you do it."

The next night, Morgan waited patiently on the porch of Doug's house. It was long past time he would be at work so she knew he wasn't home, but she couldn't seem to stop cooking. The tuna casserole and lasagna had gotten her hooked. Now she wanted to see what the consensus was about her baking.

Senior and Doug's sister and niece would be here now. Surely they would give her an opinion on her brownies.

Finally she heard footsteps near the door. A moment later it swung open to reveal a woman who was most certainly Doug's sister, Lisa. Who looked like she'd drug herself to the door.

"Hi." Lisa leaned against the door and tried to smile. "You must be Morgan."

"Yes," Morgan said with surprise. "How'd you know?"

"Not too many gorgeous redheads showing up on this porch." She leaned forward to open the screen door. "Doug isn't here, but Dad would love to see you."

"I know he's at work. I don't want to butt in on your family time. I just brought some brownies."

"Oh, god." Lisa jerked back, spun and ran down the hallway.

Morgan stared after her. Um...

She wandered into the living room. Senior was sitting with a little girl on his lap. She was reading to him. But neither of them looked so good either.

"Hi." Senior gave her a big smile. "Sick," he said pointing at Kaitlyn.

"How about you?" Morgan asked, setting the brownies on the table next to the couch. He looked pale.

"Yep," he said with a sigh.

"Oh, no." She went over to them. Kaitlyn's forehead was hot

and her cheeks flushed. "What's wrong?"

"Me and Mommy are throwing up," Kaitlyn said. "Grandpa's tummy hurts too."

Morgan looked up at Senior. "Honey, how about we get you comfy on the couch? We can let Grandpa rest."

Senior smiled but shook his head. It didn't matter to him. He was willing to risk a few germs to cuddle his granddaughter.

"This makes us both feel better," Kaitlyn said.

Morgan smiled. "I can understand that." Purely on impulse she leaned in and kissed Senior's temple. "Let me see if I can find some stuff to make you feel better."

Lisa came out of the bathroom as Morgan headed for the kitchen. "I know we've never met," Morgan said. "But you look terrible."

Lisa gave her a weak smile. "That makes sense. I feel terrible."

"How can I help?"

"You should go," Lisa said. "Before you get it. I feel bad enough exposing Dad, but I had to come over. Jeni's kids have a thing tonight and we all agreed the kids' activities were important." She leaned against the wall as if she was having trouble keeping herself up. "We made a pact."

"A pact?" Morgan asked.

"Me and Jeni and Doug. Doug especially made us promise. We would do normal parent stuff. We wouldn't keep the kids out of sports or not volunteer on committees and stuff just because we needed to be here. We agreed to make it work. But Tim's out of town and Lance and Kevin and Doug are working..." She trailed off, covering her stomach with her hand and closing her eyes for a moment.

"I know you could call Doug. The guys would cover him," Morgan said. She knew Doug had no idea his sister and niece were sick or he'd be here.

"He does so much already," Lisa said, shaking his head. "He does *everything*. Thank God he doesn't have anyone..." She trailed off, looking sheepish. "I'm sorry. That was...totally inappropriate."

Morgan felt her chest tighten. Doug didn't have anyone who needed him as much as his dad and sisters did. He didn't have a wife and kids. Because of that his sisters and their families could do what they wanted and needed to do. "It's okay," she assured Lisa. "No offense."

She wasn't offended. But she did feel like she wanted to do *something.*

"How much help does he need?" she asked, gesturing toward their dad. He couldn't hear them as Kaitlyn was reading to him again.

"Just with getting up and down, to be safe. He doesn't need to be lifted or anything, just steadied. He used to do more by himself but he had a couple of falls last year. One was bad and he broke his hip. Since then we all want someone here with him when he's in and out of the wheelchair." Lisa lifted her hand and pushed her hair back from her forehead, looking exhausted. "He needs help opening his pill bottles. If he gets sick, he'll obviously need more help. But that's the thing. He doesn't need someone constantly, but he needs someone often enough that he can't be alone for too long at once. Mostly because he'll try to do too much."

"I'll stay." Morgan heard herself say it before she thought about it, but of course, it made sense. "You need to go home. In fact, let me drive you and Kaitlyn. You shouldn't even do that. We can swing by somewhere and get some ginger ale and crackers, we'll get you tucked in and then I'll come back here. I was hoping for a card game or something tonight anyway."

She hadn't been able to make it for dinner because of a meeting with a bride and her mother for an upcoming wedding reception. They hadn't been able to meet until they had gotten off of work themselves. She'd missed being here with Doug and his family more than she could believe and the idea of not seeing any of them was too depressing.

Lisa shook her head. "I couldn't ask you to do that." She closed her eyes again, then spun and bolted for the bathroom.

Morgan smiled in spite of Lisa's obvious misery. She didn't think Lisa would argue too hard when she came back out.

Twenty minutes later, she had Lisa and Kaitlyn tucked in on the couch at their house, ginger ale and saltines on the coffee table and Disney's *Beauty and the Beast* in the DVD player. "Here's my cell number," she told Lisa, laying the note next to Lisa's phone. "Call me for anything. It's not a big deal."

Lisa smiled up at her. "I can see why Doug likes you."

Morgan paused. Doug himself had told her he loved her, but hearing his sister—not his rowdy, give-him-a-hard-time-constantly friends—tell her he liked her seemed to grab her heart. "You can?" she asked.

"Obviously you're like him. You jump in and help out however you need to. You've never even met us before and you're taking care of us."

Morgan liked that idea. She'd never met someone like Doug. Someone who was so willing to do whatever it took to be sure the people he cared about were taken care of. She wanted to be like that. She cared about these people who were important to him.

"It's my pleasure," she said honestly.

"Call if you have any questions about things with Dad," Lisa said, sleepily.

"We'll manage," Morgan said as Kaitlyn snuggled in closer to her mom and Lisa's eyes slid shut.

A lump formed in her throat at the sight.

She wanted this.

All of this. All of them. She wanted to be a part of this complicated, extended family Doug had around him.

"See you," she whispered as she let herself out of the house.

The minute she was in the door at Doug's, Senior was gesturing.

"They're fine," she said. "Asleep on the couch."

He smiled. "Thank you."

She took his hand. "No problem. How are you?"

He lifted his hand and wiggled it back and forth.

"So, so?" she clarified. "Okay, I brought ginger ale for you too."

She got him settled in the recliner with a blanket and a big yellow bowl in case he needed to throw up. Then she curled up on the couch across from him. "What did you do for a living before you retired?" she asked him.

"Ho...ho..." Senior struggled to form the word. Often he would get hung up on certain syllables or sounds. He waved a hand, dismissing that, then reached for the pen and pad next to his chair. He scribbled something, then held it up for her.

"Hotel?" she read. She looked at him. "You worked in a hotel."

"M...mine," he managed, pointing at himself.

"Yours?" She thought about that. "The hotel was yours?"

He slowly put up ten fingers.

"Ten? You had ten hotels?" she asked. How had Doug not mentioned this? How did she not know? What had happened? She sat up straighter on the couch.

Senior shook his head and held up six more fingers.

"Sixteen?"

He shook his head and scribbled on the paper.

"You had *sixty* hotels?" she asked, reading the number. "How many now?"

He closed his hand into a fist and shook his head. "Gone."

"No more?" She wasn't aware of any hotel chains that had closed. "What were they called?"

He wrote on his pad of paper again.

When he held it up she knew her mouth dropped open.

"Wyatt-Morris?"

He nodded with a frown.

She wasn't sure what to say. Wyatt-Morris hotels were still huge. In fact, there were a lot more than sixty now. Hadn't Doug told her his dad's business partner had taken his half of the company after his stroke? Doug Miller Senior had been half of Wyatt-Morris? She was amazed.

"Hang on." She went to the kitchen and grabbed the laptop computer off the table. Then she got back on the couch, tucked her feet under her and started typing.

The Our History tab on the Wyatt-Morris company website told the story. Well, at least some of the story. Not how Phillip Wyatt had stolen half the company from an incapacitated Douglas Miller, but it did talk about how Doug and Phillip's grandparents had started the hotel chain and handed it down, and how the two men had tripled the size of the chain in only nine years prior to and the staggering amount of money they had each been worth at the time of their "split".

She looked up at Senior. "Wow."

He shrugged.

She closed the laptop. "Do you miss it?"

He shrugged again. "Some," he got out.

She smiled at him. "I can't believe I didn't know this about you. I would have been picking your brain for secrets and ideas about how to make Britton bigger and better."

Senior motioned with his hand for her to go on. She shifted on the couch cushion. "You want to hear some ideas?" she asked.

He nodded.

Okay, what the hell? She told him about her ideas for the customized guest experience and then threw in some things she and Todd had talked with Jonathan about.

Doug Senior held up the pad of paper. *Bed and Breakfast.*

"A bed and breakfast?" she said out loud. "What do you mean?"

"Do it," he said, then pointed to the paper.

"They do sound more like a B & B thing, don't they?" Customizing ten guest experiences versus hundreds at once was a lot more reasonable. "But I don't work in a bed and breakfast."

"Why?" he asked.

"Because I..." Had always imagined herself in a fancy hotel surrounded by the luxury and style she'd always associated with the hotel industry, "...don't know anything about bed and breakfasts," she finally finished. But what did that mean? It wasn't that she didn't know about them. It was that she didn't picture herself there. Bed and breakfasts were quaint and small and homey. Not ritzy. Not filled with marble and crystal.

She looked out the front window of Doug's house. A bed and breakfast was like this place. Comfortable, warm, welcoming. Like tuna casserole. While the Britton was like her townhouse—decorated by an expert, no expense spared in furnishing it with the best of everything. It was like...lobster and prime rib.

It was strange how different lobster and tuna could be when they both qualified as seafood.

Senior tapped the page where he'd written *Bed and Breakfast* again, then pointed at her and nodded.

An expert in the hotel industry was telling her she should consider a bed and breakfast? Sure. That was what she should do. She'd just let go of the need for a big, steady paycheck and benefits, which of course didn't come with being self-employed. Not to mention the private jet, Egyptian cotton and fine china.

Of course, there was no rule that said Egyptian cotton and fine china weren't allowed in a bed and breakfast. She could also have Jacuzzis and massages and...

No. Good grief, what was she thinking?

Every idea would have to be hers then. She'd have to come up with everything, implement everything, take a chance on everything.

Even if it would be fun to be in full control of decisions and customer service and policies and procedures, even if it would be a challenge to entice CEOs, political figures and entertainers coming to Omaha to stay in a B & B instead of a hotel, she could never part with the security of being with a big company that could weather the ups and downs of the market and economy.

Of course, she wouldn't need the private jet if she wasn't traveling for Britton...

Just then Senior threw up in the bowl.

By the time Lance made his stop at midnight, Doug Senior had thrown up twice and was in bed with a mild fever. Lance checked on him and then said he'd stay until Doug got home.

Morgan was already curled up on the couch under a warm

blanket in another of Doug's T-shirts and boxers. "I'm good here, Lance. I can handle this until he gets here. Lisa and Kaitlyn need you."

Lance stood looking down at her, one hand on his hip. He gave her a half smile. "You're in trouble, you know."

She yawned and looked up. "What do you mean?"

"They're impossible to get over. I should know. I've been a part of all of this for nine years."

She smiled. Lance was an in-law but he was fully a part of the family. "Lucky you."

He smiled. "Doug doesn't let people get this close. He's never let another woman meet his dad."

She pushed herself up to sitting and hugged her arms around her knees. She'd assumed that, she supposed, on some level, but hearing someone confirm it made her heart thump. "He didn't invite me in. Kevin did. But you think he's okay with it?"

Lance's grin grew as he pulled his keys from his pocket. "Let's put it this way, Kevin's never done that before and I wouldn't leave you sleeping on the couch if I wasn't sure he was okay with it."

She watched the door shut, settled down further under the blanket and sighed. It felt good here. Too good. Like it might feel to be curled up in a quaint, cozy bed and breakfast...

Five minutes later she was pulled out, of her doze by the chirp of her cell phone.

She stretched her arm toward the coffee table, trying not to let the blanket slip down her shoulder. She was warm and content and was not willing to let go of either of those feelings.

She peered at the text message with only one eye open. It was from Doug.

Predictably, her heart tripped.

Heard you're staying over.

Okay, so he'd heard. From Lance? Probably. Or Lisa. Did he know his dad was sick?

You need more toothpaste, she typed back.

I appreciate you staying with Dad.

Then before she could respond he sent *I don't appreciate you using up my toothpaste.*

Grinning, she typed back, *Happy to do it.* Then she paused for just a moment before she typed, *Besides, I like sleeping naked in your bed.*

It wasn't even ten seconds before she got *Are you touching yourself and thinking of me?*

She should have known better than to start something like that with Doug. She scrunched under the blanket further, feeling hot and happy at the same time. *Of course.*

Good, 'cuz that's what I'm picturing.

Definitely hot. She wasn't sure how to respond. She wanted to tell him she was hot and wet, imagining his cock...

She was jerked away from the delicious daydream by his next message.

I have a surprise for you in the drawer of my bedside table.

Oh, boy.

She quickly pushed the blanket back and hurried down the hall to his room. *Aren't you at work?* she typed as she walked.

Which is why I'm texting and not calling. Did you find it?

She pulled the drawer open and gasped. Inside was a purple dildo. A big purple dildo. A huge purple dildo to be exact—that vibrated and rotated according to the package.

Um was all she could type back.

I know it's small compared to what you're used to.

She laughed. Only Doug.

She tossed the vibrator on the bed and slipped down the hall to Senior's room. He was sound asleep just as she'd left him. She felt his forehead and he felt cooler. Okay, this was good.

The moment she stepped into Doug's room her phone chirped again.

No using it without telling me about it.

Warmth curled through her and she barely resisted giggling. She slipped out of the T-shirt and boxers and under the covers of his bed.

Where should I start? she asked.

Are your nipples hard?

Now they were. She cupped her breast with the hand not holding the phone and rubbed over the hard tip. *Yes.*

Are you wet?

She was. But she knew Doug would have used his fingers to be sure. She slid her hand down over her stomach to her mound, then between her folds. Her eyes closed as the pad of her finger slid over her clit. Imagining Doug there with her, that it was his big finger touching her, made her moan softly.

Her phone beeped again.

Forcing her eyes open she read *If I close my eyes I can imagine how hot and wet and sweet you are.*

That made her even hotter and wetter. *If I close my eyes I can feel your tongue on me* she typed back one-thumbed.

There was a long pause and she wondered if she'd surprised him.

The next text relieved her of that idea. *Damn, girl, I'm hard enough to drive nails.*

Are you touching yourself too? she asked. She imagined it anyway. Picturing his hand wrapped around his cock, sliding up and down, she slipped two fingers into her body. She'd done this a few times but never like this, never with someone else knowing about it, right there with her step by step.

I want to but I'm not alone.

She circled her clit again and took a deep breath. *I wish you could be here. I need your hands and your mouth.*

It wasn't easy typing with one thumb but she couldn't stop touching herself now.

I wish I could be there too. But you don't need me. Make yourself come.

She could fake it. There would be no way for him to know if she had done it or not. But she wanted to do it. Not just because she was wound up and wanted the release, but because it felt so intimate to be doing this with him.

I'm going to use the present.

Good. Turn it up high.

She grabbed the dildo and immediately turned it on, pressing it where she wished she could have Doug's tongue. The vibrations immediately shot heat and tingles through her body and her knees parted.

Is your clit begging? Are you imagining me sucking on you? I am.

All she could do was gasp.

I can taste you now. I love licking deep, then flicking over your clit, then sucking you in against my tongue.

Holy... She pulled in a deep breath and slid the tip up and down the way Doug's tongue would slide.

Now slide it inside. I'm picturing it stretching you wide. I can feel how hot and slick you are.

The vibrator was thick and long. She imagined it was Doug as she slid it low and inside.

I love the way you grip on to me like you never want me to leave. When I thrust in and out I feel like you're sucking me in deeper and deeper.

The vibrator wasn't as good as Doug. It wasn't as hot and in spite of its size she didn't feel the thrusts all the way to her toes. She missed his moans and the flex of his back and butt muscles, his scratchy jaw against hers, his deep kisses.

But this wasn't terrible. Not terrible at all.

I wish I could be there, to see it stroking you deep, to hear you come, calling my name.

The vibrations rocked her deep and she dropped the phone onto the comforter. The next thrust hit *that* spot and she came, gasping Doug's name.

She lay, trying to catch her breath for several seconds before grabbing the phone.

Damn you're good, she typed.

His reply was almost immediate. *Yes, I am.*

She laughed softly. *Wake me up when you get home.*

Keep the vibrator close.

Her toes curled. *You want to watch me use it?*

Damn right.

Her toes curled a lot. *Will we have time?*

I take it as a personal challenge to prove I can make you come again in whatever time we have.

It wasn't like it ever took him very long.

I'll get the stopwatch ready too.

Brat.

I love you.

The second she hit send she cringed. *Crap.* It had been hot and playful and sexy. Now she'd gone and made it all serious—

I love you too.

And wonderful.

Morgan watched as the third interview of the afternoon crossed the lobby and left the hotel. She rubbed the middle of her forehead. Damn, this was harder than she'd anticipated.

She interviewed people all the time. She was great at reading people. She was an expert at this stuff. Hence, the fantastic staff she employed at the Britton.

Hence the fact that none of the people she'd interviewed to help out with Doug's dad had left her office with the job.

Of course, hiring someone to help take care of a man she cared about, to help the man she loved... Well, that was a little different than hiring someone to answer the hotel phone.

But it was necessary. After seeing and hearing Lisa so exhausted and feeling so guilty two nights ago, Morgan really wanted to do something. Of course, Doug should be part of this decision. As should Doug Senior. But Doug was swamped. He had too much going on. Surely she could at least narrow down the candidates, weed out the definite no's. There had to be a hundred nurses and therapists in this city who would love spending some time with Doug Senior for big bucks.

What she hadn't known before starting this search was that she was going to be incredibly hard to impress.

She'd gotten several calls after her community contacts put her in touch with the best home health agency in town. Some of the callers were women who had worked as home health aides.

She was sure they knew what they were doing, but they were unlicensed and Morgan's list of criteria included a degree in healthcare.

It also included being able to play chess, being able to make chocolate chip cookies from scratch, and being willing to listen to country music. Specifically, old country music like Johnny Cash and Willie Nelson because Doug Junior hated it and Senior could only listen when he was gone.

Some who came in about the job were professionals, some had experience, some seemed very nice. Unfortunately none of them were perfect.

She knew she was expecting a lot but, well, this was a guy she was starting to love... and she wasn't talking about Doug Junior.

Douglas Miller Senior deserved the best.

She was willing to work on this as long as it took.

As long as she found someone in a week.

Morgan dropped her head to her desk. A week.

Two days ago, Jonathan had called, wanting her in California the following Wednesday.

She knew what that meant.

It was the final test.

She and Todd would both be there to listen to the proposals from the architectural firms Jonathan was considering for the new resort. Then he'd want their thoughts. Whoever impressed him the most in those meetings would get the job. Finally.

Morgan really wanted Doug to go with her.

Not because Todd would be there—Todd held no attraction for her, at all, any more—she just really wanted Doug to go. She didn't want to be away from him and she thought it would be good for him especially. Now she'd seen how hectic and demanding his life really was and how he gave and gave and gave. If anyone deserved a couple of days of rest and relaxation it was him. She was certain everyone else in his life would agree. He'd confessed his friends had been enthusiastic about him going to Chicago with her. Surely they'd feel the same this time.

The other part—the part she didn't let herself think about much—was that she didn't know what would happen with them if she moved to California.

He couldn't move to California. She knew that. No matter how much help they hired, Doug would never leave his family.

And she wouldn't want him to. It went beyond the fact that they all needed him—his family made him who he was, the man she loved.

Which meant there were two options—one, she turn down the California promotion, or two, they have a long-distance relationship.

She could turn down the job. Of course, she could. Jonathan would let her stay in Omaha, working for him, at a job she liked and was good at. But that was as far as she could go in Omaha.

Which was fine. It really was. Or it should be.

She made a great living, she liked the people who worked for her, she was proud of the job they all did here.

But...

There was always a but. Every frickin' time she went over this in her head she came back to the but.

And it was all Doug's fault.

His words in Chicago about all of the things that could go wrong, that could affect her stability in her job had, apparently, sunk in. Every day she added more reasons to her list of reasons why she shouldn't stay in Omaha.

Omaha was not a huge city. The city worked hard to bring people to town, but it was no Chicago or Boston or Dallas. They didn't have a big-time professional team of any kind, they didn't have an international airport, they didn't have...a lot of things. It was hard to draw people to Omaha and her hotel—her job—depended on people coming to Omaha.

The economy could change, someone else could build an even bigger and better hotel, the big companies in town could decide to relocate cutting down on the people traveling in for meetings and conferences.

The truth was, her job was dependent on a lot of factors

that would be more secure in a bigger city. And if something terrible would happen to the Britton empire, her experience with the new resort would serve her well if she needed to move on.

Ironically, Doug's story about what had happened to his father had made her more aware of all of these things and how truly out of control of her financial stability she truly was.

Really, going to California was the responsible thing to do.

But she really wanted Doug. Too. More.

Which left option three—having both Doug and the job.

She was more than willing to try a long-distance relationship. *More* than willing. She had a private jet at her disposal. There had to be a way to make it work.

"Ms. James?"

Morgan lifted her head. A good-looking twenty-something guy stood in front of her desk. He wore blue jeans and a T-shirt that said, *I'm destined for greatness... I'm just pacing myself.*

Oh. Wow.

"Can I help you?" Surely no one would show up to a job interview in a shirt like that.

"I'm here about the home health job."

That about summed up her day.

"I didn't realize I had any more interviews today," she said.

"I didn't schedule an interview," he told her.

Of course he hadn't.

He stepped forward, swinging his backpack out of the way and stuck out his hand. "I'm Jay Thomas." Then he flashed her a grin.

And she realized why Jay Thomas got away with wearing shirts like that.

He was a natural born charmer.

After hanging out with Doug and his friends, she could spot one at twenty paces.

Oh, what the hell? "Have a seat, Jay. Tell me about yourself."

"I'm a physical therapy student," he said as he took a seat, "at the University Medical Center. I'm doing one of my internships with the home health agency you talked to. I overheard some of the therapists talking in the hallway."

This was going to be easy. "I'm sorry, Jay, but I'm looking for a licensed professional."

"I'm done with school in December," he said quickly. "I'm the perfect choice. I don't have any evening commitments. The job is seven to seven, right?"

"Yes, most of the time but—"

"I'm almost done with school. I'm in the top five percent of my class and I can provide references about my knowledge base."

He had a point. It wasn't like Senior was an invalid. Maybe just a basic working knowledge of strokes and their effects. She sighed. Hell, Jay knew more about strokes and their effects than *she* did, for sure.

"You've studied strokes?" she asked.

"Of course. I did a rotation at a rehab hospital where one whole floor is dedicated to stroke patients."

Oh, he definitely knew more than she did.

"Why do you want this job? Besides the money?" she asked.

"I'm going to be out of school and looking for a job soon and I'll need the experience and references," he said. "But..." He gave her that charismatic smile again, "...I am trying to buy an engagement ring for my girlfriend without going any further in debt than my student loans have put me. I'm eager to do a great job."

Uh-huh. But she couldn't help smiling back at him.

"Truth is, Ms. James, it's tough to find a job that fits around my school hours. This just sounded right up my alley so I thought I might as well stop by and see."

He looked like he was in good shape, so lifting and transferring Senior wouldn't be a problem.

Not that it was a huge concern. *She'd* been able to help him enough. Jay was also a friendly guy, he was making eye contact and he was giving well-thought-out arguments.

"I'm requiring a background check and drug screening along with your references," she said.

He smiled. "Great."

"No promises. I'm not the final decision maker."

"Okay."

"What questions do you have?"

"Tell me about the guy I'll be hanging out with."

She liked that he referred to it as hanging out with instead of taking care of, for some reason. She leaned in with her forearms on her desk and started telling him about Doug Senior—what he could do, what Jay would need to do, the general set-up with the family and how hard they all worked to pitch in.

"He has some trouble talking," she said.

"He's aphasic then?" Jay asked. "What kind?"

"Um..." She had no idea.

Jay grinned. "It doesn't matter. I'll figure out the hand signals and stuff."

"Do you play chess?" Morgan asked.

"I'm better at pitch, but that's hard to play with two people. I can muddle through chess."

Pitch? She stared at him. "As in thirteen-point pitch?" Wasn't that the game Kevin and Senior had taught her on the first enchilada night?

"I love thirteen. Ten is good too," Jay said.

Wow. "How do you feel about Gatorade?" she asked, almost sarcastically.

He gave no indication that he thought the question was weird. "Blue's my favorite."

Of course it was.

"What are you doing Saturday night?"

Jay shook his head. "Nothing special."

"I'm having a party here. I'd love to have you stop by and meet Senior and his family."

"Great. I'll be here. Will I need to wear a suit?"

"Actually, no," she said. "Wear your favorite T-shirt and jeans."

Might as well show everyone else how well he'd fit in from the very start.

Chapter Ten

Dooley watched Morgan coax his dad out onto the dance floor in his wheelchair.

No one else on the planet would have been able to do that.

He sat back with one ankle propped on his opposite knee and took a drink of champagne—*champagne* no less—and watched all of the people he loved dance and drink and laugh.

Sam and Danika and Mac and Sara were there. Ben and Jess had shown up late but they'd made it too. Even his sisters and their husbands were there. Morgan had hired sitters to watch movies and eat pizza with the girls in one of the suites upstairs. He sighed. Even though she'd spent money, including the limo that had picked them all up, she'd understood how great it was for his sisters to relax but not be too far from their kids, how great it was for them to all be there and not worry about driving, parking and unloading. Heck, he didn't even have to worry about drinking and driving—the limo would be waiting whenever they were ready to leave.

His friends, of course, were eating this up. The champagne flowed, the food was amazing, the whole environment was classy but fun, sophisticated but entertaining. He didn't remember the last time his sisters would have danced with their husbands. He didn't know if any of them had ever ridden in a limo. He loved watching them all smile and talk and laugh.

Having a chance to dress up and go out was something none of them ever did and, yes, it was fun.

"I can see why you like her," Lance said, dropping into the chair next to him as Lisa and Sara made their way to the ladies room.

Lisa and Sara had met before but never spent time together. Dooley wondered if Lance knew the *expensive* influence Sara could have on his wife.

"What do you mean?" Dooley asked. He liked both of his brothers-in-law but he and Lance got along best. It was probably the cop and paramedic thing.

"Morgan's gorgeous and loaded, what could be better?" Lance asked, cutting into a piece of cheesecake.

"She's not loaded," Dooley said. "All of this is a perk of her job." At least he didn't think she was loaded. He knew she made good money. Likely really good. But only because he knew it was important for her to have that to feel secure. Everything she'd spent or done for him or his friends was part of the job. He didn't know her personal financial situation. She dressed nicely and drove a nice car, but he'd never even been to her apartment.

He frowned at the realization. It wasn't like he was opposed to going to her place. It just worked better for her to come to his house. She didn't seem to mind. In fact, she seemed to like it. She'd stopped over the other night when he wasn't even there and then readily agreed to stay with his dad when he needed her.

He'd hoped all of that meant she was comfortable there. Maybe even feeling at home. Maybe even like staying was an option...

"You're dating exclusively?" Lance asked.

"Absolutely." He'd realized right after seeing *I love you* in her text message, after she'd taken care of his sick father and then had phone sex via text with him, that there would never be another woman for him.

"She know that?" Lance gestured toward the arched doorway leading from the hotel lobby into the Grand Ballroom where they were now.

Morgan was there with a tall, good-looking young guy. She was smiling as if she'd never been happier to see someone and then hugged him.

The only thing that kept Dooley in his seat was that his dad sat right next to Morgan in his wheelchair. She turned and clearly made introductions. The other man gave his dad a warm smile and even reached for his good hand for a handshake without blinking.

"She knows that," Dooley said to Lance.

She did. He was sure of it.

Not that he wouldn't take the first opportunity to remind her.

"So who's the guy?"

"I don't know." Dooley forced himself to keep his seat as he watched them. She'd be over soon. She'd been meeting and greeting, chatting and flitting amongst the guests all evening, but every so often she'd stop by and sit with him, talk, touch him, lean in for a kiss, and then she'd be gone again.

It was fine with him. She was in her element taking care of people, entertaining them, making sure they had a great time, which was fun to watch. She was beautiful like this.

Until now, he hadn't had a single urge to interrupt a conversation or hone in. But something about this guy made him notice. It wasn't just that he was good-looking. There were a lot of good-looking guys here tonight. Obviously the clientele that frequented the Britton believed in looking good at all times. There was something else about him.

He didn't seem to fit in here. He wore a sports jacket but it was over a T-shirt and jeans and he didn't look a bit uncomfortable. But he was almost too warm, too genuine. The way he acted—truly tickled to be here, to be invited and get to enjoy the luxury because it was a novelty—reminded Dooley of how his sisters had been acting all night.

Dooley frowned and watched the guy talk with Morgan and his dad and realized that was it. If he watched close enough he could tell which people were used to fancy parties like this and who weren't. This guy was in the latter category.

Which made him wonder all the more what the guy was doing here.

Dooley finished off his beer and watched as Morgan gave both the new guy and Senior a kiss on the cheek before she was pulled off to talk with a new group.

The guy leaned over to hear something Senior was saying,

then Senior pointed at their table. Dooley straightened as the guy turned the wheelchair and started pushing it in their direction.

It looked like he was going to figure the guy out on his own. Even better.

Morgan felt Doug come up behind her. She supposed technically it could have been anyone, but she knew it was him even before his hot whisper in her ear confirmed it.

"Your office. Now."

He grasped her upper arms, not letting her turn from where his chest pressed into her shoulder blades.

She smiled at the Mayor's wife and her friend. "Excuse me, ladies. I need to check on something."

In truth, he'd saved her from having to commit one way or the other to participating in their upcoming fundraiser for the cancer center. A worthy cause, of course, but she might not be here and that was not how she wanted the Mayor to find out about her possible relocation.

Without waiting for words from the two women, Doug turned her toward her office, one arm still firmly in hand.

"Is everything—"

"Not yet."

At his terse answer, she looked up to see his teeth were firmly gritted.

"What's wrong?"

"Not. Yet."

His answer was more forceful now and she felt her heart rate pick up. She'd thought either he'd noticed she needed rescuing or he'd just missed her. She loved that she could have him here with her but that he was capable of entertaining himself. She also loved knowing he preferred not to go too long without her.

As he pushed her through her office doorway and closed the door behind him just short of a slam, she decided this wasn't about rescuing or missing her. In fact, she wondered if she was going to need rescuing from *him* when he turned his scowl on her and leaned back against the door, obviously cutting off the only way out.

Feeling defensive and not knowing why, she folded her arms and watched him.

"God damn it, Morgan," he finally said.

She licked her lips and took a deep breath. He was clearly pissed.

"You hired Jay to stay with my dad, didn't you?"

Oh. Crap.

"Um, I met with Jay about the possibility."

"Don't lie to me," he snapped. "Jay told my dad he's excited about having the chance to work with him. What did you do?"

Her eyes widened. She'd never seen Doug like this. He was laid back. Almost too much so. He was passionate, for sure, but not...like this.

"I asked around, got some names, did some interviews. Nothing bad," she said. "I was going to discuss it with you, of course."

"*After* you discussed it with Jay obviously."

Morgan forced herself to relax her arms. She needed to be approachable, calming, reasonable. One of them did.

"Doug, you need help. All of you do. You're all trying to juggle a million things, you especially, and—"

"My dad is not a *thing* I juggle like meetings and appointments."

She shook her head. "Of course not. I didn't mean that. But you have a lot going on. You never say no to anyone. Jay is just a chance for you to get some time off—"

"What do I need time off for?" he asked. Something about his tone, and the expression on his face, made her think he already expected a certain answer.

She swallowed. "For whatever. For fun. For—"

"What—" he interrupted with a low, strained voice, "—do I need time off for, Morgan?"

She pressed her lips together. "I just—"

"Morgan," he said, his voice full of warning.

"I have to go to California," she said softly.

He visibly clenched his jaw, then relaxed it.

She could admit it sounded bad the way it was coming out. "You don't understand," she said quickly. "I want you to come, yes, but there are other times you could use Jay's help. The other night, your sister was so exhausted and overwhelmed. Jeni's kids are getting busier with activities. It just makes sense to have a back-up plan."

"Believe it or not," he said tightly. "We managed to get along just fine before you came along. Before you and your *checkbook* came along we took care of things, we got sick, we even had fun sometimes."

She felt tears start to burn and she blinked rapidly. He was totally over-reacting to this. "I'm just trying to help."

"I don't need *help*."

"But there's so much you try to do. You're one person. You can't always be everything to everyone." And she was afraid she would be the one without him when he ran out of stuff to give.

"I'm not saying it's perfect," he said, suddenly sounding tired. "But hell, you can't always *buy* a solution, sometimes you just have to *be* the solution."

"You're *always* everyone's solution!" she burst out. "You deserve—"

"Dammit!" He shoved away from the door. "It isn't about deserving something more. It's not like I'm suffering or missing out. I'm happy. I like things how they are."

She pressed her lips together and took a deep breath in through her nose. "You like how things *were*," she corrected. "Before I came along."

"I like how things have been since you've been here," he said, his voice dropping lower. "I like it a lot."

"When I'm here. And at your house. And in your bed."

"Yes."

She could see his hands clenching at his sides. "But I won't always be able to be...in those places."

"You could," he said simply. Quietly. His gaze seemed to

bore into hers.

He was right, of course. She could stay. Part of her, a big part, wanted to.

But right now, looking at him like this, hearing him say that what he wanted was to have things his way, without compromise, made her realize that even if she convinced him—by threat or bribe or guilt—to go with her, he would never be totally happy away from his life, his people. Not even for a few days. Certainly not for good.

"I was supposed to go to California next weekend. With Jonathan. But he moved it up. Now I'm supposed to leave tomorrow."

"For how long?"

For a moment her heart leapt. Would he consider it?

"Until Wednesday. I really think it's the last step."

"Which means if you don't go, you won't get the job."

She paused, trying to read his face. "Right."

Of course she wouldn't turn it down.

Dooley could see it in her eyes. She was testing him. Would he go along? Would he encourage her to go? Or would he ask her to stay?

He couldn't win.

He'd already pointed out that she could choose to stay. It was a fact. If she *wanted* to be here, she could be. Jonathan would absolutely let her continue to run the Omaha Britton. She didn't have to or need to go to California.

But he'd be damned if he'd beg her to stay. She knew what was here. If it wasn't enough…so be it.

Besides, he was mad at her.

She wanted to *hire* someone to take care of his dad. *His dad.* This wasn't someone who was going to run a cash register or shuffle papers in his absence. This would be someone spending time with and caring for his father.

"How much do babysitters for physically dependent adults charge?" he asked.

Morgan drew herself up taller and seemed to be trying to gather her composure. "Now you're just trying to piss me off."

From the pink in her cheeks he would guess he was succeeding. Good. She could be pissed, while he was heartbroken.

He'd thought she got it. She'd been there when his dad needed her. She'd pitched right in like...one of the family. She seemed to genuinely like, enjoy and care about his family and friends. God knew they all felt that way about her.

Which was all great. Until something else came along. Something bigger and better. Like a new job in California.

"You had no right to hire Jay without talking to me."

"I know. I didn't. Not really. I talked to him about the job. I asked if he was available. I never said anything more about it."

"But it's all about making it so I can go to California with you."

"No. Yes. I mean, I want you to go. That's why I fast-tracked the idea. Why I did some legwork ahead of time. But it's also about having some dependable help so none of you get stuck or have to give things up. Jeni and Tim and Lisa and Lance can do all the stuff with their kids. You can come to California with me. Kevin can go out. It's a win-win."

He tipped his head back staring up at the ceiling instead of at the woman he'd stupidly fallen in love with.

She knew his life. All of it. The good, the bad and the crazy. Still she focused on what he was giving up instead of on what he had, on what *she* would have to give up to be there with him instead of on the things he was trying to give her.

The craziest part was she was doing all this so she could have *him*. She wasn't choosing anything over *him*. She wanted him, would do anything to have him with her.

She wasn't leaving *him*.

Oh, no, she intended to have that cake and fuck it too.

He linked his hands behind his neck and sighed, eyes still on the ceiling. The sigh was full of sadness, resignation, with a touch of despair. He didn't know how he was going to survive this. "Just...go to California," he finally said, tired to his bones.

It had been inevitable. He saw that now.

Actually, he'd always seen it. It had been there, he'd just ignored it. She hadn't tried to hide it, or lie. She'd never said she wasn't going to California. She'd never said she was going to stay.

"Without you." It wasn't a question.

"I can't go."

"You *won't* go," she said.

He finally straightened, looking at her directly. The hurt was palpable.

Maybe they'd get a club T-shirt. One that said *Fuck love.* "That too."

She took a deep breath, then let it out. His hands itched, ached even, to touch her. To grab her and not let her go.

Because she was going. He knew it.

If he thought it would matter, he'd do it. But he couldn't give her what she wanted and needed ultimately. She needed security, stability. She thought that would come from money. The one thing he couldn't give her.

"I leave tomorrow," she said, chin up.

"I heard you."

She didn't say anything for a long time. Then she cleared her throat. "Well, I'd say this has officially stopped being fun."

As she stepped around him, he let her go, feeling frozen. A moment later the firm smack of the door shutting behind her jarred him out of the stunned my-whole-life-just-changed daze.

He spun, staring at the door. She was gone.

But then, she'd been gone as of the moment she'd said yes to Jonathan Britton.

Fun? It was a hell of a lot more than that.

He'd had fun in his life.

He'd never had what he had with Morgan.

This definitely wasn't fun anymore.

By the time the jet had landed in San Francisco on Sunday

Morgan had the worst headache of her life. It wasn't just from crying. Though she'd done plenty of that. But she hadn't cried for at least six hours and still her head pounded. Probably because she'd been gritting her teeth as long as the tears weren't falling.

She missed him. She was in love with him and they'd broken up. *Those* tears made sense. That feeling of loss and emptiness was expected.

It was the absolute frustration and anger she felt that she wasn't sure what to do with.

He was wrong about her and he'd so easily jumped to the conclusions he had. Didn't he know her? Didn't he want to believe the best of her? Did he not think she was as amazing as she thought he was? That was what hurt. He'd so easily believed she was selfish and self-serving, throwing her money around to get her way.

Wearily, she climbed into the back of the limo waiting for her. For the first time she didn't marvel at how great it was to travel in style. Instead she looked around at the interior, thought about how tonight the car seemed less impressive than the one she'd rented in Omaha for Doug's family and friends. She knew what it was though. She was in this car alone. It wasn't for fun, it was business. She wasn't making anyone else smile with it.

She was so screwed.

She liked glamour and glitz when she got to share it with friends, with her guests, with Doug. She loved the feeling when someone walked in and went "wow" about something she'd done, the look of pleasure on their face because of an effort she'd given.

Tipping her head back against the seat and closing her eyes she felt another tear slide down her face. It didn't take psychotherapy to figure out where that came from. It was the expression she knew her father had always been hoping for from her mom. He'd always wanted to impress her, surprise her, give her that "wow" moment.

It had never worked for him.

Now it was like Morgan was determined to prove it could happen. She was determined to make people smile and gasp and gush about something she'd done. It happened to her every day. At the Britton people would say how great their stay had been, how wonderful the extra touches were and it always made her happy. But nothing like how she'd felt the other night bringing Doug and his friends and family to the party. That had made it all a thousand times better than any other time.

Again, she didn't need to pay anyone to help her analyze that. It was because she cared about them. She wanted to make them happy because they made her happy.

Simple.

Why couldn't Doug see that?

Well, screw him.

The limo pulled up in front of the hotel as she was trying to convince herself it would be that easy to get Doug out of her system.

The hotel was a typical Britton and as Morgan walked through the tastefully elegant lobby she found herself terribly depressed.

Which ticked her off.

She loved this stuff. This was her life. She wanted to create places like this, places that guest after guest would walk into and have an emotional reaction to.

Sadness and loneliness were not the emotions she was going for.

What else could she feel though?

She was far from home, alone, and all she wanted to do was curl up on the couch and watch TV. When she'd traveled before this she hadn't left anything behind, at least nothing that was more appealing than the trip. Now that wasn't true.

"Ms. James?" The concierge approached her as the limo driver brought her bags in from the car.

"Yes?"

"This is for you." He handed her an envelope with her name on the front.

"Thank you." Heart pounding, she ripped into the envelope.

Could it be from Doug? Was he apologizing? Meeting her here?

It was from Jonathan.

Dinner's at seven in the dining room.

Dinner.

She trudged to the elevator, amazed by an overwhelming craving for tuna casserole.

Two hours later, across a table of delicious seafood, wine and chocolate soufflé, Morgan looked at her boss. Todd wasn't expected until tomorrow morning. She should have known then this conversation was more than just dinner.

"We haven't even met with the architects," she said.

"I know. I'm interested in your input with them, of course, but I've made my decision, Morgan. I want you to run my new resort."

She sat back in her chair and wondered where the rush of accomplishment and happiness was. Dammit. Instead of feeling thrilled, she felt tears prickle the backs of her eyelids. "Thank you, Jonathan."

"I'll need you out here almost immediately. Will that be a problem?"

She shook her head. Not a *problem*. She rented her townhouse so didn't have to worry about selling a house. She had some great people who could move up to manager at the Britton Omaha. Her family would be thrilled for her.

She didn't have anything keeping her in Omaha.

Unless she chose to stay.

She didn't have a ton of friends. She spent girl time with her sister, had great relationships with her staff and worked regularly with several people from the city who brought events in to the city, but she worked long hours and spent a lot of time with strangers—guests of the hotel. Some of them became regulars of course, but none were friends. Her time with them was about making them happy, ensuring things went well, doing her best to convince them to come back. It was hardly a two-way street.

Jonathan was talking about what Britton would do to help her relocate, but all Morgan could focus on was that she would have no one here. Two months ago, she would have considered that a plus. She would have plenty of time to dedicate to her work, she could stay at the resort long hours. Now, it made her sad. She liked *Castle*—she'd bought the first three seasons on DVD so she could catch up with the characters and story lines—but she wanted to watch it with Kevin and Senior.

She and Sara had talked about going shopping, she had already come up with great birthday gift ideas for Molly and Kaitlyn, and she'd been considering asking Danika to teach her how to do some fix-it-up projects around her townhouse.

All of that was separate from Doug, separate from what she would like to have with him. That might be over. In fact, she needed to assume it was. If he could so easily believe the worst of her, she was better off without him.

That didn't, however, mean she had to be without the other people she'd met and come to care for through him.

"So everything's fine?" Jonathan asked.

Morgan focused. "Fine? Yes." That was one of those words that could mean a lot of things.

"I'm surprised Doug isn't here with you." Jonathan took a sip of his scotch, watching her over the rim.

Morgan blinked at him. "Oh?"

"You seemed happy together. He seemed very supportive."

Yes, he had. When he'd essentially been paid to be there and be supportive. "Things are complicated in Doug's life. Traveling is difficult for him."

"He'll move out here with you then?" Jonathan asked.

She swallowed hard. "No. He's not able to leave Omaha."

Jonathan set his glass down beside his plate and leaned in. "That's what I was afraid of."

"You were?" She gripped her hands tightly in her lap.

"Yes. It's obvious you're in love with him. If he's staying in Omaha, I wonder how long you'll want to be in California. In fact, I'm surprised you're entertaining my job offer at all."

"Doug isn't a consideration," she said, her throat thick.

"I don't believe that." Jonathan's words were direct, but gentle.

Morgan met his gaze levelly. "Jonathan, I promise you if I take this job, I will stay and do my best for you for as long as you'll have me."

He sat back, his expression thoughtful. "*If* you take this job?"

She nodded. It was only fair, to both of them, that she think about this. "Can I give you my decision in the morning?"

Jonathan shook his head.

"No?" she asked, surprised.

"I was expecting you to decline the position."

"But I—"

He raised a hand, stopping her. "Which is why I have a different offer to make. I think this one is a better fit anyway, but thought it only fair to offer you the one you've technically been working for all this time first."

"A different offer?" She wasn't suspicious. Just curious. And maybe a little…okay, suspicious. "Like what?"

"I want you to move into a more consultative position. It will be more travel but you will be based out of Omaha. I want to send you to potential building sites for future resorts and hotels and have you do the first analysis and recommendation about each site."

That sounded interesting. Though it was unsettling how insightful Jonathan seemed. "I didn't realize there was a position like that open."

"I usually handle the initial travel. But I'm getting older and frankly, I think this would be a better fit for you. You're a visionary person, an idea person. The details and implementation are more Todd's forte. I think together you could be the perfect team for me."

She frowned. Travel the country with Todd? Even if it was just for business she didn't want to do that. "I don't know—"

"You'll be at the new site for a few days to a week at a time," Jonathan continued over her protest. "Your job will be overall site pros and cons, market analysis, competitor analysis, those things. Todd's part won't be until building is well underway. He's more of an operations specialist so won't need to be on site until well after your part of the project is finished."

Ah. Okay, that helped. "Is staying on at the Britton in Omaha an option?" she asked.

"I'd be an idiot if I didn't want you to be a part of my company in some capacity."

That warmed her. Jonathan Britton knew what he was doing and if he wanted her to be a part of it, that meant something. He reminded her of Doug Senior. She'd done some additional research on Doug's dad after learning about his business past. He'd been a big shot in his day yet all accounts said he was fair, reasonable, even friendly.

"But," Jonathan said, snagging her attention, "I'm not sure the Britton is meeting all your needs."

"What do you mean?"

"I've sensed a...restlessness from you. Your ideas for the guest experiences for instance. They're a departure from what we do now. Is that because you don't like what we're doing?"

"Of course not," she said quickly. Britton was one of the finest, if not *the* finest, hotel chains in the world for a reason. "I was thinking outside the box. As a business traveler myself, I was just trying to think of ways of making the guest experience more...memorable. Comfortable. Welcoming." None of those words were quite right and she felt the more she fumbled the worse it looked to Jonathan. She finally just shrugged. "Different, I guess. Unique. *More,*" she finished weakly.

Jonathan smiled. "I'm not against any of your ideas. They're just too homey."

"Too homey?"

"But I like the idea that you had ideas. That you're thinking outside the box. That you're using your experiences to make the hotel better. Those are all reasons I'm glad you're on this team."

"What do you mean by homey?" she said, not letting herself get distracted by the compliments.

"People don't stay at a Britton to get home-cooked meals and their favorite re-runs on TV," Jonathan said. "They stay for the elegance and luxury. It's *not* home. It's a hotel. A hotel that caters to their expensive tastes. Not to their taste for chocolate chip cookies. It's better than home."

He might be right. He'd been doing this, successfully, for a long time.

But she still liked her ideas.

She still thought a home away from home would appeal to some travelers. She wasn't thinking so much of couples or families on vacation. It was more the business traveler who kept coming to mind. The people who were on the road away from home so much that one hotel room started to blend into another. The ones who spent days to weeks on the road. The people who missed school recitals and anniversaries because of their jobs. The people who, like her, hadn't had a good casserole since childhood.

Why couldn't there be a place where they could end their day that, while there was no place like home, was more than a glitzy building full of cookie cutter rooms? Yes, the Britton rooms were gorgeous, but one looked just like another. There were no personal touches. Yes, the Britton staff members were friendly and gracious and wonderful at their jobs. But one traveler was much like another to them.

There had to be people who would find a porch light more appealing than a lobby chandelier. People who had eaten so much lobster that tuna was a welcome relief.

She sighed. Senior had been right. A bed and breakfast would the perfect place for her. She could implement all of her ideas, plan spaghetti night for Thursdays, make every room unique, and customize the welcome baskets and the room décor. Heck, what had Jonathan said? Something about their favorite TV re-runs? She could do that too.

If someone wanted to relax with chicken enchiladas and re-runs of *I Love Lucy*, she could make that happen. Then they'd come back the next time they were in town for business. They could stay on a regular basis. They could spend two weeks if needed. She could have regulars and they'd tell their co-workers and friends who traveled. They would—

"Morgan?"

She focused on Jonathan Britton, satisfaction coursing

through her veins. "Do you know what I'm especially good at?" she asked. "What I like best about my job?"

"Yes," he said without blinking. "You're especially good at and completely enjoy getting to know the guests and staff. You always take the extra step to make sure everything is just right and you love finding a way to surprise someone with the little touches."

She stared at him. How did he know all of that?

"I've read every evaluation ever done on each of my managers. Your guests and staff always gush about you, Morgan."

That was one of the best things she'd ever heard.

If she took the job traveling to scout new sites she would never get to know any guests, never have a personal hand in their stays. Yes, she'd indirectly be a part of thousands of guests' stays. But that wasn't the same. And it wasn't enough.

It was time to take a chance.

She leaned her elbows on the table and looked at Jonathan Britton, arguably the most powerful man in the hotel industry, and asked, "Jonathan, what do you know about bed and breakfasts?"

Their dinner and conversation lasted for another hour. In the end, Morgan asked for twenty-four hours to think about his offer. Jonathan agreed but she could tell he didn't believe it would change anything.

Morgan wasn't sure it would either. But before she did something she couldn't undo, she needed to talk to the one person in her life who believed in smart, rational choices over following her heart.

"Hi, Mom."

"Morgan! Hi, sweetie. What's going on?"

They talked so often there was no need for how-are-yous or other small talk. "I'm in San Francisco for work. I was offered the promotion." She appreciated being able to cut to the chase with her mom.

"That's wonderful!" her mom exclaimed.

"But I'm not sure it's what I want to do."

Her mom was quiet for a moment, then she said, "You'd be great at it." There was something in her tone though.

Morgan sat up straighter on the edge of the bed. "It's more money, travel on the company jet, great cities."

"Yep, sounds great."

She needed her mom to tell her that taking the job was the right thing to do. "Lots of perks," she said. "More money..." She trailed off when she couldn't come up with anything else.

"You said that," her mom commented.

"I know."

They were both quiet. Finally Mindy said, "When you first took the job with Britton you called and said 'here's what I'm doing, isn't it great?'"

Morgan nodded, even though her mom couldn't see her. "I know."

"Now you're telling me about a job you *might* take," Mindy said. "What's up?"

Morgan sighed. "I need someone to tell me to take it."

"Do you want to take it?" Mindy asked, instead of telling her the answer she wanted.

"I... It's more money, it's in the industry I love, I can travel."

"You've mentioned the money. More than once," Mindy said.

"There's the travel," she said weakly.

Her mom laughed. "Yes, the travel. So, the money's a big deal."

"It is, right?" Morgan said with some relief.

"I'm *asking* you. Is the money a big deal?"

Morgan blinked a few times. "Isn't it?"

"What do you want it for?"

Morgan could hear noise on the other end and could tell her mom was in the kitchen. A lump formed in her throat as water ran in the sink and a cupboard door banged shut and she had to swallow hard. Since when did kitchens and homemaking activities make her so nostalgic?

She rolled to her back and rubbed her temple. "What do you mean? I need to money to pay my rent, my car payment, my groceries—"

"But you already pay for all of that now," her mom interrupted. "What do you need *more* for?"

She heard a pan clatter on top of the stove as she thought about her question. She needed more to *have* it.

"Savings," Morgan said. "In case."

"In case of what?" Mindy asked.

"Mom," Morgan said, finally frustrated. "You of all people should know what I'm talking about. I learned this from you. Don't spend it if you don't have it, have a back-up plan, maybe two."

Things were quiet on the other end of the phone. Finally Mindy said, "I guess I did tell you girls that. But, Morgan, I don't want you to work just for the sake of money, to have more than you need just to have it."

"You did," Morgan said. "You worked your tail off just to be sure we had enough."

"*Enough*," her mom emphasized. "Not more than enough."

"You did too," Morgan protested. "In case Daddy did something spontaneous."

"But I loved those things," her mom said. "I wanted him to be able to do them, so I worked harder."

"You did *not* love them!" Morgan got up and started pacing. "You cried, you yelled, you fought."

There was a long, horrible pause on Mindy's end of the phone and Morgan felt her chest tighten even before her mom said, "Is that all you remember?"

Morgan stomped to the window to look out over San Francisco and thought about her mother's question. What did she remember?

"I remember the fights and tears," she finally said. "I remember loving and dreading Daddy's surprises at the same time. They were so fun but I always knew there'd be hell to pay."

Mindy cleared her throat. "I felt the same way." She paused, then said, "We were so young when we had you girls. We didn't know what we were doing and yeah, we didn't have a lot of money. But," she said firmly, "we always had enough. The tears and fighting..." She took a deep breath. "I'm sorry that's what you remember. They happened, but not all the time. We had lots of laughs, lots of great times. The tears were..." Her voice got scratchy.

Morgan lowered herself onto the foot stool by the chair near the window. "What were the tears, Mom?" she asked. This felt important.

"The tears were jealousy." Mindy laughed and sniffed at the same time. "Your dad was you girls' favorite. He was fun and silly and got to be there with you all the time while I worked."

Morgan frowned. "It had to be frustrating to be the only one who worked."

"No," her mom said quickly. She laughed lightly. "He was *there*, Morgan. Always. No matter what any of us needed he was there. If you were sick, he could stay with you. If you had a party at school, he could be there. I made the cupcakes, but he was there. That matters so much more."

Morgan thought about that. It was like Doug had said, sometimes you have to *be* the solution. She remembered her dad coming to her school parties. He was always in charge of games. She remembered some of the goofy stuff he had them do, how he'd get all the kids laughing and playing, even the shy ones. She didn't remember a single cupcake.

She took a deep breath. Okay, being there was good.

"But if he'd worked, you could have been there sometimes too," she said.

"Oh, honey." Her mom sighed. "Part of me wanted to, but as long as he was there I didn't feel guilty or worry. I was determined to finish nursing school, get my master's and move up at the hospital into administration."

Which she'd done.

"It all took time and commitment. I had to work long hours and crazy shifts for a while. But after everyone told me I'd ruined my life and my chance at anything good by getting pregnant and married so young, I had to prove them wrong. I wanted to show them all that your dad and I could make it. He helped me do all those professional things I wanted to do and still raise two happy, healthy, well-adjusted daughters." Mindy chuckled. "We had Maddie so soon after you to prove a point to everyone. It would have been easier and *cheaper* to wait, but we knew we could do it."

"So it was all...okay?" Morgan asked, a little stunned.

"Very okay," her mom said. "You saw tears and heard arguments, sure. Those came from fatigue and being young and jealous and sometimes guilty. Sometimes things were tight, but your dad always insisted everything would be all right and...it always was. That's why he kept doing that stuff even when we fought. Now you have a thousand great memories having nothing to do with how nice our house or car was or if we had to eat tuna casserole once a week."

Tears were tracking down her cheeks by the time her mom finished.

She was completely right.

Morgan knew then she'd trade her entire savings in for tuna casserole once a week.

And that was exactly what she was going to do.

Chapter Eleven

"I think she's stalking me."

Sara looked up from where she was playing with Ava, Jessica and Ben's daughter. "Morgan's stalking you?"

"Yeah."

Danika burst into laughter from where she was hanging photos near the fireplace.

Sara was grinning too. "Why do you think that?"

"I saw her driving away from Jeni's house the other day when I stopped by there. I saw her coming out of the Youth Center Monday when I got there and I think she was at my house last night."

"How do you know she was at your house?" Sara asked, handing Ava another block to stack.

Dooley noted neither woman was denying Morgan had been at any of those places. "I found leftover chicken and noodles in the fridge this morning and brownies on the counter."

Dani and Sara shared a look.

"What?" He sat up quickly.

"You think she's stalking you?" Dani asked, hand on her hip, her pregnant belly starting to show. "Even though she's never where you are at the same time you're there?"

"If she's stalking you, she's not very good at it," Sara said.

Dooley slumped back on the couch. Dammit. He wanted her to be stalking him. Or at least thinking about him.

"You don't seem surprised by the idea she's been at my sister's or the Center or *my* house," he said.

Sara wouldn't lie to him.

"I'm not surprised," Sara said. "I know she's been at all those places. On a regular basis," she added with a sly smile.

"She's been with you all?" He wondered why *he* wasn't more surprised. These were his friends, his family, his activities.

But if she wanted to be close to him, that was one way. He'd been tempted to just go and sit in the lobby of the Britton himself, just to be near people and things that were close to her.

"We went shopping Saturday," Dani said.

Sara had perked up. "Where'd she take you?"

"All over. But we spent most of the time in the shoe store. She got this amazing pair of..."

From there Dooley tuned out. He didn't know a damned thing about women's shoes except how they looked once they were on, and he didn't care. But he'd lost Sara. Sara wouldn't change her alliance easily, but shoes were serious.

"I saw Morgan in the dressing room between outfits," Danika said to him. "*Damn.*"

He shifted uncomfortably on the couch. Yeah, that about summed Morgan up when she was naked. Even when she wasn't.

So, she was around, in Omaha, in his life. Kind of. It was weird. She was in the lives and activities and places that made up his life but she wasn't *in* his life. Not like he wanted her to be. But she was moving to California soon so... Unless...

He sat up again. "Did she get the California job?"

Sara looked at him, then at Danika, then back to him. "Yeah, she did."

Of course she did. "I figured," he said, his chest heavy.

"You did?" Sara asked.

"She's great at her job. It's the most important thing to her," he said.

There was a beat of silence, before Dani said, "You're an idiot." Then returned to pounding nails. Loudly.

It was interesting, he mused. Danika was the first to say that.

Later that night, Dooley sat in the break room at work and tossed popcorn into his mouth with fake nonchalance. It was quiet. Very quiet. Too quiet.

He'd screwed up with a woman they all liked. Where were the opinions, the advice, the you're-an-idiot comments?

He looked around. He'd been waiting for them to say something, to ask something, to yell at him, for four shifts now. But Sam sat at the desk working a Sudoku puzzle, Kevin was reading and Mac was, apparently, watching whatever Dooley was pretending to watch on TV.

There were no comments or questions. Nothing. Even Dani and Sara had let it go after the one comment.

He scowled at the TV and chewed harder. In the past when Sam and Mac had been idiots about Dani and Sara they'd all made sure the guys knew how they all felt. They'd all known Sam belonged with Dani and they'd made sure he faced how he felt. Dooley, in particular, had seen how Mac was screwing up with Sara and he'd been sure to let Mac know.

Because he cared about them and wanted them to be happy.

So what the hell was this?

Did they think Morgan wasn't the right woman for him? They were stupid if they thought that. She was definitely the right woman. Did they think he didn't love her? That was even more ridiculous. He'd never felt, or acted, this way for anyone else. What did they think *that* was? Was it that he wasn't good enough for her? That was... Well, that was possible.

"Dammit, I thought you were my friends," he finally said, smacking the arm of his chair with his open palm.

Mac reached for a handful of popcorn, seemingly unfazed by Dooley's outburst. "Hey, man, we're good as long as you don't cry or sing."

Dooley raised an eyebrow. "If I did, real *friends* would sit through it."

Mac seemed to think about that for a moment. "'Wind Beneath My Wings'? I'm not sitting through that. Unless I had my phone so I could record it and put it on YouTube."

"How about 'Lean On Me'?" Sam piped up. "That's a good one."

"Okay, I might listen to that," Mac said.

"Or 'Friends in Low Places'," Sam said.

Dooley groaned. Country music gave him hives.

"At least go with the Beatles," Kevin said and launched into "With a Little Help from My Friends."

Dooley waited as Mac and Sam joined in for a verse. When they finally shut up he asked, "None of you are concerned about it at all?"

"Concerned about what?" Mac asked, tossing popcorn into his mouth. "Sam's singing voice has always sucked."

"Oh, yeah, and you're *American Idol* material," Sam said.

"Me and Morgan breaking up," Dooley said through gritted teeth. Seriously? Why did he hang out with these guys?

"Oh, that," Mac said.

Dooley waited. No one said anything more. "Yes, fucking *that*. Where's the 'hey, sorry buddy' or the 'I've got a cute girl you should meet' or the 'what the hell are you thinking'? You've got *nothing* to say about it at all?" he demanded.

Sam shrugged indifferently. "We figured you knew what you were doing."

Dooley scowled at them. "Since when has *anyone* in this room known what they were doing where a woman was concerned?"

They all looked at one another, unable to answer that particular question.

"So knock that shit off," Dooley ordered.

"Okay," Mac said. "Basically you're saying you don't know what you're doing breaking up with Morgan."

"Yes," Dooley said without hesitation.

"Why? You know you were right to break it off," Sam said. "You're just missing the sex."

Dooley stared at him. "I am not just missing the sex." As he said it he knew it was true with every cell of his body. Though he did miss Morgan's body there was a hell of a bigger void than that.

Mac didn't look convinced. "Really? Sex is a powerful drug."

"It wasn't just sex."

"You sure?" Sam asked. "I mean, like, what else do you miss?"

Dooley thought about that. "Everything," he finally said. "Her voice, her laugh, the feel of her skin, watching her across a room, knowing how she is."

"Hmm," Mac said thoughtfully. "Could be the liquor."

"What liquor?" Dooley asked.

"The liquor you're drinking every night because you miss the sex."

Dooley shook his head and forced himself to breathe deep. "I am not drinking every night."

"Maybe you should," Mac said with a shrug.

Dooley wanted to hit him. Too bad Mac was bigger than he was. Sam he could maybe take, but not Mac. Or Kevin. "I miss the sex," he finally said patiently. "But I miss a lot more than that."

"Why?" Sam asked. "She was stuck up. Too hoity-toity."

"Did you just say hoity-toity?" Mac asked him.

"It's accurate," Sam said. "Expensive tastes. Couldn't be bothered with Dooley's dad."

"Yeah, the minute she tried to hire that weird guy to stay with Senior I was over her," Mac added.

Dooley felt his mouth open but nothing came out. He frowned. He thought these guys liked Morgan. "You were *over* her?" he finally asked.

He knew Mac wasn't in love with her but damn, he didn't see how anyone could ever be *over* Morgan.

"Come on," Mac said. "It's obvious you have everything handled. Who is she to come in like that and try to change everything up?"

He knew it seemed that way. It seemed that way to him too. But hearing someone else say it, it felt wrong. "She was trying to make it work with us."

"I just can't figure out why she doesn't like your dad. He's awesome," Sam said.

Dooley frowned at him. "She likes my dad."

Sam raised an eyebrow. "You sure about that?"

Dooley's frown tightened. "Of course I'm sure."

"How do you know? At the first opportunity she wanted to bring someone else in to take over so she could take you out of town."

"That's not how it was," Dooley said firmly. "It was for work. It was only for a few days and..."

Sam's other eyebrow went up. "And?"

"Jay is completely qualified. And...a nice guy," he added reluctantly.

"Oh?" Sam asked.

Dooley looked away. "Yeah. Okay. He came to the house after he found out that we weren't going to hire him. He pled his case."

Sam looked like he was trying not to smile as he looked back at the puzzle in front of him. "What did your dad think of him?"

Dooley suspected Sam already knew the answer. "He likes him," he said anyway.

"I'm not surprised," Sam said. "Jay's a good guy."

Dooley sighed. "You like Jay?"

"Of course. He's hilarious, can drink more beer than Mac and knows more about Nebraska football than Kevin."

Dooley looked around at his friends. "You drank with him? You've talked football?" What the hell?

Mac shrugged. "We had to be sure that he was good enough to hang out with your dad."

"Why?" Dooley asked.

"In case you ever need a backup. I think he'd be great," Sam said.

"Me too," Mac said. "We were even thinking of taking a long weekend the four of us guys and going to see the Vikings play or something." He flipped several channels as if they were talking about nothing more than football. "Jay could cover things at your house."

"You think Jay would do a great job helping out if the four of us ever wanted to go to a football game?" Dooley clarified. As if this was a new idea. As if him needing backup had just now occurred to them. As if finding someone was just a matter of...finding someone.

Sam nodded. "Definitely."

"Oh, yeah," Mac said.

"No problem," Kevin added.

"This is all about us taking a weekend for a football game?"

"Of course," Sam said simply. "Or baseball."

"It has nothing to do with Jay being a backup in case I wanted to go, oh I don't know, to California with Morgan," he said.

"Nah." Mac tossed more popcorn into his mouth. "That's never going to work out."

It wasn't? Of course he'd been thinking the same thing, but hearing someone else say it sucked.

"Why?" Again, he was shocked and annoyed they were letting go of what had happened between him and Morgan so easily.

Mac shrugged. "She wants to live in California and you want to live here. Obviously that's not going to work."

"It's not about living in California," Dooley said, slumping deeper into the chair. "She wants this job."

"Why?" Sam asked. "Job sounds boring. Catering to fancy-shmancy rich guys? Yuck."

"Fancy-shmancy and hoity-toity?" Mac asked. "What's going on with you today?"

Dooley stared at the beer commercial on TV without seeing it. Somehow, Sam's description didn't feel right. On the surface, that did seem like what Morgan did, but something nagged at him.

"That's not what she does," he said before he'd thought it all out.

"What does she do, then?" Mac asked. He commandeered the entire bowl of popcorn.

"She takes care of people."

Sam snorted. "For money. The Britton's not a charity, you know?"

"We take care of people for money," Kevin pointed out.

Sam threw his pencil at him.

"Well, we do," Kevin insisted. "None of you are here for free are you?"

"What about the Center?" Mac asked. "We all volunteer down there. We take care of the girls. You help out with Senior. We don't get paid for that stuff."

"We get compensated though," Kevin said. "It's not money, but we get cake and cookies and laughs and fun and appreciation and the reward of knowing we've done something good."

Mac rolled his eyes but he didn't argue. There was no argument. It was all true and they all felt the same way.

"Morgan tries to make people feel comfortable and relaxed even when they're away from home. She tries to make them happy. She does it for money, but..." He trailed off as his thoughts came together.

"But?" Kevin prompted.

Dooley turned to look at him. "She does it for money because she thinks that's what *she* needs most."

"Which is why you'll never be able to be together," Mac said, propping his feet on the coffee table and tossing a handful of popcorn in his mouth.

Dooley sat, lost in thought. Morgan liked doing things for other people, but she'd seen her dad's efforts met with sadness and anger from her mom when it cost the family. In Morgan's mind, she'd found a way to take care of people, to make sure they enjoyed themselves and had fun, but without the risk of those negative reactions. There was no expense for her personally to see people have a good time. The best of both worlds.

Pulling himself out of his realizations he looked around at his friends. "Really? We're not going to talk about this? You're not going to encourage me to go after her? To show her there are other kinds of security than money?"

"Why would we do that?" Mac asked, munching on his popcorn, his eyes never leaving the TV.

"Because I love her?" Dooley said. "Because I'm miserable without her? Because she'll be miserable without me too, because even though she'll have the job and the money she thinks she wants, no one will ever love her or make her happy like I do?"

He watched as Mac's mouth spread into a wide grin. Dooley glanced at Sam and Kevin, seeing big grins on their faces too.

They'd gotten him.

They hadn't needed to do the talking. He'd talked it all out himself.

"You guys are dicks."

Mac chuckled. "No wonder we get along with you so well."

"I screwed up," he said. "I get it. Now how do I fix it?"

"You go to California," Sam said, as if it was obvious. "You told her you wouldn't leave for her but you will. You have to."

"How can I leave?" Dooley pushed up out of the chair, the same old frustration welling in his chest. "Damn, that hasn't changed. I can't just move to California."

"Right. Your only back up is that weird guy, Jay, that Morgan interviewed," Mac said.

Dooley shrugged. "Jay's not weird. It wasn't that. It wasn't about Jay at all."

"It was about..." Sam prompted.

"Me over-reacting," Dooley admitted. "I was pissed," he said in his defense. "She was willing to give everything up, all of *us*... Me. She had a choice and she didn't pick me."

"You just said you understand that she can't help how she feels about money. She just doesn't know there are other ways of being secure," Sam said.

"How do I show her that?" Dooley shoved a hand through his hair. He'd thought he *had* shown her that.

Sam laid his puzzle book to one side and looked at Mac. Mac set the popcorn bowl down and sighed. "We're not sure. We've been talking about it, but...as long as what's most important to her is in California and what's most important to you is here..." He sighed again. "We're not sure."

Dooley frowned at them. "You know, when you were both

being idiots about love *I* actually *helped* you."

They both looked sheepish. "We know," Sam said. "Sorry, man."

Dooley paced the length of the room. Great. The only thing they'd accomplished was proving to him he did want her back. "Okay," he said turning to face his friends. "Here's the thing. I have to find a way of showing her we can have the best of both worlds."

"Sounds good," Sam said.

"Great plan," Mac agreed.

"How are you going to do that?" Kevin asked.

They all just looked at each other.

Fuck.

Dooley paced again. How was he going to do that? He could take her traveling, they could stay in nice hotels, he'd buy her diamonds. Then at the end of the day they'd curl up on the couch and watch TV with his dad, have breakfast with his nieces and spend a lot of time with these guys and their families.

How did he show her how great it would be?

"Hey," he asked as a thought hit him. "What did Richard Gere do at the end of *Pretty Woman*?"

Mac chuckled. "What are you talking about?"

"What did Richard Gere's character do at the end of the movie to get Julia back?"

Sam laughed. "Why does that matter? *You're* Julia."

Dooley crossed his arms as they all laughed. "No," he said, when they'd quieted. "I'm the guy who screwed up and needs to grovel."

"He's got a point," Mac said.

"He got a nice suit, flowers, a big diamond ring and took a limo to her house, climbed the fire escape and proposed," Kevin said.

"I don't think he prop—" Sam started, then cut off and said quickly, "Yep, that's right, big proposal."

Okay, so evidently Gere hadn't proposed after all. Still, the happily ever after was implied. He could build on that. "Where do I get a limo?"

"It's gonna cost you," Sam said.

"Oh, yeah, big bucks," Mac said with a nod.

"You sure you want to go there?" Kevin asked.

"Yeah, yeah, I'm cheap, I don't spend money, blah, blah, blah," Dooley said.

"Well..."

He sighed. "I don't spend money *frivolously*," he said. "But I hardly think winning the heart of the only woman I'll ever love is frivolous." He stared at each of them, daring them to give him a hard time. "Do you?" he asked the group.

"No."

"Of course not."

"Not at all."

That's what he thought. "Where do I get a limo?" he asked again. He had money and if it took every last dime he owned to win Morgan back, he would. "Do you think Sara will help me pick out a ring?" he asked Mac.

Mac rolled his eyes. "Will Sara be willing to go to a jewelry store with the sole purpose of buying something big and expensive?" He chuckled. "Is the ocean wet?"

"Okay, so I should do that first," Dooley said. "But then—"

Kevin's phone rang just then. He pulled it out, frowned at the display and answered it immediately. "Morgan?"

Doug's heart thumped and he forgot everything else. Why was Morgan calling Kevin?

"What do you mean don't freak out?" Kevin asked with a frown.

Dooley started toward Kevin, fully intending to rip the phone from his hand. Something had happened, involving Morgan, that might freak him out?

"You were *robbed*?"

Dooley immediately changed directions, pulling his keys from his pocket, he headed for the door. Kevin could handle the phone call part of this. *He* was going to handle the rest. Whatever it was.

"Are you okay?" Kevin asked.

Dooley's gut clenched and he almost stopped walking. He wanted to hear her answer. But it didn't matter. Okay or not, he was going to her and he couldn't do anything about 'not okay' until he got there.

"Of course you're shaken and scared, Morgan," Kevin said soothingly.

Dooley gripped his keys hard in his hand and forced himself to keep walking. He just had to get to her. From there they'd figure everything else out.

Morgan was in his life now and, while she might hire or buy something for whatever problem she was having, in his world *he* took care of things. Of her. And she was going to learn that one way or another.

"Get Conner to cover me," he told Sam as he yanked the door open, "and call Jay to go over to Dad's. Tell Kevin I'll call him for details when I can."

"Where are you going?" Sam called after him.

"To the airport. To California. To Morgan."

Not one of his friends tried to stop him as the heavy break room door swung shut behind him.

Morgan took a deep breath and combed her hair back from her face with her fingers. She hadn't said the word robbed to anyone but the cops. Saying it out loud now made her shake—partly from the creepiness of it and partly from the anger.

It was her fault. She was in and out of the bed and breakfast so much with the renovations she had forgotten to lock the door behind her when she ran to the store for more paint. Most of what had been taken was small and replaceable. She was pissed about the iPod but the power tools were basic. What she was most upset about was her missing laptop.

Oh, and that someone had been here and taken things that belonged to her.

Had they been waiting for her to leave? Watching to see when the place was empty? That was creepy. But so was the idea they could have shown up when she was there. Alone.

Yeah, she had a power drill and she wasn't afraid to use it but...

She shivered. She wasn't sure she would have thought to use it, frankly. The bed and breakfast wasn't completely isolated, but it also wasn't a bustling business area. Being here alone, distracted by the renovations and deaf because of the iPod now seemed less than bright.

Of course, now she wouldn't have to worry about the iPod.

"I'm shook up," she admitted to Kevin.

"Of course you're shaken and scared."

Yes, shaken and scared. Definitely. And pissed.

She would have rather called Doug—in fact, she'd dialed twice—but Kevin was good too. Comforting, supportive, concerned. It especially felt great when he said, "We're on our way."

She glanced at the clock. "You're working, aren't you?"

"We can get a crew to cover," he said. "We'll be there in twenty minutes."

It was silly. She was fine, the cops had been here, the theft was relatively small. But she did want them to come. Especially Doug. Kevin would bring Doug, she was sure.

"Okay. Thanks."

Nineteen minutes later Kevin, Mac and Sam were on the porch of her bed and breakfast. No Doug.

"You sure you're fine?" Kevin asked, pulling her into a hug before she could even answer.

"I'm not hurt. I'm pissed. And freaked out."

"What'd they take?" Mac started examining the front door while Sam moved into the eventually-would-be lobby and living room.

The guys had been there before. In fact, they'd been helping with some of the renovations. Morgan had asked Sara to help her shop for furniture, flooring and window treatments. Sara had brought Dani who had immediately started identifying things that needed to be updated and making lists of needed supplies. She'd gotten the guys involved and from there things had really started to take shape.

Morgan still couldn't believe it. She didn't want them to work for free, but the only thing they'd let her do in return was cook. There were no other available contractors for at least six weeks and since emptying her savings account to buy the place and renovate, she didn't have much left.

Besides, she got the feeling they enjoyed it. As Jessica had said, they would have all been hanging out together anyway and they might as well make themselves useful while they do it. Morgan had to laugh at that. She'd never met a group of people who made themselves more useful to more people than this group. She was thrilled to spend any amount of time with them. Even without Doug.

She didn't know what he was doing while they were here and she never asked. She'd hoped they'd drop comments or hints, but no one ever slipped.

Which was just as well. She missed him plenty all on her own.

She tuned back in to the conversation in time to realize Kevin and Mac were discussing new security options for the B & B and Sam was on the phone with what sounded like the police.

"Who's he talking to?" she asked, gesturing at Sam.

"Oh, one of our cop buddies. Seeing if they know everything yet."

"They said—"

"Theft of opportunity. Some kids who happened to walking by and got curious, found it unlocked, etc, etc.," Sam said, snapping his phone shut. "They found them walking a few blocks away." He stopped in front of Morgan. "They don't think you have anything to worry about. Still, a security system is a good idea."

Okay, theft of opportunity. That felt a lot better than someone staking her out. "Locking my door when I leave is also a good idea."

Sam gave her a smile. "Yeah. That too."

The guys launched into a discussion about who they should call to get a system installed right away. Five minutes later Sara and Danika showed up.

"Oh my God, Morgan," Sara gushed, grabbing her into a hug.

"We have to get a security system installed," Danika said eyeing the doorframe.

Chuckling, Sam wrapped his arms around her from behind.

And just like that Morgan was crying.

It was part adrenaline, she knew, but it was also this amazing bunch of people. They were here for her. She'd said less than ten words to Kevin over the phone and they'd all shown up. They'd left work for her and now they were all here debating the best way to keep her safe.

It didn't matter which security system she got. She could spend the maximum amount of money and nothing would make her feel as secure as they did.

If only Doug were here.

She sniffed as she realized that no matter what these people did for her, it wouldn't be as good as if Doug was here doing it.

But he would be.

He didn't know what was going on or he'd be here. She knew it as surely as she knew she'd never get over him. She'd never not need him. She'd never not want him to be here.

But if he didn't know about this then it must mean he wasn't with them when she called. They'd been at work. Why wasn't he with them?

She grabbed Kevin's shirtsleeve and tugged him to one side. "What's wrong with Doug?"

He looked surprised. "Nothing."

"Is Senior sick? Or one of the girls?"

"No. Nobody's sick, Morgan."

Everyone had quieted and were focused on her and Kevin. She didn't care. "Then what's wrong? Why wasn't he at work with you?"

"He was at work with us."

"Then why isn't he here?" For just a moment her stomach

dropped. *Maybe he doesn't want to come.* But almost immediately she realized that couldn't be true. He would be here if he knew.

"He's...um..." Kevin rubbed a hand over the back of his neck and looked at the other guys.

Sam shrugged. "You told us to let him go," he said to Kevin.

"Let him go where?" Morgan grabbed Kevin's arm again. "Where is he?"

Kevin let out a breath. "California. Or on his way anyway."

She stared up at him for a moment. Was he kidding? Or was there something in that statement she was supposed to understand? Because she didn't. "Why is he in California?"

"For you," Kevin said.

"But I'm not in California."

"What's going on, Kevin?" Sara asked. "Since when is Dooley in California?"

"Technically he's not there yet. The plane's just taking off," he said, looking at his watch. "But as soon as he heard something had happened to Morgan he took off, hell bent to get to her."

"She's right here," Sara said, propping a hand on her hip. "Why didn't you stop him?"

"I wanted both him and Morgan to see what he's willing to do," Kevin said. He looked completely unapologetic. "Now he doesn't have to be in California to be with her, but I wanted them both to know he was willing to be."

"Who's with his dad?" Morgan asked.

"Jay."

She wasn't sure how to react. She was relieved at first. Jay was a great guy and would take great care of Doug Senior. She was annoyed too. That had been her idea from the beginning. But mostly, she was amazed. Doug had left everything and gone to California to be with her when he thought she needed him.

He was right. She did need him.

But she needed him right here.

"When are you going to tell him?" she asked Kevin.

"In my defense, he didn't give me a chance to tell him. He

started for the door the minute he heard me ask you if you were okay and he stormed out after I repeated you were robbed." Kevin looked at the other guys. "He said he'd call me for details when he could right? He hasn't called."

"So you're just going to let him get on a plane, fly to California, on a ticket that's got to be expensive, get in a cab and go to the Britton and *then* find out I'm not there?"

"Isn't it romantic he just up and left to be with you?" Sam asked.

"It is," she admitted. In fact, it made her feel...like dancing or turning cartwheels or...something. Doug hadn't been laid back and hadn't been worried about money. The ticket had to have cost over five hundred dollars. Probably a lot more. The whole thing showed that his concern, his feelings for her, were so important they made him act spontaneously, without thought or worry about consequences. Being with her when she needed him was the only thing that mattered.

Now she just had to convince him she needed him all the time.

"All the way to California and the hotel he'll be thinking how he can't wait to see you and how worried he is and how none of the rest of the b.s. you were disagreeing about matters," Kevin said. "Then he'll find out you're not only fine, but you're here in Omaha—to stay—and he'll be thrilled." He stood grinning at her as if he'd announced she'd won the lottery.

"When will he be back?" Morgan asked.

"Sometime tomorrow, I'd say."

That gave her some time. "What did Richard Gere do at the end of *Pretty Woman* to win Julia Roberts back?" she asked.

The guys all looked at one another with smiles. Then Mac said, "Funny you should ask."

Dooley didn't trust himself to talk to Kevin without ruining a very nice, long-term friendship. So he called Sara.

"You told me she was in California."

"I did not."

"You said she got the job." He was sure she had said that. But according to the front desk attendant at the Britton, Morgan hadn't been back to San Francisco since she'd met with Jonathan.

"She did get the job," Sara said, sounding huffy. "She just didn't *take* the job."

He gritted his teeth. "You didn't think to clarify that?"

"I figured she should be the one to tell you. Or not."

The "or not" bugged him. "Why wouldn't she want me to know?"

"Maybe she was afraid you'd think it was all for you."

"That she wasn't taking the job?"

"That she was staying in Omaha."

"She's..." That stopped him. "She's staying in Omaha?"

"She bought a bed and breakfast. Drained her savings account."

He frowned. What the hell was going on? "She just gave a huge donation to the Youth Center," he said. Ben had told him about it two days ago. "Ten thousand dollars."

"Only like a hundred of it was hers," Sara said. "She raised the rest."

"Raised it?"

"She knows a lot of influential—and wealthy—people. She got them all to donate."

He had no idea what to say. "She spent her entire savings on a bed and breakfast?"

That seemed right somehow.

"Almost every penny," Sara confirmed.

"Then why am I in California?" he asked, keeping his voice even since he was in the lobby of the nicest hotel in San Francisco.

"Kevin felt you both needed to know what she meant to you."

"She means everything." It was crystal clear to him. Even before he'd gotten on the plane.

"Then get your ass back here and tell her."

There were, of course, no return flights until the next morning and by the time he walked through his front door it was well after noon. Jay and his dad were playing a video game. Dooley did a double take. Even his dad was playing, with a controller that had been rigged with duct tape, twine and a piece of wood, then fit over the arms of his wheelchair.

"That's cool," he said distractedly.

Jay glanced at the contraption. "Thanks. Though I'm starting to regret it. Your dad is awesome at Avenging Angels."

Senior grinned.

Dooley shook his head. "Hey, Jay, can you stay?"

"Sure. What's up?" His eyes were firmly on the TV and he leaned right then left quickly as he dodged enemy missile fire.

"I need to go propose to Morgan."

Jay took a direct hit as he and Senior both pivoted to look at Dooley.

"Yeah?" Jay asked.

Senior was watching him intently.

"Yeah," Dooley said without pause.

"Okay, great, man. Take your time." Jay gave him a big grin.

Dooley looked at his dad. "What do you think?"

There were tears in Senior's eyes as he nodded and gave Dooley a thumb's up.

"You know about the bed and breakfast, don't you?" Dooley guessed.

Senior smiled.

Dooley shook his head. Morgan wasn't just in all of their lives—they were in hers. He loved that.

He headed for the phonebook and started running through to find a limo service. Apparently there wasn't a lot of call for limos at one p.m. on a weekday because for an extra fifty bucks the driver agreed to pick up a dozen roses on his way over. Once that was arranged Dooley headed for his closet and his tux.

He was patting his pants pocket, relishing the feel of the little black velvet box inside, when honking and the sound of an ambulance siren erupted outside.

Still barefoot, his shirt unbuttoned, his tie hanging loose, he took off for the front of the house, heart pounding. Was it one of his neighbors?

He ripped open the door and was down the steps and halfway across the yard when he realized the ambulance—or something that looked a little like an ambulance—had pulled up in front of his house.

The thing had once been an ambulance, he was pretty sure. It was confirmed when his friends piled out of the front and back. But it was covered in streamers and balloons and ribbon and a huge piece of cardboard on the side that read "Will You Marry Me?"

He knew he looked like an idiot standing in the middle of the grass, half dressed, staring but...well, what was he supposed to do?

Then Morgan climbed out of the back of the ambulance.

"Hi."

She was smiling brightly at him and she looked delicious. She was wearing khaki capris, a red T-shirt and sandals. Her hair was pulled back into a ponytail and the only trace of make-up was the lip-gloss on her lips.

"Hi."

"Here's the thing," she said. "I would have loved to show up here in a limo in a great dress with flowers, give you tickets for some amazing trip, and make this a big production. But I've got nothing. I sank everything I have into the bed and breakfast. This is the only unique vehicle I could afford, this is what I'll be wearing from now on, we won't be taking any big trips for a while and I could only get this." She handed him a single rose. "But I don't care about the money." She moved closer and reached for his hand. "I want to be rich in all the ways *you* are, with friends, laughter, support and love. I'm money poor, but will you marry me anyway?"

He stared at her. *She* was proposing to *him*? With an ambulance?

"I..." Just then a long black limo pulled up at the curb and parked nose to nose with the ambulance. The driver got out with a huge bouquet of red roses and started toward them.

Dooley looked back at Morgan. "I, um, had something planned too."

Her eyes were wide. "I see that."

He grinned. "Here's the thing," he said, repeating her words. "I do have money."

Her eyes got wider. "You have money?"

"Nothing like Britton's got, but I don't spend. I save obsessively. I invest. My dad is the best with investment advice. So, I have money. That I want to spend on you. Not because you expect it, but because it will make you smile. You've learned something about what real security is, but I've learned something too—there are lots of ways to take care of someone. We can go on great trips, stay in fancy hotels, eat amazing food and also live here, with all of these people we love, and eat macaroni and cheese and watch *Castle*."

Her eyes were teary when he looked at her.

"Marry me, Morgan."

"Of course." She sniffed. "Yes. Absolutely."

He pulled the ring out of his pocket and opened the top.

Morgan gasped. "Oh, Doug, it's too much." She covered her mouth with her hand.

"Hey, it's my money," he teased. "Nobody tells me how to spend it."

She ignored the ring for a moment, stepped close and wrapped her arms around him, burying her face against his neck. "I can't believe you went to California," she murmured.

He put his hand against the back of her head, relishing the silkiness of her hair, the way she molded her body to his, and how he wanted this for the next hundred years. At least. "I can't believe you're surprised by that." He realized she was shaking and he pulled back. "What's wrong?"

"I'm overwhelmed."

"By the ring?" he asked. It was gorgeous. Sara had approved of it via picture on his phone sent to hers.

"By everything you've given me."

"The roses? The trip to Hawaii?" She hadn't even seen those tickets yet.

She sniffed and turned slightly, watching Mac, Sam and Kevin laughing and joking near the ambulance, then looked over Dooley's shoulder to where Senior and Jay were watching from the porch. "I guess I should have said every*body* you've given me."

His heart expanded in his chest to the point it was hard to breathe and he just gathered her close.

"By the way," she said after a moment of holding him. "I was wrong. This is still really, really fun."

He drew in a deep lungful of her scent, then he felt a huge grin stretch his lips. "Yeah," he agreed. "And you ain't seen nothin' yet."

About the Author

Erin Nicholas is the author of sexy contemporary romances. Her stories have been described as toe-curling, enchanting, steamy and fun. She loves to write about reluctant heroes, flawed heroines, sex with food and happily ever afters. She does not like to write dark moments, synopses or bios. You can find Erin on the web at www.ErinNicholas.com, ninenaughtynovelists.blogspot.com, on Twitter (@ErinNicholas) and even on Facebook (when necessary).

How to make a strong man fall hard? Refuse him.

Worth the Risk
© 2012 Karen Erickson
Worth It, Book 2

Hunter Worth lives life to the absolute fullest. As vice president and head of brand marketing for Worth Luxury Goods, he's brought his family's business firmly into the twenty-first century. Ruthless yet charming, he's now set his sights on the sexiest member of the marketing team. First thing on his agenda? Seduction.

Gracie Hayes needs her job at Worth—and she's not about to let the gorgeous owner and her direct boss distract her—again. Orphaned, and with a rough childhood behind her, she's worked too hard to compromise everything for a fling, no matter how tempting. Independent, strong and resourceful, she will fight off Hunter. She has to.

Flirting, stolen kisses, a few nights of scorching hot sex...Hunter has all that in mind and more with the delicious Gracie. He never figures he'd fall in love or that she'd deny him. How will Hunter convince Gracie he's the one for her?

Warning: Contains yet another one of those sexy, bossy Worth brothers, though this one is too full of charm for his own good. Watch as he falls hard—and watch as she tries her hardest to dodge his every attempt at seduction.

Available now in ebook and print from Samhain Publishing.

It's all about the story...

Romance

HORROR

www.samhainpublishing.com

CPSIA information can be obtained at www.ICGtesting.com
Printed in the USA
BVOW080957140513

320673BV00008B/16/P